The Thin Man's Poison

by

Randall Jarmon

MIKVELK Publishing, LLC
mikvelk.com

The ISBN for *The Thin Man's Poison* is 979-8-9879542-4-9. The ISBN for the ebook version' is 979-8-9879542-5-6.

The Thin Man's Poison is entirely a work of fiction, which is to say it is entirely a product of the author's imagination. The organizations, places, activities, and events in the story either do not exist, or, if they do exist, are used in entirely fictitious ways. So far as the author is aware, both neural cascade and Lars Brent's wonder drug do not exist. Any character's resemblance to any person, living or dead, is purely coincidental.

This is the 2023 edition of T*he Thin Man's Poison.*

MIKVELK Publishing, LLC
mikvelk.com

At MIKVELK, we use Readers' Favorite as a vital step in our company's quality control. Near the launch of a new title, we send the story to Readers' Favorite for their feedback. We use what their reviewers tell us to make sure a new story is as good as we think it is. Below are excerpts from Readers' Favorite's feedback on The Thin Man's Poison. *The boldfacing was added by us at MIKVELK.*

"... The Thin Man's Poison by Randall Jarmon is **an edge-of-your-seat thriller with lots of romantic suspense built in for good measure** ... The characters are perfectly developed ... **If you love suspenseful mysteries, you're going to love this and you won't want it to end."**

--- Anne-Marie Reynolds for Readers' Favorite

"...**I love the tension in the narrative, the pace of the story, and the overall feel of it** ... The actual suspense is pretty amazing ... **It is a novel that is worth reading well into the night.**

--- Rabia Tanveer for Readers' Favorite

"...**The romance part of the story is brilliantly developed and it enhances the conflict.** The Thin Man's Poison is a well-crafted story that features rock-solid characters and a clever plot. It was, for me, an exciting read."

--- Romuald Dzemo for Readers' Favorite

"... **a gripping novel filled with romance,**

action, suspense, and thought-provoking content. I loved the characters ... There were great villains throughout the plot … **The areas of conflict were absolute perfection and the ending was a punch in the air moment.** This novel will be hard to forget even when the final page is turned."

--- Lesley Jones for Readers' Favorite

"... The Thin Man's Poison is the type of novel that will translate well as a movie … The romantic angle between Brent and Mila Rossi adds spice to the narrative whenever Brent takes a break from tracking assassins. **Mila Rossi is not the typical trophy girlfriend, but rather a woman who is, in all measure, Lars Brent's equal. This is a fun and memorable romantic suspense thriller.**"

--- Vincent Dublado for Readers' Favorite

Five Years Earlier

The Montreal Mob spent freely to assassinate one of Sanjay Haranya's sons. They recruited the six deadliest assassins in Haranya's native India, paid them lavishly, and flew them by private jet to Vancouver, Canada. The city's Little India district was home not only to Sanjay Haranya's family, but also to their secretive business empire.

Few Canadians knew how profoundly rich the low-profile, tightly-knit Haranya clan was. Even the Montreal Mob, ever eager to sell its "protection" services to highly profitable Canadian businesses run by immigrants, discovered the Haranyas only recently. When the Mob ordered family patriarch Sanjay Haranya to pay, he refused and went to the Vancouver police.

The police did their best, guarding the Haranyas round-the-clock for a week. Then the police randomly assigned a few officers to surveillance for another week. A Vancouver city budget analyst thereupon declared the Haranyas demonstrably safe and the city's police intervention fully successful. The Haranyas' *ad hoc* police protection evaporated like morning fog, leaving the family on its own.

The Montreal Mob had expected that. That's how it always went with the most stubborn of their best prospects. By now the

Mob had a process for such recalcitrance. The Mob promised to kill a key member of whichever business resisted. The Mob told the business beforehand to hire private guards, set alarms, or whatever.

The firm inevitably did so. Yet a targeted company's precautions never mattered. In each such case, the Mob used a full kill team comprised of proven assassins. Such profoundly lethal talent in such uncommon numbers overwhelmed any obstacles. The Montreal Mob's evil reputation grew with each success.

Now it was Sanjay Haranya's turn to learn this lesson. The Mob told him one of his sons would die. It would happen before a certain date and in a certain way. Then, the Mob said, they and Sanjay Haranya would be even. They'd start over. He'd pay protection money or lose another son. Maybe they'd just go after one of his two daughters, said the Mob. That might be fun. He had pretty daughters.

The executive jet transporting the six hired killers landed in heavy rain at a private airstrip outside Vancouver. A luxurious, customized shuttle van pulled alongside, driven by a thin, bearded man wearing a raincoat over his chauffeur's uniform. He bowed to show respect, identified himself, and held his big umbrella for each assassin as the killers walked one at a time from the private jet to the waiting van.

Inside the van, a high-end sound system played Bollywood's most popular songs. A cooler held iced beverages, including Asia's best-selling beers. The killers also found hot samosas awaiting them. All six were pleased. It was, one assassin crowed, as though England's queen had sent her personal butler!

After a few minutes, the killers were settled into the van, each of them warm, dry, and comfortable. The driver was not. His raincoat, uniform trousers, and shiny shoes were soaked from the cold, heavy rain. Even so, the driver meekly closed his umbrella and loaded their luggage into the rear of the van without complaint.

By the time he finished loading luggage, two of the killers were on second beers and half the food was gone. Merriment was breaking out inside the van as the driver, now shivering and dripping wet, climbed into his seat. A small puddle of water formed around his feet.

He politely announced over the van's speaker system that he'd been told to take his distinguished passengers to the Opulent Tower, which was Vancouver's best hotel. Would that be satisfactory to them? he asked.

An older man who seemed in charge of

the kill team said the Opulent Tower would be fine. The driver thanked him for confirmation, raised the luxury shuttle van's privacy partition, and drove off. One of the six passengers began a bawdy story the other five killers found hilarious almost right away.

A minute later the van driver triggered hidden canisters inside the van's well-sealed passenger compartment. Poison gas escaped unnoticed. The killers died in ten seconds through a neurological phenomenon called neural cascade. In all the world, only the van's driver could induce neural cascade. His secret poison left no trace.

The driver switched the sound system over to classical music and turned away from the city, while the van's ventilation system flushed toxic gas from the passenger compartment. An hour later the van drove onto a remote stretch of Pacific Ocean beach. With nobody around for miles, the driver positioned the killers' bodies on the beach in a circle, feet toward the center, each corpse face-up. He moved arms so that the dead men seemed to hold hands while lifeless eyes stared skyward. The unrelenting rain would wash away footprints and tire tracks.

Since the victims appeared to have engaged in a strange ritual, their deaths easily made the front page of Canada's leading tabloid. That was how the Montreal Mob learned its invincible assassins had failed.

Both Mob leaders and Canadian authorities suspected foul play. The forensic analysis that followed became the most rigorous in Canadian history. In the end, the small legion of scientific experts involved all said the same thing: Poison definitely wasn't involved. The six men died of natural causes. Maybe the cold rain somehow triggered their deaths. Nobody knew.

A day later, Sanjay Haranya called the Mob's leader. If the Mob ever again threatened a Haranya, Sanjay said, Mob leadership would begin dying of natural causes.

So it was that, five years ago, the deadliest assassins in all of India were killed by the deadliest man in Canada. He'd pay a high price, though, for rescuing the Haranyas. He'd known that beforehand.

Defending them, in his mind, meant never commercializing his revolutionary poison. The pharmaceutical implications, though breathtaking, now would never benefit him. Given his unique background, applying for the essential patent could link him to the six inexplicable deaths. Not right away, of course, but within several months of the patent application.

Yet the Haranyas were his friends.

Protecting them had been the right thing to do.

Today

1 Despite cold, rainy weather, the best restaurant in Vancouver, Canada was again filled with the city's rich and famous. Only they could afford the luncheon menu, which was superb and priced accordingly. With dozens of beautiful people about, nobody would have paid attention to ordinary-looking Lars Brent, even though he'd finally whitened his teeth.

Forty-something Brent sat alone at a backwall table. He was a thin man whose slight frame would lift him six feet high when pulled himself erect. His straight gray-brown hair was neatly combed, his gray-brown beard neatly trimmed. Thick-rimmed glasses and an undistinguished suit gave him a mid-career civil service look. Only Brent's intelligent eyes suggested there might be something special about him.

In fact, two things were special. First, he was far, far smarter than anyone in the crowded restaurant, except for one woman he didn't think present. Second, Brent made his living by killing assassins.

That afternoon he took his usual precaution. Many of the restaurant's tables offered a splendid Pacific Ocean vista. He sat in the restaurant's back corner, barely seeing front windows, let alone ocean beyond. He did, however, have the room's best view of entrances and exits. His keen eyes inconspicuously scanned the crowded dining area as he sipped a legendary wine.

He came here often, though, and now felt a little too safe. He somehow didn't see Mila Rossi until she'd walked close to his table. That bothered him. Rossi shouldn't be there, he thought. He'd have slipped into the kitchen and out the back door had he noticed her sooner. He knew she'd have one of the Agency's goon teams with her.

Even so, he smiled and stood.

She smiled back warmly and held out her hand for him.

"I hope you're surprised, Lars. You've no idea how hard it was sneaking up on you."

"It's been a long time," he said, shaking her hand.

He pulled out his table's second chair for her. She'd have kissed him, but he was too quick. They sat down together.

Brent waved to a nearby waiter, who took Mila's drink order. Mila asked for the red wine her friend drank. He was, she said, an accomplished wine snob. Mila announced it with such a wonderful smile that being called a wine snob pleased Brent.

He'd always liked Mila. She'd

supervised his work twelve years ago, back at the little off-the-books Alabama laboratory where they alone invented toxins for America's spies to kill America's enemies.

Mila Rossi was two years older than Brent, impeccably well-dressed, and forever a beautiful woman. She had marvelous dark eyes, and honey-blond hair curling at her shoulders. Today she wore contact lenses. He remembered her with wire-rimmed glasses, designer jeans, and a ponytail. The smile was the same, though. So was the good cheer.

More importantly, Mila Rossi remained far and away the most intelligent woman he'd ever met. It was probably dangerous staying at the table with her, he thought, but he didn't care.

"So, Mila, how many minders do you have lurking around me?"

"Guess. Let's see if you're still clever."

He looked around, but only for a moment. It was easy once he paid full attention.

"The big man seated up front, with his cellphone set to selfie mode so he can watch me with his back turned. Also, the guy who just came in the main entrance. Ex-military. He halfway marches when he walks. And you'd have a woman someplace. You'd think I'd overlook her."

"Right on the first two. And right about a

woman. Which one's she?"

He looked puzzled, but soon smiled. "The brunette bartender. She just ignored a tip somebody left her so she could watch us. How'd you ever place somebody behind the bar?"

"I'm told it took two big bribes. And it didn't hurt any that she's pretty and worked bar jobs in college. Somebody thinks you're very, very dangerous."

"Sounds like your escorts are a snatch team. Are you planning to kidnap me, Mila, or just lure me into your bed?" His eyes twinkled as he said it.

She treated him to one of her little, happy laughs. Her bedding him was a preposterous suggestion and they both knew it.

"*Neither* ... Although you came close to getting kidnapped for only forty-eight hours. That's what Charlie Hexler told me."

"He's still alive?"

"Charlie's why I'm here, even though I've been gone from the Agency eleven years. I left not long after you did. But you wouldn't know that since you've ignored me ever since."

"Sorry. I thought you were still one of them. I'd have invited you to lunch had I known you left. Then I'd have asked about your younger sister."

He smiled again. She laughed again, this time louder and with appreciation in her voice.

"Thank you, Lars. I feel better. And my younger sister's married. You're too late."

"Story of my life. So, why are you hanging out with Charlie Hexler, Mila?"

"A week ago Charlie showed up on his own at my university. I'm a professor of pharmacological chemistry now, Lars, but save that long story for next time. Charlie, out of the blue, asked me what I thought of his plan to kidnap you so he could offer you a job."

"And what did you say?"

"I told Charlie that idea was crazy. You're a Canadian and this is Canada. There'd be serious repercussions to a kidnapping. Besides that, he planned on using six guys. I told him you'd kill at least half of them. I said it would be easier to let me contact you on his behalf."

"And here you are."

"Yes! But he's also in town. The minders, as you call them, are really to protect him. He's waiting for you in a conference room two blocks away. I'm to tell you to walk there, with the minders tagging along. But I made Charlie promise you and I could have lunch first."

"How thoughtful of him. Are you coming with me to the conference?"

"No. I have to catch a plane back home in four hours. Even full professors get stuck with eight a.m. classes these days."

She batted her eyelashes at him and smiled.

"In case you don't already know, Mila, the Agency and I officially haven't liked each other since I left. Why would I talk with Charlie Hexler? Or why doesn't he just call me?"

"Two excellent questions! The answers are 'I don't know' and 'I don't know.' I'm here since Charlie paid me more for two days work than I make in two months. I don't know much."

"Any idea how Hexler found me? Just in case I don't want to be found again?"

"He told me it was facial recognition. They still have your employee badge photo from when we all worked in Alabama. Charlie said to tell you he can remove that picture and any others of you from U.S. government databases."

"Can he?"

"Who knows? Consider it unsupported assertion. He also said to tell you he has three contracts. Each one's for five million American dollars. Half now, half on completion. There's another million U.S. dollars for expenses. I guess you'd get that now. He didn't say, though."

"What's he want?"

"That's all he said. Everything besides what I've told you is too secret for me to know, and, of course, too secret to discuss here."

"Does Hexler still look the same?"

"He's mid-sixties now. Small wrinkles around the eyes. His hair's all there, but it's gone gray. Contact lenses and some expensive dental work. But the same weight and still ruggedly handsome. The same ice blue eyes. You'll recognize him right away."

"What do his other minders look like?"

"I don't know. I met the two guys in the room with us when they led me into the kitchen from the rear. Then I waited five minutes for them to get into position. They told me the brunette behind the bar would be one of them. As to the rest, I didn't see them, but Charlie said there were three more."

Brent frowned and looked momentarily at the ceiling. He looked back at Mila. Then he said, more to himself than to her, "I don't like it."

His words alarmed Mila, who suddenly, unmistakably looked very worried. She lowered her voice and leaned toward him.

"Then I've made a horrible, terrible mistake ... Lars, I thought my being here might keep you out of a fight with Charlie's guys. I'm *so very sorry* if I've put you in danger!"

She said it from the heart. Lars sensed that and was kind with her.

"Not a problem, Mila. These things happen in my business. Don't blame yourself."

He smiled reassuringly. Mila smiled back, but immediately returned to being worried. She reached into her purse and withdrew a thick envelope. She held it below the table where only Lars could see it, her beautiful eyes locked onto his.

"Lars, I've got fifty thousand U.S. dollars in this envelope. It's what Charlie paid me. Take it all. Use it to get away." Mila looked resolute.

Brent smiled kindly again. "Thank you. I owe you one, Mila, but it won't be necessary. And I already plan on buying us both lunch. Settling the bill might even help me get out of here."

"You'll call the local police to escort you out? Tell me you'll do that, Lars."

"No. I have to make a point first. Put the money back in your purse."

Her eyes pleaded with him for long seconds. Then she sighed and gave up. The envelope went back in her purse.

"You're being stubborn, Lars." She frowned at him.

"I am."

She rolled her eyes, frowned again, but said nothing.

"Mila, for most of our time together you were in charge."

"So?"

"Therefore, it's my turn. I get to be in charge for lunch."

She laughed softly in spite of herself. "Okay. You can be in charge for lunch."

She tipped her head and awaited his direction. She was back to looking happy.

"Mila, write down for me the phone number Hexler told you to use."

She took out a pen and paper, wrote down the number, and slid it across the table to him.

"Lars, should I be worried about you?" She yet again looked worried.

Lars pocketed Hexler's phone number. "Nope. This'll be easy. Now, let's have lunch."

They did so. He set about putting her at ease, quickly succeeding since he knew her so well from long past. During the meal, Lars and Mila relived their two years spent at adjacent lab benches making super poisons. Lars made Mila laugh often during the meal. Their collaboration at the Pentagon's tiny Advanced Toxins Research Center had left many good memories.

Two and a half hours later, their lunch was over, their table was cleared, and their bill was paid. When the taxi Lars had called for Mila showed up out front, the restaurant was almost empty. She slid her business card across the table to him.

"Here. Stay in touch this time."

"I will. Do you recall what you're to tell Hexler?"

"Yes. But Charlie won't care what I say. He's interested in you."

"Good. That's as it should be."

"Lars, you're sure you don't need me to stay?"

"Yes. I actually need you to leave. Do it cheerfully, point toward where Hexler is, smile at Hexler's two guys, but don't smile at the woman. Act like everything went perfectly well."

"Goodbye, Lars."

She stood. He stood. This time she kissed his cheek.

"Lars, sometime in the days ahead, call me so I know you're safe. Promise me that. Otherwise, there's no way I'll look happy leaving here."

"I promise. Now, show your gorgeous smile and get out of here." He made himself smile.

"Goodbye, Lars." She, too, made herself smile, first for him and then for the others.

Mila walked alone from the restaurant, got into the taxi, and was driven away.

2

Working for Hexler made the pretty bartender a goon in Brent's eyes. She and the two male goons exchanged puzzled glances when Mila left. Rossi was supposed to send Brent to Hexler. The goons were supposed to follow. What, they wondered, should they do now that Rossi had gone and Brent had stayed? Soon the three were texting each other.

Lars Brent summoned a waiter. Brent ordered four gourmet Irish coffees and two of the restaurant's cookie plates. He further said the female bartender should not only make the drinks, but she and her two friends should join him. The other bartender easily could cover for her.

Lars asked for one more thing. He wanted the three to join him in the restaurant's private dining room, which he'd be happy to rent for the next four hours. Brent gave the waiter six hundred Canadian dollars for making the arrangements. He said to give the woman bartender two hundred dollars, the other bartender fifty dollars, and keep the rest himself.

The happy waiter told the woman

bartender, who texted somebody. Probably, thought Brent, the two male goons, who now sat together at a table near the front entrance. Before making the drinks, she removed her apron and pulled a cardigan sweater over her official restaurant shirt. She walked to Lars' table and sat down.

"That's a big tip. Thank you. But what makes you think I know those two guys?"

"I know Charlie Hexler. He'd travel with the standard Agency six-pack of bodyguards. Two will stay with him. I'd guess that's still protocol. That leaves four. One's watching the rear and the rest are watching me. Getting you behind the bar, by the way, was a nice touch."

"I don't know any Charlie Hexler."

He sighed. "Look, if you play dumb, I'll go talk with those two beefy guys at the front door. I'll tell them you're just an airheaded woman too naive to take seriously. I'll say I'd rather deal with them than a boneheaded rookie like you. Got that?"

"Yeah. No comment."

"If I said those nasty things, I'd be lying. But the lies would still end up in your mission's after action report. Those guys'll have to write down what I told them, and you'll look bad. Still want to play dumb?"

She glared at him. "Let's pretend I know Hexler. Let's pretend he wants you to follow us to a place two blocks from here. And let's pretend that blonde told you this."

He looked amused. "You give her too much credit. She's been out of the game for at least a decade. I guess Hexler knew that'd make her gullible. She told me what Hexler said to tell me, which is less than you think. I then told her what a great job she'd done for Hexler and promised to follow through. We had a nice lunch and discussed old times before I sent her on her way. Like I indicated, I don't deal with rookies."

"I watched you two. You didn't act like she's a rookie."

He looked disappointed with her.

"You're much too worldly for that. She's a former co-worker I haven't seen for many years. And she's still hot as can be. I intend to sleep with her."

The she-goon smiled. "Good luck."

"Thank you. Ready to hear what I want from you, besides Irish coffee?"

"You're not going to say sex, are you?"

"Nope. Not yet, anyway. I first have to deal with Hexler. He and I don't like each other much, but his offer's intriguing. It's worth talking about for sure. But it's not worth talking about in the place he wants to use. Can you guess why?"

"I hope you're not afraid of me. Maybe you fear my two musclebound friends?"

"No. I often eat here. It's safe for me because I have my own friends nearby."

"I don't see them."

"You wouldn't. The landlord provides an armed security officer. He's watching us on closed circuit TV. I did him a big favor once. My other two friends are beat cops for this area. I donate generously to their union. Their union rep gave me their phone numbers. It's not hard to be safe once you know how Vancouver works."

It was 100 percent pure bluff, but Brent bluffed well. She believed him.

"Why don't you want to meet where Hexler does?"

"Canadian mobsters use that room. It's an excellent bet the cops have it bugged."

It was another competent bluff.

"Hexler's guys swept it this morning."

"Won't matter. You've got a cellphone tower on the building's roof and microwave ovens in the employee canteen nearby. The lobby guards run a metal detector, operate radios, and have some kind of bomb sniffing x-ray thing. There's so much stray electronic radiation that sweepers never work reliably. The best they can do is tell you the room *might* be secure."

"Okay. Maybe you're smarter than Hexler said. So, how do we all walk away happy?"

"I'll tell you where we'll all meet. Hexler won't go there until somebody on his team checks it out. That means the two door guys, you, and I'll be waiting here close to an hour. Then we'll all get into the same taxi. I thought Irish coffee and cookies would help us wait."

"We don't drink on duty. You know that."

"Tell Hexler I insisted. Everybody's acting too edgy. Irish coffee takes the edge off."

"How do you know I'll put whiskey in anybody's drink but yours?"

"Yeah. There is that. But I knew from the first you'd be the one who'd make trouble."

She smiled and Brent went on.

"Don't put any whiskey in. Bring the bottle---make it the finest this place has---and a shot glass. I'll put a big shot in everybody's coffee. Everybody's but yours. You get two big shots."

She smiled even more. "Are you trying to get me drunk?"

"Well, you're not wearing a wedding ring. You're hot. Are you between boyfriends?"

"Maybe." Her eyes twinkled.

"In that case, I'm pouring you three big shots instead of two."

Lars Brent knew how to charm a she-goon when he had to.

3

Much happened in the next fifteen minutes. One he-goon checked out the restaurant's private dining room and gave the other he-goon a thumbs up. That he-goon called Hexler. Hexler cursed a lot, but said he'd deal with Brent at the second location. The outside goon, stationed at the restaurant's back door beside pungent garbage cans, gratefully caught a cab for the new location. He'd be Hexler's scout.

While she-goon made alcohol-free Irish coffee to Brent's specifications, the unassuming waiter set two plates of cookies on the private dining room table, placed napkins nearby, and left. Lars Brent, wearing his big smile, met the wary he-goons at the dining room door, shook their hands, and offered them seats. They felt safe. Each carried a pistol. Brent seemed unarmed.

She-goon brought in the coffee and the bottle, closing the private dining room's thick door behind her. Brent poured one and a half ounces of whiskey into each glass mug. He poured three ounces into she-goon's mug since, he told the men, bartenders could always drink bar patrons under the table. He invited everyone to add more whiskey at their own discretion. When Lars added a second shot to his own mug, the men laughed and did likewise. The he-goons found the prospect of any she-goon out-drinking them highly amusing.

Lars spent the next several minutes telling them about the room where he'd meet Hexler. He said it was atop Vancouver's tallest office building and part of a private club. Renting the room was so expensive one could always reserve it on short notice if willing to pay the price. Perhaps they saw him text the concierge minutes ago? They hadn't, but were now well into the cookies and didn't much care about the room.

As Lars described the view from the conference room, the first he-goon passed out and tumbled from his chair onto the carpeted floor. The second he-goon tried to draw his pistol, but also passed out and tumbled to the floor.

She-goon looked at Brent with both astonishment and terror in her eyes. He leapt up and caught her before she fell from her chair. Then Brent lifted her up, carried her to the dining room's long leather sofa, and gently positioned her against one corner of it. Satisfied she wouldn't topple, he pulled a dining table chair over to the sofa and sat down opposite her.

"Don't be afraid. I'm not going to hurt

you. If you can blink your eyes, do that twice to show you understand me." She blinked twice.

He smiled reassuringly.

"I used a proprietary drug completely unknown, even to anesthesiologists. I've made myself immune to it so I delivered it subcutaneously this time. The drug's ideal for lethal injections, but the potency levels I gave you and your friends won't harm you. Those two guys got exposed when they shook hands with me. Your dose was on handle of your Irish coffee mug. Blink your eyes twice if I'm being clear."

She blinked.

"Good. In about six hours the two guys will come around. They'll have no side effects. No headache, no nausea, no degraded cognition. Nothing bad. Again, blink if you've got this."

She did so. The fear and astonishment were mostly gone.

"You got the lightest dose and I only induced temporary paralysis in your large voluntary muscles---mostly just your arms, legs, and neck. That's why you're still awake, but unable to move. I need you to tell the doctors and your friends not to worry. Got that?"

Two more blinks.

"Almost done. I'm going to write a phone number on your arm. I'll write it on your friends' arms, too. Give that phone number to

Hexler. Tell him it's secure and untraceable. He should text me when he's ready to have a serious conversation. Okay?"

She blinked.

"I think we're done. Remember, you three will all be completely back to normal soon."

He took out a little bottle of what looked like hand sanitizer, squeezed less than a drop on his finger, and touched it to her neck.

"Time to sleep. You'll wake up in about four hours."

Her eyes no longer held fear. Medical doctor that he once was, Lars Brent communicated well with patients facing the unknown. Seconds later, her eyes closed.

Brent first wrote on their arms the number for one of the untraceable burner phones he kept available. He prepaid the phone time by the minute. Nobody knew he made the payments.

Brent wiped his fingerprints from everything he'd touched in the private dining room. Hexler likely had his prints, but Vancouver police didn't. He didn't worry about prints in the main restaurant. So many prints were everyplace out there the police would never isolate his.

He ignored the holstered he-goon guns, but collected cellphones. He unlocked he-goon phones by swiping them across he-goon fingers. Lars set the unlocked phones to airplane mode so nobody could erase them with commands from afar. He also disabled he-goon phone lock screens. Later Lars would study the two phones' contents.

He couldn't unlock the she-goon phone and left it behind.

Brent calmly walked from the private dining room, found the waiter, and offered him another two hundred dollars to ensure those in the room weren't disturbed by anyone in the next four hours. Lars had ready a story as to why that was necessary, but the waiter didn't ask. The two-hundred-Canadian-dollars part was all he cared about.

Brent got his raincoat, umbrella, and tweed cap from the coat room. He disappeared into urban Vancouver---fifteen minutes before Hexler's scout discovered there was no conference room atop the office building Brent had identified.

4

It took Charlie Hexler all the rest of that day to quench his fury. He needed a second quench early the next morning. It was almost lunch time before he could text Lars Brent. Hexler settled into a comfortable chair in his comfortable hotel room. He picked up his own untraceable burner phone and one-finger typed:

Ready to talk. When? How? Where?

To Hexler's surprise, Brent texted back right away:

1400 hours. Face to face. Kerala Emporium II in the Little India district. Ask for the Adoor meeting room upstairs. No cellphones. No bodyguards. No recorders. Guns are optional since Canada's such a violent nation.

The last part was a joke. Hexler laughed in spite of himself.

Hexler had never been to Vancouver's Little India district, but liked it immediately. It had bright colors, vibrant crowds, and exotic aromas. It reminded him of four years spent undercover in India, working out of the American consulate in Mumbai. Little India, he told himself, held so many wonderful delights---plus reliable Canadian restaurant inspectors! He'd return for dinner.

He easily found Kerala Emporium II. It was a two-story structure and large by Little India standards. The store's shelves displayed the very latest electronic gadgetry, all of it attractively priced. Eager shoppers clogged the aisles and good-naturedly haggled with the Emporium's knowledgeable sales reps.

Hexler left his Agency bodyguards and

cellphone outside, but kept the vintage Walther PPK .380 caliber pistol he wore in a shoulder holster beneath his sport coat. Once inside, he was told to take a narrow, dark flight of stairs to a second floor conference room. Inside, he found Lars Brent wearing what passed for business casual in Little India.

It was a brightly lighted, windowless room. Lars stood by one end of a simple conference table that could seat ten. A big mug of tea was before him. Strange, but pleasant incense wafted from a little burner. It and a modern-looking teapot shared the small table in one corner.

"Take any chair, Charlie. Help yourself to tea. I just brewed it."

Hexler ignored the tea and sat at the conference table end opposite Lars. He deliberately studied authentic Indian tapestries on the walls before deigning to look at Lars.

"Charlie, I've got the room for four hours. Since you and I might struggle to stay civil, I suggest we spend the first hour discussing why we don't like each other."

Hexler scowled. "You think an hour's enough?"

Brent shrugged. "Maybe. However, the Agency---indeed, all of the NATO countries together---only produced five truly extraordinary assassins in the past sixty years.

Three are now dead. That leaves you and me, Charlie. We ought to be friends."

He waited for Hexler to lash out at him. Hexler did, but with less intensity than Brent expected.

"I'm not sure you're that good a killer, Lars. You're still a youngster."

Surprisingly, Hexler then smiled ever so little.

Brent smiled back slightly more.

"There is that. Anyway, you go first. What pisses you off about me Charlie?"

Thin smiles evanesced.

"Where do I begin?" Hexler looked upward and actually seemed to think hard.

He then stared straight at Lars, as if looks might kill.

"Lars, you created this magical poison, used it five times in the field for us, and then quit the Agency."

"Nobody would listen to me, Charlie. I had to use the poison in the field to prove it. Even then nobody'd listen to me. Almost everybody wanted to use snipers. The rest wanted to use bombs. Why stick around where you're not wanted?"

Old memories, most of them bad, came flooding back for Hexler.

"Maybe because it was your job to stick

around, Lars. Or maybe because you took the formula for your super-poison with you. *Or maybe because Mila and I got a trainload of Agency Office of Personnel Manipulation shit dumped on us when you left.*"

Hexler was red-faced now and his fists were clenched.

"Okay. Thanks for your candor, Charlie. How about if I take those things one at a time?"

"Please do. It'll remind me why I feel deeply pissed off."

He leaned forward to reinforce his lingering scowl.

"Charlie, my job description was one of those federal personnel office fantasies. It was written by somebody who didn't understand the work and wasn't cleared high enough to ask about it. They used a pollution techie job and changed the word 'pollution' to 'poison.'"

"It wasn't that bad, Lars … almost that bad, though. The job analyst was a moron."

Hexler mellowed a little. Even after forty-plus years of government service, federal bureaucracy bothered him.

"And my job description had gross misconceptions and omissions. Also, Charlie, Mila'd just become my supervisor then. There were only two of us in the entire lab, but for some reason you made her a lab supervisor."

"Had to. Mila was a fish out of water and ready to quit. Nonetheless, she had superb instincts for supervision. Making her your supervisor was my attempt to keep her with the Agency."

"But you put her in the job before she ever could've been ready for it. Mila's likely the World's smartest woman, Charlie, but she knew nothing about job descriptions, fed-speak, and that sanctimonious rabbit warren they call Personnel. Bottomline: I was pretty much free to do whatever I wanted and I did."

"*You can't just up and quit*, Lars. If you'd been a U.S. citizen, you'd have been thrown in jail."

He went back to full scowl.

"So, why'd the Agency hire a Canadian like me, Charlie? All I had to do was cross the border and be outside your grasp. You could've extradited me, I guess, but that would've meant telling the World what I did for you. Your dumbass Personnel people should've seen it coming. They're your real problem. Not me."

"But you *quit*, Lars. *Q-u-i-t*. You're missing the point."

"When I quit, you didn't have me around to explain poisons. So what? Nobody'd listen to me anyhow."

"*You took your lab journal.* You know, Lars: that vital logbook for recording daily explanations of what you did and how you did it. Even Mila couldn't figure out what you'd been doing without that journal."

"No, Charlie. *I left the lab journal.* The entries were short and vague because they made no difference. The lab tests I did were like a roller coaster moving a hundred miles an hour. The results changed not long after the journal ink dried. I didn't bother writing it all down."

"You could've at least explained to Mila what you were working on."

"I tried, Charlie. Mila will tell you that. But it took six days a week in the lab to keep up with me. Your bureaucrats had Mila overloaded with budget revisions, safety reports, five-year crystal ball sessions, parking lot privileges, a goofy savings bond drive, and more. It was so much Agency administrative crap that even the smartest woman in the world couldn't keep up. Mila felt like she was standing in front of a firehose."

Hexler sighed. "The Agency Office of Personnel Manipulation sucks."

"Yeah, Charlie. AOPM sucks big-time. And after about six months, I didn't write down the details of what I did. It all stayed in my head. Otherwise, I'd have been creating reports I didn't need, Mila didn't want, and you didn't understand. I did us all a favor."

"Where'd you leave the journal?"

"In lab safe number three. My journal was worthless to me. Why bother taking it?"

"Your office was searched and inventoried. The journal wasn't on the list."

"That's *very* hard to believe. Did Mila do the inventory?"

"No. She was off for a week's training on some stupid personnel priority. Maybe hiring by quotas. That's long been good for three wasted days per year."

Lars smiled. "AOPM sucks, huh?"

"Yeah. We at least agree on that."

"I guess that's good because we've come to the hard part. A category five federal shitstorm hit you and Mila when I left, right?"

"Big time. Orchestrated on high by Blanche Pierre. Then the Agency's assistant deputy director for personnel. Now the Agency Office Personnel Manipulation Director. Ever a four-star bitch."

"She's still a U.S. senator's daughter-in-law, Charlie. Still free to be mean as a snake and shamelessly two-faced."

"You're description's too nice ... Lars, it was pure hell for about two months after you left. I missed my annual raise for two years over that and got exiled to India. My wife hated the Indian consulate life so much she left me."

Hexler seemed less angry. Lars sensed

Charlie coming around. Charlie hadn't missed his ex-wife. Nobody had.

"Sorry about that, Charlie. Back then I couldn't imagine you or Mila taking any flak."

"Now, that one's *very* hard to believe, Lars."

Even so, Charlie apparently wanted to believe it.

"Not hard at all, Charlie. I poisoned five world-class bad guys. One in Tahiti, three in France, and one in Morocco. It was done in four weeks, which everybody but you and I thought impossible back then. You were my trainer and also my field controller. You should've been a hero five times over, regardless of what I did afterwards."

"The world's not fair, Lars. It didn't turn out that way."

"Pierre made you the fall guy?"

"Yeah. For years, Pierre's covered up the personnel outrages of Agency pooh-bahs. She had lots of IOUs to call in from them. The week after you left, it was all Pierre's fault. Two weeks later, it was all my fault. The top floor's superb at protecting itself."

"What happened to Mila?"

"Not much. Pierre tried to frame her first. I opened my big mouth, though, and pointed out that Mila was not only new to the

Agency, but new to the job. They gave her a pass and went looking for some other scapegoat. I was the only candidate."

"Again, I apologize. I'd have come back and testified somewhere or other if I'd known that happened. Once you're out of the Agency, though, you hear nothing that's going on inside. Not if you leave the way I did."

Hexler shook his head.

"You'd have been arrested for stealing secrets. You couldn't have reached Alabama."

Lars laughed softly. "Charlie, you and I are assassins. We move freely where others can't. We both know I could've come back. But you couldn't bring yourself to ask, could you?"

Charlie smiled. "I couldn't. It was easier just staying mad at you, Lars."

Charlie smiled more, and said, "It's always easier for a loose cannon like me to be mad at a loose cannon like you."

It was a turning point. Hexler marked it by looking at his watch.

"I feel marginally better and we're running out of time to gripe. What's eating at you?"

"The snatch team you sent. Charlie, you and I butted heads dozens of times while those five bad guys got killed. Same for when you gave me your crash course in how to hunt and kill. But I always thought I could trust you. Sending six goons put me in serious danger. Suddenly, I couldn't trust you. Why the goon team?"

"That was Pierre's idea. The mission we'll talk about soon involves you killing people again. She got it assigned to her oversight, partly to make sure nobody can ever fault her. She'll watch everything you do, making certain it can be blamed on me, if necessary."

"Pierre knows nothing about running field missions."

"She doesn't have to. It's called federal executive career development. You can be in charge of an aircraft carrier these days without ever landing a fighter plane on a carrier at night. Hell, you don't even have to be a pilot. When quotas bump up against commonsense, quotas win. I'd bet a year from now Pierre's daddy-in-law will decide Pentagon Personnel should be run by a woman with field intelligence experience. Somebody like Blanche the Bozo."

"I'm not doing anything if Pierre's my controller."

"I'd be your controller. Lucky me. I'm retiring soon. It's an open secret. That means I won't be around to explain how I did not screw up if you fail. See how this works?"

"How did Mila show up yesterday?"

"That was my idea. I couldn't talk Pierre out of a snatch team. I think she wanted to video your agreeing to one-sided terms. Tough guys were supposed to hold you before a camera."

"They wouldn't get that far."

"Agreed. I knew you'd destroy a snatch team. It would've been an international incident Pierre would've blamed on me."

"You made sure it never came to that. Since you couldn't warn me yourself, you got Mila to do it?"

"Exactly. She's a single parent who needs the extra money. Mila's husband dumped her two years ago, so she was open to a couple days of consulting work."

"*Her husband dumped her?*"

Brent couldn't imagine any sane man leaving Mila.

"Yeah. Hard to believe, huh?"

"Damned near impossible to believe."

"It was a case of midlife crisis meets midlife stupid. He left Mila for some hot young floozie. He died in a car wreck months after the divorce. His estate and any insurance somehow all went to Ms. Floozie. Child support somehow stopped. Ask Mila if you want specifics ... By the way, Mila liked the prospect of seeing you again, Lars. That last little bit's off the record."

"Understood. Thank you."

"You're welcome. Anyway, I told Mila I wanted her to help me have you kidnapped. She immediately knew that was a tragically, horribly, awful idea. I let her talk me out of it. She might have told you she was in this for the extra money, but protecting you was more important to her. And that part's also off the record."

"I didn't even hear you say it, Charlie. Thanks, though."

"No problem. So, what do you think so far?"

Lars laughed softly. "Charlie, I think you're even trickier than you were years ago."

"Thank you."

It was lofty praise coming from Lars.

"And that, Lars, is the story of how Mila kept three or four snatch team guys alive."

Lars shook his head.

"You're wrong, Charlie. I'd have killed all six. Then I'd have gone after you."

"You think a young pup like you could kill an old dog like me?"

"Nope. I'm a realist, Charlie. I know we'd have killed each other simultaneously."

Lars said it with a good smile, though. Charlie smiled back. They were friends again.

5 Four years earlier, the three Volkov brothers concluded their Russian military careers. The brothers were natural athletes, who quickly had become *Spetznaz* superstars. Such prowess didn't go unnoticed. They soon were transferred into Russian military intelligence, where they underwent intensive training well beyond what even the *Spetznaz* received.

The skills thus acquired were tested and honed by dangerous missions in dangerous places. It was a ruthless selection process, meant to develop extraordinary assassins the Russian government could rely upon as unofficial need arose. The very few persons who survived the vetting were taught to move undetected in both the West and the Developing World. That included ongoing language instruction. The Volkovs thus became fully proficient in French, undertaking clandestine missions in France's former colonies or in France itself.

They killed separately or together. Unarmed Volkovs routinely walked alone where local police traveled in groups while carrying automatic weapons. On a typical mission before their retirements, one, two, or all three Volkovs would be sent to eliminate distant enemies who thought themselves well-guarded. The result was always the same. Whomever the Volkovs were told to kill died on schedule. Often that target's entire security team died, too.

When the Volkovs retired from military service, lucrative employment overtures came their way, some of them from powerful French mob bosses. Even so, the Volkovs chose to become freelance assassins. Their first job arrived the day after they went into business. They finished it flawlessly by week's end. More jobs soon followed and met comparable success. European drug dealers seemed forever in need of the Volkovs' grim talents.

Although the brothers limited themselves to regions where either Russian or French was spoken, the demand for their services grew steadily. They began charging three million dollars per kill, half down and half on completion. Fewer jobs came their way at this price.

The Volkov brothers intended that. Now financially secure for life, they focused on their reputations. One or two kills per year would suffice provided the kills seemed impossibly difficult to others. The Volkovs meant to become living legends in the shadowy, lucrative world of international contract murder. Their Russian government careers, in their eyes, had merely presaged their true destiny.

Each brother lived in a different country, maintaining a sanctuary for each other brother in case that person had to flee. They also identified on-call experts who helped them with useful technologies. The brothers paid generous finders' fees for new jobs, never meeting with clients. A few trusted, well-placed intermediaries funneled contract kill jobs to the Volkovs.

Arkady, the eldest Volkov, told his brothers they'd soon be offered three big contracts. Contracts like these, he said, only went to world's foremost assassins. In Arkady's view, the Volkovs at last had been accepted as the best of the best.

6 To Lars' mild surprise, coffee lover Charlie Hexler stood up and poured a mug of tea. He sipped, sipped again, and looked at his mug with satisfaction.

"That stuff's good. If you poisoned it, I'll die happy."

"I thought you'd think that, Charlie, so I let you bring a gun."

Hexler and his tea mug returned to the table.

"I'd shoot you in the last five seconds of my life, right?"

"Actually, you'd have ten seconds. But, yes. Now, ready to talk business?"

"Yeah. First big piece: Assure me, Lars, that you're not recording us."

It was a late for such assurance in light of Hexler's heartfelt condemnation of Agency Personnel, but he cared little. He'd be retired before Personnel's tribe of finger-pointers could write charges---if they ever found out, that is.

"This is the most secretive place in Western Canada, Charlie. It's a long story. Ready?"

"Sure. I could use some extended good news." He sipped tea in anticipation.

"Charlie, Little India's controlled by five families. The largest and most powerful's the Haranya clan. They own the Emporium and more, but you'd never know it. The Haranyas are among the most secretive businesspeople anywhere. They even have their own spies throughout China's electronics industry. The retail area below us is the best place you'll ever find to learn about next year's cellphones. You've maybe guessed that already?"

"The sales clerks all seemed smart, if that's what you mean."

"Very smart. About half are electrical engineers. The rest mostly are back office types. They all rotate through just to stay in touch with the customer. A few more are security experts recruited from elite military units."

"These Haranya guys are tied in with the Mob, maybe?"

"Too bad Sanjay Haranya didn't hear

that. He's the clan patriarch and he'd laugh hard. Even the Montreal Mob doesn't take on the Haranyas. The last such attempt was five years ago. The Mob sent its dream team of killers to assassinate a Haranya, but the goons all mysteriously expired when they got here. Their deaths bewildered Canadian medical examiners, who finally declared the goons died from natural causes."

"You killed the goons?"

"Let's just say the killer, if there were one, had to be extraordinarily skillful with poisons. Sanjay and his family are very good friends of mine. Unofficially, that is. That's the only reason we get to use this special room."

"What's so special about this room."

"First, we're sitting in a Faraday cage. There's a copper grid in the walls, under the floor, above the ceiling. No electronic waves go in or out. When you and I came up the stairs, we walked through sophisticated antenna loops in the walls. I told the Haranya guys to ignore your gun. They found no cellphone. No electronic watch, either. The watch part's unusual, but once I said you're a dinosaur that way, they weren't concerned."

"Okay, Lars. You're safe from me. How am I safe from you?"

"Look at the edge of the table. There's a black button and a little white light. See them?"

"Yeah."

"I've got my own button and my own light. So do other places at the table. If you want to know if you're being recorded, push the button. The light glows once if no recording's detected. It also flashes steadily---all the lights at the table do---the moment any electronic transmission is discovered. This room's for pencil and paper only, Charlie. No tablets. No computers. No phones. That's all pretty amazing given that multimillion dollar deals take place here at least several times a quarter."

"This store's a big business?"

"It's one of several sizable businesses the Haranyas control. They're diversified. One of their other businesses sells sophisticated spy gear that would impress the Agency no end. It would even impress the Chinese, who are more demanding. The Haranyas sweep this room constantly. That's part of how they test new technologies."

"We're safe then." He sounded convinced.

"We're very safe. Now, Charlie, tell me what the Agency wants me to do."

7

The Volkov brothers were connected in a secure video conference, each man thousands of miles from the other two. This time the eldest brother, Arkady, was participating during the middle of his night. He lived alone in Tahiti when not helping effect the two high-profile assassination missions the brothers jointly undertook each year. He sat before his laptop in pajamas, Sumatran coffee in his cup, Turkish cigarette in his mouth.

Arkady Volkov was fifty years old, but still might be mistaken for the *Spetsnaz* colonel he once was. He had Volkov brother good looks and athletic build. Although he worked out hard and often, tonight he felt sleepy. At the video conference's outset, he had told the middle brother that next time he'd be the one participating by night. Arkady was unofficial boss of the three so there was no discussion. The middle brother just nodded his acquiescence.

The middle brother, Grigori, was two years younger than Arkady and fully awake. He lived in Montreal's Russian immigrant section, where it was daytime. Though athletic like his two brothers, his wire-rimmed glasses and longish hair made him look professorial. He was the best planner among them.

That left brother Stepan, who was three years younger than Grigori. He looked somewhat like Grigori, but without Grigori's intelligent eyes. When Arkady and Grigori first discussed becoming freelance assassins, they'd been uncertain if Stepan should join them.

While they loved him in a brotherly sort of way---the Volkov family had always been close---Stepan's work in brutal corners of Russian intelligence had changed him. He seemed to enjoy killing more and more with each successful mission. His two brothers had feared Stepan's fiery bloodlust would be incompatible with their own methodical, dispassionate approach to murder.

They'd discussed that with Stepan. A heated argument began, but ended when Stepan swung a wine bottle at Arkady's head. Arkady calmly blocked his brother's arm and then beat Stepan to within an inch of his life. Afterwards, Arkady and Grigori gently, lovingly nursed him back to health. There'd been no lasting trauma, no broken bones, no ruptured organs. Even so, Stepan's full recovery took much rest, long discussions, and more of each.

Something unexpected happened on the fourth day: Stepan broke into tears. He cried long and hard, repeatedly apologizing. He said he'd been such a fool. He had, he said, no desire to ever endanger his brothers. They could leave him behind, but he hoped they wouldn't. He wanted to be with them, to help them, and---if they'd let him---to kill with them.

Arkady and Grigori left the room and had a long talk. They returned to Stepan and invited him to join them on their first mission.

They said they'd all see how that went. Afterwards, all three brothers would decide if they should remain a three-man team. For Stepan, it was the beginning of a new life, one with single-minded focus on emulating, supporting, and protecting his brothers.

The change in Stepan became fully evident that mission when four armed bodyguards surprised Arkady and Stepan from behind. Stepan jumped between them and his eldest brother, attacking the four with a ferocity Arkady had never encountered. Stepan killed all four men, even though they were bigger than he and well-armed.

He was wounded three times. Arkady halfway carried him from the fight scene, following Grigori's flawless escape plan. That plan took them to an unscrupulous physician's home. He patched up Stepan enough that an equally unscrupulous private pilot could fly the brothers to safety.

Never again did his brothers question Stepan's competence. Never again did Stepan question their careful preparations. Because of his brothers' prudence, Stepan survived his wounds. Because of their foresight, Grigori---waiting on the target's likely escape route---terminated their target as she fled. The brothers should've died that fateful night. Instead, they became even more formidable.

Now, during the videoconference, Stepan fingered his brown hair and blinked his dull eyes. A sustained sip of beer followed. It was good beer, brewed in Belgium only five blocks from Stepan's apartment. He opened up a small notebook, picked up his pen, and sat ready to take notes when Arkady began. Stepan would burn the notes later---his brothers knew that---but writing notes better fixed things in his memory. Stepan needed that extra help and more.

"This job proposal's from Beacon. The targets are important men, always with three or four bodyguards each. The kills have to be made before the American presidential election. We'd have fifty-six days left if we accepted the contract tomorrow."

"How much per kill, Arkady?" asked middle brother Grigori.

"Our fee's four million per hit. We also get a million for expenses and keep any expense money that we don't use. We get half the fee and all the expense money up front. The rest's paid on completion."

Grigori looked surprised. "Thirteen million's a lot of money, even for us. What's the catch?"

"Beacon says they want some stagecraft. We'd plant evidence making it look like Russian government assassins carried out the hit." He laughed softly.

"Guys like we used to be?" asked Stepan. Sometimes he did not get a job's novel aspects on the first time through.

"Yeah. We make it look like the work we used to do."

"Any idea who's the client?" asked Grigori.

"Nope. Beacon doesn't know. For big jobs, he won't talk about a hit unless there's a go-between separating him from the client. He insists clients stay anonymous."

Arkady snuffed out his cigarette and began taking another from its European-style box. About once every six months Stepan told him smoking was unhealthy. Arkady agreed and ignored each warning.

"Why won't Beacon tell us?" asked Stepan, who handled none of the administration. It was mostly Arkady who made financial arrangements. It went with being in charge.

"He's being careful," explained Grigori. "Suppose there's a go-between and the client wants to ensure no trails lead back to the client. The client just whacks the go-between. Beacon's survived in this business by ensuring he's never the go-between closest to clients."

"He's being smart?" asked Stepan, as a light belatedly flickered behind his eyes.

"Yeah, Stepan," said Grigori, who was more patient with Stepan than Arkady was.

"Has Beacon told us where yet?" asked Grigori.

"Where could change by the day, but it'll be in Canada. Beacon says we'll have all the intelligence we need for each job."

"I like Canada," offered Stepan. "Lots of Canadians speak French."

Stefan occasionally said things too obvious to mention. He mostly excelled at ferocious violence and absolute loyalty. Those virtues mostly offset the pointless observations he made.

"Anything else before we vote?" asked Arkady.

Grigori shook his head. Stepan thereupon did the same.

"All in favor say so."

Arkady and Grigori professed themselves in favor simultaneously. Once Stepan was sure what his brothers wanted, he joined in. Arkady notified Beacon of their decision an hour later. An hour after that, the first payment reached the offshore bank the brothers used. They also received a link to the Dark Web encrypted chatroom holding information to plan the kills.

8 Charlie shifted position in his conference room chair before explaining to Lars Brent what the Agency wanted. The shifting revealed the .380 Walther PPK in his shoulder holster. Neither he nor Brent cared.

"My turn for a long story, Lars. The proposed mission's like your first one, but you'd only have to eliminate three assassins before they strike. The money's good. The intelligence you'd need's at least average. Not yet great, but sure to get better. But put that and even more aside for now. Let me begin with some mystery. The Agency doesn't know who ordered the hits you'd have to stop. We don't even know why the hits were ordered."

"But the Agency has its theories?"

"Mainly one theory, Lars. Pierre says the Agency's official, tenuous speculation of the week's that somebody wants to dramatically worsen Russian-American relations."

He stopped, mistakenly thinking a dramatic pause might help.

"I already don't get it."

Charlie sighed. "My fault. I rushed the story. Let's start over with some background."

"Let's do that."

"Lars, the U.S. and Russia have had an increasingly stormy relationship in recent years. 'Stormy' as in typhoons are 'stormy.' Russia rattled sabers at NATO, cheated on a nuclear arms deal, and buddied up with Iran. Moscow seized Crimea, sort of seized southern Ukraine, and deviously acquired American uranium. Lesser outrages took place, but you get the idea."

"I do."

Lars' tea was getting cold so he took a big sip. He'd grown serious about good tea and liked it hot.

"Meanwhile, the U.S. applied serious economic sanctions and harangued Kremlin leaders. The phony Russian collusion *imbroglio* didn't help whatever dialogue ensued. Also, U.S. efforts to stop Russian gas sales to Germany raised Russian hackles. And, of course, the multifaceted disaster that is Syria made both sides angry."

"And now somebody wants to dial back the temperature?"

"Actually, both the U.S. and Russia quietly seek that. You see, both sides have kept their adult diplomats in the room, even when the youngsters staged food fights. The adults are finally being listened to by people at the very top."

"Why?"

"First, neither side wants things to get worse. Nobody who remembers the Cold War wants to recreate it. Second, there's huge trade opportunity at stake. The U.S. sells things

Russia needs. Russia has the mineral wealth to buy them."

"I think you're telling me that Russia and the U.S. should be the best of trading partners."

"They would be in a sane world, but the World's only sane in fits and spurts. We're now somewhere between a fit and a spurt. U.S.-Russian relations are at a tipping point and could get either much better or much worse. Nobody knows which."

"I still don't get it … Charlie, if the U.S. and Russia want better relations, why wouldn't they have just go out and have better relations?"

"Because other nations don't want that. Other countries fare better if the U.S.-Russia relationship gets worse. Other nations might want to sabotage U.S.-Russian *rapprochement*."

"The Agency actually thinks that?"

"Some of it does. Certain smarty-pants analysts think that, but not all of them. Not yet, anyway. This assessment's from Her Insufferable Highness, the AOPM Director."

"Charlie, do you believe anything that comes from Blanche Pierre?"

"Forget about Pierre. I'm telling you about current smarty-pants thinking."

"I sense a convoluted explanation ahead."

"Not convoluted, Lars. It's easy to

follow. There are only two key pieces. I'll tell you why some nations do worse if Russia and the U.S. get along well. That's the first piece. You'll need about half a mug of tea to keep up."

"The tea aspect sounds okay." He took another sip from his mug.

"The second piece's how some nation might make the U.S. angry at Russia. That second part takes less than half a mug of tea … Ready to begin?"

"Yeah. I can't wait. Tell me who might want America and Russia mad at each other."

"Take China first. They have a gazillion people and not much land. Right next door is Russia's Siberia, which has a gazillion square miles and not many people. Suppose China decided to quasi-invade Siberia like Russia quasi-invaded Ukraine."

"The Chinese won't invade. Russia has ICBMs."

"China's building better ICBMs. Remember, Lars, China's figured out how to build and market superb smartphones. Russia's not there yet. If you can't win at smartphones, you can't win at missiles. Not long-term, anyway."

Brent decided his tea was too cold to drink. He rose and walked to the room's high-tech, electric teapot, ready for a refill. A thought struck him midway. He looked back toward

Hexler.

"Let me guess the next little piece, Charlie."

"Guess away."

"If the U.S. and Russia were buddies," Brent suggested, "the U.S. just might withdraw from NATO? Maybe so they could use the NATO money for health care back home?"

"Pierre says some smartypants think that. And if the U.S. leaves NATO, Russia can shift lots of troops from its border with Europe to its border with China."

"Thus, for China, invading Siberia gets easier if these Russian troops stay in Europe. China wants both Europe and America to see Russia as a grave military threat to Europe?"

"Yep. So think some Agency smarty-pants imagine in their pointy little heads."

Brent finished with the high-tech teapot and returned to the table.

"Okay, Charlie. I guess it follows Germany might not want America trusting Russia. That way Germany can keep America picking up the tab for German defense while Germany puts its own money into German health care. How's that sound?"

"That sounds exactly like the smarty-pants epiphany."

Brent sat down at the table and drank

some tea. Hexler thought about getting more tea, himself. It was good, but any more caffeine that late in the day would keep him awake at night.

"May I presume the Agency thinks only China or Germany or both might try to derail any near-term Russian-American *rapprochement*?"

"Let's just say those are possibilities, Lars. We're not done with the first part yet. I'm still identifying for you countries that might want poor relations between the U.S. and Russia."

"Are there many others?"

"Sadly enough, there are. Suppose Russia and America warm up to each other and Russia goes shopping in the U.S. Whatever America began selling Russia would no longer be bought by Russia from someplace else. Japan, France, Korea---or any of the little countries punching well above their weight on trade---could lose business."

"I get the point."

"Good."

Charlie shifted position. His gun was pushing against his ribs.

"So far, I've said there may be unknown third parties that want bad relations between the U.S. and Russia. Not bad enough to start a nuclear war, but bad enough to worry people about war. Got it?"

"Got it."

"Next I'm going to tell you how some unknown nation can ensure U.S.-Russian relations become really lousy really soon. Not lousy to the point of war, but still genuinely stinking bad."

"Is half a mug of tea enough for this part, Charlie?"

"Lars, don't give me that skeptical look of yours. The beard makes it even worse."

"It's just the beard, Charlie. I'm being open-minded. Tell me how to make Americans exceedingly angry at Russians."

"First off, remember a U.S. presidential election'll be held in roughly two months. For almost sixty days, there will be serious, big-time opportunity to change what American voters think about Russia. Our unknown nation plans on doing that."

"These three assassinations somehow make American voters so angry that U.S. politicians react?"

"More like over-react. Nobody accuses Washington of precision."

"And the Agency knows about all this how?"

"Hypothetically speaking --- you remember how hypothetical conversations go,

Lars?"

"Yeah. We never discussed for real what we discussed. We were just amusing ourselves with idle speculation about what might happen. Charlie, the room's not bugged. You don't need to go hypothetical on me."

"Humor me, Lars. Hypothetically, there are about seven persons in the Western world who broker high-level hits. The Agency tries to keep hit brokers under electronic surveillance. NSA does, too. But these seven guys hire top-level consultants who know the surveillance tricks we know. We miss broker conversations much more often than we listen in."

"Yet the Agency still picked up something that might require my help?"

"Yeah. There'll be three high-profile hits. The killers speak French. The hit broker's somebody at France's Montreal consulate. Our guys intercepted about half of the messages exchanged."

"Who are the targets?"

"For now, let's just say they're high profile individuals sure to be missed."

"The hits would occur in the U.S.?"

"No. They're to be in Canada. A big convention begins in Quebec City soon. The messages and bits of messages we intercepted mentioned it specifically. Also, there'd be backup plans in case they don't get all the kills made in Quebec City. The backup part's just me guessing."

"Good guess. What's the secondary kill site you'd use?"

"Ottawa. A day after the Quebec City convention, the likely targets will testify at one hearing or another in Ottawa for two days, before flying back to their well-protected home bases. Counting the time in Ottawa, the killers have about six days of good opportunity."

"You're thinking they'll invest the usual prep time?"

"Yep. No freelancer wants to make a hit without a week to get ready. Two weeks would be better still."

"So, Charlie, you expect they'll spend roughly two weeks preparing to kill at each location? Maybe a month of work altogether?"

"I'd guess three weeks at most since the targets don't change. They'll study the Quebec sites first. Conventions present easier kill zones than Ottawa hearing rooms these days. But, of course, the hits could be when targets enter or exit buildings at either place. And there are airport opportunities. All the usual VIP vulnerabilities."

"Why would anybody blame the kills on Russia?"

"There'd be phony evidence left behind showing the Russians ordered the hits. The goal's to make ordinary American voters furious with the Kremlin."

"I still don't get it. American voters are always halfway furious about something these days. Mostly, it's about each other. Since outrage is normal, who cares if they're angry?"

"Lars, American politicians care. American voters have huge leverage before elections. Since a U.S. presidential election's coming up two months from now, U.S. politicians would have little choice but to come out strongly against Russia in the wake of the assassinations. Expect competitions over which candidate can promise to hurt Russia the most, short of sending troops or firing missiles. The Russians will claim innocence, but nobody'll believe them. Not after they've bungled some high-profile assassinations outside Russia in past years."

"So, somebody'd create a backlash by making three kills look like Russian dirty work?"

"Exactly."

Lars looked at the ceiling, closed his eyes, and very quickly played back Charlie's story in Lars' powerful memory. He tried to listen between the lines when he did so.

"Charlie, let me sum up what I think I heard you tell me, even if I still struggle to believe it. Start with the tipping point piece.

Following the U.S. presidential election, Americans and Russians will become good friends for a couple of years, or they'll hate each other at least that long. It could go either way. You think some nation will send a kill team to turn ordinary American voters fervently against Russia. Have I got that part right?"

"Yes." Charlie leaned forward with anticipation.

"And you have no idea which nation's paying for the kills?"

"No, but the smarty pants are working on that."

"Okay. Ignore that for the moment. Maybe you can tell me why *faux*-Russians would kill anybody while in Canada. Conventions occur all over the world. Corporate big shots can testify pretty much anyplace anytime. Why Canada?"

"It's happy little Canada, land of goodwill to all. There's so little espionage and terrorism here that Canadian law enforcement's not terrific at catching spies and assassins. Don't get me wrong. You've got good counterespionage guys, Lars, but they've far too little real-life experience to be terrific. It's like comparing combat veterans with the best new arrivals."

"You look down your nose at everywhere outside the Beltway, don't you

Charlie?"

"Mostly, except that I might really get to like this Little India place of yours."

9 The three Volkov brothers were again connected by secure videoconference. This time Grigori attended during the middle of the night from his apartment in French Canada. Grigori moved every six months. He always rented expensive apartments no more than four floors up. He kept rappelling gear under his bed, in case he had to leave by a window.

This time Stepan participated from his own apartment somewhere near Paris. He looked a little hung over, but it was early in Paris. He'd probably just awakened, Arkady thought, given Stepan hadn't yet bothered to shave.

Arkady, as usual, began their proceeding. "Has everybody received the file I sent you? The one with the information from Beacon's client?"

They had. Grigori nodded after Stepan grunted.

Arkady said, "The targets are two drug company execs and one Russian dissident. You've seen their biographies and what's known of their security arrangements. You've seen their schedules for nine days. Tell me your thoughts?"

That really meant asking Grigori's opinion. Grigori was the deep thinker. Stepan could sometimes locate good restaurants and average hookers, but mostly did simple, repetitive tasks.

Grigori said, "My initial thought's that we don't want to kill the CEOs one right after the other. As soon as we snuff one, it'll suggest we're after top executives. Best, I think, to kill the dissident second. That'll suggest the killers might randomly choose targets. The CEO we take out last would feel marginally safer that way."

"Both CEOs will be available at the convention," said Arkady. "What if we could get both at once? The right bomb in the right place would do that."

Grigori replied, "If we can blow them up when they're in the same men's room, ten pounds of plastic explosive would work. The intelligence Beacon sent us isn't precise enough for using less explosive. No small kill charges this time."

"Would a much bigger bomb work? Maybe we could blow up an auditorium with them in it?" asked Stepan, trying to participate.

Arkady waited for Grigori to answer their brother. Grigori would be more patient with Stepan than Arkady would. Somebody who'd been an elite Russian army assassin as long as Stepan had shouldn't need to ask such a question, Arkady thought.

Arkady made a tally mark on his legal pad. It was how he kept track of Stepan's useless comments. If Stepan earned ten marks, as he rarely did, Arkady would gently rebuke him. Arkady always waited for ten tally marks, though. Stepan became sulky when criticized. It was easier to let him waste nine tally marks worth of videoconference.

Grigori patiently said, "It depends on the auditorium, of course, but it'd take something like a hundred pounds of plastic explosive if we stuffed in ball bearings or nails. Otherwise, make that at least two hundred pounds of plastic explosive. Even the Montreal Mob can't provide much more than twenty pounds on short notice. If we use bombs, they'll need to be somewhere around ten-pounds or less."

Then Stepan had a relatively good idea. His brothers were pleasantly surprised.

"The Mega Pharma convention's in a high-rise luxury hotel. Do you think hotel security's good enough to check the elevator shafts for bombs?"

Grigori looked pleased. "I'd say it's fifty-fifty. Somebody'd do that for sure if a head of state were staying there. Otherwise, I think they'd rely on door locks and, maybe, on motion sensors. They'd also check for bombs twice a year or whenever they have to make full elevator inspections. In between inspections, they'd ignore shafts unless sensors went off there."

"Maybe we should check out the elevators when we get to Quebec for our reconnaissance?" suggested Arkady.

"Yes," responded Grigori. "I'll put that on the list. What about ceramic knives?"

"They'd have bodyguards around them," said Stepan. "Probably a bodyguard screen at least three yards out and one person in close at arm's length."

Arkady gave Stepan a second tally mark.

"Bodyguards just mean two or three kills instead of one," explained Grigori. "Remember how your team did things in Kiev long ago, Stepan. Two men each took out a bodyguard. That left a hole in the target's security perimeter. You walked through with a knife. A big success for you back then, huh?"

Stepan looked pleased. It had been a big success. Once he'd fatally stabbed the target, he and two colleagues fought their ways out of the room. Mostly, that meant pushing reporters and camera crews aside while pretending to be security officers, charging after the supposedly fleeing assassin. All three got away in the confusion.

Arkady said, "Can Montreal's Mob get

us exotic poisons? Maybe radioactive polonium? Or thallium?"

Grigori added to the action item list he'd been keeping.

"I'll try, but I doubt it. I'll ask the St. Petersburg Mob, too. Government controls on poisons are still looser in Russia."

Arkady said, "We could always use dioxin or ricin. Somehow we'd poison one of these guys. I guess we'd shoot the third, just so we don't use the same tactic more than once?"

"Shooting at least one of them's a nice idea," said Stepan.

Stepan was a superb sniper---so much so that Arkady made no tally mark.

"We can get whatever sniper stuff Stepan might need from the Montreal Mob," Grigori assured them.

Arkady began to wrap things up. "Remember, this videoconference is just the first pass. Nothing tactical is definite yet. But I think we know the kill plan is either two CEOs followed by the dissident, or CEO-dissident-CEO, correct?"

Both men nodded.

"We'll use three ways to kill if we can and we'll need both cities."

Both his brothers again nodded.

"Then, I think we're on schedule. Let's

meet in Quebec City," said Arkady. Minutes later they ended the videoconference.

10

Lars glanced at his watch and suggested he and Charlie take a restroom break before going on. Five minutes later each returned to his table end.

"Charlie, you said the mission intelligence was average. Not great, but average. Since what you've told me so far falls well short of average, I guess you're about to disclose good stuff. Lots of good stuff, even. That might bring the Agency's overall contribution up to average. Up from remarkably inadequate so far, that is."

"Lars, I said 'average,' not 'perfect.' It's all relative. My version of 'average' might surpass your version of 'perfect.'"

"I hope so. I'm not feeling good about this job yet."

"You will. For one thing, you'll like the challenge. You'd be going up against all three Volkov brothers."

"Who?"

"Spoken like an untutored civilian from flyover country. I'll enlighten you."

"Please do that, Charlie."

"The Volkovs are ex-Russian government assassins. Two are very smart and very ferocious. One's not-so-smart, but even more ferocious. They were trained to speak French and made hits in French-speaking areas on behalf of Mother Russia. I'll send you the encrypted folder once you take the job. The paper version's a half-inch thick."

"You've got facial pictures? Fingerprints?"

"Only recently. Our adults are working with adult Russian diplomats to stop the Volkovs. All of a sudden, we've access to much of the Volkovs' Red Army files. We've got their old Red Army photos, former aliases, and their fingerprints. We can track them with facial recognition. Well, we sort of can track them. Maybe half the time at best."

"No doubt they know the standard ways to thwart facial recognition."

"Unquestionably. Every now and then we figure out where a Volkov was a couple of days ago. The dumb one's easiest to follow. But there are still plenty of gaps in our knowledge. We can fill some gaps with artificial intelligence. Sometimes our techies can predict where the Volkovs are headed. Only sometimes, though."

"Maybe the Volkovs follow patterns when they kill?"

"They've all got superb infantry skills. They're excellent with guns, knives, fists, and explosives. They also might be the ones who poisoned a cartel boss and his bodyguards. It was a simple poison. Cyanide, arsenic, something mundane like that. They seem to prefer fists. No brass to recover. No gun to hide. And each one's a top-flight martial artist."

"I need locations, Charlie. I can't kill what your folks can't find."

"Finding the Volkovs will get much, much better once they enter Quebec City or Ottawa. Both places are overflowing with indoor facial recognition cameras. Fewer cameras outside, though, but still enough of them."

"Winter tends to keep crooks indoors."

"Good. Maybe the Volkovs will go inside with everybody else. The extra cameras will be waiting for them. So will Major Kati Barska, U.S. Army Signal Corps. Think of her as your new shadow. She'll handle IT for you. Finding the Volkovs will be her job."

"I work alone, Charlie. You know that."

"Barska's Blanche Pierre's idea. Pierre handpicked her. You're stuck with Barska."

"Okay. Tell her to stay twenty miles from me. I'll text her if I need anything. That'll work."

Hexler shook his head, rolled his eyes, and said nothing.

"Charlie, tell me how I'd get operational intelligence and support during the mission."

"Ask Barska. All that comes through her by order of Blanche Pierre."

"Is Barska any good?"

"I, personally, have no idea. Pierre thinks so."

"Pierre's a knucklehead."

"Her Senator daddy-in-law says she's brilliant. Within the Agency, that makes it official. Anyhow, you're stuck with Barska just like I'm stuck with Pierre. Be happy like me."

"Not so fast. I want to see Barska's army file and anything else you've got on her."

Hexler reached into a pocket and slide a thumb drive down the table to Brent.

"It's all there. I had Blanche's chief flunky dump every record we Feds have about Barska onto that thumb drive. The password's your middle name in lower case, with a capital letter 'L' after each syllable."

"Thanks. You don't have something like this on the Volkovs do you?"

"Nope. The Agency smarty-pants didn't get around to it. Tell Barska to gather up whatever else's available."

"I haven't agreed to work with Barska."

"You will. The job pays five million for each Volkov you kill, with half up front regardless. There's a million for expenses, all of it upfront."

"The price is right. At least somebody realizes how hard this could be."

"You've got to keep Barska by your side if you want the money."

"Swell. What's she look like."

"Brunette. Sexy. About five years younger than you. Barska's your bartender friend."

11

The international pharmaceutical industry convention in Quebec City would be held in the Old City Tower, two blocks from Quebec City's popular historical district. The Old City Tower rose thirty stories. It was not only the city's newest hotel, but also its most luxurious. The Volkovs, however, would stay in separate rooms at a cheap hotel six blocks away.

Grigori would make the brothers' indoor reconnaissance of the Old City Tower. Arkady would plan outdoor escape routes from the CEO assassination or, maybe, from the CEO assassinations. Stepan would remain in his room in tactical reserve.

The Volkovs believed Western law enforcement still had no pictures of them. However, someday they would, and facial recognition then would spot one of them---

probably Stepan---once in awhile. That being so, Grigori and Arkady thought it prudent to divert any emerging police interest to somewhere in Quebec City far from where the Volkovs' would be working.

The next day Stepan left reserve status for the kill mission's first dangerous task. He would travel to the opposite side of Quebec City, where Friends of the Deer Tick had scheduled their last outdoor protest before Quebec's autumn began feeling like Washington, D.C.'s winter.

An unruly crowd of three hundred surprisingly ill-mannered Canadian agitators was anticipated. Some in the Canadian media forecast a bitter confrontation with police---an encounter characterized by foul language, vile hand gestures, and scofflaw littering. All the major Canadian networks would have camera crews present to record the disruption.

Stepan's job was repeatedly showing his face among the demonstrators, but not staying anywhere among them for long. He would also walk past various security cameras near a particular budget hotel. As the brothers easily discovered online, the demonstration's organizers would stay there. Canadian police would deploy extra surveillance in that area.

Stepan's deliberately erratic approach would take him through ten miles of city. That morning there was no chance facial recognition would identify him before he intended. It was cold enough to wear his jacket collar up and bright enough for sunglasses. His hat, which he wore low on his forehead, proudly displayed the local hockey team's logo on the brim.

After walking randomly for several blocks to check for anyone following him, he hailed the oldest taxi he could find. Grigori had discovered online that ride sharing apps had seriously damaged the Quebec City taxi fleet's income. The smallest operators by now routinely deferred maintenance and body work. Few of these tiny companies had extra money to install the passenger cameras the big company cabs carried.

No taxicab video record was made of Stepan during the ride from his side of Quebec City to the far side of Quebec City. He initially would've given the cab driver an average tip. Too much or too little, Stepan had assumed, would help the driver remember him.

However, after one look into the driver's glassy eyes, Stepan doubted she'd remember anybody. He tipped two dollars less. It was like giving himself a lottery ticket. He felt clever.

The demonstration crowd was still assembling. Organizers made fund-raising pitches as latecomers drifted into the pack. Some demonstrators passed out placards.

Others culled the prettiest of the crowd's women and led them to the front of the parade being formed. The group would sing, chant, wave fists, and snarl on cue. It had to be over in an hour, organizers said, because few public restrooms were nearby.

Stepan located four surveillance cameras. He removed his hat, pocketed his sunglasses, and hiked past all four like a baseball player rounding the bases in slow motion. He also waved at activists along the way, shook hands with some of them, and handed two others what looked like envelopes of cash, but actually were packets of deer tick fundraising brochures.

A third bystander got a large manila envelope that really did hold cash. Another thin packet of cash went to a clean-shaven man Stepan thought an undercover cop, given the man's shiny black shoes, big shoulders, and recent haircut.

Stepan climbed on a sidewalk bench and took video of the crowd as it began its one-block march to a parking lot, where a Hollywood has-been would lambast the usual corporate villains, desperately hoping to revitalize her career. Somebody with a bullhorn began leading the songs, which were warm-up for chants to come.

Hat still off, Stepan jogged to the

organizers' hotel from the activists' demonstration assembly area. As he knew, running would make him stand out from the slow-shuffling pedestrians.

At the hotel, he found an organizers' table set up in the lobby, just as the activists' website promised. Stepan presented an envelope of cash to the ranking Deer Ticker, got a receipt, and abruptly left.

Outside the hotel, he walked into a public library. In its restroom, he reversed his jacket and donned a bright cap advertising a Lake Ontario fishing boat charter service. Stepan left by the backdoor, sliding on a different pair of sunglasses as he exited.

The facial recognition cameras Stepan had passed each produced a haystack of data that morning. Computers labored hard that afternoon sorting through the haystacks for interesting needles. One computer flagged video of Stepan taken when he had uncovered his face. Other computers, thus alerted, soon found Stepan video of their own.

Quebec City police analysts notified Provincial officials a suspected terrorist had been seen among Deer Tickers. He'd given them money, too.

12

Brent and Hexler still sat in the Haranya conference room. Charlie again looked at his watch.

"Lars, we gotta get this done. Is Barska the only obstacle?"

"I need some time, Charlie. I want to read Barska's file. I should look at whatever pictures the Web has of the Quebec City and Ottawa sites. I need to know why my gut's already so uncomfortable about a chance at sixteen million U.S. dollars. Be patient."

"I don't do patient anymore, Lars. I'm an upper paygrade Agency demi-poohbah now. And it's not U.S. dollars. Pierre is offering you sixteen million Canadian dollars."

"You're kidding. Mila said U.S. dollars."

"Mila mistakenly might have assumed U.S. dollars."

"Mila doesn't make errors like that, Charlie."

"Well, maybe I got careless explaining to Mila what I wanted her to say. So what? Just ask for more money. Ask for Swiss francs or Icelandic krona, if you want. The Agency can pay you in just about anything. Maybe even bitcoins."

"If I do this, I want thirty million Canadian dollars."

"Ridiculous. Sixteen million U.S. dollars

at today's exchange rate equals roughly twenty million Canadian."

"I included a hefty bullshit tax, Charlie. I don't like your changing the currency on me. I don't like babysitting Barska. And I don't believe your guys can find the Volkovs, anyway."

"We'll find them. I'll figure out some kind of payment to you if we don't. Pierre'll go along with that."

"I don't want Barska around. She can log into whatever she needs from a thousand miles away. She doesn't have to be across the hall from me."

"Pierre was thinking you and Barska would travel as man and wife. Or maybe as man and girlfriend, since it's Canada. Pierre wants Barska right next to you. Like in the same king bed."

"Why?"

"Pierre doesn't trust you. My opinion---and Pierre hasn't said this---is that Barska's to report on you."

"You'd be my controller. Why don't you do the reporting on me?"

"I would. Pierre doesn't trust me, either. I'm just an easy guy to blame if the operation turns from promising to tragic. I'll be retired soon and unable to tell my side of things."

"Ready for my big problem with all this, Charlie."

"Sure. I'd have guessed sixteen big problems. You've got that skeptical brow wrinkle you used to do."

"I only look that way around you, Charlie. Anyhow, I don't get why you even need me. You could use Agency terminators almost for free."

"Nope. We can't use them, Lars. They're ours. They're Americans. If this mission blew up in the Agency's face, it would look like U.S. government agents went to war with Russian government agents. That'd be *de facto* proof the U.S. government not only needed to fight Russia, but was already doing so. There'd instantly be zero hope of good trade relations."

"So, if I did the work and things blew up, it'd only look like Canada fighting Russia?"

"Even better. It might only look like a single Canadian hitman against three freelance hitmen coincidentally born in Russia. And to your average American voter, Canada's relationship with Russia is Canada's problem, regardless. A Lars Brent fiasco never would become an issue in the U.S. election."

13

Charlie Hexler shifted in his chair again. He had begun doing that every few minutes, by Lars' estimation. Charlie's posterior had spent enough time on his wooden chair.

"Charlie, I'll contact you tomorrow. I've got to understand Barska's file first."

It was not an unreasonable position.

"Okay. I'll tell Pierre you want more money. She'll be really mad about that. I like seeing Pierre mad, if she's not mad at me. I'll probably even enjoy watching her gag as she swallows your outrageous fee, Lars."

He smiled, thereby signaling Blanche Pierre would pay more.

"And you'll figure out what I get paid if the Agency can't locate the targets?"

"Yeah. I'll work on that. I'll try to get Blanche apoplectic before lunch. That'll spoil her meal. I'll meet with her later about a contingency payment to you if the Agency can't find the Volkovs. I'll spoil her dinner, too."

Charlie then said his codename would be Old Dog. Did Lars want to be Needles again? Lars did. Next Lars gave Charlie an offshore bank account to use once they reached agreement. Both expected a suitable deal, Barska and Pierre notwithstanding.

Old Dog handed Needles a piece of waterproof flash paper, which burned almost instantly when lit. On it were Dark Web chatroom URLs, secure phone numbers, and secure email addresses. They also agreed to use the *Cryptobag* app to encode their email conversations.

At that point, they'd gone as far as necessary that day. Old Dog asked Needles where the best Little India restaurant was, the men shook hands, and Lars walked out into the street with Old Dog and his patient bodyguards. As Charlie's team continued on toward the restaurant a few minutes distant. Lars went into the Emporium and out its rear entrance.

Before Lars got back inside, though, Old Dog turned and looked briefly over his shoulder at his former protégé. The Volkovs were the best evil talent out there, so far as Charlie could tell. He wondered if he'd ever again see Lars alive.

14

Once back in his comfortable Vancouver hotel room, Charlie thought hard about the danger Lars would face. The thinking helped. He reminded himself all over again that Lars was up to the challenge.

He played back in his head memories of their extended conversation. Most of it seemed fine, but the lab journal piece needed attention. He should check whether Lars lied about that.

The next morning Charlie called Senior Journeyperson Classified Federal Documents Archivist Grade IV Ruby Dobbins. She had, for thirty some years, kept track of classified documents at the super-secret Alabama chemical weaponry facility where Lars and Mila worked.

Charlie had been a frequent visitor to the facility back in those days. That's how he and Ruby met. He couldn't see her over the phone, but she still wore a size eight dress and dyed her hair red. Rubies, she long ago told him, should be red.

Ruby remembered him as soon as he said 'hello' on the telephone.

"Charlie Hexler! It's been like forever plus a day. If you'd waited three months, you'd have missed me. I'd have been retired and out of here."

"Good to talk with you again, Ruby! And if you left in three months, I just might've retired two weeks ahead of you. I might start talking to a travel agent soon."

"No, you won't, Charlie. People do that online now. Unless you're rich, that is. But maybe you're rich now, huh?"

"Nope. I'm just another downtrodden Fed taking Washington, D.C. cattle trains to work. I'm like a million others, except I urgently need your help."

"Well, Charlie, you'll get my serious help. I remember you buying five cases of candy bars from my daughter to support the Frontier Girls. She's a Frontier Girls leader now and you're one of her heroes. She tells her girls about you at the start of each fundraiser."

"I'm flattered. Maybe my sweet tooth's a good thing. Anyway, do you remember Lars Brent? He worked in the tiny, little lab Mila Rossi supervised."

"Yes! A skinny Ph.D. who was always polite. In two years he went from clean shaven to a mustache to a goatee, and talked about a full beard when he left. Did he ever grow one?"

"He's got one now. And he's still skinny. We're talking about the same guy. Ready for my questions testing your memory to its outer limits?"

"Fire away. I'll either know it or I'll look it up. These days I mostly look it up."

"Lars was working on some sort of super-advanced compound. It was revolutionary. When he quit, he tells me, he left the lab journal for his work in his lab safe. Safe three, he says. Can you confirm that?"

Charlie heard computer keys click. "Can't confirm it from memory, but I'm typing away. I have kept superb records of the whereabouts of every secret document created at this facility in my well over thirty years here. I record creation, custody, and destruction. Of course, you already know that, but saying it gives me time to type."

"I'd rather listen to you than be put on

hold. No problem."

"Thank you … and here it is on my almost-obsolete computer's screen. Lars did create a lab journal. You need the date?"

"Probably not. I mostly need to know if he took it when he left. He says it stayed at the lab in safe three."

"Gotta go to another screen … There. Well, it looks like he's wrong. His office was inventoried the day after he left. Between eight-twenty-three a.m. and eleven-fifteen a.m. Must have been pretty thorough to take them that long."

"Did Mila do the inventory?"

"No. And that's strange. But she could've been absent. I could check her attendance cards, but they'd take a few hours to dig out. Time cards that far back are on microfilm in another building."

"Thanks, but don't bother. I'd bet Mila was away at some kind of supervisory training. I can just ask her."

"Okay. I won't look up her time cards. And there's a little more information here. The inventory of Lars Brent's office was conducted by Blanche Pierre. She did it all by herself with one security guard watching. One supervisor/ manager and one guard make up the minimum inventory team allowed."

"And the inventory doesn't show any lab

journal from safe three?"

"No."

"That's really odd, Ruby. Lars was emphatic about leaving the lab journal. He said he had no use for it, and wouldn't have bothered taking it even if he were allowed to."

"You believe him?"

"You know, Ruby, I do. It's a gut feeling I've got about this situation."

"And I bet part of that feeling's because you don't like Blanche Pierre at all, do you?"

"Ruby, I'm now officially a mid-level Federal demi-poohbah …"

"Charlie, don't con me. I never heard you moved up. Demi-poohbah, my foot!"

"Ruby, consider it classified. But, if I were retired and not a demi-poohbah, I'd agree that I don't like Blanche Pierre even a little bit. I'm not retired yet, though. Ask me in three months."

Ruby laughed. "You're talking with an old friend now. You're safe. And your old friend, like everybody else here who knew Blanche Pierre long ago, still despises her. Lighten up."

"I'll lighten up ... I sure wish you'd found that notebook, though. Now I might have to grab Lars by the beard and shake him hard enough to loosen dandruff."

“Don’t do that yet, Charlie. You know Federal computers crash every now and then?”

“Yeah. The grand poohbahs then pay a gazillion bucks for civilian consultants to restore some department’s files. Happens on a small scale every two years or so where I work.”

“Same at this facility. That’s why offices like mine still keep all the handwritten, clothbound ledgers used to record secret documents. Some of those ledgers have been here longer than I have.”

“I’m not following you. Remember, I’m getting old, Ruby.”

“No older than I am. You’re still perfectly fine. I just haven’t explained yet. You gotta listen, Charlie. Be patient.”

“Okay.”

“A lab inventory’s copied onto a paper form. For the inventory of Lars’ lab, both the guard and Blanche Pierre had to sign the form. Then, when they’d finished, Pierre would’ve gone back to her office and the guard would’ve come here. He had to do that within his next two hours at work. I’d have copied the inventory results from the form into my ledger. He’d have verified it and we’d have both initialed.”

Charlie thought a moment. “Ruby, are you suggesting the computer record might have been edited by somebody? Maybe by Blanche Pierre?"

"I'm not suggesting that at all. We gotta be careful how we say this, Charlie. What I am saying is only that the paper ledger is always taken as the better record if it conflicts with the computer. The ledger has numbered pages. You can't remove a page to delete an entry. But deleting entries is easy on a computer. You see what's coming here?"

"Yeah. And I love it. You'll check to see if the computer record of the lab inventory is the same as the ledger entry?"

"Yes. You just need to wait about an hour longer. Call back then. And one more thing."

"What?"

"In the year ahead, I'd be really pleased if you bought more candy bars or whatever from some nice little Frontier Girls."

15 Grigori sat alone in his room at the nondescript hotel the Volkov brothers now used. He studied the engineering drawings filed with the city when the Old City Tower was built. These drawings were public property and any citizen could buy copies from the city at nominal cost. A Montreal Mob flunky had acquired a full set of drawings on Grigori's behalf.

Because elevators required safety

inspections, the engineering drawings included full details for the elevators. Grigori quickly learned the Old City Tower had six modern, high-speed passenger elevators. There also were two freight elevators for employee use only. CEOs didn't use freight elevators, he thought. No point considering them.

To hotel guests, each of the six passenger elevators seemed only a small chamber with a floor and ceiling nine feet apart. However, underneath each elevator four unseen motor/generator units, one at each corner, helped the chamber's heavy cable pull it upwards. On the way down, these units generated electricity for the next lift.

On the top of each passenger chamber was the elevator's process controller, a computer supervising the box of high-voltage switches beside it. In the dark elevator shaft, this roof-mounted equipment resembled a small refrigerator bolted to a large microwave oven. Two fans circulated air over the switches and their controlling computer. Both fans had air filters that required monthly replacement.

A hotel technician then used a handheld remote control to position the elevator at its maintenance station between the second and third floors. He would lock the elevator in place, open its shaft's maintenance access door, and safely step a small platform with railings and a safety chain. From there, the technician could step safely onto the elevator chamber's roof. Once on the roof, changing air filters became easy.

Grigori Volkov was primarily interested in the maintenance station for each elevator shaft. Volkov knew either police or hotel security or both would routinely have a bomb-sniffing dog inspect each elevator chamber. Placing a bomb in the elevator's chamber, while possible, would fail. A dog would find it before the target entered the elevator.

Alternatively, the bomb could be sealed in black plastic and hidden underneath the technician's station's safety platform between the second and third floors. Even a bomb-sniffing dog would not detect well-packaged explosive that high up.

It would be easy for someone with Grigori Volkov's technical skills to detonate the hidden bomb as the elevator chamber passed by it. In the semi-confined elevator shaft, the bomb's effect would become deadlier, he thought. Five pounds of plastic explosive alone would suffice since elevator fragments would work like shrapnel.

Grigori studied engineering drawings in his hotel room until evening, when whomever maintained the elevators would've departed for the day. Better still, many guests would've left the hotel for restaurants, bars, and entertainment.

Grigori made his way to Old City Tower. He easily found the second floor entrance to its maintenance corridor. The corridor was like a hidden hallway running behind the walls of guest rooms. Air ducts, steam pipes, plumbing, and conduit ran the length of the corridor, bringing utilities to the rooms. The corridor was entered through one of the windowless metal security doors at either end. Grigori only had to pick one lock and easily did so.

As the drawings had shown him, there was no alarm system for the maintenance corridor. That meant no motion detectors, which at first surprised him. On reflection, though, it made sense. The utility lines had automatic shutoffs. A terrorist might sever all of a single corridor's pipes, wires, and conduit, but the confined damage would hardly matter given so many other Old City Tower rooms. With relatively little at stake, the corridor didn't need an alarm system.

Grigori stepped inside and walked to the corridor's middle, where the individual elevator shaft maintenance doors were. Grigori opened one such door, using a standard elevator key like firefighters had. He smiled as he examined the technician's platform immediately behind the door. A bomb easily could be taped underneath it.

The bomb should, Grigori thought, be the size of an Old City street cobblestone. He'd plant two such bombs, hiding each beneath its shaft's technician platform. The next day, he'd arm one bomb, Stepan would arm the other. A motion detector attached to each armed bomb would set it off. Detonation should occur, Grigori decided, a quarter-second after the elevator chamber roof entered the bomb motion detector's field of awareness.

He pulled out his cellphone and checked signal strength. As anticipated, he had four-bars. A luxury hotel like the Old City Tower had phone signal repeaters in each elevator shaft. At Old City Tower prices, guests expected uninterrupted phone calls when using the elevators.

Grigori closed the shaft's maintenance door and went looking for the big circuit breakers that shut off power to individual elevator shafts. He found them farther down the maintenance corridor, right where the building drawings indicated.

The day of the attack, Grigori decided, Arkady would be on the second floor, dressed as a maintenance technician. Just before the long, mid-morning break, Arkady would throw the breaker switches for four elevators, which immediately would stop in place. Arkady would walk from the maintenance corridor after squirting glue into the corridor's access door locks.

Hotel maintenance persons arriving to troubleshoot the four, suddenly dysfunctional elevators initially would think the door locks had merely stuck. Grigori thought five useful minutes might elapse before they sought permission to break off a lock.

Meanwhile, the convention attendees---and especially CEOs needing to contact their offices---would be returning to their hotel rooms by the two working elevators vulnerable to bombs. The Volkovs should be able to kill one target for sure. They might even murder both.

Such was their initial plan. Though already viable, it would be repeatedly refined. Volkov planning always proceeded that way. Grigori said that was why Volkov plans always worked.

16

Needles returned to his comfortable Vancouver apartment. As usual, he checked that no one followed him. As usual, he checked his apartment's sensors and cameras. All was well.

Once safely inside, he uploaded Charlie Hexler's thumb drive files, sending them to a well-encrypted corner of the Dark Web. Nobody would ever find Barska's records there. Even if someone did, though, Needles would have the data safely tucked inside five layers of Haranya-furnished super-encryption.

He'd return the thumb drive to Charlie tomorrow.

Lars Brent poured a good glass of wine, streamed classical music, and started electronically flipping through the many pages of Kati Barska's story. He first noticed she'd only recently become a brunette. Her hair had been black upon her entering the army right after college. She'd been a blonde in between. He preferred her as a blonde, but didn't really care.

She'd attended a bottom-quartile state school on the West Coast, studying both biology and computer science. For some reason he couldn't imagine, she'd made time for ROTC. Her grades were good, but not great. No sports. No sorority. No clubs, unless one counted ROTC. No marriage before graduation or afterwards. Possibly a loner like him, he thought.

She'd been to the usual army schools. First an introductory course for the signal corps. Next came parachute training, which he supposed evil army personnel trolls made her attend. She finished the course and---he flipped forward before returning to his page---had never jumped from an airplane since. Sensible woman, he told himself. He wouldn't have gone to parachute school in the first place, personnel trolls be damned.

In the years that followed, she went to a routine, midlevel course for officers, graduating in the middle of the pack. He wondered why only the middle. Army courses didn't strike him as difficult. The colonels that came and went at his Alabama facility long ago had seemed intellectually undistinguished. Maybe Barska decided to have a good time as an army student. That assumed anybody could be happy in an army course, he thought. He couldn't.

He remembered army officers were supposed to be in charge of troops every now and then. In between troop assignments, they went to schools like Barska had, or they performed standardized, repetitive staff work. They had to, simply as a way to keep busy. He'd been surprised the army had so many more officers than it needed to oversee its troops. Apparently, the extras would replace casualties and rapidly staff new troop units in time of war.

Anyway, the army, in Needles' not very nice opinion, looked ridiculously labor-intensive. At the Alabama chemical warfare facility, the troops had seemed to take fifteen hours of work and make it last all week. He'd been amazed they'd painted so many rocks. Needles couldn't imagine a career of such activity. He'd have needed alcohol to endure it.

Then Barska's career path began looking good to him. She'd spent very little time in troop units. Mostly she'd worked with civilian contractors on Pentagon software projects. Indeed, she never seemed to have more than one foot in the army for very long. To Needles, that meant she definitely wasn't a rock painter. He found himself grudgingly developing respect for her. He even thought she might not like the army very much. That prospect elicited more respect.

He focused his search engine on the contractors Barska had experience with. To his surprise, some of them were impressive! She must have held a sky-high clearance, maybe even as high as the one he held in Alabama. She also seemed to have excellent aptitude for getting one vendor's software app working with another vendor's app.

He began to see in her what Blanche Pierre presumably saw: Barska surely could get the surveillance cameras in City A, the surveillance cameras in City B, and artificial intelligence someplace else all interacting harmoniously. That might even be why army Personnel trolls had spared her from rock-painting competitions and forced marches to nowhere.

Once he had a general idea of her career, he turned to her medical records. Brent had been a neurologist before getting a doctorate in pharmacological research. A neurologist like him might, he knew, learn something important from what doctors and nurses had written under their assumption of iron-clad confidentiality. If she took any medicines, he'd know why.

He found she'd kept her bodyweight under control. That meant diet, exercise, and good enough genes. Maybe it meant self-discipline. He imagined her jogging and lifting light weights by herself, given nothing indicated she'd ever played team sports. Further indication of a loner, he told himself. If he had to work with her, it would help immensely that she were low maintenance. Loners often were, he believed, so Barska might be.

She had been treated for venereal disease twice, the occurrences coming two years apart early in her career. She'd been lucky, not picking up one of the incurable STDs. Apparently she learned her lesson. No recurrences had been diagnosed. Also, no pregnancies, which was to be expected given her chronic use of birth control pills. She needed corrective lenses to see both up close and far away. Her hearing, though, was perfect. Bloodwork results were in the right ranges.

He was satisfied with her medical history until he got to its end. Entries in her file ceased two weeks ago, even though she'd been overdue for a mandatory biennial physical. The last entry was especially interesting. It prescribed a medicine almost no physician encountered.

Needles whistled softly. Barska wasn't who she seemed. He wondered if Charlie knew that. The bigger question was whether what Needles had just learned even mattered. Halfway into another glass of wine, Needles concluded Barska's deception wasn't a deal breaker.

Lars Brent decided to accept Charlie's offer, provided its good money became much better money. He went to bed and slept soundly, confident he'd somehow overcome treachery sure to lie ahead.

17

The next morning Charlie called Lars, doing so just as Lars was about to phone Charlie. Charlie was pleased Lars would take the job. They arranged to meet that morning so Lars could sign a long nondisclosure form. It'd only be an electronic form, Charlie said, but would evoke happy paperwork memories.

Before Lars could say he hated federal government forms, Charlie changed topics.

"I checked on that lab journal you said you left in safe number three of your lab."

“I’m surprised. That sounds like work, Charlie. How’d you go back twelve years?”

“I asked a friend. It turns out the official federal computer says there was no such lab journal in safe three or anywhere else in your lab. The inventory on the computer screen’s very clear to that effect.”

“Well, Charlie, it was there. I can’t explain it’s not being recorded.”

“Ah! You can’t, but I can. I know almost exactly what happened. Ready to listen?”

“Yeah. Ready and eager.”

“The inventory of your lab was made by Blanche Pierre with a security guard watching. The inventory results---which were just a fancy list of items found---went two places. One place was a government database. The other place was a ledger maintained by an old friend of mine.”

“There’s a hardcopy record of the inventory?”

“Yes. And in case of conflicts between the hardcopy and the computer record, the hardcopy always wins. The hardcopy shows your lab journal was found locked up in safe three.”

“Just like I said?”

“Yep. Just like you said. But it gets more interesting.”

"How?"

"There should've been a record of that super-secret journal's location every time it changed rooms. No record was kept, though. The government doesn't know where your lab journal was after it went missing in the inventory. Could've been anywhere onsite. It might've gone offsite, but that's unlikely. Anybody caught taking a journal offsite faced felony charges."

"So, for awhile my lab journal was someplace onsite. Is it still there?"

"Nope. It was destroyed two months after the inventory. And here's where things get fascinating. Destruction of journals required incineration, and lab journals almost never get destroyed. They indicate who invented something first. Therefore, they affect patent rights. The incinerator team carefully logs each lab journal it burns. They recorded your journal's arrival at the burner room two hours before it became ashes. The journal's destruction's certain."

"How'd it get to the incineration team? Didn't somebody have to authorize destruction?"

"Sort of. But high-ranking government executives each had their own little yellow burn box with a lock on it. They handled highly classified documents only they could see."

Charlie paused to let the suspense mount. This was one of his best moments in months.

"Go on, Charlie. My journal went to the incinerator after being in whose office burn box?"

"Blanche Pierre's personal office burn box."

"She'd been using my lab journal without following procedure?"

"Looks that way. It's not conclusive, but her possibly using it's not even the good part. Ready for the point of this long story?"

"Yes. Very ready and very curious."

"Lars, here's how a lawyer might see it: You, a government employee, invented a radically good new poison. You explained it in your journal …"

"Charlie, I didn't explain it very well at all."

"Not a problem. The only two people who know you cut corners are you and me. I've already forgotten all about what you just said. Got that?"

"Yes. Thank you."

"Don't even tell Mila what wasn't in the journal. And you're welcome. Ready for the rest?"

"Yes. I'm feeling overwhelmed. Do I need to sit down?"

"Maybe. You see, as a government employee, your invention would belong to the government. You therefore wrote down the recipe and left it behind when you quit. It was the government which not only ignored your work, but also destroyed it. You now have a much stronger claim to owning full rights to your invention. They effectively threw away all evidence of their potential rights to your invention when they threw away your journal."

"Could Pierre make those hardcopies you found disappear?"

"Nope. My friend can authorize duplication of documents that must get extra-special protection from fire, tornadoes, and so forth. She made three photocopies of the hardcopies that show what I told you. They're in three different government storage buildings labeled as something else. I'll email you the precise locations soon."

"Charlie, this is a better outcome than I could ever have imagined. How do I thank you?"

"Easy. You're going to buy ten cases of Frontier Girl cookies or whatever annually. Order them through a nice lady who's retiring to Florida soon."

18

All three Volkovs planned to be at the Old City Tower when the bombs went off. They'd flee the building in the predictable panic after the first blast, expertly blending into the crowd of fleeing civilians. Police wouldn't interfere with the exodus in the few minutes following the blast. However, within hours investigators would closely examine surveillance video of everyone passing through every hotel exit.

The Volkovs' first precaution would be covering their faces. Arkady planned to leave the area via jogging trails through a large park nearby. He'd wear a hooded sweat suit, as though he'd been working out in the hotel's little gymnasium when the blast came. All Arkady had to do was keep his head down and his hood up.

After a three-mile run, which was nothing for an athlete like Arkady, he'd locate the backpack he'd have hidden. Out of sight, he'd switch to a different, windproof running suit. He'd pull on a knit cap and sling the backpack over his shoulder. He'd hail two or three cabs, walking a block or more between each such ride, checking for tails as he went.

His two brothers initially would exfiltrate together. Stepan, waiting across the street from the hotel, would be joined by Grigori. They would walk off, with Stepan staying fifteen yards behind Grigori. They did not want to seem together. When Grigori slowed down to a normal walk, Stepan would. When Grigori jumped on a city bus, Stepan would.

Two or three buses later, with some walking in between to check for tails, Stepan and Grigori would go their separate ways, each to a different motel. Arkady would already be at a third motel. Each Volkov would change into an expensive business suit and drive his own rental car to Ottawa, relying on an untraceable cellphone to coordinate with the others. Each also would carry a silenced .45 caliber semiautomatic pistol during the trip, just in case.

19

The morning after meeting with Needles in Vancouver, Charlie Hexler was back in Washington, D.C. The Agency'd sent one of its private jets for him, which meant he'd been able to stretch out a little during the night-time flight back home. He still didn't get more than an hour of good sleep in his military transport passenger seat. Agency jets looked impressive on the outside. Some were impressive inside, too, but they were reserved for Agency employees in the top paygrades. Demi-poohbahs like Charlie roughed it.

Feeling stiff and greasy all over, Hexler took a cab from the airport to his townhouse. He showered, dressed, and walked to his favorite local restaurant.

During his usual, hearty breakfast, Charlie planned what he'd tell Blanche Pierre at their one p.m. meeting in her office. There was at least a remote chance she's get angry enough to have a stroke. Pierre was both a heavy person and a heavy smoker. Her little black heart, Charlie told himself, just might burst after a minute of unrestrained fury.

He was hoping for at least five minutes of total rage, turning Pierre's face dark red. Once, long ago, it briefly had resembled a large bruise. He savored that memory. Pierre, he suspected, back then had even bitten her tongue trying to spew out invectives at hyper-speed. Oh, to have had a camera running! Anonymously posting one of Blanche Pierre's megaton tantrums on *MugShot* would have ranked among his long career's best moments.

It would come down to how well he crafted his message. This afternoon Charlie couldn't just say that Needles had *requested* more money. No! That was too tame, he told himself. He'd tell her Needles *demanded much, much more money*. That wording was more likely to infuriate her. It would sound even better if he said Needles, *whose U.S. legal status was still questionable, had arrogantly, tyrannically demanded she pay a far greater sum*.

Then he'd wait and make her ask him what the additional sum was. Not getting all the information right away from anyone annoyed her. When he, Charlie Hexler, didn't promptly give her all the information, it annoyed her even more. Though marginally civil when together, Hexler and Pierre despised each other.

He'd thereupon pull out his notepad, estimate exchange rates aloud, and work it all out. He'd round up or down to get thirty-six million Canadian dollars. No. He'd quote the price as thirty-six million Canadian dollars and seventy five Canadian cents.

The seventy-five cents would, of course, seem like silly precision. She'd glare or---better still---rebuke him. He'd then say Needles had told him to add the seventy-five cents as a message for the Agency. She'd demand to know what the message was. Needles hadn't said, Charlie would tell her. That way the seventy-five cents would eat away at Pierre all day. Maybe even all night. She obsessed on little things like that.

Hexler finished his stack of three pancakes. They'd been awash in maple syrup, which he loved. Now halfway through his meal, he turned to the generous mound of corned beef hash. Calories and sleep, he reminded himself, were interchangeable. More of one somewhat offset less of the other. His breakfast today helped him plot. With that assurance, he went back to crafting the most objectionable demands he could contrive.

Upon finishing the hash, Charlie had a big smile on his face.

It was one-thirty p.m. when Charlie Hexler left Blanche Pierre's office. The smile he had carefully suppressed during the meeting was creeping back. Their meeting had gone exceptionally well. Pierre burst into one of her legendary damnation monologues, cursing toward three of her big office's four corners. Charlie credited himself with a solid three-bagger.

Pierre shouted, threw a notebook, waved her arms, and pounded her desk. Her face was so red after fifteen minutes that it resembled the bruise of yore. Her hand became so battered from desk pounding that it swelled. Spittle flecked her computer screen.

He had stayed sympathetic throughout, took notes on his little pad to show concern, and nodded agreement repeatedly. In between nods, he adroitly modified his planned presentation to add greater edge. It was a truly satisfying session---almost as good as interrogating a particular terrorist years ago in Mumbai.

He left the Agency headquarters

building, grinning all the more. Charlie walked to his car, but didn't drive off. He waited five minutes, wondering if Pierre's heart had finally sputtered out under massive emotional strain. He hoped paramedics would show up.

When none did, he shrugged and drove back to his townhouse.

Pierre had agreed to Needles' inflammatory terms. Charlie knew she would since she clearly had no choice. Nobody but Lars could stop the Volkovs before U.S. elections occurred.

She had also agreed to a demand Charlie had added on behalf of Needles. Charlie thought he owned Lars that. This little bit of icing added to Needles' oversized cake would offset for Lars any lasting repercussions of Blanche Pierre's wrath.

Charlie's townhouse in Alexandria, VA made a burner phone call to Needles' apartment in Vancouver, BC.

"Needles."

"This is Old Dog. Good news. Meet me online in three minutes."

"Understood. Needles out."

Three minutes later they were in an encrypted Dark Web chatroom. Nobody else would ever read their messages.

<u>Old Dog</u>: *The Big Bitch agreed to your extravagant terms. The package is now worth thirty-six million Canadian if you complete the full job.*

<u>Needles:</u> *I'm speechless. That's six million Canadian more than I asked for. How did you get me that much money? Are the Volkovs bringing their cousins to help them?*

<u>Old Dog</u>: *Nope. Still only three Volkovs to kill. You get ten million Canadian for each Volkov killed. Clear on that?*

<u>Needles</u>: *Yes. Thirty million Canadian for three kills.*

<u>Old Dog</u>: *Then, on top of that amount, you get six million Canadian dollars for expenses. That brings the grand total to thirty-six million Canadian dollars when you succeed.*

<u>Needles</u>: *What if your guys can't locate the targets for me?*

<u>Old Dog</u>: *Each failure to locate gets counted as an actual kill by you.*

<u>Needles</u>: *Charlie, that's almost beyond belief.*

<u>Old Dog</u>: *Yeah. For a little while, Pierre was literally choking over target location.*

<u>Needles</u>: *Sounds like you almost killed Pierre with words alone.*

<u>Old Dog</u>: *Nope. It wasn't that gratifying,*

but it was close. She had a full glass of water on her desk. She drank most of it with some kind of pill. Spilled the rest down the front of her. The pill must have saved her abominable life.

Needles: I guess I get all the expenses and half the three fees up front? The rest on successful completion?

Old Dog: Twenty-one million immediately. Just send me your account number.

Needles: This package is six million Canadian more than I asked for. How come?

Old Dog: Well, you deserve it. Big Bitch ended up viscerally hating you after I presented your terms. The six million makes up for your incurring her wrath.

Needles: I don't get it. She already hated me.

Old Dog: Your terms might have sounded severely unreasonable and monumentally arrogant to her. Believe me, she now hates you much more.

Needles: Funny! We see again why you never had any future as a diplomat.

Old Dog: Couldn't help myself. She's got no choice but to accept your terms.

Needles: You seem happy.

Old Dog: More than happy! I wish I could adequately share that heartwarming

Agency career moment with you, but words fail me. However, feel spontaneously joyful, if you can.

Needles: Okay. I'll do that. When do I meet my female coworker?

Old Dog: That's mainly up to you. She's officially still recovering in Vancouver, Washington. A government ambulance brought her and the two big guys back into the U.S. before she woke up. They're all fine, by the way. The big guys are highly pissed at you. Your coworker's highly impressed with you. I'd guess you've got a good chance to screw her if you're into purely recreational sex. She's supposed to be easy that way.

Needles: Where'd you hear she's easy that way?

Old Dog: From the venerable confluence of Agency gossip and Pentagon gossip. Otherwise known as the senior drones in Agency Personnel, all of whom hate the Big Bitch. They've long been my kindred spirits. And your new coworker's apparently not been very selective. She even had a couple of Feebee boyfriends. In among some contractor boyfriends, that is. Nothing's lasted long with her.

Needles: This coworker's not my type.

Old Dog: Good for you. Think seriously, instead, about a certain blonde with strong maternal instincts. Take that as more of the good advice I've showered upon you.

Needles: *Thank you. I'll do that.*

Old Dog: *You're welcome. Back to your new coworker. How should I send her to you?*

Needles: *Well, the Mega Pharma convention in Quebec City is the Volkovs' first chance to kill. It looks like we all start there. The convention's in the Old City Tower Hotel. Tell my new coworker to get herself a room near the restaurant on top and to get me a room above the lobby below. That way we'll have a staging area close to each of the hotel's likely hit zones.*

Old Dog: *Got it. What else?*

Needles: *Have my coworker do whatever's necessary to access the hotel's surveillance systems and its guest register.*

Old Dog: *She'll have to get some Agency hackers on it. So far the Canadian government's out of the loop on this. We need to keep it that way if you can.*

Needles: *That suits me fine. I don't' want Canadian police coordinating with me on anything. The less they know about me, the better.*

Old Dog: *I heartily agree ... And I think maybe we're done for now?"*

Needles: *Almost. Tell my coworker to use*

one of the three email addresses I set up. She's to contact me once she's made the room reservations. And thanks for the extra six million. I'll remember your help with that. Expect a very big thank you once you retire and are out from under government rules on outside compensation.

20

Mila Rossi's flight back to Washington, D.C. got her home after her two teenagers had gone to bed. Mila paid her kind, grandmotherly neighbor for babysitting. She also gave her a little bottle of top-grade Canadian maple syrup Mila had found at the airport.

Mila checked on her sleeping teens, changed to pajamas, and poured the glass of wine she'd been thinking about since her plane took off. Charlie's big wad of Canadian dollars would catch her up on credit card bills, but the mortgage was still touch and go. Mila wouldn't even think of buying herself a glass of wine on the plane.

She felt exhausted. The only good part of her day had been seeing Lars again. Those very few hours had been refreshing, delightful, and---she finally admitted to herself---romantic. She would probably never forget that luncheon.

Even so, Mila had worried about Lars in the taxi to the Vancouver airport. She worried at the airport. She worried more on the flight home while grading graduate lab notebooks for her pharmacological chemistry course.

She worried about him now, too. She felt sure he was hunting assassins again. Lars was good at it. Twelve long years ago she'd been told about the five assassins he eliminated in amazingly short order.

But Charlie Hexler might be working against Lars this time. Mila liked Charlie. He sometimes treated her like the daughter he never had. She knew, though, that Charlie'd been the Agency's best assassin ever. Until Lars came along, of course. Charlie had trained him.

She could think of nobody more potentially dangerous to Lars than Charlie. Was Charlie hunting Lars? That sudden thought sent such a chill down her spine that she took two big sips of wine, hoping to redirect her powerful mind. It didn't work. She still worried.

Acutely aware of how little she could help Lars, Mila sighed and looked at her watch. She finished her wine in one big swallow. Then Mila Rossi climbed into bed, thought briefly about Lars, and fell fast asleep.

21

After his call with Charlie, Needles packed a suitcase with clothing, toiletries, a razor, clutter, and various poisons disguised as something else. The chemical delivery tools he would use---including needle-like micro sticks of his poison---were hidden in the suitcase's walls, in the heels of his gym shoes, and in his leather briefcase's handle. His belt, his wallet, his cellphone case, and his ink pen held tablets, powders, and more of his one-of-a-kind needles.

He also carried his tablet-keyboard-combination computer, which mostly was filled with eBooks and encryption software. Needles kept all his serious data in the Dark Web's cloud. Two passports in other names, corresponding credit cards, and fifty thousand Canadian dollars went into the cleverly designed pouch he'd wear under his shirt.

He called the short-notice private jet service he used and told them he wanted to take off for Quebec City in an hour. No problem, they said. If you paid what Needles paid, you got that kind of service, which also came without airport screening.

He checked his offshore accounts and found the money Charlie promised already there. This time it arrived from some fictitious company in Barbados. He redirected the disguised deposits to other offshore accounts. It took ten minutes he'd rather not have lost, but the money became untraceable. One of Sanjay Haranya's sons had helped him set up the transfer routine.

His taxi pulled up. Needles activated his townhouse's high-end surveillance system and locked the door behind him. Somehow that reminded him he still hadn't called Mila. Instantly, he was mad at himself. He thought about calling Mila from the plane, but realized she already would be asleep. In her two or three unguarded moments at their recent lunch, Lars thought Mila had looked tired. He rightly imagined her single-parent life a hard one. She should be allowed all the rest she could get tonight, he told himself.

He would send her flowers, though, once aloft. It'd be his apology for not calling as soon as he should've. Mila had liked roses. He'd send her a dozen red roses. Better still, he'd send her three dozen roses---one dozen for each full or partial day of delay. He smiled as he anticipated her reaction.

22

The brothers now had three rooms in the budget-priced Francophile Hotel, which was three stories high, in need of paint, and mostly without surveillance cameras inside. Hotel security appeared limited to an elderly poodle asleep behind the lobby desk. For the Volkovs' purposes, the place was ideal. It also sat between two competing small diners that struggled to outdo each other coating French fries with gravy and cheese curds. Stepan could have played his favorite cellphone games in either diner all day and been blissfully content.

Nonetheless, Stepan was in his room, studying a road atlas for Canada. His job was to identify three escape routes from Quebec City to Ottawa, one route for each brother. He'd carefully print out driving directions for each brother. It was low-value busy work, but it kept Stepan out of the way while the older brothers plotted murder.

Grigori and Arkady now met in Grigori's room, which was slightly larger than Arkady's and had a better radiator.

"I don't see how we get both CEOs with one bomb," admitted Arkady. "Once a bomb goes off, the survivor's security team'll rush him outside. There'd be a couple of security guys waiting in a car for just such an emergency. Huge companies spend freely to protect big shots."

Grigori concurred, and then said, "I think we still should use two bombs, even though the second one's unlikely to kill the second CEO. If the second bomb explodes soon after the first, it'll be a good distraction. We can escape even better. And if they find the second bomb before it blows, it's almost as good a distraction. Leaving the second bomb in place isn't a problem."

"Okay. We'll use two bombs. We'll arm

them both when a target gets on the elevator … You know, Grigori, that means we don't need both you and Stepan watching the elevators. One guy could arm both bombs."

"Yeah ... I should've seen that sooner. What should we do about Stepan?"

Arkady seemed pleased to have a good answer.

"I had our Montreal Mob contact make up employee badges for both of you, just in case. I can get another building maintenance outfit right away. Quebec hotels try for a standard look. Stefan could be a new maintenance guy putting out-of-order signs on the elevators I shut down, just before convention sessions go on break."

Grigori said, "That'd work. There's a janitor's closet fifty yards from the elevators and around a corner. Stepan could take his maintenance outfit off there. He'd be wearing street clothes underneath. He'd meet me outside across the street and we'd exfiltrate together."

Arkady said, "And now we're at the big question: How do we get one or both CEOs to step into a working elevator during the break? Why would they want to go upstairs?"

Stepan's role in their tentative plan was about to change again.

23

Mila Rossi had endured a terrible day. She'd graded student papers most of the morning. Grading was always dreadful, but especially so when she had to coach native-English-speaking students on their utterly dismal writing. That meant typing out long comments to help them with basic skills they should've acquired by eighth grade.

It was almost always the grading that drove good faculty into retirement, she thought. Each year the incoming students seemed worse. Each year grading seemed harder.

Her afternoon was spent in a faculty meeting. Professor Blowhard, as she privately called the department's senior member, again explained at length how the university's administration in years long past had thwarted his inspired academic initiatives. Their arrogant subversion of his enlightened efforts long ago had, he implied, led to the university's present urgent Problem X. Mila supposed that next month he'd discourse on urgent Problem Y. Eventually, he would get to Problem Z and afterwards, she imagined, switch to knock-knock jokes.

Nobody but Mila paid attention to Professor Blowhard's monthly soliloquies. Others simply caught up with their cellphone tasks. Mila felt sorry for Blowhard, though, and quietly endured his pointless ramblings rather than avert her eyes.

After Blowhard held forth, the Department Chair called a short break even though the meeting had barely started. That allowed participants, the Chair said, to eat the hard candy and potato chips she'd placed on a side table. There were also sugary drinks since, she asserted, sugar was converted into brain energy given the presence of vegetable oil and salt.

After their sugar, salt, and corn oil fixes, the faculty turned to committee reports that ranged from the trivial to the irrelevant. Professor Blowhard briefly nodded off.

Following the faculty meeting, a self-righteous undergraduate came by Mila's office to argue for an "A" on a paper Mila had assigned. Mila explained the student hadn't handed in the assignment and thus received an "F." The student thereupon argued fervently for a "B." The young woman was, she said, not only a legacy student, but also on an athletic scholarship, as if all that should dictate academic standards. Mila referred her to the Student Social Justice Ombudsperson, who dealt with both grading disputes and undergraduates' tender feelings.

The traffic on the way home was worse than usual because of roadwork, accidents, and a bemused herd of deer on the roadway. Traffic crept along as angry adults all around Mila blew car horns at each other with the fervor of angry children.

She finally made it home. Mila wearily climbed from the car, hauled out the canvas bag of student projects left to grade, and walked to her front door. She turned the door knob, certain she'd be arguing with her teenage son after no more than fifteen minutes. Then, once her son had softened her up, her teenage daughter would start in.

She smelled the roses before she saw them.

"Mom! Some guy named Lars sent these."

The daughter waved at Mila the card accompanying the roses. Daughter, unbidden but curious, had opened it on mother's behalf.

"He says he's sorry he didn't call and will phone tonight … So, Mom, what's this all about? This Lars guy must be really rich, huh?"

Mila missed everything her daughter said after the first "Lars," losing herself in happy disbelief. She smiled, put down her bag of student projects, and went to make dinner. She'd marvel at the roses later, once her inquisitive daughter wasn't there watching her.

Today, Mila said to herself, was a perfectly wonderful day!

24

Lars checked into the recently renovated Old City Tower under an assumed name. He asked for, and received, a room halfway up the tall building and at the end of the long hall. That made his room as far as one simultaneously could be from the pool, the gym, the restaurant, and Kati Barska. Once inside his sanctuary, he separated his computer keyboard from its screen and began using the screen alone as a tablet. It was the perfect way to read information recently sent him on the Volkovs.

He liked their military backgrounds. Twenty-some years of military culture forever permeated one's habits, thinking, and being. Never again would the Volkovs look completely like civilians, however hard they tried. There'd be tiny signals each Volkov wasn't who he seemed. Needles made the most of tiny signals. He was, after all, superb with biochemistry and often worked at the molecular level. Tiny signal analysis was easy.

He already thought the Volkovs wouldn't try sniping. Even in urban settings, snipers needed at least four hundred yards of distance from the target to reliably escape. They couldn't find a shooting position that far from the hotel. Neighborhood rooftops were studded with surveillance cameras. Empty apartments with hotel views might be almost nonexistent given both the desirable location and Quebec City's chronically tight real estate market.

Besides all that, the extended overhead cover by the front door, though meant to catch snowfall and rain, would stop most bullets. Lars thought professional ego would be involved, too. Anybody could shoot a rifle up close. Such a kill would impress no one, and might even lower the fee the shooter could obtain next time.

On to the next threat. Lars easily decided they wouldn't use handguns up close. Everybody knew what a handgun was. The shooters would be detected as soon as their guns came out, making both their mission and their escape highly uncertain. They might slaughter a few dozen innocents---though that was harder than it sounded---or they might take hostages. Either way led to the same result: The attackers would be gunned down or captured. Given all the bodyguards in attendance, they'd be gunned down. Nope. No handguns.

They might try poisoning food, but without access to the kitchen area he thought that unlikely. Hotel security would use cameras in the kitchen. Supervisors would check on cook behaviors and hotel Personnel would check on cook backgrounds. Also, it was not so unusual to get a food taster as part of a high-end bodyguard team. There were even little handheld gadgets to check for simple poisons like cyanide, arsenic, and whatever else was sold for rodent control. The gadgets also easily detected anything radioactive in the meal.

The Volkovs could resort to the Russian cliché of stabbing somebody's leg with a cane or with an umbrella. It was an old tactic easier by the year to defeat. Some little company even sold puncture-proof gaiters that were worn under ordinary trousers and came to the wearer's knee. Another problem was the metal detectors that'd be used at the convention. Umbrellas would get inspected along with everything else. Some umbrellas still concealed thin swords.

Aerosol poisons would work. The right spray in one's face from the right distance at the right angle would suffice, assuming one could cope with any breeze present. Correctly addressing all those variables before bodyguards reacted would be difficult for the Volkovs. They might even poison themselves along the way. Success took theatrical skill and aerosol training, in addition to icy cold nerves.

Needles could kill with aerosol toxins ten times out of ten. Rookies would fail seven times out of ten. The Volkovs simply weren't in his league that way. No aerosols, he thought, even if they could acquire the right chemicals. Getting poisons for most people was prohibitively difficult. He, on the other hand, formulated his own poisons from scratch in his lab.

He preferred a toxic needle of his own design. It delivered a poison of his own design, a poison only superficially similar to the one he'd invented in Alabama. Stick one of his exotic needles anywhere in the victim's body and death would occur in ten seconds. His needles were never found in their victims and death had always been attributed to natural causes. The way Lars Brent killed was extraordinary. The Volkovs weren't that sophisticated. Even the big Mega Pharma companies weren't that sophisticated. So, no high-tech needles.

He stood, walked to the incompetent little coffee machine cowering on a shelf, and brewed a cup of unpromising hotel room coffee. It proved worse than expected. He shrugged, sat back down, and continued analyzing the Volkovs' options.

Knives and fists wouldn't work for them. The Volkovs would be superb with both but dared not get that close. There'd be bodyguards all around. There'd be a layer of hotel security hovering outside the rings of bodyguards. The Volkovs' escape would end at the hotel lobby. Even if they fled the hotel, Quebec City police would be arriving outside to greet them. So, no knives. No fists.

Ramming the CEOs with a vehicle wouldn't work. That was silliness. Whatever armored-up limousine each CEO traveled in would easily survive the collision. Who knew? Maybe a its airbags wouldn't even deploy.

That left only a bomb. He took another swallow of insipid coffee, kicked off his shoes, and began streaming classical piano music over his computer. He leaned back into his hotel room's comfortable chair, enjoying the intellectual challenge of high-stakes murder.

How, he asked himself, could he kill one or two CEOs with one or two bombs?

25

To her surprise, Kati Barska woke up feeling refreshed after Lars Brent sedated her. She would be fine, said the U.S. government medical team which debriefed her in Vancouver, Washington.

She grudgingly repeated four times what Brent said. Didn't the Feebees know how to listen the first time? she asked herself on three occasions. She endured two precautionary blood tests. She listened to her stomach growl during the two hours it took some doctor to authorize her eating oatmeal. Oatmeal! She told the doctor she hated oatmeal and declined his gracious offer.

Two hours later the big guys woke up. The various debriefers left Barska alone to focus on them, so she wandered down the hall to the hospital cafeteria. She'd forgotten about money, but found Brent had left her wallet untouched. He'd also left her cellphone in her sweater pocket. Brent wasn't all bad, Barska thought. He already was four and a half tons nicer than either the Feebee jerks or the medical jerks.

Barska ordered a double hamburger, extra fries, and coleslaw along with an extra-large lemonade. She told herself it was about a million calories, most of which would show up on her thighs tomorrow. No matter. After what she'd been through, she deserved some red meat and more. Not only that, but coleslaw calories didn't really count since they were from a vegetable.

She lingered over her forbidden feast before sauntering back to the debriefing area. The jerks were still talking to the pair of Agency guys. That was good. Better still, the Jerk-in-Charge didn't seem above the rank of major. There was little risk in sneaking out. If the jerks needed to bother her again, they could try surface mail.

She found a somewhat secluded corner of the hospital parking lot and called Charlie Hexler. He gave her Lars Brent's instructions: book two reservations at the newly renovated Old City Tower and notify Brent which room he'd have. Then she'd fly to Northern Virginia, pack a suitcase, and fly to Quebec City. Since she hadn't been issued a laptop for the Vancouver snatch-team job, she should bring her own computer to Quebec City.

Hexler said to *hurry*. She could sleep on the planes, shower in the hotel, and live on airline food as opportunity arose. *Hurry*. He abruptly ended their call.

Barska held her cellphone at arm's length and raised her middle finger at it. Then she called her real boss.

26

Mila Rossi had just cleaned up after dinner. She sat down in her living room, where her son was playing a video game on the TV screen. Her daughter was lost in a novel. Both teenagers seemed oblivious to the world around them until Mila's phone rang.

Her daughter put her book down halfway into the first ring. "Is that Lars?"

Even Mila's son paused his video game, something which almost never happened unless he were hungry. He turned mother's way.

Mila wrinkled her nose at them, stood up, and answered her phone.

"Hello."

Everybody already knew who the caller was.

“Hi, Mila. This is Lars.”

“Lars! So good to hear your voice. This means you left without difficulty?”

Two pairs of teenage eyes focused intently on Mila.

“I did. Uh, is this a good time to talk, Mila? Or should I call back later?”

“Now’s a perfect time. However, to avoid an audience of two, I’ll take this call in my office. Just a moment.”

She wrinkled her nose again and went to her office. She closed her door, crushing daughter’s vibrant hopes of hearing mother talk with mother’s boyfriend. Well, daughter conceded, it could be her boyfriend. Mom acted sort of in love for an old person.

Mila sat at her desk. “I’m now alone. They won’t listen at the door, even though my daughter’s bursting with curiosity about those gorgeous roses! Thank you, Lars! The flowers are indescribably beautiful and they smell heavenly!”

She finished with a big smile.

“I’m glad you liked them. I’m hoping they let me state a fact and ask a question.”

“Okay. I’d say three dozen long-stem roses gets you that much for sure.”

“First, Mila, lunch with you was wonderful. I’m hoping we can do it again after the presidential election, which is as soon as I'll be back in the U.S."

"I'd love having lunch again. Thank you! And one of these days, you'll have to come here for dinner, Lars. My two teenagers will probably insist on it."

"Consider it done. Ready for the question? It's sort of serious."

"Ready," she said, with sudden concern. Mila sensed what would come next.

"Mila, I thought you still took off your wedding ring to protect it from damage in the lab. I didn't even notice it missing. Why didn't you tell me you were divorced?"

She sighed. "Lars, it's not easy to come right out and say it to an old friend. Not yet, and especially not to you. I didn't want to spoil our time together."

"Is that all?"

She decided to be candid.

"No. I guess I still felt guilty---like it was all my fault somehow."

They both knew that whatever he said next would matter.

"I met your husband years ago, Mila. I was careful to never say anything, but now I can assure you the divorce was 100 percent his fault. Beaufort wasn't worthy of you. He never was."

"Thank you, Lars."

She blinked and wiped one eye. Then she wiped the other eye.

"You're welcome ... I was too blunt, huh? Another of my socially awkward moments?"

"You did fine. What makes you think you're the only one who has socially awkward moments?"

"Mostly, I base my opinion on empirical data I collect myself. Like now. You're still too nice to tell me."

"Lars, I delight in your eccentricities. You're too hard on yourself."

"Well, maybe. Or maybe not. But I sometimes don't know what to say. Like now. I want to ask you to go on an extended date."

Mila rolled her eyes.

"Lars, I think I know what you mean, but you'd better tell me."

"I thought maybe you and I could go away together for a week. Or for just a weekend so you're at less risk of being stuck with me too long."

"One room. One bed?"

"It did cross my mind, I admit."

She laughed gently.

"And after it crossed your mind, it kept right on going out your ear. Lars, you and I are *not* sleeping together unless we're married. Want to hear my two reasons?"

"Yeah. I'm hoping to talk you out of at least one reason."

This had become a delightful conversation for Mila, just as Lars knew it would.

"First reason: I have two teenagers to raise, which includes guiding them through the very serious perils of sexual temptation. I---actually, *you and I*---must set good examples."

"Okay. That one's hard to talk you out of. Is the next one easy?"

"About the same. You and I both already know that, when it comes to sex, *you're every bit as puritanical as I am*. Whatever gave you such a preposterous idea?"

Lars smiled. He could sense genuine affection in her voice. After so many years, though, he'd needed to check that she felt as she always had. The weekend away suggestion---which he'd hoped would fail---had been that check.

"Social awkwardness, I suppose. So, you'd sleep with me if we were married?"

"Eagerly. But you can't propose yet, Lars. I need to see if you're still the same person you once were or even better. And my kids will want to interrogate you ten times. They're becoming little puritans in regard to sex. They'll soon be inflexible that way--- like you, Lars!"

"So, you're not going to sleep with me?"

"Not without a wedding ring."

"Expect a whirlwind courtship after the election, Mila. I'll ask Charlie for advice."

"You should be coaching Charlie. He's still a bachelor. And does this mean you and Charlie are friends again?

"Yes. Charlie and I now expect to die of something besides each other."

"Good! I love you both---in different ways, of course."

"And I love you, Mila. In the way that matters most. There … I wasn't sure I could get that out tonight. It sort of came out on its own. Are you mad at me?"

He'd become serious. She became serious, too.

"Of course not! I'm never mad at you. At least, not for long. My problem is I'm worrying about you again. About the dangerous work you do, Lars. Are you ready to retire yet?"

"Will it help my chances of marrying you?"

"*Yes*. Very much so!"

There was unmistakable hope in her voice.

"Then I'll retire after the election. As

soon as the vote's counted. How's that?"

"I'd like that, Lars."

Suddenly daughter knocked hard on mother's office door.

"Mom, your son ate all the ice cream. *He didn't share again and he's being obnoxious!*"

That was followed by, "It's your fault. *You drank all the juice. And you're obnoxious!*"

Their confrontation immediately grew louder.

"Lars, I have to go. Can you hear my two teenagers arguing?"

"Yeah. You're needed. I'll call you weekly, if you'll let me."

"I'd like that. Goodbye, Lars."

Without missing a beat, Mila Rossi went into mother mode. She opened her office door, saying, "You two *stop* fighting and get ready for bed, *now!*"

She stepped from her office with purpose in her stride and a frown on her face. Neither was easy for Mila given the song in her heart.

27

Stepan was in his drab hotel room, sometimes looking at maps, and sometimes watching a porn channel on the room's television. Mostly he watched porn.

Grigori and Arkady Volkov were in Grigori's modest hotel room with their computers on their laps, but had moved their chairs closer to the room's single window. The light was better, although they now sat farther from the room's radiator. Their feet already felt the chill, but they were Russians. They faced cold stoically.

"Beacon's just provided excellent intelligence," said Arkady, smile on his face.

"It's about time Beacon gave us something," growled Grigori, who'd been complaining about Beacon's unknown client on and off for two days.

"Yes. But the client's made up for it. Anyway, before we go into Beacon's stuff, tell me what you found on the Web."

Grigori pushed his reading glasses up his nose, changed computer screens twice, and mostly read from the notes he'd taken.

"Let's start with the CEO for Bowel-Wow," said Grigori. He referred to the world's leading source of generic gastrointestinal medications.

"He's that gray-haired, skinny guy even taller than his bodyguards?"

"That's him. The Web shows he's got a trophy wife, nice kids, and a cute dog. I paid for one of those quickie Web searches for any court records related to him. No arrests. Nothing else useful. We can't lure him upstairs to a hooker's room."

"And the other guy? The barrel-chested gnome who runs Happy Pill?"

"About the same story. If there are skeletons in his closet, we won't find them."

"That's it?"

"That's it. See why I've spent two days pissed at Beacon's client for lousy intel?"

"Yeah. But that client just came through. Cheer up, Grigori."

"Okay. I'm cheerful."

He still looked disgusted, though.

"A short tutorial first: Drug patents eventually expire. Until then, the drug company owning the patent can charge whatever it wants and get away with it."

"So their legendary price gouging's legal?" Grigori still didn't understand capitalism.

"Yes. Until the patent expires. Once the patent expires, anybody can make the drug and sell it for less. They call them generic drugs once they're off patent. But these drugs, even in generic form, are still very complicated and usually hard to make. Not many companies in the world can do it well enough on a large scale."

"No doubt those companies charge less than the company which invented the drug?"

"Yes."

"You know, if they can sell for less than the inventing company, they could sell for less than each other. They'd undercut each other's prices down to pennies per pill?"

Grigori began feeling better about capitalism.

"Yes---if they let it go that far. Suppose the biggest ones secretly agree to only lower prices just enough that there seems to be competition. They'd all earn more money that way."

"Why not just agree in the open?"

"Because those agreements would be illegal. They're called price fixing. Governments outlaw price fixing because it makes voters pay more. The penalties for being caught fixing prices can be astronomical."

"Maybe Beacon's client thinks one of these companies fixes prices anyhow?"

"Precisely so. The client, whoever the client is, thinks Bowel-Wow's a big-time price fixer. Now, let's see how sneaky you can be, Grigori."

"I can be very sneaky," he said with pride.

"Excellent. Pretend you're the CEO of Bowel-Wow. From time to time you have to communicate with the CEOs of the other price-fixing companies. How would you do it?"

"I might use encrypted email?"

"You might, but you probably wouldn't. The U.S. government's NSA would decrypt the message once they found it. I'd bet they look for such things regularly given the massive fines the government could rake in. Same for the EU. Try again."

"Well, I wouldn't meet privately with the other CEOs. That would be interpreted as price-fixing by lawyers."

"Yes! You'd only meet in public places, like this industry convention or maybe on some industry panel testifying openly before Congress. You'd always have witnesses present to swear you never talked with the other CEOs about prices. Keep going. You're getting close."

"I'd only communicate with the other CEOs through an intermediary and nothing would be written down."

"Bravo! That's how Bowel-Wow's CEO does it. The intermediary is the Honorable Rufus Benedict, one of the newer members of the Canadian Parliament. Here's his picture."

Arkady turned his computer so Grigori could see the screen.

"He looks like Stepan!"

"He does. Stepan would need a mustache. We'd have to trim his hair a little around the ears. But, through a partially opened door or in dim lighting, Stepan could pass for the intermediary every time if Stepan slouched like Benedict in that photo."

"Somehow Stepan becomes bait to draw Bowel-Wow's CEO to the CEO's hotel room? Maybe he'd leave to meet Stepan there during the break?"

"Exactly … Well, almost exactly."

28

During her whirlwind trip from Vancouver, Washington to Alexandria, Virginia, to Quebec City, Canada, Kati Barska had no time for a shower, let alone a leisurely hot bath. She'd only brushed her hair three times and had chewed gum instead of brushing her teeth. Three hours into her journey, she wanted to scratch Charlie Hexler's eyes out.

She made the hotel reservations and emailed that information to Lars Brent, who'd be called Needles. Charlie Hexler would be Old Dog. Her codename, which she hated, was Grunt. Charlie---make that Old Dog, she thought---had explained Grunt was an affectionate term for someone in the infantry. She'd thereupon suggested Sparks, since she was signal corps, but he said he'd already registered Grunt for her. She'd given her phone a middle-finger salute at the end of that call, too.

Once finally in her Old City Tower room, she drew her long-awaited bath, intent on a good soak before anybody could tell her what to do. She even turned off her cellphone. She couldn't use it much longer, anyway. Old Dog said she should get a couple of burner phones. That would probably mean hiking around Quebec City. *Ugh!* She already thought it an over-hyped place, distinguished mostly by old buildings, unsliced bread, and too many people speaking French.

She slid into the welcoming tub. Kati Barska washed her hair, bathed herself, leaned back, and soaked. She soon decided she needed to have a man. It had been too long since the last one. Nonetheless, she needed a really good man this time. The last several had been too fat, too old, or too young. All had been too eager. None deserved more than a "C" for coital technique, and she had to show two of them some of what to do! They'd been untutored, fumbling idiots.

Lars Brent would be exactly the opposite in bed, she speculated. He looked fit. Without that silly beard of his, he'd look halfway handsome. Most importantly, he was a neurologist. He knew precisely how her nervous system worked and could stimulate her to unimaginable sexual bliss. He'd already given her the best nap she'd ever had.

In due time, she climbed from the tub, toweled off, and began drying her hair. In among the clothes she'd brought were three short skirts, two tight sweaters, and escort-class lingerie. She would, she thought, be working with Brent for something like thirty days. Kati Barska, based on much prior experience, was confident she'd seduce him in less than a week.

29

Needles had been in his chair long enough to finish his Old City Hotel room's disappointing coffee. He set the cup aside, folded his arms across his chest, and stared at the sky through the full-length window on the room's opposite side.

So far, he'd concluded the bomb would be explosive with shrapnel wrapped around it. That way the bomber could kill the same number of persons with less explosive. He asked himself how big the bomb would be.

A military hand grenade had only a few ounces of explosive wrapped with serrated wire. If you were standing within five yards when it exploded, there was a fifty-fifty chance you'd be killed or wounded. For the world's armies, wounding one's target was usually better than a kill. Both the victim and somebody who'd care for the victim were taken out of the fight.

Nonetheless, 50 percent was a lousy percentage for an assassin. Who wanted to get paid his full fee only half the time? A grenade-sized bomb wouldn't work well enough for the

Volkovs. Also, anybody could toss a grenade. Whatever the Volkovs did would have panache.

It would take something the size of a sixty millimeter mortar shell to get sure kills at a bursting radius of five yards. Certain world battle zones were awash in sixty millimeter mortar shells, but getting them into Canada wouldn't be easy. A small, private jet might work best, Lars thought, but pilots reckless enough to haul arms could make more money hauling drugs. Even if they stubbornly hauled arms alone, they'd find something more profitable than mortar shells. Pipe bombs could work as well and nobody paid much for a pipe bomb.

Anyway, the bomb would have to be at least as big as a flashlight using two "D" cells. That settled, how much bigger would it be? Blowing up the hotel was out of the question. The Volkov's didn't have an army's firepower behind them. Not even an army squad's firepower. More importantly, the specific attack location would determine the size of the bomb.

There was an underground parking area. Could that be a viable kill zone? he wondered. Getting a car bomb into underground parking might sometimes work, but not at the Mega Pharma meeting. Their industry was almost unimaginably lucrative. Not even the defense industry's corporate security was better funded.

There'd be dogs sniffing whatever entered the underground parking area. He told himself to ignore the underground parking area.

The next biggest prospective target Lars could imagine would be the convention center ballroom, which could seat three or four hundred attendees. It was a confined space, and any significant blast was more effective if confined. Once again, one could use less explosive if one wrapped shrapnel around it.

Nevertheless, the two targets could be at opposite ends of the cavernous room. If even some of the corporate security people thought about bombs, VIPs not on the stage would be seated far apart. He had already checked the speakers lists and industry association officers list. The two targets would be in the audience.

The Volkovs would figure that out, too. Two bombs would be better than one for reaching the whole room, but two bombs would be twice as hard to hide. He supposed the Volkovs would adopt the same rules of thumb he'd use, and go with a single hundred-and-fifty-pound bomb near one executive or the other. One still might get both with luck.

As a practical matter, the Volkovs would never get any bomb that big into the room. Even if they did, a bomb-sniffing dog would do a walk through before executives entered. The dog would find any explosive inside any first floor room, including whatever might be in the kitchens. It'd be the same outcome, for the same reasons, at the restaurant atop the hotel.

That meant a lesser bomb somewhere between the second floor and the top floor. It wouldn't be in janitor closets or the gym or the pool area. Both dogs and security officers could check those areas without unduly invading guest privacy, so those areas would be checked often.

Rule out the top, the bottom, and the public areas, he thought. That meant the most one would need to blow up at one time was a typical luxury guest suite---roughly two standard rooms with a gypsum board wall between them. Two pounds of plastic explosive with shrapnel would do it. Four pounds at most. The bomb would the size of a one-quart milk carton.

Finding the target's suite would be easy. Placing the bomb would be hard. The suite would've been swept by the company's security detail traveling with the CEO. They'd likely leave an armed officer in the room whenever the CEO was out. Even if they didn't, it would be simple to set up alarms and cameras in the empty room.

There'd be lateral maintenance passageways sometimes called pipe chases. These would be unseen, walled off corridors that held steam pipes, conduit, air ducts, and plumbing. The corridors would be sealed at each end with a security door.

Even if a bomber got past the door, the corridors all had steel-reinforced concrete ceilings, floors, and sidewalls. Setting off a bomb inside the pipe chase corridor would not appreciably damage any rooms on the other side of the steel-reinforced concrete. In fact, Lars speculated, if there had to be a bomb blast, hotel management would prefer it be in a pipe chase.

There were two emergency exit stairwells. Someone using them was never more than half a floor from an exit to the next floor up or the next floor down. Victims therefore weren't easily confined to a kill zone, even if they could be lured into the stairwells. Also, each stairwell had greater volume than the hotel ballroom. Bomb blast wouldn't reliably reach its target.

That left the elevator shafts. Each shaft, itself, was loosely comparable to an emergency stairwell. It was just a long vertical space, that space traveled by metal boxes called elevators. Each such box was unlikely to hold more than fifteen or twenty persons. Luring a target in among those persons didn't look easy.

Even so, he thought about the elevator shafts for much longer than the other possibilities. The killers would know which upstairs floor the target would get on and off the elevator at. Maybe one could detonate a bomb there.

Lars decided to look closest of all at the elevators.

30 Kati Barska did her makeup, finished dressing, and stood before her room's full-length mirror. She liked what she saw. The short skirt called attention to her shapely legs. The tight sweater accentuated her ample bust. She also wore a little too much eye makeup. If all that failed to get Lars Brent aroused, she'd sit down opposite him and cross her legs carelessly. She'd bed him by dinner, she told herself, and looked at her watch.

Barska next opened her email expecting to find an encrypted message from Brent. There was none, which suggested to Barska he might be shy. She hadn't bagged a shy one in years. Brent might be more fun than anticipated. The thought made her smile.

Barska decided to write him:

Needles,

Ready to go. When do we meet? I suggest using my room. The view's spectacular.

Grunt

She frowned at her codename, but clicked the "send" icon. Barska's eyes stayed on the screen. Any moment now, she thought. Somebody shy like him would want her to make the first move. Fine. She'd just done that.

Five minutes later, her screen was unchanged. She mumbled something and picked up the television remote. She could see the TV screen from where she sat. If she had to wait on Brent, she might as well make it interesting. Barska soon had one of those in-room porno movies running. She couldn't understand the French words, but moans and gasps in French meant the same thing in English.

Thirty minutes later the porno film's female performer had gone through three standard sex acts, two weird sex acts, and approximately six partners. Barska found it hard to count the partners since the film's lighting was so poor. She thought it only marginal pornography. No, she told herself, it wasn't even marginal. She'd almost switched channels to English-language cable news when her computer dinged to announce an email.

It was from Needles. She eagerly opened it.

Grunt,

Welcome to Canada.

Stay in your room. Schedule maid service no more than twice a week. Use room service meals. Have the concierge send up whatever else you need. Otherwise, keep your door locked. Your first priority's being safe. Your second priority's being unseen.

The third priority's hacking into the hotel computer surveillance system the lobby guards use. Old Dog says you can run a facial recognition application from your computer using the hotel's camera feeds. For the time being, monitor the first floor and the front of the building. Now's about when the bad guys will scout for kill zones and escape routes.

Next, see if you can tap into the police blotter or whatever the locals call it. You're looking for a daily events log. The police will have something like that for recording anything they deem unusual. Maybe something suggesting bad guy activity will get logged.

Finally, search the Web and prepare capsule biographies for the three targets. The Web's vast. Chances are good you can find information Old Dog's people don't have yet.

The mission will be like a stakeout until the convention starts. Stay alert.

Needles

Barska read the message three times, cursing to herself each pass through it. She was faced with all work---all boring work!---and no play. Even though it was only their mission's first full day, she already disliked Needles.

31 After sending Barska instructions from the hotel room she'd reserved for him, Lars rang Charlie Hexler's burner phone twice and hung up. Minutes later the two men met in an encrypted Dark Web chatroom. They relied on their laptop computers' voice recognition, which meant they could communicate in text as quickly as they could dictate to their laptops.

Needles: *I'm still studying the hotel layout, but it's a good bet they'll use a bomb in an elevator shaft. They'll place it far enough above ground level that bomb dogs won't smell it.*

Old Dog: *Why no guns?*

Needles: *There's nowhere good to snipe from outside. They might be able to get up close inside, but there are bodyguards all over. I'd say getting an aimed shot off is a fifty-fifty proposition at best. And, of course, they'd never get away afterwards.*

Old Dog: *A bomb makes sense to me. And how's Grunt doing?*

Needles: *Can't say yet. She just got her first assignments by email.*

Old Dog: *The NSA guys are inside the firewall for whatever you Canadians call your provincial anti-terrorist group. I'm reliably told Stepan Volkov showed his face a day ago on the other side of Quebec City. He gave some deer tick preservation clowns a couple of envelopes.*

One envelope contained cash for sure. It was all very obvious.

<u>Needles</u>: A diversion?

<u>Old Dog</u>: Maybe. They might just be trying to provoke a reaction. That way they could tell if anybody's interested in them yet.

<u>Needles</u>: And what'll they conclude?

<u>Old Dog</u>: So far there's not enough to justify a big search. The Canadians are staying passive. Just facial recognition surveillance for now. That could change without warning, but at present the Volkovs ought to feel safe.

<u>Needles</u>: This hotel's the best choice. The kill attempt will be here.

<u>Old Dog</u>: If you say so. And that's it at my end. Happy hunting.

<u>Needles</u>: Thanks. Needles out.

32

Needles rode the his first elevator up and down between the lobby and his floor in the hotel's middle for three trips before he was alone in the elevator car. He finally could get the pictures he needed.

When doors for the car opened at a floor, there was a half-inch gap between the floor's door frame and his elevator car. He used his cellphone's tiny camera to look up and down through the gap. He took similar pictures to the left and right. His cellphone camera flash was bright enough that he could examine two-yard-long slivers of shaft in each direction. He repeated this process for each passenger elevator, randomly sampling to keep the analysis manageable.

The cumulative results yielded major insights. Needles realized the concrete shaft wall nearest each elevator door opening was uniformly smooth. For each of the mid-hotel levels he examined, there were no brackets, hooks, or ledges suitable for holding a bomb.

Nor could someone attach a bomb to the elevator car sides using magnets. While the elevator car had a steel frame, the car's siding was polymer and aluminum to save weight. The car also did not have recesses, panels, or ceiling sections that could be opened without special keys and special tools.

The Volkovs could always put on mountain climbing gear and repel down the side of the shaft from some upper floor's elevator portal. It'd be time-consuming, dangerous, and difficult. It'd be easier to just climb atop an elevator car someplace designated for ordinary elevator car maintenance. Somewhere, he supposed, the designers had provided a convenient way to change ceiling lights, inspect cable connections, and examine motors.

Whatever maintenance station existed would be near the bottom of the elevator's shaft. Nobody would want to work on the cab's underside while hanging from it thirty floors up. Better to work on elevators in the elevator pit at the shaft's bottom or, maybe, a maintenance station near the second floor. Either way, it would be someplace where guests didn't see the work being done. Who knew? Some paranoid guest might infer from the routine maintenance that all the elevators were dangerous and required serious repair.

If the Volkovs wanted to place a bomb on the elevator cab top or tape a bomb on the elevator cab bottom, they'd use the cab's ordinary maintenance location. That being so, Needles now didn't really care where the bomb was. The key piece was getting it to detonate when one or both CEOs entered the elevators rigged to explode. One actually had to see them get into an elevator cab. Only then could the bomber push his bomb's trigger.

Needles thought they'd keep that part simple. The person who watched passengers enter the elevators also would detonate the bomb. There were only two ways for that person to watch the elevator: in person or with a camera.

It was time to contact Grunt again.

33

Kati Barska grew bored with her hotel room not long after being confined there. She even lost interest in the room's splendid view. Further still, Canadian television, she told herself, was ridiculous! Her TV set only had two channels with English-language programming, and so far they'd carried either Canadian talk shows or Canadian newscasts. Having no more than nominal appreciation for all things Canadian, she found either offering tedious.

With no serious entertainment on her horizon, it became easy to concentrate on tasks Brent had given her. Her hacking skills were about average, but more than sufficient for present purposes. All she had to do was find the login screen for whatever hotel software she wanted to access. Then she connected to an NSA server far away and pointed one of its powerful programs toward the targeted login screen.

The NSA program would deploy all classical firewall breaching routines, including a sophisticated password-guessing routine. Some special NSA algorithms would also be applied. Usually, all that software worked very well from afar.

If the software failed, she'd try the working file for the exotic program's next update. In this file were the most current hacker routines, some of which had been posted to the Dark Web only days earlier. They were still being fully tested by NSA IT geeks for exotic malware. Standard procedure was to complete such testing before releasing suitable updates to the field.

But those in the field sometimes faced urgent needs of national importance. Then it was better to risk a little malware than failing in a mission-critical hack. Malware could always be cleaned up later by Agency security utilities downloaded to the field operator's PC. It would be the field operator's call---in this case, Kati Barska's call---whether to use the newest updates.

This time the basic program was enough. It broke into all the hotel accounts, including the financial accounts, the entire guest management system, and the maintenance accounts. Barska also could access every surveillance camera in the hotel. It turned out there were over two hundred of them.

Needles called ten minutes later for an update. She gave him the good news. He said he'd come to her room in eight minutes. She should show him the camera coverage of the lobby's elevator area.

Grunt's heart leapt! This might be her big chance for the therapeutic sex she needed---a heart-pounding, sensual escape from staid, dreary Quebec City! She touched up her hair and makeup. With only two minutes to go, she looked in the mirror and decided to undo one more button on her blouse. Then, with seconds left, she gave her neck a strategic dab of perfume.

Needles knocked at her door right on time. She opened it with a big smile. He smiled a little and walked in.

"Nice place," he said.

She closed the door as he walked to the window. Needles said her room looked bigger than his. He looked in the single closet and proclaimed it larger than what he had. He looked in the bathroom and said it was likewise bigger. Not much, he thought, but at least a foot longer. Barska never realized he cared nothing about their room dimensions. He just wanted to be sure nobody was hidden there.

Barska realized her computer was still on a round worktable in one corner. There were two chairs at the worktable. She had been using one of them.

"We can sit on the couch," she said. "I can tell you from experience these two chairs get uncomfortable."

She smiled and started to move her computer.

If they sat on the other side of the room, she knew, the short skirt would ride up on its own once she leaned back into the deep cushions. Also, if she bent down to the couch's coffee table, her blouse would open to reveal the swell of one breast.

Needles said, "No problem. I won't stay that long."

He sat at the little worktable in the chair next to the one she'd been using. Her only option was to sit down in the other worktable chair. That meant her legs would be under the table and her blouse would remained closed. She decided to offer him coffee in approximately five minutes. Coffee implied the coffee table by the couch. She'd get him to move.

"Show me what the security cameras around the elevators see."

She did so. He watched intently, often asking her to switch back and forth between close-up images and the broad views hotel security seemed to prefer.

"Does hotel security run its own facial recognition?"

She brought up the control panel for the facial recognition software the guards could use. Needles took the mouse from her and moved a cursor over the various facial recognition panel buttons. He was quite pleased to find a box would pop up to explain whatever button the mouse pointer indicated. Barska watched him read in French every little box for every little button. He did so in silence. It annoyed her.

Finally, he said, “Let’s look at the facial recognition log.”

“What’s that?” asked Barska. She knew, but was tired of being ignored.

“It’s like the pull-down destination menu on your browser. It shows what you looked at within some time period.”

He opened the log, studied it, and closed it back up.

“As I thought. They’re not using facial recognition much by the elevators. But they’d be able to if they wanted.”

“Why are they able?” she asked, mainly to keep him talking.

“The hotel gets a picture of every guest at check in. There’s a camera behind the lobby desk. But they don’t bother applying facial recognition near lobby elevators. And I think I now know why.”

He leaned back in his chair, as though having reached an important conclusion, and spoke before she could.

“The camera angles are all wrong. Whoever put in the lobby cameras mounted them high, possibly to deter tampering. Anyway, hat brims mask faces when cameras look down from that high angle. A simple ball cap would be enough to prevent your being recognized."

"I don't understand."

He browsed the hotel computer's guest management menu as he spoke.

"The Volkovs will use an elevator bomb. That solves lots of problems for them, but it creates a very big problem. Somebody has to watch who gets in the elevator where the bomb is."

"There are six elevators. They'll watch all six?"

"No. Not that many. I imagine they'll somehow take half the elevators out of service. There's probably someplace one of the brothers can throw switches to turn off electrical current to those elevators … Add that to your list. See if you can figure out where the Volkov brother will go to interrupt elevator power. It'll be on the two or three bottom levels. Some kind of maintenance area, I'd guess."

She wrote the latest task in an open notebook by her computer.

"What if they just shut down the elevators with software?"

"It's not their pattern. You might do that. I imagine the Volkovs don't know how, but you're right. They could get some consultant of theirs to hack into the hotel system and disable elevators ... Yeah. I missed that. Good thinking on your part. See if you can shut down elevators with your computer. Don't do it yet. Just tell me if you can."

She made another note. "Okay."

"Now, the next question is whether a Volkov would stand by the elevators. Their other option is planting their own spy camera at the elevators."

"Cameras are tiny. It could be anyplace."

"The spy camera's very big problem's battery life. Cameras are hard on batteries. If they transmit their images to the Web, as they would, the battery wears out even quicker. To get long-term device power, the easiest way's to hook your camera and transmitter up to the building electrical system. Overhead light fixtures are hard to reach. It's easiest to find a floor-level plug that the janitor might use when vacuuming. You can swap out the plug faceplate with another one that's got a camera-transmitter unit inside. It takes about two minutes to make the swap."

"You've done that?" Barska looked impressed.

"Twice. But better stuff's on the way. In a year, nobody'll do plug tricks anymore."

"How do you know all this?" She still looked impressed.

"Smart friends."

He finally smiled a little.

"But back to the outlets," he said.

He began looking at the camera feeds for both the elevator doors and lobby area nearby. Thirty seconds of silence passed.

"Nope. They won't use a floor-level plug. The plugs are all in the wrong places. Sometimes you'd be looking at the back of people rather than the front. The rest of the time, the plugs are too far away. There's no zoom function. You'd only get thumbnails of heads, and thumbnails look sort of alike. That's especially so if you've got a crowd milling around."

Barska thought a moment. "That implies a Volkov standing by the lobby elevator doors. He'd be somehow ready to detonate a bomb?"

"Yes. The easy way's to send the bomb a code with a cellphone. There's cellphone repeater coverage all up and down the hotel elevator shafts. Alternatively, the Volkovs could buy a device that sends a trigger signal directly. Pay enough for a bomb and you can get a tiny little transmitter not much bigger than a guitar pick."

Barska was now so interested she forgot about coffee.

"Then what do we do?"

"We can be sure they'll attack during a break. Watching the elevator's less conspicuous with a crowd around you. Somehow the

Volkovs will trick a CEO into taking an elevator up to his room during one of the conference's four breaks. They'll try to blow up the elevator cab as he goes. That means one Volkov at the elevators watching for the CEO to get on. Since we know what the Volkovs look like, I can get that one for sure."

"You'll be in the lobby during each break?"

"Ideally, just for the first break. The Volkovs will try to kill then, if feasible. That way they've more breaks left to try again if something fails."

"Where will the other Volkovs be?"

"Well, if they can't shut down elevators by computer," he reminded her, "one Volkov will have to trip big mechanical circuit breakers from someplace in the hotel."

"You'd kill the circuit breaker Volkov after you kill the lobby Volkov?"

"I'll try."

"Sounds difficult. Can you run fast?"

He laughed softly. "Possibly not that fast. But we'll have another opportunity. After the explosion, the surviving brothers will flee the hotel. I doubt they'll have a room here---please check me on that by using the lobby desk registration pictures---and they'll want to be long gone when half the Quebec City police force shows up. I might be able to get them across the street."

"They'll go that way?"

"Maybe. Maybe not. These are ex-military types. There's a park that way. They'll feel safe in among trees, I think. Soldiers like boondocks."

She nodded. He smiled again. For the first time since he'd entered the room, she got the friendly smile she wanted. Not only that, but he said, "Good work so far, Grunt."

"Thank you. I was about to make some coffee. Can you stay for a cup?"

Strangely, she mostly wanted to talk with him now. What was he like as a person? she wondered. Was he seeing anyone?

"Can't. I have important calls to make. Since the convention starts in two days, I have to get a lot done. One more thing, though. It's important."

"What?"

"You have a big disadvantage on this mission, Grunt. You're far too pretty."

She smiled, hope rising within her.

"Thank you. At least, I think I should thank you."

He smiled back.

"You're welcome. You might not like what comes next, though."

"Okay. I'm already preparing myself."

"The Volkovs aren't nice family guys. They're used to getting sex for money or just taking what they want, and one of them's supposed to be ruthless that way. You don't want them hitting on you. You don't even want them noticing you."

"I stay in my room with the door locked?"

"Yes. Also, have the concierge buy you a set of clunky shoes, along with orthopedic stockings. Have the concierge get you a long, ugly dress one size too large. Don't wear makeup and find some way short of cutting it to make your hair look awful."

A very nice surprise she thought! He seemed genuinely to care about her safety.

"Yuck!"

She feigned a scowl, but only for a moment. Her smile returned.

"Okay," he said. "That's it for now. I'll phone tonight to see what you've discovered."

He rose and was halfway to letting himself out before she could stand. He stopped by the door and pointed to the bolt, to the chain, and to the lock's button.

"Remember, lock them all."

He smiled. She promised to keep the door locked. She smiled. He left.

Outside her room, he talked to his to his

cellphone as he walked away.

Send text message to Dragon Lady. Grunt's computer is a KopiKat model 4000. I can get her out of her hotel room if your technician gives me two hours' notice. Needles

34

The Volkov brothers called Stepan into their room. He took a seat and pulled out his notepad. He'd again take notes and again destroy them, thereby enhancing his memory.

"Let's begin," said Arkady, "It's time to change our evolving plan."

He proceeded to tell Stepan about the price-fixing CEO's go-between, who looked like Stepan. Grigori by then had taken from the Web a capsule biography for the Honorable Rufus Benedict, member of the Canadian Parliament. The biography had a recent picture of the man.

"Yeah," said Stepan, looking surprised. "That guy could be me."

"Grigori will take you shopping this morning for an expensive suit," said Arkady. "You'll also visit a good barbershop. We'll do the walk-throughs and rehearsals this afternoon."

"Okay. What, specifically, do you want from me?"

"We'll attack the first day of the convention at the afternoon break. We're only going after the Bowel-Wow CEO. He leaves a bodyguard in his hotel room when he's not there."

"How do you know that?" asked Stepan.

"A maid cleans the room. I used the fake police detective ID Grigori had made up for me. Once the maid finished the room, I asked her in the hallway about the guy staying there."

"Okay. There'll be a bodyguard in the room. Then what?"

"Thirty minutes before the afternoon break, you knock on the room's door. The bodyguard will open it, though maybe only a few inches. Make sure he gets a good look at your face. You'll be wearing a false mustache, by the way."

"I don't have a false mustache. Nobody told me to bring one."

Stepan said it defensively, not wanting to look bad. If his brothers lost confidence in him, he had nobody.

Arkady sighed. "I'll get you one. Don't worry."

"You want the bodyguard to think I'm the Canadian politician?"

"Yes. We'll rehearse what you say. It'll be something like, 'Tell Wesley that Rufus needs to meet him here during the next break. Tell him it's urgent.' And then you just turn and walk away."

"What if the bodyguard asks questions?"

"He probably won't. But if he does, just say something like, 'I only talk to your boss. If I tell him to fire you, he will. Just do what I said.' Then walk away."

"Are you sure he'll just let me go? Just like that?"

"Yes. He'll be suspicious. He'll call whoever's in charge of the security team downstairs with the client. If you came back later, the whole team would be there waiting for you."

"Am I coming back later?"

"No. Take the emergency stairs out of the building. Put on a hat and pull off the mustache. Wear sunglasses. Wait for Grigori across the street in front of the hotel. There's a bus stop there. Stand fifteen yards to the side of it."

"Which side? East or West." Stepan had his pen poised to write down Arkady's answer.

To Arkady, it felt like training a pigeon.

"The East side. That way the bus driver won't think you're waiting for the bus. The driver will ignore you if you're not exactly at the bus stop."

"Okay. Fifteen yards to the East."

He read the fifteen yards part from his notebook, closed his eyes, and said it to himself. Then he opened his eyes, ready for the next critical fact.

Grigori smiled at Arkady, who didn't notice.

Arkady said, "That's all you have to do, Stepan."

"What if somebody tries to stop me in the hallway or on the stairs?"

It was one of the usual dozen tiny-detail questions Stepan would ask before a mission. Grigori smiled again. Arkady saw the smile this time and stayed patient.

"Tell the person to follow you into the emergency stairway. Say nobody'll be there to see the money you have for him."

After block printing Arkady's guidance nearly verbatim, Stepan looked up. "How much money do I give him?"

Arkady sighed. "None. Simply kill him and continue down the stairs."

35

Needles emailed Grunt early the next morning, instructing her to spend from noon until two p.m. outside the Old City Tower. She should spend thirty minutes on each side of the hotel, determining how the Volkovs would withdraw from the building after the attack. He said it would also give her practice being unattractive. Grunt had laughed at the last part. She then made a serious effort to comply with Needles' directive.

At two p.m. the same day, Needles went to an encrypted Dark Web chatroom, where he awaited the Dragon Lady. Dragon Lady was the codename for Jenny Haranya, the forty-something Eurasian beauty married to Sanjay Haranya's eldest son, Kenneth.

It was surprising to some that Jenny Haranya was the family empire's heiress in waiting. Everybody in the family liked Jenny. They all liked Sanjay's five sons, too, but the sons were super-techies. Sanjay's daughters now lived in India, where they did sophisticated market research they enjoyed. Only Jenny loved top-level management as much as her father-in-law did.

Needles and Dragon Lady had immediately realized what essential resources they could become for each other. Each had carefully cultivated their business relationship over the years. This time it was Needles who needed help.

<u>Dragon Lady</u>: *I have good news.*

<u>Needles</u>: *Your team finished?*

<u>Dragon Lady</u>: *Fifteen minutes ago. Grunt's computer now has a datalogger chip soldered onto its motherboard. The datalogger's*

the newest version for spies. Shall I describe it?

Needles: *Please.*

Dragon Lady: *The little chip's essentially undetectable, even to most KopiKat laptop repair technicians. It records every keystroke Grunt makes on the keyboard. It even works for the touchscreen keyboard if she uses that. The chip will store a full terabyte of keystrokes. It waits for your signal and uploads its keystroke data to the Web.*

Needles: *There's some sort of dashboard I can use, right?*

Dragon Lady: *Right. If you go to our usual, untraceable download page, you'll find a file named "n_file_17.exe". Install it on your computer, and you'll see the dashboard for controlling the datalogger chip. I'm told it's self-explanatory. You won't need more than ten minutes to figure it out. The technician says only two minutes. The ten-minute part's my being conservative.*

Needles: *This sounds like a wonderful device.*

Dragon Lady: *Yes, but I'm not done. It's even better than wonderful.*

Needles: *How?*

Dragon Lady: *From the chip's Web dashboard, you can control Grunt's computer. You can partially take over the critical heart of her machine's operating system. Then you can turn her computer microphone on or off. The chip will send what the microphone hears to wherever you want it sent whenever the computer's online. You set it all up from the dashboard.*

Needles: *What if she's not connected to the Web?*

Dragon Lady: *If she's offline, but the machine's powered up, the chip will try to hack into anybody's router that's nearby. The hacking's not super-sophisticated. I'm told only about two hundred thousand common passwords get tried. However, it seems to work about one time in three according to our tests. People almost everywhere are careless with passwords.*

Needles: *One time out of three's much better than nothing.*

Dragon Lady: *Also, the datalogger can keep storing keystrokes and audio even if not connected. Some better-than-military compression's involved. Eventually, you'd run out of storage space. Kenneth says it would take at least a month, though.*

Needles: *Can't Grunt somehow detect that I'm recording her over her own microphone?*

Dragon Lady: *I'm told three firewall features and two hardware features should prevent somebody controlling her microphone.*

The chip overcomes all five features. It simply bypasses them. She won't notice. Anytime she goes online, you can make her machine play any of the tricks it knows.

Needles: Thank you! I owe you another one.

Dragon Lady: You do! I'm going to let you to repay those favors all at once. I just need your help finding a nice man in his sixties to marry Sanjay's sister.

Needles: I tried. I only knew that chemist in Ottawa. Auntie thought he was a wimp.

Dragon Lady: She did. I should have told you more about Auntie. Therefore, I now will tell you: She has seen every John Wayne movie ten times. She's very, very intelligent. And don't forget, she's quite beautiful, even at sixty-three.

Needles: She is quite beautiful. She broke the wimpy guy's heart.

Dragon Lady: He was too fragile. I asked Auntie about that. She tried hard not to hurt his feelings. On objective grounds, she was thoughtful and polite. Maybe too honest, though.

Needles: And where's that leave us?

Dragon Lady: You have another friend that looks like a good fit for Auntie.

Needles: I give up. Who?

Dragon Lady: I'm thinking about that

guy you met with in our conference room. Sixty-something. Handsome. Athletic build. He seems like a John Wayne type.

Needles: You refer to someone I call Old Dog. Auntie would hate me forever if I set her up with him for a date. It might be so bad that she'd even hate you for a little while.

Dragon Lady: He carried a gun. That's a good start. It's John Wayne-ish.

Needles: He's stubborn as a mule. Auntie would find him overbearing.

Dragon Lady: That's not all bad. Usually it's the other way around on Auntie's dates ... Is he tough? Could he win a fistfight with an average guy thirty years younger than he is?

Needles: Ten times out of ten.

Dragon Lady: Then I think Auntie would find him very sexy.

Needles: I doubt it. He'd find her sexy, though. Until she started telling him what to do.

Dragon Lady: Auntie's late husband never let her boss him around. She liked that about him. She misses a strong man in her life. I think the strong women of her generation might even prefer the strong men of her generation. Anyway, she does.

Needles: I suggest scheduling her to meet with Sanjay once a month for counseling. He's a very strong man of her generation. He could give her advice.

<u>*Dragon Lady*</u>*: My mother-in-law and I tried something like that. Auntie drove Sanjay nuts. He ordered me to get Auntie married. I now have to give him an Auntie marriage forecast at each of my monthly business goals meetings with him.*

<u>*Needles*</u>*: It's really that bad?*

<u>*Dragon Lady*</u>*: It's at least that bad. Will you help me?*

<u>*Needles*</u>*: I can't do much until the mission's over. Old Dog's involved in it.*

<u>*Dragon Lady*</u>*: Understood. And may I say that his helping you makes him an even better prospect? Auntie also has watched the James Bond movies over and over.*

<u>*Needles*</u>*: Well, don't get your hopes up. I'll find some way to have Old Dog take her to dinner. Probably in Little India. He absolutely loves Little India.*

<u>*Dragon Lady*</u>*: Splendid! Thank you, Needles! Thank you so very much!!*

36

Arkady and Grigori had planned to kill the Bowel-Wow CEO during the half-hour morning break on the convention's first day. However, they couldn't get Stepan ready in time. He could say his twenty-words, but not convincingly. He also had difficulty with the "If

I tell him to fire you, he will" part. Stepan in his entire life would never have thought to say such a thing. He'd have simply killed the person. Stepan wasn't even marginally subtle.

His brothers needed all morning and part of the afternoon to get Stepan's lines right. Mostly, Grigori did the coaching. Even so, Arkady ran out of patience with Stepan. Stepan sensed as much, becoming anxious and defensive.

Grigori suggested Arkady work on something in Grigori's room while he and Stepan continued. Arkady left. Stepan did better almost immediately. Not even halfway well, but better. It took until two p.m. before Stepan could convincingly mimic the Honorable Rufus Benedict.

Nevertheless, his repeated inadequacy in front of his brothers much unnerved Stepan, who perspired when nervous. By the time he finally could get his words right, he'd sweated through most of his dress shirt. Worse still, his heavy sweating overcame his false mustache glue. The mustache fell off soon after Arkady returned to the room.

There was another problem. The perspiration overcame whatever deodorant Stepan had applied. Arkady wondered for the first time if Stepan even used deodorant. Grigori also noticed. He suggested their attack would go better if they waited until tomorrow. Arkady agreed and Stepan wisely remained silent.

That settled, Stepan showered, grateful to be alone. Arkady left to get Stepan's shirt expeditiously laundered, pressed, and lightly starched. Grigori carefully rinsed and dried the mustache with a hairdryer set to low power. Fortunately, he had enough of the theatrical makeup cement left to stick it back on Stepan tomorrow.

All the brothers knew it was essential to kill Bowel-Wow's CEO tomorrow. Stepan would lie awake much of the night worrying about his debut as an actor.

37

Brent would've been no match for the Volkovs if the fight were limited to guns, knives, or martial arts. He relied almost entirely upon poisonous needles nobody else used. Each was like a tiny ice pick two inches long: a needle-thin stick of hard poison mounted in a wooden grip.

Each needle started out as the high-strength glass tubing found in chemistry laboratories. If carefully heated and stretched, the tubing would become extraordinarily thin, but still remain hollow. Brent stretched the ultra-thin tubing himself and cut it into lengths only one and a half inches long. Each length would become a high-tech needle.

Getting the liquid poison into the tube was simplicity, itself. Brent relied upon capillary action for atmospheric pressure at sea level. He heated his poison to nearly its boiling point and dipped the glass tube into it. That brought half a drop of low-viscosity poison up to precisely half an inch from the top of his tube section. Half a drop was plenty since less than a hundredth of a drop easily would kill a three-hundred-pound male athlete.

Brent cooled the ultrathin glass tubes with their liquid still inside. It had taken some serious trial and error to do this without cracking the glass. He finally determined an air quench, as he called it, in an ordinary household freezer was best. It developed a crystalline structure in the poison, making the toxin glossy white and harder than glass.

The next part was the most difficult. The thin glass tube casing kept the poison from making direct contact with the victim's flesh. Brent had to remove the glass tube from the thin, hard stick of poison inside it. He had started out trying to use micro-saws and high-precision grinding wheels to cut the glass away from the poison. Most of these early efforts failed, with the needle breaking apart from the vibration. Brent switched to laser machining and nearly always succeeded in removing the glass tubing from almost the entire poison stick.

He left just enough glass tubing that the poison stick remained attached to the half inch of tubing still free of poison. Most of that empty half inch would be mounted in the needle's wooden grip. Though much greater care was needed, that final step would be like seating an ice pick's metal spike into its wooden handle.

The wooden handle was an inch-long piece of hardware store dowel, one-eighth inch in diameter. Brent used a watchmaker's drill to make a hole down the center of the dowel, but only three-eighths-inch deep. He gently pushed most of the empty tube portion into the hole. The tiniest bit of paraffin wax in the hole kept the needle in place.

Needles held his weapon with its dowel grip between two adjacent fingers. By now he could use any two fingers on either hand. If he held his hand palm down, the needle's poison spike would point downward from between his fingers. The slightest push into the target's skin would send the lethal poison spike fully into the target.

Next, and in one fluid gesture, Brent would flick the little bit of dowel sideways, causing the needle not only to snap free of its handle, but also to fragment beneath the skin. Fragmentation further distributed poison below the victim's skin, where it was quickly absorbed by the bodily fluids present.

Absorption didn't affect kill speed---neural cascade required only a few molecules of poison beneath the skin---but hampered forensic analysis. Two minutes after an attack, and usually sooner still, the little micro stick of deadly poison inside the target had dissolved without attendant discoloration or swelling. Bits of poison thus were never found. Sophisticated examination of tissue, blood, and fluid would not find the poison, either. Since forensic analysis knew nothing of neural cascade, forensic analysis never looked for it. Also, there were too few of the telltale molecules for modern day forensic instrumentation to detect, even if it did look.

Ideally, Brent disposed of the wooden stub by dropping it into one of his leather-lined coat pockets for destruction later. Otherwise, the needle stub could safely be tossed aside, sure to go unnoticed or misunderstood. When he killed multiple targets at once---as he had on one occasion---he tossed stubs freely.

Because the soluble poison had very high affinity for water, ordinary humidity would turn needles limp in minutes. Brent therefore kept each needle in an air-tight vial until just before its use. The vial, in effect, became the needle's holster. These vials were small glass tubes, melted shut at one end. They escaped detection in all varieties of airport scanners, just as the high-tech poison residue went unnoticed in all manner of forensic tests.

As impressive as the needles were, the poison Brent used was even more amazing. Indeed, it was revolutionary---so much so, it already had prompted a serious plan to kidnap him, torture him, and kill him in the weeks ahead.

38

Needles began the convention's first day at four a.m. by altering his key parameters for facial recognition. The basic idea was to create uncertainty about portions of the face not easily changed. Oddly enough, the distance between pupils of the eye was so standard that facial recognition mostly ignored it. Instead, facial recognition programs looked at the harder points of the face. In other words, they looked at facial tissue not easily reconfigured at will.

The cheeks, for example, would be ignored. Someone instantly could suck them in or puff them out. Hairlines were also useless. Thirty seconds with a comb, or thirty seconds in the wind, and apparent hairline moved dramatically. Eyebrow dimensions were also misleading.

In contrast, the tip of the nose, the width of the nose, the point of the chin, the distance between cheekbones, and the center of the lower eyelid were relatively immutable. A person's facial recognition signature was his or her unique combination of measurements taken among these facial landmarks. Some of the later surveillance camera applications also considered skin texture, but Brent was sure the Old City Tower's owner wouldn't pay for that upgrade. Almost nobody did.

He therefore changed his "immutable" measurements. A short plastic tube inside each nostril slightly widened his nose while actually helping him breathe better. He always put those tubes in when using a disguise.

Ordinary wrinkle cream tightened the skin of his lower eyelids, reshaping that portion of his eye. Cellphone earbuds made it hard to precisely tell where his ear openings were relative to the top of his ears, which his longish hair already obscured.

His full beard did the rest. It kept facial recognition from precisely finding the tip of his chin or the precise width of his cheekbones. If somebody's database held his Alabama laboratory ID picture, the dimensions taken from that picture wouldn't match those for Brent's lightly modified face. In facial recognition terms, he couldn't possibly be the Lars Brent anybody's computer might know.

He was dressed like a convention attendee, having registered late as Wendell

Puckett, M.D., paid the late fee, and thereby acquired a conference badge like everyone else's. He hung it from his official convention neck lanyard. Before leaving his hotel room, he ate two meal-replacement bars, which he washed down with two cups of in-room coffee. It made an uninviting breakfast, but Brent wanted a light meal. He was in hunter mode now, with high-tech kill needles cleverly holstered about his body. His senses were keen when he reached the lobby.

He would live in the lobby most of the day pretending to work on his cellphone. That made him look like fifty other lobby visitors, most of whom actually were working on their cellphones. He made restroom visits whether he needed to or not. He bought a newspaper, pretended to read it, and threw it away. Two hours later, when he was surrounded by another fifty cellphone devotees, he bought a different newspaper and pretended to read it, too. His lunch and dinner were more energy bars. He sporadically watched wall-mounted TV screens report the same news stories dozens of times.

It wasn't much fun. Even so, in these and other little ways, Brent looked perfectly ordinary. Nobody noticed him staking out the lobby near the elevators.

39

Frequenting the hotel lobby the entire first morning of the convention had given Needles plenty of time to ponder. Late afternoon of the convention's first day, after finding a temporarily empty nook of the vast lobby, he called Grunt about one of his ideas. He spoke softly with nobody nearby. Only Grunt would hear him.

He said, "Can we talk somewhere private."

She said, "Sure. I know a good, little place. I'll meet you there."

It was a code. Minutes later they were using the *Cryptobag* apps on their burner phones. That meant they could dictate encrypted emails to each other with the app's voice recognition capability. It was only a little slower than encrypted chat and equally secure.

Needles: Are you there?

Grunt: I'm here and wearing my dowdy dress. I look awful.

Needles: Good. Congratulations.

Grunt: Thank you.

Needles: Can you hack into the hallway cameras outside of the two CEO rooms?

Grunt: Sure. I'm leaving the hotel security system dashboard open. Just give me fifteen seconds per floor to access any floor's cameras.

<u>Needles</u>: Watch the CEO hallways during both of the long breaks in the convention tomorrow. Tell me if a Volkov shows up.

<u>Grunt</u>: Are you expecting them?

<u>Needles</u>: Hard to say. But I'm pretty sure I'll kill whatever Volkovs are near the elevators. I'd bet there's only one there. I'd have to be lucky for a second one to arrive.

<u>Grunt</u>: Okay. I'll watch hallways.

<u>Needles</u>: They'll have a backup plan. When they don't hear a bomb go off, they'll expect the CEO somehow made it safely to his hotel room. They might try to gun down him and his bodyguards in the hallway outside his room.

<u>Grunt</u>: Can you stop something like that?

<u>Needles</u>: Maybe. It depends on whether I get to the Volkovs before or after they've started shooting. So, tell me if you see them on the CEO floors or even traveling up to those floors. It'll only be during a break. If the Volkovs start shooting, they'll want their targets out in the open ... One more item.

<u>Grunt</u>: What?

<u>Needles</u>: If the Volkovs run from the building, which way will they go?

<u>Grunt</u>: In my opinion, they won't go south. That means getting down a two-hundred-foot cliff, and even the easier ways take too long. Besides, once you get down to river level,

the river pretty much boxes you in. There's no place to run.

<u>*Needles*</u>*: So, where?*

<u>*Grunt*</u>*: I'd say north. Both east and west have advantages, but north has more of those advantages. That's where the crowds are. That's also where more hiding places are.*

<u>*Needles*</u>*: My thoughts, as well. If I don't get all the Volkovs inside the hotel, be ready to tap into police surveillance cameras north of here. I'll need you to lead me to any Volkovs that get away.*

40

At eight p.m. on the first day, Grunt reported the CEOs safely back in their rooms. Lars left his comfortable chair and headed toward the lobby elevators nearby. That was when his cellphone vibrated. It was Charlie. Lars left his earbuds in for the call.

"Lars, can you talk in the clear now?"

"Yeah. Somebody might walk by, but I'll be suitably cryptic."

"Understood. What's your status?"

Brent quickly reached the elevators and pushed an "up" button.

"Three traveling sales reps nobody likes haven't shown up yet."

"You've got your sales assistant looking for them elsewhere in the hotel?"

"Correct. My sales assistant hasn't seen them, either.

"It seems to me that all three being late looks strange. Not alarming yet. Merely strange."

The empty elevator compartment's doors opened. Brent stepped in, pleased that his phone still worked. He pushed a button for two floors above his mid-level hotel room, just in case anyone was watching the floor numbers displayed above each elevator door. He would walk down the fire stairs to his room.

"Like you say, Old Dog. It's strange. But their absences could be illness. Could be some sort of logistics snafu. Could be something else. I'm betting they'll be here tomorrow."

"Then tomorrow's a long day for you and your sales assistant. I've got my own two assistant salespersons at a budget hotel. They can help you sell if you say the word."

"You weren't supposed to do that. That's not how I work. Consider me highly pissed." He didn't sound highly pissed, though. There was warmth in his voice.

Old Dog seemed to entirely miss the warmth.

"Then sue me. I'm just trying to look out for a youngster like you."

Nobody joined Brent for the short trip upward. The doors opened. He looked up and down the hall before leaving the elevator. He then walked briskly to the nearest fire stair entrance, talking as he went.

"I feel better, but now you owe me. You can make us even, though, if you have dinner with a beautiful woman."

"Why would I have dinner with the well-built blonde who mainly likes you?"

"Not her. Somebody your age. I've been asked to arrange it."

"Who would I have dinner with?"

"A woman who's still so smoking hot you won't know she's your age."

"Who?"

"It's a secret. Besides, we're on an unsecure line."

"Where?"

Brent was in the stairs now and almost to his floor.

"A little place reminiscent of Mumbai, but farther north. You pick the restaurant. I'll pay for dinner."

"I don't like blind dates. Sticking you with the dinner tab warms my heart, though."

"Just remember this woman's drop-dead beautiful. She'll be embarrassed being seen in public with an ogre like you."

Brent was almost to his room. He'd already taken the room key from his pocket so he could enter quickly once he reached the door.

"I'll think about it. I first need to figure out which restaurant's the most expensive. And there'd be a hefty bar tab, even if I were the only one drinking."

"No problem. It's the chance of a lifetime for you."

"Like I said, I'll think about it. And it's time for you to get back to selling."

"Yeah. Sales are good. Goodbye, Old Dog."

Needles deftly opened his room door and stepped inside as he said it. Nobody noticed. Nobody noticed most of what he did. He was superb at avoiding attention.

41

It was the second day of the convention. The well-rehearsed Volkovs were ready to kill the Bowel-Wow CEO. Needles was ready to kill Volkovs.

The morning break would be from nine-thirty a.m. to ten-fifteen a.m. Convention attendees would surround large tables bearing coffee and pastries outside their meeting rooms. All the tables were near the lobby elevator area. For forty-five minutes, Grigori would be able to find the Bowel-Wow CEO, and Needles would be able to find any Volkov watching the elevators. Needles didn't know which Volkov he might find, but didn't care. He'd memorized the faces of all three brothers.

At seven-forty-five a.m. Needles, dressed like any other male convention attendee, sat in the lobby "reading" his first newspaper of the day. His burner phone was connected to Grunt's burner phone.

Again unattractively attired, Grunt sat before her laptop in the safety of her hotel room. Like Needles, she wore earbuds. Her screen was sectioned into quadrants with a different surveillance camera feeding each quadrant. By now, Grunt operated the hotel surveillance system better than the guards, themselves, did. She adroitly switched from camera view to camera view.

"I've changed screen views. I'm watching the hallway outside the Bowel-Wow guy's room, the hallway outside the Happy Pill guy's room, the basement elevator pit, and the second-floor utility area. How's that?"

"Perfect," said Needles.

"Did the CEOs and their bodyguards all go to breakfast?"

Needles hadn't told her, even though she'd told him when they left their rooms.

He forced himself to smile noticeably as he spoke into his earbud headset, like a traveling executive might if checking in with his wife at home. "I think so. I can't see the dining area from here, though. Anything else?"

"Negative. Grunt out."

Ten boring minutes passed for them both. At nine-twenty a.m. Grunt said, "A guy walked to the second-floor maintenance corridor. He's so far got his back to me and the focus isn't terrific. Wearing a maintenance jump suit. Short hair or maybe even bald. Athletic build. Might be Arkady."

"I'd bet on it. Good! Try to keep track of him. I doubt I can leave here for another forty minutes. At least they're finally making their move."

"Understood. Grunt out."

At nine-twenty-five, Grunt said, "I think maybe Stepan's in the hallway outside the Bowel-Wow CEO's room."

"Understood," said Needles.

"The guy in the hallway's knocking on the door. It's Stepan for sure."

Needles slowly folded his newspaper and thought about drawing one of his holstered poison needles. He could hid it under the folded newspaper. Before he finished his thought, though, Grunt spoke.

"Stepan said something to the bodyguard in the room, with the door only partially open. Stepan stayed in the hall. It took less than ten seconds. Stepan's walking back the way he came."

"Follow him by camera as best you can. If you have to, ignore the elevator pit for now."

"Understood. Stepan's taking the fire stairs down. You might be able to get him in the stairway. It's the one on the southwest of the building."

"Don't I wish. I can't leave here until the third brother's located. I've got to stay between Grigori and the CEOs. But who knows? Maybe Grigori and Stepan will come to me."

A minute passed.

"Stepan just left the fire stairs on the lobby level. Get ready. He could be at your part of the building in thirty seconds."

Needles drew a poison needle from its small scabbard, hiding it within the pages of his folded paper. Once a needle was drawn, he had to be very careful where its point was. Lesser assassins might easily prick themselves, and especially so if nervous. Needles, in contrast, was calm and controlled. He did, however, make himself smile briefly as though recalling a joke. Even the one little half-smile made him look far less like the killer he was.

"Stepan just left the building ... He's going across the street. Toward a bus stop over there. If he takes a bus, I might lose him. Even after I tap into the police surveillance cameras."

"No problem. Forget about Stepan. He's not important now. If he were, his brothers would've kept him in the hotel to help them."

"Okay. I've stopped watching Stepan's bus stop. I now have one screen quadrant free to watch something else. The lobby desk area maybe?"

"Yeah. Do that for now."

Seven tense minutes passed, during which the drawn needle absorbed moisture. Needles pushed it back into its scabbard and dropped the scabbard into his leather-lined pocket.

Needles then said into his earbud headset, "Grigori's here. He just came in. That means nobody's in the elevator pit. Shift your elevator pit camera to the convention rooms. The break starts in five minutes. You should see bodyguards enter the lobby refreshment area and then the CEOs, with the rest of their bodyguards."

He drew a fresh needle from its tiny glass scabbard.

Soon certain convention area doors opened and two hundred attendees walked briskly out of their sessions, most of these persons heading toward the break area refreshments or toward the restrooms farther away.

Needles rose and walked into the swelling crowd. He moved calmly in Grigori's direction, a slight smile on his face. It was time for him to kill an assassin. Needles saw each such execution as his personal gift to mankind. Needles was uncommonly generous that way.

42

As Needles approached Grigori, Arkady pulled four of the elevator power switches inside the second floor maintenance corridor, shutting down power to those elevators shafts. He inserted a padlock into each of the four switch handles to "lock them out." Locking out was a safety procedure universally used by electricians working on high voltage machinery. Removing someone else's lock was all but unheard of. It would take at least an hour for hotel management to authorize breaking Arkady's padlocks off.

Arkady removed his maintenance worker coveralls in the privacy of the maintenance corridor, revealing the jogging suit underneath. Before leaving the corridor, he dealt with its two door locks, squirting fast-acting acrylic glue into each. Nobody would get through the doors to the elevator power switches anytime soon, he thought. They'd also have to pry one of the metal doors open first, and that destructive act would require further management authorization.

His part finished, Arkady walked calmly down the fire stairs and left the hotel. Outside the hotel, cloudy, drizzly weather awaited him for his long run through the nearby forest of an extended urban park. He casually ran off, as though starting his daily exercise routine, except that Arkady would keep well off the running trail local joggers normally traveled.

For the Volkov brothers, everything so far was going perfectly.

43

Needles was ten yards from Grigori when four elevators ceased to function. The lighted panel over each elevator door affected went dark. Big clutch-like brakes in the elevator pits groaned slightly as their shafts lost power. The brakes locked heavy cable counterweights into place, simultaneously stalling four elevator cabs between floors. The frightened passengers used their elevators' emergency phones to call lobby security, briefly overwhelming the two security officers on duty.

Needles knew what would come next and quickened his pace.

Grigori stood across the lobby from the working elevators. He wore a hat and a rain coat well-suited to the weather outside. Nobody but Needles took notice of Grigori as he tapped away at his cellphone.

Brent realized Grigori might be arming bombs. He walked faster and soon stood in front of Grigori. Brent's open right hand held the poison needle. It was tucked between two fingers, perpendicular to the palm, point down.

"Grigori, old friend!" Needles said.

Grigori Volkov looked up from his phone in total surprise as Needles' right hand clapped against the left side of Volkov's neck. Needles concurrently extended his left arm, as though about to hug Grigori, while the right hand stayed in place. To anyone watching, it looked as if one old friend had just affectionately greeted another old friend. Hardly anyone watched, though. Either the elevators or the refreshments held the crowd's attention.

"Welcome to Quebec," said Lars, reaching for Grigori's cellphone as he spoke.

Grigori tried to hold the phone, but couldn't. His last thought was to punch Brent, but his arms no longer worked. Fury would have clouded his face, but that was numb, as well. Then his legs collapsed and he fell to the floor unconscious. He died seconds later.

Brent took three side steps away from the body. It was seconds later before anyone happened to look down and see Grigori's corpse on the floor. Brent used those seconds to make sense of Grigori's phone screen, which showed two simple on-off switches. Lars tapped both switches into the off position as he walked away.

By then, four persons were trying to revive Grigori, and four others were summoning EMTs, ambulances, and other conventioneers. It was a Mega Pharma convention, after all. Medical practitioners of all sorts attended.

Brent changed settings on Grigori's phone so it couldn't power off or lock up on its own. He walked from the hotel into its parking garage. His rental car awaited him there, his suitcase already in the trunk. He called Grunt.

"The middle bad guy's dead. Any idea where his brothers are?"

"No. We're getting some unexpected help, though. Old Dog called. I told him there was no sign of the other two in the hotel. He said he has about thirty guys in Washington secretly tapped into Quebec City surveillance cameras of all sorts. Did you know about this?"

"No. I'd have told them to butt out and stay away. That's why he didn't tell me, I guess. We don't always see eye to eye."

"Well, there's chaos in the lobby. Paramedics just came in. Somebody's news camera crew's taking pictures. You'd better get out of the hotel."

"I'm already gone. Any clue where the two brothers went?"

"No. I've got three-quarters of my screen going up and down police cameras on the three main roads through the City. Picture quality's mixed. Most intersection camera angles are better for reading license plates than faces. I don't expect to find much useful."

"Okay. Shutdown and destroy your burner phone. I'll destroy mine, too. We go to our alternate phones in thirty minutes, got that?"

"Understood."

"Go out through the lobby. Police will swarm in and then swarm out. Plan to leave soon after they swarm out. And keep wearing your ugly suit."

She smiled at that. "Anything else."

"Don't worry about Old Dog. I'll deal with him. Concentrate on your own exit."

"Understood."

"Needles out."

44

Needles drove to the edge of Quebec City before pulling off the road. His first call on his new burner phone was to Old Dog, telling him to meet in their usual place. Minutes later they began an encrypted *Cryptobag* email session.

<u>Old Dog</u>: *Congratulations on getting Grigori.*

<u>Needles</u>: *Thanks. I hear you've got two platoons of Agency hotshots gazing at Quebec camera feeds instead of gazing at their navels.*

<u>Old Dog</u>: *You think you're too important. It's more like one platoon. And some of them are*

just trainees. All in all, it's a pretty half-assed effort to assist you. Don't get your hopes up.

<u>Needles</u>: *I won't. This was Pierre's dumb idea?*

<u>Old Dog</u>: *100 percent. Did I mention she doesn't trust either one of us?*

<u>Needles</u>: *Were your two Agency guys watching the outside of the hotel?*

<u>Old Dog</u>: *Yeah. One spotted Stepan at the bus stop and followed him into a crowded bus terminal before losing him. The other guy was tapped into police security cameras. He reported Arkady getting onto a running trail in the park nearby. I told him to forget about Arkady and help look for Stepan.*

<u>Needles</u>: *Why give up on Arkady?*

<u>Old Dog</u>: *Because back when you were hunched over your first chemistry set, I was an off-the-books Marine killing guerilla movement leaders in jungles. You don't know much about parks and boonies, do you?*

<u>Needles</u>: *What's there to know about a big bunch of trees?*

<u>Old Dog</u>: *In this Quebec City park there are some surveillance cameras, but not many. They'll all be along the one or two trails though the park. Arkady will stay well off the trails, running cross-country. He's probably got civilian clothes on under the sweats. He'll pick the right place---somewhere unlikely to have*

cameras---and creep out of the forest the right way.

<u>Needles</u>: *He'd get back into the city unobserved?*

<u>Old Dog</u>: *Yeah. It's not even hard.*

<u>Needles</u>: *New topic. I might need to bring Mila into this. I'd do so after Ottawa and before the U.S. election.*

<u>Old Dog</u>: *Why? Mila's not a trained killer like us. She's strictly killer support---or she once was. Now she's a single mom working as hard as she can to keep her house.*

<u>Needles</u>: *I need a faster-acting poison. Grigori was within seconds of killing that Bowel-Wow CEO. Only Mila can help me with the chemistry involved. It's tricky.*

<u>Old Dog</u>: *If you send her anywhere even remotely dangerous, I'm going to surround her with thirty Agency contractors. And I'll stand next to her myself.*

<u>Needles</u>: *I get that. We think the same way Mila's safety. What I've got in mind won't be dangerous.*

<u>Old Dog</u>: *I feel much better.*

<u>Needles</u>: *Good. Next item. Tell me about the Ottawa kill zone, or maybe kill zones. What are the tactical constraints on the Volkovs there?*

<u>Old Dog</u>: *I thought you were sent the full*

smarty-pants work-up on all that.

<u>*Needles*</u>*: Nope. All I know is what I saw on the Web.*

<u>*Old Dog*</u>*: Damn! I'm gonna kick somebody's ass into orbit over this. You should've had that information yesterday at the latest.*

<u>*Needles*</u>*: Interesting ... When do I get it?*

<u>*Old Dog*</u>*: Well, if you're still in Quebec City, you'd first better get the hell out of there.*

<u>*Needles*</u>*: I know. You taught me that.*

<u>*Old Dog*</u>*: Yeah. There's hope for you. Spend at least another hour getting away and then call me. Call in the middle of the night or whenever. I'll have all the answers. Or, more accurately, I'll have all the supposed answers that are currently available. It's just Agency smarty-pants work. Don't expect profound wisdom.*

45

Both remaining Volkovs, now traveling in separate rental cars, were driving from Quebec City to their modest hotel accommodations in Ottawa. It was a six-hour trip. The plan had been to check in with Arkady at two-hour intervals along the way. When Grigori didn't, Arkady waited thirty minutes and called Stepan.

"Something may be wrong. Grigori

hasn't phoned me. There's been nothing on the radio about a bombing, either."

"I could go back and look for him," suggested Stepan.

Arkady thought Stepan's offer well-meant nonsense. Stepan was an unthinking weapon to be pointed at a target. Nothing more. If he went back to Quebec City, he'd have no idea what to do upon arrival. No, thought Arkady after a moment's reflection. Stepan would find multiple things to do, all of them stupid.

"Don't go back," said Arkady, keeping his scorn in check. "There may be a good explanation. Just keep driving. I'll pull over soon. There's a place ahead that'll have public Wi-Fi. I'll see if there's anything on the Web that might explain Grigori's delay."

Arkady then warned Stepan not to call Grigori's burner phone---not until they were sure Grigori was the one who'd answer.

Fifteen minutes later Arkady was online. He checked the New City Hotel website, but found nothing. He'd expected that. The hotel would be loathe to tell the public anything bad ever happened on its premises.

Next Arkady tried Web pages for TV news stations, for two Quebec City newspapers, and for the city's police department. He found nothing that pointed to Grigori. He became certain, however, that neither bomb had gone off. The police would find them, he told himself. Somebody'd wonder if the elevators had experienced more than power lock outs.

He turned to the Mega Pharma convention Web page. There he discovered a recent article lauding four conference physicians, who'd responded immediately when an unknown person suddenly died from an apparent stroke in the hotel lobby. The article was mostly nice words from some public relations minion, who gushed over the humanitarianism, expertise, and responsiveness of the four conventioneers. The writer went on to say equally nice things about all the other conventioneers.

Arkady supposed the article was just Mega Pharma sucking up to those who prescribed its products. No surprise there. The short article was never meant to be about the victim of the apparent stroke. It was all about capitalist marketing. He frowned in disgust.

However, once he knew there'd been a dead body, Arkady knew exactly how to proceed. He searched the Web for state-run morgues nearest the hotel. He assumed a stranger's unexplained death would require an autopsy

Using a false name, he called the morgue nearest the hotel. Arkady explained that his cousin had gone to visit a friend at the Old City Tower and was now missing. He feared the worst given his cousin's medical history. Then he described Grigori and asked if somebody fitting that description had been brought to the morgue. It would have been in the last thirty-six hours, Arkady said. No longer.

Arkady got lucky right away. The morgue supervisor---Arkady guessed that was her role---asked if he could describe an unusual tattoo on the man's arm. Arkady did, and then convincingly seemed to struggle against grief.

Could he visit the morgue to identify the body? asked the supervisor.

He explained he was calling on his personal cellphone from deep in the American South. While he couldn't reach Montreal quickly, he knew who could. Then he named a fictitious next of kin. He claimed not to have her street address, but knew she lived in Halifax. Struggling again with apparent grief---it was good acting---he thanked the supervisor and ended the call.

Trained killer that he was, Arkady would grieve his brother later. For now, he cursed as he sat in his car outside the diner in a small, all-night truck stop. Nobody noticed his rage, but somebody eventually would if he didn't control his face. He made himself appear calm.

At least, he told himself, they hadn't

identified Grigori. That meant the Russian government still hadn't given foreign law enforcement the Volkovs' military identification photos or fingerprints. The thought comforted him.

46

Lars Brent wanted to be in Ottawa before Kati Barska arrived. While she made the six-hour drive by car, he used his favorite private jet service. His plane was waiting for him only ten minutes outside Quebec City. As usual, he bypassed airport processing. The pilots knew him only as Mr. Jones, who always tipped them well. Four minutes after Lars boarded, the jet was at cruising altitude. Ottawa lay twenty minutes away.

In the total privacy of the aircraft's luxurious cabin, Needles picked up the handset for the plane's satellite phone. It cost something like fifty dollars a minute to make calls this way, but Lars didn't care. He was calling Mila.

He reached her as she drove home through Washington, D.C. traffic.

"Hello," she said.

Her voice sounded even more beautiful at fifty dollars a minute.

"Mila, it's me. Can you talk fifteen minutes?"

"Sure. I'm in traffic. I've got you on my

little car's speaker system."

"Is it safe to talk on the phone in traffic?"

"I think it depends on the speed. This traffic's moving at twenty miles an hour. I'm safe."

"Good. I want to hire you as a consultant."

"Me? Lars, if the work's easy, just tell me. I'll do it free for old times' sake."

"Nope. I need help with my proprietary poison. It kills in ten seconds if delivered as a toxin needle."

"*Wow!* Lars, do you realize how amazing that is? Your poison's even faster than a bullet to the heart. Well done, Lars!"

She said it with genuine admiration.

"Thank you, Mila. I need it to work faster than a head shot. Well, almost faster. Two seconds at most, but I'm shooting for instant death. No pun intended."

"Is that even possible?"

"Yes. The poison induces neural cascade."

Mila was so stunned she almost failed to stop when a truck ahead of her did. Almost.

"*You're kidding*. Tell me this is *not* a joke, Lars."

"I'm not kidding."

She still struggled to believe him.

"A neural cascade has been the ultimate goal of people like us forever, Lars. *It's supposed to be impossible.* Are you thinking about the same thing I am?"

"Yep. A neural cascade. The poison touches any nerve cell. That nerve cell not only shuts down, but also orders other nerve cells to shut down. It's not about what the poison does to the nerve cells so much as about what the nerve cells do to each other. The brain dies instantly once the nerve cell suicide chain reaction reaches it. That's what happens, Mila. A neural cascade."

"Lars, I'm so proud of you!" she gushed. "I mean, I always knew you were a genius. Way beyond genius even, *but this!* A neural cascade's like science fiction. Years ago, you and I couldn't cause death in less than thirty seconds. And that took a three-milliliter injection!"

"That was then, Mila. Now I've got a four-level toxin. The levels loosely mimic those for heroin. A little of it relieves anxiety. A little more of it kills pain and sedates just like opioids, but without any side effects. It's completely non-addictive. More still brings you to the next level, which is a general anesthesia suitable for surgery. No headache, nausea, or cognitive degradation. The final level's the weapon---a poison that kills in ten seconds."

Mila almost ran into the truck again.

"Lars, don't say anything else for two minutes. I'm so amazed at what you told me that I have to pull off the road before I hear anymore. I'm not even safe in creeping traffic."

It took her ninety seconds to do so. Far away, Lars Brent imagined the look on Mila's face and smiled. She had looked at him in something like unabashed wonder about once a month years ago. She always recovered quickly, though.

Not this time.

"Lars, are you still there?"

"Yes."

"Okay. Lars, just to be sure I'm not dreaming this, I'm going to repeat it back to you. Ready?" She still had her unabashed wonder look.

"Yes." He still imagined her with that look and smiled again.

"Your poison at maximum level triggers a neural cascade the moment it hits a big nerve. Have I got that right?"

"Almost. Even the tiniest nerves will do."

She whistled softly. Mila Rossi almost never did that.

"Lars, this is *phenomenal!* I don't see how I can help you. I'd gladly help, but, frankly, I'm only human. What you've done is superhuman and then some."

"Thank you."

She said nothing.

"Mila, are you still there?"

"Yes! Sorry. I'm sitting here with me eyes wide and my mouth open."

Then she laughed at herself. "You know, Lars, I hope nobody's watching. I must look like a little girl who just discovered chocolate."

"You've done that before. That look's one of many aspects I love about you, Mila."

"Thank you … Okay. I've got my composure back. Tell me how a mere mortal like Mila Rossi can help you?"

"Here's the problem: The more I use of an essential ingredient, the faster the poison kills. But if I use too much, the poison leaves a residue that could be detected by autopsies."

"You want to get the residue down to what? About five parts per billion?"

"Even less. Five parts per billion might work fine for the next few years, but forensic equipment keeps getting more accurate. Before long, I'll need residue below two parts per billion."

Another low whistle.

"Lars, there's one part per billion of everything in everything else. Close to that, anyway. How will you ever get poison residue that low?"

"Well, it's easier than it sounds. Some of the components appear in the body anyway, even if there's no poison. They won't look odd. It's only one molecule that's causing trouble. I need to get it below the two-part-per-billion threshold."

"I'll gladly help you, Lars. But it already sounds impossible. Don't pay me much."

She said it with a big smile.

Far away, he smiled back.

"Not impossible, Mila. The problem's cause lies in the production of the poison. It's a complicated process demanding extraordinary precision---just the sort of chemistry you like."

Her eyes sparkled. "Yes! I do love those problems. Maybe I should pay you."

"Nope."

"You realize, Lars, I'd be starting off a thousand miles behind you."

"Yes. But you'd catch up quickly. I know you Mila. It'll be easy."

"Okay. I have my own lab at the university. Technically, it belongs to the department, but nobody else can understand it. I also brought in the mega-grants that paid for it. About half the room's for wet chemistry. The rest is for computerized simulations of chemical reactions."

"Perfect. I'll be working from exactly the same sort of lab. Can we videoconference as we work?"

"Yes. Don't expect a proper lab coat. I'll be wearing jeans again. My lab's informal."

"I'm sure you still look fabulous in jeans. Mila. Try to wear tight ones."

She laughed softly. "I won't comment on that. What about the simulation software?"

"I'll be running the latest version of *ChemTronix*. That's version fourteen."

"Splendid! I installed version fourteen last week. Lars, this'll be fun."

"Yeah. It will be. What's your consulting rate, Mila?"

"I have to give the university an obscenely big cut. How's a thousand dollars an hour sound? Or maybe one dollar an hour since I'm staring off a thousand miles behind you?"

"How much do you need to pay off your mortgage?"

"Lars, that's a sore subject. Don't joke."

"I'm not. Either you give me a number, or I'll just pay you an even two million dollars. It would be for two days of consulting."

She said nothing. Mila was back to sitting with her mouth open and her eyes wide.

"Mila? Are you there?"

She snapped out of her astonishment,

thought a moment, and asked, "Lars, I already know you're not expecting me to sleep with you for this money. You'd better tell me that, though. Just so we're both very clear that I'm not becoming your mistress."

"I'm not expecting you to sleep with me until we get married. If you'll ever marry me, that is. I'm hoping to get that lucky someday."

"Lars, you can't propose yet. We're still getting reacquainted, remember?"

"Yeah. I know that … Get out a pencil and paper. Tell me when you're ready to write."

"Okay ... I'm ready."

He sent her a twelve-digit number. Then he gave her a Web URL.

"That's your new offshore bank account. Your password's the colorful nickname you gave that old car you drove to work in Alabama."

"Okay. But I'm an American. Am I allowed to have an offshore account?"

"I think so. Nonetheless, you can move the money wherever you want. Be sure to get some legal advice, though. I mean, what do I know about U.S. law? I'm Canadian."

She laughed. "Lars, this is very generous of you, but I can't let you do this."

"Nope. This is *not* generous."

He paused a moment, wondering if he

should say what he really felt. He took the risk.

"What you did in Vancouver was generous, Mila. Back then you offered me all that cash and you couldn't afford to give me any of it. Don't talk to me about generous."

She was touched. She even wiped one eye.

"Thank you, Lars." She said it softly.

"You're welcome. Besides, I figure I'll get half of it back as community property when you marry me."

She laughed. "Who knows? Maybe you will. Want to know what's left of my mortgage?"

"No. It doesn't matter. I was only kidding about the mortgage. I thought you might not tell me so I just transferred an even two million dollars to your new offshore account."

"Lars! I don't know what to say ... *Thank you!* ... And now you've made me start to cry!" Her voice choked up a little. It was one of those very happy, too-few-in-a-lifetime cries, though.

He understood. "You're welcome. And don't get too excited. It's only two million Canadian dollars. Not U.S. dollars."

47

Lars landed at a private airport half an hour outside Ottawa. A high-powered luxury rental car awaited him. He drove off toward Ottawa, but stopped midway in a big parking lot. Lars looked at his watch. It still wasn't too late for calling Old Dog.

Charlie Hexler awaited the call. "Hello."

"It's me. Ready to meet online?"

"Yeah. See you in two."

Two minutes later they were in the same Dark Web encrypted chatroom:

Old Dog: Let's start with an update. My guys had tapped phone lines to the provincial morgue nearest the Old City Tower. Grigori's body's there. Somebody pretending to be his cousin called. Most likely Arkady since Stepan's too dumb to act out the caller's part.

Needles: So, we've got Arkady's voiceprints now. That might be useful.

Old Dog: Yeah. Maybe. Also, the Canadians don't know yet who Grigori is. Up to now, everybody thinks he's just a John Doe who had a stroke. The autopsy might be tomorrow. Maybe the next day.

Needles: Anybody find an elevator bomb yet?

Old Dog: Both of them and within the hour. That's all very hush-hush. The Canadian counterterrorism guys are handling that information themselves.

Needles: How are they doing?

Old Dog: I grudgingly admit they're doing quite well.

Needles: Next topic. What can you tell me on the situation in Ottawa?

Old Dog: Both CEOs will stay at the hotel I told you about. The dissident's across the street. I made you a reservation in each place. Use your Kevin Grakowski ID to check in where the CEOs are. Use your Gerald Flynn ID where the dissident is. Want me to repeat that?

Needles: No. I got it. What else should I know?

Old Dog: The two CEOs will be testifying in a government building that's set up for high security everything. I'll text you the basic details. The government building's not a good place for the Volkovs to make a kill unless they're suicidal. The hotel looks easier, except everybody in Ottawa security anything is watching elevators now.

Needles: What about the dissident? Begin with who this guy is.

Old Dog: It's not a guy. She's Svetlana Rutskaya. Pretty. Articulate. About my age. She tells anybody who will listen about corruption in the Russian government. Dissidents back home send her a steady stream of evidence to support her charges. So far, she's gotten five or six Russian political hacks fired. A couple went to prison. Only a couple.

<u>Needles</u>: She's here and the bad guys are in Russia. Who in Russia pays attention to her?

<u>Old Dog</u>: Millions of Russians, that's who. The internet's everywhere. So is satellite TV. When the Western press covers her, her claims get broadcast back home in Russia. A battalion of Russian politicians hate her and the rest of them don't like her much.

<u>Needles</u>: How many bodyguards does she have?

<u>Old Dog</u>: Maybe one. I say "maybe" because she hangs out with an athletic-looking guy who's either her bodyguard or her boy toy.

<u>Needles</u>: Arkady will see her as a soft target. I'd bet he unleashes Stepan on her.

<u>Old Dog</u>: I agree. Arkady might even hope Stepan gets killed then. Younger brother has got to be a headache. He also knows too much about his older brother. Arkady can't risk Stepan going out on his own after this mission.

<u>Needles</u>: Can you have your local asset set up facial recognition around the hotels?

<u>Old Dog</u>: Already done. My asset's a retired Agency super-techie. She's got superb experience and easily tapped into the police, traffic, and ATM cameras. Maybe a few more cameras besides those. Just the public area ones, though. No bedrooms or anything.

<u>Needles</u>: That's enough. I'll have Grunt's facial recognition program watch inside both

hotels. Things will go fast once we find the Volkovs.

48 Kati Barska and her rental car would reach Ottawa hours after Needles. At the moment, she was in the parking lot of a distant truck stop with her laptop out. She also was in an encrypted Dark Web chatroom that neither Needles nor Old Dog knew about.

She drank some more coffee and took another bite of her grab-and-go cheeseburger. For truck stop food, it was quite good. Even for restaurant food, it was okay. Not quite up to Old City Tower room service, but you can't have everything, she thought.

She looked at her watch. Necromancer would enter the chatroom in two minutes if he, or maybe she, were on time. Barska thought Necromancer was probably a man. Somebody authoritarian, like the asshole lieutenant colonel she'd once worked for---the one after the asshole colonel she'd worked for. Two buzzcut little Hitlers in a row, she told herself. She should've put in for a transfer to someplace overseas.

Her laptop beeped at her. It was time to start.

Necromancer: Report.

Barska winced. That's how the asshole colonel would've started off. Report!

<u>Grunt</u>: Grigori Volkov's dead. I made a copy of lobby camera video showing Needles killing him. However, the camera angle was wrong and the camera wasn't all that good. Also, Needles is almost unbelievably smooth. You won't be able to tell he made the kill even if you know he made the kill. Volkov just seemed to drop.

<u>Necromancer</u>: What's Needles told you about his poisons and his tactics?

<u>Grunt</u>: Nothing.

<u>Necromancer</u>: That's unacceptable. I need all you can learn about his poison and how he uses it. You were told that. Do I infer you've not seduced him?

<u>Grunt</u>: He's kept me watching security camera video and far away from him. I wasn't even allowed out of my room. And he's 100 percent all about business. The guy's like a robot. Robots don't care about sex with worker bees.

<u>Necromancer</u>: I'm disappointed in you.

<u>Grunt</u>: Then you're disappointed. Get over it. What I did was the best anybody could do so far. And this job's not finished. There's still hope for pillow talk.

<u>Necromancer</u>: Do you know where Needles will be in Ottawa?

<u>Grunt</u>: Of course. I made the reservations for us. He'll probably be in room

307 of the Glass Walled Tower. That's the hotel the two CEOs will use. He might some of the time be in room 217 of the Brick Front Hotel, where the dissident stays. Brick Front's lots less comfy. I expect he'll mostly stay at the Glass Walled Tower.

Necromancer: My people still can't find his face in the databases. Did you get a good picture of him?

Grunt: I've got lots of pictures of him in the hotel lobby waiting for a Volkov. I'll send you the best three.

Necromancer: Do that. Anything else we need to discuss?

Grunt: I hate this chatroom stuff. When are you going to send me a mobile phone with top-level encryption capability? Or---better yet---one of those encrypted satellite phones?

Necromancer: Never. You shouldn't even ask, but you're new to intelligence work. Therefore, I'll explain. You never want such a device in your possession. Needles might see it. Worse yet, if the Canadian police get suspicious of you, they'll take your car apart and they'll take your room apart. If they found spy stuff, you'd be in a jail cell that same day. Got it?

Grunt: If you say so.

Necromancer: I say so. Any more questions?

Grunt: No more questions.

Necromancer: Rush those pictures along. Necromancer out.

Barska gave her laptop a middle finger salute before closing it up. She enjoyed the rest of her burger and lingered over her coffee. She finally drive off to Ottawa at a leisurely pace.

Necromancer was definitely an asshole, she told herself. He could wait for his damned pictures until she was settled into her Ottawa hotel room. To hell with him, or maybe her.

49

Arkady got two rooms in a cheap motel outside Ottawa. Stepan in one room alternated between map study and video games. Arkady in the other room systematically worked through Web information on the Ottawa government building where the CEOs would testify. After an hour of rapt attention, he felt both tired and discouraged. The government building was a little fortress. The CEO kills would have to occur in their hotel.

He stood, dropped to the floor for twenty push-ups to clear his head, and again sat before his laptop. It was so much easier, he thought, when he had Grigori to help him with the cerebral side of their work. Grigori had been their best planner, but at least his own skills were close.

He turned his attention to the dissident. She seemed to crave publicity, he decided. The

Web held dozens of pictures and videos from her public appearances. Arkady studied the images, much more interested in the persons around the dissident than in her. Her security budget, he concluded, must be tiny. Bodyguards would look at the crowd, not at her. He saw nobody who even might be watching the crowd.

Her meager security budget also was wasted. Whoever was responsible for her safety let crowds get much too close to the podiums and platforms she used. Why, he briefly wondered, did she always stay on some sort of stage? Then he realized she was quite short. She'd want to stand on something when news cameras were running just so she'd seem to be at lens level.

He found no pictures of her wading into adoring crowds. The crowds weren't really large and "adoring" overstated things. Half those present seemed to be reporters. They were young reporters, too---the ones assigned to less-important stories while gaining experience.

It would be easy to shoot her from within a small crowd and get away, especially with another man nearby covering the shooter. It should be easier still to shoot her as she walked out onto whatever stage she used. One often could do that from various places backstage. Shooting her from behind a curtain, which sometimes might be possible, had appeal.

There'd be less chance the audience might see the shooter.

He thought killing her first could distract attention from the CEOs. The dissident's murder would seem politically motivated. The CEOs, to be very sure, oversaw lobbyists and corporate propagandists. However, the CEOs weren't really political figures. Their testimony would be from the context of commercial experts, not political experts. Nobody would soon connect her death to their deaths. Meanwhile, police focus would be blocks away from the CEOs' hotel.

He abruptly decided what should be a simple assassination of one old woman was getting much too complicated. He didn't have time for complexity. It would be quickest---and therefore best---to send Stepan into the woman's hotel room with nothing more than his bare hands.

50

After his chatroom session with Old Dog, Needles had time to write computer code. In about three hours, Kati Barska would check into her hotel room. He didn't know if she'd begin hacking into cameras then, but she'd at least go online to ensure viable Wi-Fi connection. Once she was online, he'd empty the keystroke information in her datalogger by using the Web dashboard Dragon

Lady had described. He'd reset the datalogger cache to zero, making ample room for whatever else Barska said or typed.

He also would turn on the laptop microphone. He admitted to himself he should have done that sooner, but he had wanted to write his code first. The resulting little program would ensure whatever the microphone heard would be sent to one of his cloud accounts. It was not a hard program to write, but not all that easy either, because of the exotic security measures watching over his cloud accounts. Even for him, getting past the firewall alone was tricky. He had waited for leisurely, uninterrupted quiet to focus upon the programming.

He had the necessary code finished in time. When Barska signed on in Ottawa, Needles turned on the microphone and heard her moving about her room. He easily uploaded her keystrokes for the past three days and then disconnected.

Scrolling through Grunt's keystrokes, he found hundreds of camera commands sent to whatever software she'd used. There also were URLs for porn sites, keyed-in data from making their Ottawa hotel reservations, and some online room service orders. Grunt, he decided, was a hearty eater. She apparently had, to her credit, avoided alcohol while doing her camera work.

He found her half of the conversation with Necromancer, since that was all she, herself, had keyed in. That conversation in the datalogger's Barska-only format read:

Grunt: Grigori Volkov's dead. I made a copy of lobby camera video showing Needles killing him. However, the camera angle was wrong and the camera was not all that good. Also, Needles is almost unbelievably smooth. You won't be able to tell he made the kill even if you know he made the kill. Volkov just seemed to drop.

Grunt: Nothing.

Grunt: He's kept me far away from him, watching security camera video. I'm not allowed out of the room either. And he's 100 percent all about business. The guy's like a robot. Robots don't care about sex with their worker bees.

Grunt: Well, then you're disappointed. Get over it. What I did was the best anybody could do so far. And this job's not finished yet. There's still hope for pillow talk.

Grunt: Of course. I made the reservations for us both. He'll probably be in room 307 of the Glass Walled Tower. That's where the two CEOs will be. He might some of the time be in room 217 of the Brick Front Hotel. Brick Front is lots cheaper and less comfy. I expect he'll mostly stay at the Glass

Walled Tower.

Grunt: I've got lots of pictures of him in the hotel lobby waiting for a Volkov. I'll send you the best three.

Grunt: I hate this chatroom stuff. When are you going to send me a mobile phone with encryption capability? Or---better yet---one of those encrypted satellite phones?

Grunt: If you say so.

Grunt: No more questions.

Needles was intrigued by the results. Too bad, he thought, there was so little available. Grunt unmistakably was spying on him while helping him. But for whom? Old Dog already had his photo. Grunt wasn't doing this for him.

Right now, though, he needed rest. Needles knew that sleep was as important as reflection when hunting killers. Being mentally alert helped keep him alive. He quickly got ready for bed, throttled down his powerful mind, and soon was fast asleep.

51

Arkady awoke next morning at six a.m. He texted Stepan to eat breakfast alone. Arkady further said they should stay away from each other for now. If they saw one another, they should act like strangers unless they'd planned to act otherwise. That way, if one of them fell under surveillance, the other might not. Then the one undetected might eventually catch any stakeout team stalking the other.

It was a tactically reasonable story, Arkady told himself. It also kept Stepan away. Arkady was tired of explaining the obvious. That had been Grigori's job, not his.

Arkady made coffee and pondered how to kill his three targets. The woman dissident would be easiest by far. The boy toy wouldn't seriously interfere. At most, the boy toy was just a gym rat with a few bar brawls under his belt. Stepan could handle the dissident alone.

He and Stepan would work together, he decided, to kill the two CEOs. It would take both to get through a locked hotel room door before guards inside drew their guns. They'd need some advice on opening a locked door that quickly. Once Arkady had pictures of the actual locks and chains, he'd send them to his technical consultant, Sasha. Sasha would know everything about defeating hotel room doors, chains, and locks.

For the actual killing, Arkady and Stepan each would use a silenced .45 caliber pistol. Arkady already knew from similar kills that each brother would draw his gun *after* the door opened. They had little choice. It always took two persons to open a door without breeching equipment or explosives, either or which made too much noise and wasn't all that fast, anyway.

He and Stepan each would need both hands free while opening the door.

The bodyguards would have guns, of course, but they'd draw them too late if he and Stepan entered the room both quickly enough and quietly enough.

Arkady showered and dressed. He oiled his pistol and headed off to breakfast. After a good meal, he'd walk around inside the Glass Walled Tower. It would just be a reconnaissance this time, but he'd still take his gun. As an ex-infantryman, he knew targets sometimes appeared fortuitously. He might get lucky.

52

Needles also awoke at six a.m. He was in the Glass Walled Tower room Kati Barska didn't know about, registered there under a name she also didn't know. After a shower, he'd have breakfast sent up, he thought. As he climbed from bed, his cellphone buzzed.

"It's me. Old Dog. Meet me in the usual place in three minutes."

"Make it ten minutes, unless you want to talk before coffee activates my brain."

"Okay. Ten minutes. Old Dog out."

Nine minutes later they were in their encrypted Dark Web chatroom. Needles poured his second cup of do-it-yourself coffee as Old Dog began.

<u>Old Dog</u>: Good news. I didn't want to wait on this. My retired agent not only has tapped into the relevant camera feeds for both Ottawa hotels, but she's also got a way you can do the same.

<u>Needles</u>: You mean a way that doesn't require Barska?

<u>Old Dog</u>: Yeah. I'll email you a link. Go there and download the app you'll install. In another email I'll provide the codes you enter into the installed app. My retired agent will talk you through it over the phone if you need help. She says you won't need her, though.

<u>Needles</u>: Then what?

<u>Old Dog</u>: Then you'll be seeing on your computer the hotel hallways, lobbies, etc. *You'll have a menu of choices. Barska can watch whatever she wants. You can watch whatever you want. I tried this software two hours ago. It's addictive. I got so interested I let you sleep.*

<u>Needles</u>: I look forward to using it. I'm assuming that, with all this remote hotel inspection you did, you've reached some conclusions?

<u>Old Dog</u>: Yeah. No bombs for the CEOs. Everybody will be looking for bombs in the Glass Walled Tower. Even in the Brick Front Hotel, their one or two security guys will have seen the elevator alerts and bomb warnings.

<u>Needles</u>: I think I'll agree with that after

more coffee. Too soon to decide now. What else?

Old Dog: Either Arkady or Stepan could walk into the dissident woman's hotel room and kill her without using weapons. The smart way would be making it look like she accidentally fell and hit her head. Arkady might do that. Stepan will just strangle her or snap her neck.

Needles: And the CEOs?

Old Dog: Our two bad guys won't have much time to kill both CEOs. I'd bet Arkady and Stepan do one room together and then right away attack the second room. There'd be a bodyguard at each door to frisk them and one more bodyguard inside each door. Basically your standard Agency approach, but without Agency guys.

Needles: You think neither Arkady nor Stepan will carry a gun into the room?

Old Dog: They won't have to. Once inside, they'll sucker punch the bodyguards and take their guns.

Needles: Sounds hard to me. I'd bet they go in with guns.

Old Dog: Going in unarmed won't sound hard to them. They're ex-Spetsnaz. For them, this approach will look easy.

Needles: You seem to be thinking that, once they kill a Mega Pharma CEO, everybody in security'll figure out another Mega Pharma

CEO might be next. That's why the Volkovs can't get one CEO one night and come back the next night for the other.

<u>Old Dog</u>: *Right. The Volkovs must kill both CEOs quietly and within minutes of each other. They can get the woman the day before or the day after. The day after might be marginally better.*

<u>Needles</u>: *Why marginally better?*

<u>Old Dog</u>: *Hotel murders are rare in Ottawa. There'll be lots of press attention. For a little while, anybody in hotel security will be more careful. If two teams of CEO bodyguards get even a little more careful, that little bit matters. Those guys are good.*

<u>Needles</u>: *And if the Brick Front Hotel's one or two bodyguards get marginally better, it won't even be noticeable?*

<u>Old Dog</u>: *That's how I see it. And they might not get any better. To them, a couple of hits in a luxury hotel will seem as relevant as two hits on the moon. It's not a world they identify with.*

<u>Needles</u>: *Wait a minute while I think this through. I feel caffeine kicking in. I'm getting smarter.*

Old Dog waited for three minutes. He was about to suggest a cold shower complement to the caffeine, but Needles typed first.

<u>Needles:</u> *I think you're right. Thanks. I'll*

keep looking for flaws in your thinking, but right now I don't see any.

Old Dog: Now you owe me.

Needles: Uh-oh.

Old Dog: We can talk about that later. After you whack a couple of Volkovs.

53

Arkady casually walked through the Glass Walled Tower, making an unobtrusive reconnaissance. Beacon had forwarded target information. It told Arkady which of the hotel's four hundred and thirty rooms the executives were in, and nothing else useful. Even so, knowing which rooms to attack was essential intelligence.

Arkady expected each set of bodyguards to be inside their CEO's large suite rather than patrolling the hallways and stairs outside. His walk-through confirmed as much.

Arkady was especially interested in door locks. He stopped outside a room door left open as housekeeping worked. While the housekeeper cleaned the shower, Arkady took cellphone images of the electronic room lock's outside, inside, and bolt plate. He also photographed the heavy-duty door chain. He'd send the pictures to Sasha.

Images taken, he continued his tour. He saw four of the hotel's lobby security guards, which was more than expected. He quickly realized it was a shift change. Soon only two guards were at the lobby station.

He hadn't been impressed with any of the guards. They were overweight, over-groomed, and over-friendly. Arkady would have bet money all four couldn't find Afghanistan on a map without a search engine. These weren't tough Canadian combat veterans. These four, he told himself, probably got promoted in-house from pastry chef apprenticeships.

Not only that, but their colorful uniforms were better for holding a crease than concealing a gun. The guards might have firearms locked up somewhere nearby, but this was Canada. Any locked up guns might well be unloaded. Cupcake commandos, he sneered.

He learned where the fire alarms were, just in case he needed a distraction. He determined which custodial staff areas had ordinary locks he could pick. He examined every first floor exit and every underground parking garage exit. He discovered that there was only one, old-fashioned metal detector in the hotel. It was at the main entrance to the meeting room area, and therefore no concern of his. That revelation made for a very bright spot in his day.

He inconspicuously photographed those who carried up room service, made beds, cleaned hallways, and replaced lightbulbs.

These persons seemed to wear standard uniforms sourced locally and but little altered. He could get such uniforms if need be.

He captured a good image of an employee badge from only a few feet away. It was a simple plastic badge of ordinary design. He, himself, could make a convincing replica in an office supply store.

He turned his attention to the hotel's exterior. He quickly identified enough surveillance cameras to understand hotel security's camera strategy. He found the bus stops. He saw where taxicabs lined up for doormen to hail them. He walked nearby streets and alleys, determining how police and ambulances would approach the hotel.

Arkady went across the street for lunch, spending a full hour eating at a table by the little cafe's big front window. During that time he watched the front of the Glass Walled Tower, noting, among other things, how many times police cars went past. He also contacted Sasha by encrypted email. How, Arkady asked, could he very quickly get through the locked hotel suite door and its chain? Sasha soon emailed him the explanation needed.

Arkady walked back across the street, and back through the Glass Walled Tower lobby to see if the guards remained as alert as at their shift's start. He found them halfway so. One of the two guards stood behind the guard desk and sometimes scanned the lobby intently. The other sat behind the guard desk and read something. Probably a cookbook, thought Arkady.

He left the Glass Walled Tower. His mid-afternoon would be spent reconnoitering the dissident's hotel.

54

After further reflection on his conversation with Old Dog, Needles concluded the Volkovs would team up to attack one CEO's hotel room, and then move quickly to attack the other CEO room the same way. They'd attempt killing everyone in each room to eliminate witnesses.

They would, he decided, avoid using guns until inside a CEO's suite. Even "silenced" firearms fired in the hallway would be heard in nearby rooms. If necessary, the Volkovs would resort to something quiet in the hallway---something like knives or hand techniques. Maybe even a club. They were so good with all three they'd feel no need to shoot anyone outside a CEO's suite.

He thought both men would stand in the hallway looking toward the CEO's door, ready to spring into the room and start shooting. They would use their hands first to open the door and then to draw their guns as they lunged inside. Needles by now thought Old Dog mistaken about the guns. It mattered little, though. If Needles were both quick and quiet, he could attack unnoticed from behind the Volkovs whether their guns were holstered or not.

He zoomed in a hotel surveillance camera on one of the electronic door locks for a CEO suite. The lock was just like the one on his room and relied on electronic codes. One needed either a plastic key that looked like a credit card, or a smartphone with the hotel's app installed. One rubbed either key or phone against the lock's plastic disk, which was the size of a poker chip. The plastic disk's logic circuits confirmed the key's or the phone's signal was valid, and then retracted the lock's heavy bolt. There'd also be a heavy door chain to overcome.

Arkady and Stepan had to get past the room's door quickly. Two seconds at most, Needles thought. Otherwise, somebody inside would draw a gun. Lars had no idea how the brothers would do that despite the hotel's electronic locks, but Dragon Lady would know. Soon she and he met in their usual Dark Web encrypted chatroom.

Dragon Lady: This is a nice surprise. Is Old Dog ready to date Auntie?

Needles: No, but it's very likely. I need two more days.

Dragon Lady: Wonderful! But enough of

Auntie for now. How can I help you?

Needles explained he thought two high-end assassins would try opening a hotel room to shoot everyone inside with suppressed pistols. That would only work if they could quietly get past a high tech door lock and a door chain, neutralizing both in a total of two seconds or less. Was that even possible? His room had the same door lock and heavy chain. He sent Dragon Lady images of them.

Dragon Lady: Interesting! This lock can be opened with the usual plastic keycard or by using the hotel company's smartphone app. Very high tech.

Needles: Can it be defeated quickly and quietly?

Dragon Lady: Yes. I can give you the general explanation. If you need a very technical explanation, I'll get Kenneth.

Needles: A general explanation's fine.

Dragon Lady: Let's begin with how the lock works. Both the fancy keycard and the hotel's even fancier smartphone app create a tiny electronic unlocking signal. The signal first tells the door to wake up and pay attention. The signal next provides not only a unique code for that door lock, but also a command to open. If the unique code matches what's stored in the door look, the door opens.

Needles: So, I only have to intercept the

electronic signal sent to the lock when the hotel guest last opened the door?

Dragon Lady: That's the idea, but here's the tricky part: Everything occurs at extraordinarily low power levels. The cellphone and card both send the same nano-wattage little pulse. Its range is barely two inches, so somebody using a phone signal grabber someplace down the hall will never detect it. You literally have to intercept the signal from no more than two inches from the door's plastic disk when the room guest opens the door.

Needles: How do I get that close?

Dragon Lady: You don't. You instead stick an inconspicuous little plastic button below the door lock. If you center it well, it looks like a part of the lock. The little button will record to its very, very limited memory the signal sent to open that door look. The memory only holds the most-recent five signals sent from the keycard to the lock. Use the last one sent.

Needles: Clever. How do I upload the door signal stored in the button to my cellphone?

Dragon Lady: There's an easy-to-use app. You can turn it on, walk past the door, and let bluetooth on your phone grab the button's information as you pass by. It's quick and easy, but the tiny battery in the plastic button's quite weak. You'd need to replace the entire button after three or four of these bluetooth transfers.

Needles: *These little stick-on lock buttons must be difficult to get.*

Dragon Lady: *Very difficult! We're the only commercial source in Canada and we require a serious background check. Even so, the Montreal Mob sells them. I think they buy cloned devices someplace in Asia. That's what I've heard from our people in Asia.*

Needles: *There'd still be some sort of door chain to deal with.*

Dragon Lady: *There would. If you have thirty seconds of time and can open the door about an inch, you can remove the chain with a coat hanger and a rubber band. You can find Dark Web videos showing the technique.*

Needles: *There'll only be two seconds to get through the door.*

Dragon Lady: *Then they'd just use bolt cutters on the chain. Less than one second if the guy's strong and quick. Compared to the lock, the door chain's easy.*

Needles: *Thank you. You've overcome a big obstacle for me!*

Dragon Lady: *You're so welcome! I'm delighted to help someone about to solve my Auntie problem.*

55 The dissident and the man often accompanying her both stayed near the Glass Walled Tower. Their hotel, called the Brick Front Hotel, marked the abrupt onset of Ottawa's low rent hotel district. In return for much reduced room prices, patrons accepted stained carpets, fading paint, noisy plumbing, and whimsical heating.

Brick Front security was marginal. Hallway and lobby cameras were average, door locks less so. Although the locks used early-generation key cards, they secured old wooden doors set in old wooden frames. Last year a petite woman kicked in one of the doors while drunk.

Arkady made his customary reconnaissance. Needles simply examined the Brick Front Hotel through its security cameras. He and Arkady independently concluded that breaking down the door was the best way into the dissident's room. Both men planned for that approach.

Arkady by then knew all about defeating electronic door locks in the Glass Walled Tower. He had called Sasha's Montreal Mob contact and paid their ever lofty prices. In return, the Mob rushed him two button-like devices, one to stick beneath each door lock.

Arkady stuck both buttons under their respective CEO door locks. He walked past each door while wearing a hat and a raincoat, looking like just any hotel guest headed outside the hotel. He barely broke stride to place each device. Nobody noticed.

Needles, with some artful help from Old Dog's people, booked two more Glass Walled Tower hotel rooms. Each was directly across the hall from a CEO's room. That meant Needles now had a room on both the twenty-fourth and twenty-fifth floors. He told Barska, who was on the twenty-eighth floor, about these rooms.

Needles quickly moved himself to the twenty-fourth floor. He checked its CEO's door lock for a button-like device and found one. Minutes later he found a second button for the CEO one floor up. That implied the Volkovs were still waiting for the devices to record several signals from each lock's being opened and closed. He told Barska to keep only the CEO hallways and connecting stairways on her screen.

Needles, concealing a small pen knife in one hand, walked past the upstairs CEO's door. He stopped long enough to poke the button device with the point of his knife. Doing so destroyed essential circuitry inside the device, but without the damage being visible to anyone standing before its door. Too late to do anything about it, the Volkovs would discover their button had failed them for the upstairs CEO's door. That would force them to attack only the CEO room on the next floor down---the room opposite Brent's.

Brent would be waiting inside his door for the killers. He would step behind them in the hallway as they set about opening the CEO's door across from Brent's.

56

Needles quickly grew bored as he waited in his room opposite the CEO suite. He decided he might as well use the time to contact Old Dog by secure chat. Soon they were again on the Dark Web. Needles gave Old Dog an update on the mission. Then:

Needles: I'm almost afraid to raise this topic. I owe you one, though. How do you propose I make us even.

Old Dog: It's simple. I just want a picture of this blind date you have in mind for me. I'm particular. I'll give you an answer after you give me a picture.

Needles: You're getting timid in your old age, Charlie.

Old Dog: I prefer to be called "prudent." When do I get my picture?

Needles: If you can wait five minutes, I might be able to find her on the Web. I'll send you a screen shot. Otherwise, I'll have to ask somebody and I don't know when I'll hear back. It could take a full day.

Old Dog: Let's start with the five-minute approach.

Needles went to another screen and searched for Auntie. He made a screenshot of her best picture and sent it to Charlie by email.

Charlie opened the email while Needles waited on the line.

Old Dog: You're right. She really is a stunner! ... What's the catch?

Needles: No catch, Charlie. That image might be your first glimpse of your true love.

Old Dog: What's her name?

Needles: That's secret until right before your dinner date.

Old Dog: I'll just use facial recognition on her picture.

Needles: I already thought of that. Assume I made the image a little longer, a little wider, or both. All the critical dimensions might be distorted.

It was another effective bluff. Charlie wouldn't bother with facial recognition. He probably would not have bothered with it, anyway.

Old Dog: She looks amazingly good! And she's my age?

Needles: Give or take a year.

Old Dog: You're still paying for the drinks and for dinner?

Needles: Yes. And also for the tip.

Old Dog: Does she really look as good as her picture?

Needles: She looks at least ten percent better.

Old Dog: Why's she still single?

Needles: Her husband died two or three years ago. You're lucky she's still single. I guess she has very high standards.

Old Dog: Why would a woman with very high standards settle for me?

Needles: I'm going to give her a richly embellished description of you.

Old Dog: Okay. I'll do it ... but if this is a hoax, I'll tell Mila dreadful things about you!

Needles: No trickery. And congratulations, Charlie! You made the right choice.

57

After Needles told Kati Barska which hotel areas to watch, she set her computer screen up accordingly. Then she halfway ignored it. She had something more important to do. Grunt opened up a Dark Web chatroom:

Necromancer: You're late again.

Grunt: Had to talk with Needles. He expects to kill the last two bad guys within hours.

<u>Necromancer</u>: This time try to get better video of the kills.

<u>Grunt</u>: The security camera feed angles can't be adjusted much. They are what they are.

<u>Necromancer</u>: I've questions about the two men Needles sedated when he sedated you.

<u>Grunt</u>: I did like you asked. I contacted both guys anesthetized with me. I paid them for the relevant doctor reports on them. I sent that to you. What more do you need?

<u>Necromancer</u>: I require more information on what you experienced.

<u>Grunt</u>: We can talk about that after you pay me for the medical reports I sent you on the two guys knocked out when I was. The money's not in my account yet.

<u>Necromancer</u>: Be patient.

<u>Grunt</u>: Okay. I'll be patient. In fact, let's both be patient. If you want to know more about what Needles' chemicals did to me, you can wait until you pay me.

<u>Necromancer</u>: I am so disappointed by that statement. However, in the interest of haste, I'll move some funds around. This will take about two minutes. You might as well open up your bank account on your smartphone so you can watch the money arrive.

Ninety seconds passed.

<u>Grunt</u>: The money just showed up. What

more do you want to know about how Needles' chemicals affected me?

Necromancer: Have you received ordinary anesthesia before?

Grunt: I was given anesthesia by intravenous drip when they took my wisdom teeth out. Is that good enough?

Necromancer: Yes. Did you have any side effects?

Grunt: Only two side effects. Nausea was one. I vomited while I was under. The dentist had to clear my airway. I vomited again about an hour after I woke up. The second effect was a splitting headache when I awoke. It went away after the pain pills the dentist gave me took hold.

Necromancer: How long was it before Needles' chemicals made you feel numb?

Grunt: He said the chemicals were on the outside of my Irish coffee glass. I went numb between five and ten minutes later. The two big guys passed out entirely then. Within seconds of each other, even.

Necromancer: Did he identify the drug he used?

Grunt: He didn't mention a name for it. He said it was proprietary. This was all in my report. Did you or anybody important read it?

Necromancer: I read it. So did my chief

research pharmacologist, if you must know. She wanted me to confirm certain key points of your story.

<u>*Grunt*</u>*: So your chief research pharmacologist, whatever that means, is the person making me repeat all this? Tell her how patient I've been.*

<u>*Necromancer*</u>*: I'll think about it. Anything else to cover now?*

<u>*Grunt*</u>*: No. And I gotta concentrate on hallways and stairways. I might have a final report tomorrow. After I get my final payment, that is. Grunt out.*

58

At eight p.m. both Needles and Grunt drank coffee to keep alert. She was on her second cup. He was on his third. Thank goodness, thought Needles, one could order pots of room service coffee. The alternative was the hotel's in-the-room coffee adventure kit. He'd told Grunt to use room service for coffee, like he was, if she wanted real coffee.

Grunt liked Needles a little better after that. While waiting for room service coffee, she thought about sleeping with him. Her fantasies lasted a barely a minute. The mission was almost over. Necromancer would pay her more for having sex with Needles, but Grunt thought the clock had run out.

At eight-forty-five p.m. Arkady entered

the hotel's bar and sat in a corner. He ordered a beer and spent twenty minutes drinking it. Stepan, meanwhile, walked the streets surrounding the building. He had a pair of bolt cutters slung out of sight on a piece of string underneath his jacket. Both men looked for any unexpected activity by bodyguards, hotel security, or police. Neither man saw anything disturbing.

At nine-fifty-five p.m., just as the bar was closing, Stepan and Arkady converged at the hotel lobby elevators. They took the same elevator to the floor just beneath the lower CEO's floor. When the doors opened, they looked up and down the empty hallway before stepping off. By now they had hats pulled low on their foreheads. Each man wore vinyl gloves. They entered the nearest stairway and climbed to the twenty-fourth floor. Their first CEO room was there.

Arkady took out his cellphone and readied it to retrieve the stick-on door button's data and, almost right away, to open the room door. Stepan undid the string holding the bolt cutters underneath his left shoulder. Once Arkady opened the door lock, Stepan would cut the chain in a second or less. Both Volkovs were confident Stepan could do that.

Barska saw them first, just as Arkady peeked from a fire stairway. Grunt already was connected to Needles by cellphone. They wore their earbud headsets.

"Arkady's arrived. Your floor. North stairway. Do you see him?"

Needles was only a split second behind her. He stood up from his laptop.

"I see him. Looks like this is it."

The two Volkovs stepped into the hallway.

"Stepan's with him," said Barska. Needles had told her to be his narrator since, as he stood poised by his room's door, he wouldn't be able to see the Volkovs well. He stepped to his room door, drawing two of his needles from their little belt sheaths as he went.

"Understood. Ready to kill. Tell me when both men stop in front of the CEO's door and are looking toward it."

"Five seconds," said Barska. "Four … Three … Two … One … NOW!"

Needles held one needle in each of his hands as he silently stepped from his room into the hallway. A thin wooden dowel grip was between two adjacent fingers of each hand. If he held his hands palm down, the actual poison spike of each hand's needle pointed downward, like a single fang of a venomous snake.

In no time he stood behind the brothers as they focused their attention on the CEO's door. Needles slapped Arkady's neck from behind as Arkady fumbled with his cellphone. Arkady turned around in surprise, dropping the phone.

Concurrently, Barska began the count Needles had asked for.

"One … two …"

Between "one" and "two," Needles struck Stepan in the neck with his other hand. It took astonishing speed on Needles' part. Stepan held the bolt cutter with both hands and instinctively raised it like a club to retaliate.

"Three … four …"

Needles sprang backward and took two steps to the side. It was Arkady that worried him. The man was much bigger and stronger than Needles and far smarter than Stepan. Arkady no doubt knew what was happening.

"Five … six … seven …"

Needles needed a ten count before the poison would kill. Arkady drew a knife from somewhere. Needles only saw the ceramic blade and not its hiding place. Arkady stepped toward Needles, but with suddenly heavy feet. The poison already affected his movement.

"Eight … nine …"

Needles changed direction, darting to Stepan's side, thereby putting Stepan between Needles and Arkady. Arkady cursed softly and pivoted, his knife edge again pointing toward Needles. Concurrently, Stepan began swinging the long-handled bolt cutters like a club.

Stepan did that with one hand. Stepan's other hand reached toward Needles with a quickness Needles had never imagined possible from the dim-witted thug. One way or another, it was almost over. Stepan held Needles in place as Arkady lunged anew. There would be no outrunning that lunge.

"Ten."

Grunt said it as Arkady was still in full motion. Needles blocked Arkady's forearm with his, thereby pushing the knife away from Needles' body. Arkady dropped dead as he did so.

Stepan began to bring the bolt cutters, which he held high, down hard on Needles' head. The blow would have crushed Needles' skull, even though Stepan was already moving slower. Stepan, however, hesitated. He was visibly shocked at his brother's instant, unexpected collapse. Barely a second later, Stepan dropped dead, himself.

"Eleven … twelve."

Needles hadn't looked directly at the hallway camera throughout the encounter. He didn't do so now, either.

"They're dead. Notify Old Dog. I'll meet you at your location in two hours. Needles out."

Lars Brent picked up Arkady's cellphone. The hallway was still empty, so he didn't need to pull a nearby fire alarm for distraction. Needles stepped back into his hotel room opposite the CEO's, his face still well-concealed. In seconds he again wiped any fingerprints from the few things he'd touched, took his computer, and exited the room.

He had left no trace. The hallway security cameras mostly missed his face. Even had they caught his face, he'd taken precautions against facial recognition. From Needles' standpoint, it was another perfect kill.

Just another day at the office, he told himself, as he walked calmly down the fire stairs and then toward his room on the hotel's middle level---the room Barska still didn't know about. However, his favorite poison definitely took eight seconds too long. This time that delay had almost meant his death.

59

Once inside his room in the hotel's middle, Needles opened up the settings on Arkady's phone and turned off those security features he could. He put it on airplane mode and dimmed the screen. That would keep its data intact until Dragon Lady's technician could do a full forensic analysis.

Needles made the necessary phone call to Dragon Lady.

"Hello," she said on a burner phone. She sometimes used three or four burner phones a day, but always made sure Needles had a working number for her.

"It's me," he said, knowing she'd recognize his voice as easily as he did hers.

"Two items. First, Old Dog eagerly looks forward to dinner with your friend. Maybe a week from now. No more. I'll call soon to make arrangements."

"*Wonderful!*" said Dragon Lady. "Thank you. Thank you. *Thank you!*"

"You're very welcome," said Needles, pleased with her reaction.

"You can't see me, but I'm doing my happy dance."

"Good. On to the second item. I need the doctor to make an urgent house call."

"No more happy dance. I'll get right on it. He's waiting in the Big Guy's private jet with the pilots." She referred to Sanjay Haranya's personal aircraft.

The "doctor" was one of her husband's brothers, and the Emporium's expert in forensic analysis of anything electronic that had a memory. An average user assumed data in a phone's memory chips was gone forever once deleted. In reality, only the phone's awareness of that data disappeared, meaning the phone couldn't access it. The data still existed in a chip until enough other data got stored on top of it. Dragon Lady's expert would connect Arkady's phone to a special computer program and read whatever was in each storage location.

The expert also would decrypt whatever was encoded, or at least most of it. By day's end, Needles would know many, if not all, of the phone's secrets. Needles didn't expect to learn much, however. Arkady was a high-end pro.

"Thank you," said Needles. "I'm finished if you are."

"Then we're finished. Dragon Lady out."

Needles took out his laptop and went to his datalogger dashboard, hoping Grunt's computer was still on line. It was. He quickly uploaded keystrokes Grunt had made at her keyboard since his last datalogger dump. Again, he could only see what she'd typed and nothing anyone else had typed. He soon found this:

Grunt: Had to talk with Needles. He expects to kill the remaining two bad guys within hours.

Grunt: The security camera feeds can't be adjusted much. They are what they are.

Grunt: I did like you asked. I contacted both the two guys anesthetized with me. I paid them for the relevant doctor reports on them. I sent that to you. What more do you need?

Grunt: We can talk about that after you

pay me for the medical reports I sent you on the two guys knocked out when I was. The money's not in my account yet.

<u>*Grunt*</u>*: Okay. I'll be patient. In fact, let's both be patient. If you want to know more about what Needles' chemicals did to me, you can wait until you pay me.*

<u>*Grunt*</u>*: The money just arrived. What more do you want to know about how Needles' chemicals affected me?*

<u>*Grunt*</u>*: I was given anesthesia by intravenous drip when they took my wisdom teeth out. Is that good enough?*

<u>*Grunt*</u>*: Only two side effects. Nausea was one. I vomited while I was under. The dentist had to clear my airway. I vomited again about an hour after I woke up. The second effect was a splitting headache when I awoke. It went away after the pain pills the dentist gave me took hold.*

<u>*Grunt*</u>*: He said the chemicals were on the outside of my Irish coffee glass. I went numb between five and ten minutes later. The two big guys passed out entirely then. Within seconds of each other, even.*

<u>*Grunt*</u>*: He didn't mention the name of the drugs. He said they were proprietary, so maybe they didn't even have a name. He called it a cocktail, so I guess he mixed things together. This was all in my report. Did you or anybody*

important read it?

Grunt: So your chief research pharmacologist, whatever that means, is the person making me repeat all this? Tell her how patient I've been.

Grunt: No. And I gotta start watching hallways and stairways. I might have a final report tomorrow. After I get my final payment, that is. Grunt out.

He didn't have time to go through whatever audio her computer's microphone had sent to his cloud account, but Brent right away knew who Necromancer was. Only one Mega Pharma company had a female research director. Brent had heard her speak twice at conferences. Necromancer could only be Valhalla's CEO, Vlaski Peeters, or somebody very close to him. Probably just Peeters, thought Brent. Peeters would be safer if he alone controlled Barska.

Brent leaned back in his chair, folded his arms, and gazed overhead. So, he thought, it was finally happening. It'd taken Mega Pharma years longer than he'd expected, but now one of them would soon send goons his way. Grunt's involvement was just prelude.

They likely were being very cautious, he thought. If he knew what they were up to, they'd speculate, he might release the recipe for his poison to the public domain. He wouldn't do that. They'd anticipate he wouldn't do that, but they could never be sure. Against such uncertainty, they'd be subtle. They'd offer no warning. They'd use intermediaries like Barska to spy on him before doing anything overt. With half a trillion dollars at stake, they'd be very careful.

Lars Brent needed Mila Rossi's insight now more than ever. Nobody but she could help him figure out the chemistry in time.

He'd also need Charlie's help more than ever. Serious killing lay ahead.

60

Kati Barska had one more chance to bed Lars Brent. When he arrived at her door, two hours after his very impressive kills, she would make the most of their meeting. She'd wear a full, snug slip from her escort-class lingerie collection and matching underwear. She'd answer the door in her slip and say she was late getting ready.

Then she'd give him a congratulatory kiss. If that weren't enough to ensure Nature took its course, there was always the full bottle of whiskey she'd had sent up just in case. Kati was even better at seduction than at hacking. She didn't expect to need the whiskey.

Needles knocked at her door right on time. Grunt mostly stood behind the door as she opened it, since someone in the Saskatchewan family two rooms down the hall might peer out. Needles walked right past her, checked the bathroom and closet for hidden persons, and turned around. He didn't seem surprised Barska was but partially dressed. He also stood beyond range of the kiss she'd intended.

"You won't need your ugly dress anymore. Put something else on and get ready to go. We need to move you into another room right away. You're no longer safe here."

She frowned at him. If anybody could spoil a romantic moment, he could! Without a word she threw on a blouse, skirt, and jacket. Then she did her shoes while sitting in a chair. She had recovered her momentum by then. Barska made sure he had a look up her leg as she pulled one shoe on.

It changed nothing. He remained all business. She quickly closed her suitcase, packed her briefcase, and slung a designer leather purse over one shoulder. He carried her luggage for her. They were out the door not even a minute after she'd flashed her panties.

"Where are we going?" Barska asked as they walked briskly to the elevators.

"I'll tell you when we get there. This'll all make sense in half an hour."

They went to the midlevel room he'd rented for her only fifteen minutes earlier. The room had a king-sized bed. Her hopes rose as soon as he set her luggage in one corner.

Needles gestured for her to sit in one of two chairs at the room's little table. She did so as he locked the door. He took the table's other chair and began.

"I rented this room under the name Kim Blevins. You'll need to remember that name."

"Kim Blevins. Got it," she said.

"I paid in advance. You can stay here seven nights if you want. No need to checkout. There's good access to the street if you need to leave in haste. If you look out the window, you'll see where the taxis line up. Think of them as getaway cars, if you need one. Get food sent up from a different restaurant each day. Just about all the ones near here deliver. Okay so far?"

"Yes. Why's my safety a big deal? The mission's over."

"We'll get to that. First, who do you work for?"

"I'm a major in the United States Army Signal Corps. You want my service number?"

"Kati, I don't have time for games. I requested your Army file when they told me you'd be coming along. The last page or two were missing. That's because you've been medically discharged. Less than a month ago, I think, but it doesn't matter."

"I'm in the Army, but I'm attached to the Agency temporarily. You want to call somebody and check? I've got a phone number."

"I'll need that phone number. Write it down for me."

She took out a pad and pen, wrote the number and extension, tore off the page, and pushed it across the table to him. He pocketed the little piece of paper without looking at it.

"The tip off's the last medicine recommended for you, assuming you could get into clinical testing. Sequilphaznost is an experimental drug developed by some very smart guys in Poland. It's undergoing U.S. trials, but won't hit the market for about a year. That assumes the trials work, which they probably will. In my opinion, this will be the best medication ever for the serious schizophrenia you have."

"Looks like there's some clerical error in my file."

She looked nervous.

"Nope. Without one of those pills each day, you're statistically likely to commit suicide within a few weeks. They promised you these pills if you'd spy on me, right?"

"I want a lawyer."

"Good luck with that. I kill people, Kati. I don't get them lawyers."

Fear washed over her face.

"You're going to kill me?"

"I'm not. Be sure of that. For one thing, I don't need to. I think I know who put you up to this and I'm sure they'll eliminate witnesses. They'll soon try to kidnap me and, after learning some secrets I have, they'll try to kill me. I once thought they'd stop short of attempting murder, but now I know better. Anyway, if they'd kill even me---and I'm the goose with golden eggs they want---they'll surely kill you. Within two or three weeks. No more."

"No, they won't. I'd go to the police."

"And tell them what? You'd be somebody who was somehow given a bottle of pills that maybe would keep her alive. I'd bet there's no real record where the pills came from. Also, the Agency at most might concede they used you for surveillance somewhere in, say, Calgary. Someplace you never were. They'll be as puzzled as everyone else. Meanwhile, you'll run out of these very, very expensive pills. You won't be able to buy more. Nobody will have to kill you, Kati. Schizophrenia will do it if these guys wait six weeks."

Her hands now gripped her chair armrest so tightly her knuckles were white.

"Of course, if they want you dead sooner

than six weeks, that's easy. They'd have you put on jeans and carry a daypack they'd provide. There might even be a lunch inside. They'd take you off into some isolated rural area, and make you swallow two or three of your pills. That done, they'd leave you by yourself, along with a compass, map, and directions. You'd walk back toward town and die along the way from the overdose."

She seemed puzzled by that part. He answered her question before she could ask it.

"The death would look like your very incorrect response to a sudden flare up of your illness. The forensic team would think you overdosed yourself in a fit of deep depression or sudden panic. Their conclusion would be credible. Too much Sequilphaznost is so dangerous the clinical trials are creeping along extra slowly. They're taking precautions not usually needed."

She finally believed him. "What can I do?"

He opened his briefcase and took out a bottle of four hundred very little pills, a thick envelope, a pad, and a pen.

"Let's start with the pills. There are in the world of pharmaceuticals places that manufacture locally in small batches the same medicines made in big manufacturing sites far away. These little places are called compounding pharmacies. Mostly, they make simple generic medicines in tablets of exactly the dose somebody needs.

"But a world-class chemist can quickly make almost any prescription drug there is if he's careful. Those locally made drugs---which might be complex---can actually be purer and better standardized than Mega Pharma manufacturing sites anywhere could make. Mine are, anyway."

"You made what's in the bottle?"

"Yes. Days ago in somebody's lab near here. Once they have everything set up and waiting for me, it doesn't take long. The pills are chemically equivalent to the pills you were given. They're exactly the same molecule prescribed for you."

He pushed the pills across the table to her.

"Thank you."

"You're welcome. Whoever hired you might continue to give you pills. Remember, though, that whoever hired you wants you dead. They're determined to kill me and you're now a witness connecting them to me. They might give you a bottle where each pill's as strong as three ordinary pills, even though they'll look the same."

"Who's behind all this?"

Brent did not want Barska able to

blackmail Valhalla or Peeters. That'd get her killed for sure and would complicate his own plan.

"Too soon to tell you that. Besides, knowing who's behind this won't help keep you alive. It might even put you at greater risk."

"Are the pills you're giving me poisoned?"

"No. That'd be too much trouble. As you know, I have undetectable poisons available. My stuff's better poison than a Sequilphaznost overdose ever could be."

"What happens when the bottle of pills you made runs out?"

"I expect Sequilphaznost will be on the market by then. Just go first to a doctor and then to a drug store. Meanwhile, watch this website every day."

He wrote a URL on a sheet of paper and handed it to her.

"What's this?"

"That's the U.S. Food and Drug Administration's Web page for the most recent information on Sequilphaznost. If it's declared unsafe, the warning will appear there right away. Then go see a psychiatrist and ask for help. Be sure to pick a good one. Your kind of schizophrenia's difficult to diagnose and treat. Find somebody with at least five years experience treating schizophrenia."

She was silent a moment.

"Will I live? Can I ever have a normal life?"

He smiled reassuringly. "Yes. There are a great many people living ordinary, happy lives who need help adjusting their brain chemistry. It's nothing to be ashamed of. It's nothing to be afraid of, either. I think you'll be okay if we can just get you through the next three weeks. I'll have dealt with the bad guys by then."

He slid the envelope across the table to her. It held three hundred thousand Canadian dollars.

"And what's this?" she asked as she opened it. Her eyes grew wide upon seeing the money.

"That's to help you through the next three weeks and the twelve months afterwards. You're out of a job now, right?"

"I got discharged a week after I was diagnosed. The Army sent me to the Agency's Personnel Department. Agency Personnel said there was no job I could do with my disability."

"They lied to you about that."

"Agency Personnel said nobody'd ever renew my security clearance. But there was a temporary project I could do."

"This mission we're on now?"

"Yes. Personnel got some doctor to

furnish the medicine I needed. For a little while, I had hope. At least, until today."

"You can still have hope. In fact, you should."

It was the doctor in him speaking. Barska looked relieved.

"Right. Lots of new hope. I guess I have you to thank for that, so thank you."

"You're very welcome. Next item. Does anybody besides us know about the Dark Web chatroom we used?"

"Only Old Dog. He might have told someone, though."

"No. Old Dog's perfectly discreet. That website's still safe. I'll check it daily for a month or so. If you think you're in trouble, send me a message and explain why you sent it. I probably will hand that message off to people you can trust. Those persons will identify themselves to you with the code word 'signal corpse.' Not 'signal corps,' but 'signal corpse.' Nobody will guess that. Okay?"

"Yes."

"Have you turned off your computer's location routines?"

"Yes. Just like you said."

"And you've got a VPN tunnel so nobody can tell where your computer is?"

"Yes again."

"Good. Keep your laptop with you for now, but realize whoever'll be coming to kill you will also want to destroy your computer. In a week or less, remove the laptop's battery and lock up the computer somewhere safe. Buy another computer with cash. The bad guys will want you to take them to your old computer before they kill you. You might delay your death that way. Any delay's precious to both you and whoever's coming to rescue you."

She nodded. "I'll do all that. Thank you again."

"Next topic: Who were you reporting to about my poisons?"

"His---or maybe her---codename was Necromancer. I never met the person. We just talked in a chatroom."

"Did you keep transcripts of those chatroom sessions?"

"Yeah. I wasn't supposed to, but I wanted some leverage in case they didn't pay me. You want the transcripts?"

"Yes. Can you send them to me?"

"Gladly. Just give me an email address."

He wrote down an address, gave it to her, and turned to his final question.

"Do you remember who you talked with in Personnel? Their names weren't in your file."

"I only talked with one woman there, an

executive named Blanche Pierre. She was really nice. She's also the one who referred me to Old Dog. Two days later you made me take a nap."

She smiled only a little. It was, however, enough good cheer that Needles thought Grunt would be okay---assuming, of course, he could effect certain very dangerous outcomes.

61

Needles left Grunt's hotel, took a cab across Ottawa, and checked into a comfortable motel not far from the airport. Once in his room he took out a burner phone and called Charlie.

"Old Dog on an unsecured phone. Talk to me."

"It's Needles. Can you meet me in the usual place? We'll need an hour."

"That's a long time. I might get tired before we finish."

"Very funny. See you in three minutes. Needles out."

As it turned out, Old Dog needed four minutes to meet Needles in their Dark Web chatroom.

<u>Needles</u>: *Why so slow today?*

<u>Old Dog</u>: *I'm tired already. You'll ask if the Agency paid you for the last two kills and I'll have to go check. It's tedious.*

<u>Needles</u>: *Nope. I received all the thirty-*

six million Canadian dollars. You feel young and spry again?

Old Dog: Yes, and that's good. I have a big date to get ready for.

Needles: Ready to copy?

Old Dog: Send it.

Needles read him the account code for Old Dog's new offshore bank numbered account.

Old Dog: What's this?

Needles: That's access information for your new offshore bank account. There's six million Canadian dollars in there for you. Use it to become younger. You know: hair implants, liposuction, little blue pills. Maybe a facelift.

Old Dog: Very funny, yourself. I'll have you know I'm fully functional. I'm just more deliberate about it. But thanks. And you don't need to pay me. I negotiated that six million for you, not me. I thought it might help gorgeous-looking Mila find skinny-looking you attractive.

Needles: The money's all yours, Charlie, and richly deserved. Sending you the money a little bit early's the first part of my two-part effort to get you feeling indebted to me.

Old Dog: You're going to ask for a favor, right?

Needles: A big one, but you'll like it. Ready for the second thing to make you feel indebted to me?

<u>Old Dog</u>: *Ready and waiting.*

<u>Needles</u>: *I have for you the information on your big date. She's Louise Haranya. You two will be going to the best restaurant in Little India for dinner. Watch your inbox for the details.*

<u>Old Dog</u>: *I'm watching. Send them.*

Needles provided a detailed schedule for what he said would be a magical evening.

<u>Needles</u>: *Next item's the big favor.*

<u>Old Dog</u>: *Wait while I steady myself. Okay. Tell me.*

<u>Needles</u>: *I'm about to start something you don't know about. It requires your help.*

<u>Old Dog</u>: *And what would I do?*

<u>Needles</u>: *Get the Agency to fire you. Then help me extort a vast fortune from one of the world's most powerful companies. To do that, we might need to kill some bad guys in self-defense. If it all works, you'll be even richer than you can imagine. Else you might be dead.*

Thirty seconds passed with no reply from Old Dog. To Needles it seemed an eternity.

<u>Needles</u>: *Are you still there?*

<u>Old Dog</u>: *Yeah. All this sounds like physical exertion. I'm feeling old. You'd better cut straight to the good part of this proposition.*

<u>Needles</u>: *Gladly. I think we can get*

Blanche Pierre fired or much, much worse.

Old Dog: Amazing! I suddenly feel young and adventurous. Tell me more.

62 Not long after Charlie became a full partner in Lars Brent's plot, Lars called Dragon Lady's husband, Kenneth. He was Sanjay's eldest son, Sanjay's top technical advisor, and the smartest electrical engineer Lars had ever heard of. Sometimes, Dragon Lady had told Lars, she just stood and marveled at how utterly brilliant her husband was with anything electronic. Those moments lasted, she said, until she remembered he couldn't keep track of his socks.

Kenneth Haranya picked up on the second ring.

"Hello, Lars."

"Hi, Kenneth. I'm calling to ask about electronic surveillance."

"One of my favorite topics. Ask away."

"I need to bug a conference room. It'll be swept for bugs before being used for a particular conference. It'll be monitored during the conference for incoming and outgoing transmissions. There might even be a Faraday cage around the room."

"Interesting. I suppose somebody'd check continuously for laser splash on any window the room has?"

"Yeah. Can't use that trick. How many more tricks do you have?"

"Only one good one. It needs a masonry wall for one side of the conference room and an unused room on the far side of that wall. You bore a thin hole through the wall. The hole's a crude waveguide. You aim the hole toward the part of the conference room you're interested in. If you have people at a table, one hole might pick up only one person. Two persons at most. There'd be a sophisticated microphone in the unused room. That microphone records the tiny little nano soundwaves coming through the hole."

"Sounds like a lot of work."

"It is, and some highly complicated mathematics go into locating the hole. But you do all this to keep the microphone outside the conference room. That way any electronic leakage from it doesn't get through the wall. Sweeping devices inside the room will never detect it. Also, sound waves unlike radio waves, can go right through a Faraday cage."

"Is the hole in the wall big enough to see?"

"If you're looking for it, yes. We've tested this a couple of times in our lab. You need a hole a quarter inch in diameter. This approach works best if you hang artwork or something on the wall to disguise the hole."

"And you can hear clearly what's going on in the room?"

"You can hear one person per hole. Maybe two. You might be able to catch three voices if you have a computer massage the jumbled signal of the third voice. Even then, the third voice result's not very good and might not hold up in court."

"Kevin, I don't think I can get a hole drilled that well or that soon."

"Where's this conference going to be?"

"Anywhere in the world I choose."

"Lars, I know of five conference rooms with holes already drilled. Lots of holes, even. As of last month, the holes all were still undetected. The rooms are in Europe, though."

"Where in Europe?"

"There's an airport conference room in Marseilles, France. There are two hotel conference rooms in Berlin, Germany. There's a train station conference room in Zurich and, finally, a restaurant conference room in London. There doubtless are more such rooms. These are the only ones I, personally, can vouch for."

"Can you arrange for me to use the room in Marseilles if money's no object?"

"Easily. I'll get you the best price I can, but I know these guys, Lars. Their price still will be about 200 percent too high."

"Not a problem. And no discounts for me this time, Kenneth! This is a rush job. Only about five days notice, I'd guess."

"Again, not a problem. Glad to do it. Email me the details. The bugs'll be in place and fully tested forty-eight hours later. I'll keep one of my guys in Marseilles until you're done. He'll be in the unused room during the conference, just in case you need tech support. How's that?"

"Perfect! Kenneth, you're astonishing! I'll tell Sanjay that yet again, too."

63

After her phone conversation with Lars, Mila Rossi felt wonderful. Even her teenagers sensed as much. The next evening she took them out for dinner at a nice restaurant. Mila hadn't done that since her divorce two years ago. She never felt she could afford it. But now she had two million Canadian dollars in the bank. It was, she told herself, more than a million U.S. dollars!

The day after dinner with her kids, Mila checked currency exchange rates sporadically throughout the morning, just in case exchange rates were volatile. Apparently they were not. That meant she'd time to think about what to do with her money.

It was the thinking that spoiled things for

her. She realized she'd have to find a lawyer so she could get the taxes right. Then she'd have to move the money to her local bank, and maybe that was the wrong place. She'd need both serious legal advice and serious investment advice.

Any new financial advisers would ask where the money came from. So would her local bank. One of the young faculty members she knew had said as much, explaining the questions were to fight crime. Her colleague was applying for a mortgage and had to show all his money came from a legitimate source---a source, for instance, other than money laundering or drug profits or terrorism or whatever. Mila thought it'd be like having to prove herself innocent.

Would she need a letter from Lars? Would merely identifying him get him into trouble? But how could she do anything without identifying Lars? Maybe the lawyer, whoever that would be, could tell her.

There was another problem. What did Lars expect in return for all that money? He said it was hers outright. He sounded like he meant it. But did it require her tacit agreement to marry him? She hadn't agreed to anything like that! Not yet, anyway. What would happen if she spent the money and then decided Lars wasn't right for her? What if the kids disliked him?

She quickly decided not to touch the money until her many questions were answered. That decision comforted her through lunchtime. By mid-afternoon, though, she was asking herself if she should give the money back.

She'd no idea how to make that happen, of course, but Lars would know. She'd let him handle it. Way back years ago, he'd always read some of *The Manhattan SomeTimes* business section and nearly all of *The Snooty Journal*. He probably still did and knew all about financial things. She was just a chemist. He wouldn't expect her to know financial stuff. So, he'd not get mad when she asked him to move the money back to his account.

Or would he get mad? Was she being hasty? Was she procrastinating? Losing the money wouldn't be terrible. She didn't really have it, anyway. It was still on some Caribbean island. Losing Lars, though, might be the biggest mistake she'd ever make. What should she do? she asked herself repeatedly. The next day she decided to call him.

He answered on the first ring.

"Hi, Mila. What's up?"

He already knew what was up. He understood Mila that well.

"Lars, we need a serious talk about the money you sent me. Can we do that now?"

"Can you wait on the line for two minutes? I'm going to send you an email first."

"Okay. Two minutes … "

"There. It's on its way. Promise me you won't open it until I say you can."

"Okay … Lars, why can't I open it?"

"Because, at the right moment, I think it'll help us. It'll help with the serious talk you wanted. Tell me why you're worried."

"I didn't say I was worried."

"Never mind. Just tell me what's on your mind."

It all came out then. Lars was a good listener. He reflected back, prompted her as necessary, and demonstrated empathy. It was a little easier since he'd anticipated this call.

"So, what should I do?" she finally asked.

"Keep the money. In about two days we'll connect our labs via videoconference. We'll find a way to make one of my poisons kill instantly. It now takes ten seconds. That's too long."

"I might not be much use, Lars. You're talking about work I did long ago."

"You're still doing it. I infer that from your published research."

She laughed. "I have almost no published research. I'm surprised you found it."

“That’s because almost all your research projects have been proprietary work for Mega Pharma. They gave you millions to build your special lab, Mila.”

She laughed again. “They did. Almost all of it went for equipment. The university’s greedy president took most of the rest for university overhead. And I, the lowly principal investigator, was allowed to do fascinating work for minimum wage. Well, maybe twice minimum wage. I sort of got a raise.”

“You should quit that job, Mila.”

“I should. I’m routinely exploited. But the hours are flexible and my kids need to finish high school. Someday I’ll quit … I guess you’re wondering why somebody like me who needs money’s reluctant to accept it from you, huh?”

“Nope. Before you called, I already knew why.”

“No, you didn’t ... Not all of it.”

“Okay. Time to open up the email. Tell me if I accurately summarized in my email all of your concerns before you voiced them.”

She opened the email and read it to herself. He had precisely summarized her thinking! It was like a magician’s trick. She stared briefly at her computer screen with her mouth and eyes both opened a little too wide, and then recovered.

“How’d you do that?”

"I can read your mind, Mila. Go ahead. Admit it."

She laughed. "That's scary. When do I learn to read your mind?"

"Soon, I'd guess, if you let me marry you. You were always good at reading people, Mila. I'm only good at reading you. Well, you and maybe Charlie. He's an open book."

She laughed longer. Then she became serious.

"Your email says you fully understand I might decide I'm not able to marry you for whatever reason. If so, you said, there'd be no hard feelings and I should keep the money. Did you mean that?"

"Every word of it." He also sounded serious.

"Lars, you don't have to give me that much money for two days of work."

"Nope. It's not the effort that's important, Mila. It's the value added. Your research has been almost entirely on the side effects of Mega Pharma drugs, right?"

"Yes. But it was proprietary, unpublished research. How'd you guess what it was about?"

"It's an easy guess. If you can make poisons, you can make antidotes to those poisons. Antidotes are just chemical countermeasures against harmful chemical effects. Same skill set. It was a simple transition for you, Mila. I'd bet you're so good at it that you really don't have to work very hard. That's why being exploited hasn't mattered much to you. The university president has no idea how brilliant you are, does he?"

"No. Not even close ... And thank you, Lars! That's such a nice compliment coming from you, the man who almost always was one step ahead of me."

"Only half a step, Mila. And only sometimes. I was catching up with you as often as you were catching up with me. You're still too modest."

"Perhaps. Anyhow, the university's greedy president thinks I work harder than I do. Don't' give away my secret."

"I won't. And are you beginning to see why I'm happy to pay you what I did? It's not the effort you put in, Mila. It's the results you achieve---the value you add, in other words. Tell me if I need to argue with you about this."

"You don't. But you still paid me too much."

"I paid you too little. I actually wanted to send you four million dollars for the two days, but I figured I'd never get you to accept it. You'd have been suspicious."

She smiled wonderfully, unseen to Lars.

"I would've. You're reading my mind

again, aren't you?"

"Yes. I expect to know days before you do that you're finally ready to marry me."

She sighed. "Lars, I do love you. But I'm not ready yet. I have to get this right for my kids as well as for you and me. You seem to be okay with that, however ... Are you?"

She was back to being serious.

"Yes. You're a very sensible woman, Mila, and waiting makes good sense."

"Thank you ... I now feel so much better, Lars! Even though I've no idea what to do with all that money you sent me."

All the same, she was smiling as she said it.

"Just leave it there for now. I'll send you by overnight mail another twenty-five thousand Canadian dollars for expenses. You'll need that for a software add-on you might not have yet, and also two pairs of tight-fitting jeans for your lab work."

"Lars! What do you mean by tight-fitting?"

"At least as tight as you wore in Alabama."

"Hmm. I didn't think you or anyone else noticed. Clearly I was thinking about science while you were thinking about … never mind. I'm not going there. Nope! Not there at all."

"Mila, let me tell you where I think we now stand. First, you know I love you, right?"

"Yes. And you know I love you."

"Good. Our stars begin to align. You also need to promise me you won't worry about the offshore money for a reasonable time."

"How long's a reasonable time?"

"No more than two weeks. We'll need to have a very serious financial discussion before long. You'll like it, though. It'll also make what I sent you seem like middle school lunch money. Wait two weeks."

"You've become so mysterious, Lars!"

"But I love you."

"Okay. Since you love me, I can handle 'mysterious' for two weeks."

"And the final point is you'll wear tight jeans for our video conference."

"Lars, you're terrible! I might wear *comfortable* jeans. I'll probably have my kids in my office watching me work through the lab's big window. That's how I sometimes do child care during lab sessions. They eat snacks, do homework, and play on my office computer."

"Maybe a short skirt instead of jeans? Or at least a skirt that's above the knee?"

She blew him a kiss. "There. Do you need another kiss or is one enough for now?"

"I need another."

She kissed the air again for him.

"And now we should hang up, Lars. Otherwise, you'll start talking about bikinis."

"Really? We can discuss super-sexy Mila Rossi in a bikini?"

He became very happy.

"Goodbye, Lars."

She ended their call, even happier than he was.

64

Lars called Mila the next morning. She was sitting at her kitchen table grading student papers. Her teenagers had left for school and she didn't have to be on campus that day.

"When would you like my general, introductory overview of neural cascade?"

"How about now?"

She pushed the papers aside and moved a yellow legal pad before her.

"Okay ... One day years ago I was ironing my shirts when the phone rang."

"Oh, this already sounds good. I like men who iron their own shirts."

"I thought you'd approve. Anyway, I forgot to turn the iron off. When I came back after the phone call, I burned my finger on the hot iron."

"That must have hurt!"

"It did. My body went through the

obvious sequence: The burn occurred, a nerve in my finger reported the injury to my brain, my brain decided to withdraw the finger, and sent the finger muscles a message to jerk away from the iron. It all took milliseconds."

"Somehow this sequence got you to neural cascade?"

"Yes. You see, moving the finger away from the iron was so obvious, it didn't need figuring out. So, why ask the brain to make a decision? What if the finger's nerve cells had told the brain what to do and the brain had obeyed them to save time?"

She put her pencil down, closed her eyes, and moved her lips slightly as she silently talked herself through the implications. Mila often did that when mastering some big, new idea. Lars could even see her in his mind. He waited until she was ready to proceed.

"Lars, if the brain didn't have to think it through, the process would've gone faster. And if the finger tissue's burning away, every millisecond matters. You make it seem plausible, Lars. The nerves did the thinking and told the brain what to do?"

"Well, that was my basic theory---my starting point, if you will. I began to wonder if nerves sometimes gave orders to the brain, instead of the brain making the decisions. Just for simple reflexes, that is. Peripheral nerves aren't equipped for complex analyses."

"But they could react instantly to, say, electric shock?"

"Yes. If so, maybe they'd tell the brain what to do."

"Lars, you found a way to make the nerves give orders to the brain, instead of the brain giving them the orders? You made the nerves issue their own commands?"

"Yes. Sometimes yes, that is. Remember, nerves don't have a lot of processing power. But deep inside our beings, down at the molecular level, nerves have a mechanism for giving very simple commands to the brain. My poison hijacks that mechanism."

"Nerves can tell the brain to kill itself?"

"They can, but it takes the right chemical---and it's a very complicated, manmade chemical---to make the nerves issue a suicide command the brain would follow. Nerve cells would never do this without my complicated poison molecule making them do it."

There was silence. Mila was talking to herself again, reviewing what Lars had said. He easily imagined wonder filling her eyes. She finally did one of her soft little whistles that he liked.

"Lars, this is starting to sound too complicated to explain over the phone."

"The actual chemistry's every bit that complex. That discussion goes better in a lab, but it can wait. For now, the big challenge might be fighting off disbelief. It was for me."

"I admit I'm struggling. People in our field don't think about nerves like you do!"

"Unquestionably."

"And I'll have to unlearn some of what I know ... This is sooo radically different from everything we did in Alabama."

More silence. Mila was talking to herself again, but not for long.

"Lars, my head's spinning. You'll have to hold my hand every step of the way."

"I think I'd like that."

She laughed. "I might like it, too. Thank goodness there's only one simple command for me to understand!"

"Sorry. There are four commands, but the same chemical deals with them all. At a very low power, my drug tells the brain to be happy. Worry goes away. Take the drug to its next power level and one safely falls asleep. Go up another power level still and the drug acts like an anesthesia. Actually, it's much, much better than what's available today. And---at maximum power level---the drug creates neural cascade and the person dies quickly."

"At least I only have one chemical and

four levels to understand."

She laughed at herself as she said it. Understanding one chemical and four potencies seemed worthy of a lifetime's research. Even with Lars coaching her! She whistled softly again.

"There's a little more. There's an antidote. More like a regulator, really. It can throttle back the effectiveness of the drug. The antidote thus can protect against neural cascade."

She was silent again, working through more little girl wonder. Her eyes were wide.

"Lars, I won't be able to think about anything but you this morning! I won't be able to grade a single paper today!"

"Good. I like you thinking about me. Maybe someday you'll even dream about me."

Mila sighed. "I already do. You're such a distraction for me, Lars!"

65

Business magazines for years ranked Belgium-based Valhalla Pharmaceutical the largest company in its industry. Valhalla's longtime Managing Director, Vlaski Peeters, for those years had cause to feel smug, and often did. Today, however, his aristocratic face looked worried.

Peeters sat in his big office behind a

polished mahogany desk sizable enough, with but few modifications, to kennel a pair of wolfhounds. Before him sat Peeters' Security Director, who looked like the former state intelligence assassin he once had been. Security, as they called him, was a fit-looking man in his late fifties with short blond hair. His face frightened children and his disdainful stare intimidated adults. He sometimes smiled, but only if cued by Peeters, whom he idolized. They shared similarly evil temperaments.

"Tell me about Barska," said Peeters.

"The kill team got to her room soon after Brent eliminated the last two Volkovs. Barska was gone."

"Maybe they should've moved sooner?" asked Peeters, more from curiosity than recrimination. Peeters merely sought to understand how top-flight Montreal Mob assassins had failed to murder an ex-army desk jockey.

"Since the Prague work wasn't finished, I used the Montreal Mob. Usually, they're a good choice. They find good people, but even their best people aren't up to my team's skills. Not even close. To make up for that, I told them to send three killers to take out Barska."

Peeters knew Security referred to the murder of a European Union regulator traveling in Prague. The kill had to look like an accidental death and convincing accidents took longer.

"The Mob took too long assembling the three-person team?"

"They did. They assigned their three best contract killers. One guy had to fly back from French Guiana. We lost a day, but for an acceptable reason."

"Barska had a computer. It might've been a government computer. Ask Blanche Pierre if she can have it traced somehow. Maybe it reports its location to the Agency."

"I've already called Pierre. She said Barska's government computer was turned in when Barska was discharged from the Army. Also, the Agency would never issue a short-term temporary contractor like Barska an Agency computer. She had to use her own computer."

"You still have the Montreal Mob looking for Barska?"

"Actively so. Both the three killers and other operatives the Mob brought in. The Mob also bribes somebody in the Ottawa police to report useful voice or facial recognitions."

"That can't hurt ... You'll get some private detectives showing Barska's picture at rental car places, the bus depot, and the airport?"

"Already done. They've been at it about

six hours. No new developments yet, which tells me she hasn't gone far. We'll find her, overdose her, and bring back her computer. Barska's way out of her depth. She'll screw up soon."

66

Old Dog had bought into Needles' plan as soon as he understood it. Two hours later, Old Dog sat at his laptop, composing a personal email to Blanche Pierre. Ideally, it would plunge her into life-threatening fury, driving her blood pressure to deadly new highs. As a practical matter, though, he thought he'd only induce a desk-pounding hissy fit.

He fleetingly considered addressing the email to *Her Narcistic Highness*, but that would disclose his nefarious intent. The poohbahs would take Blanche Pierre's side if he began like that. Charlie would be subtle.

He therefore wrote *Dearest Blanche*, knowing that alone would compel her saying something obscene. Blanche Pierre preferred her title when addressed by underlings, and the word "dearest" coming from him might make her gag. So far, so good, Charlie thought.

I hereby request all my accrued vacation be approved, beginning with tomorrow. Thanks. Charlie

Charlie thought it a promising start. Before anyone at his level took vacation,

Blanche Pierre insisted on thirty days notice, even though Federal regulations didn't exactly require it. Even when she got thirty days notice, she typically disapproved anything over two weeks. She'd discover quickly that Charlie had requested his full seven weeks of accrued time off.

He felt good all over as he pressed the "send" icon.

It turned out that Blanche Pierre was at her desk when her inbox beeped. It was, she saw, email from Charlie Hexler. The very thought triggered a deep, persisting frown. She opened the message and, sure enough, pounded her desk. She cursed as she hit the reply icon and vented:

No. I don't approve vacation by email. I can meet with you in four days and you can explain to me then why you think you need vacation when the Agency has so much important work for you.

B. Pierre

Things looked promising, thought Charlie, as he read her response. He almost had her composing an intemperate, reckless response that would reflect poorly on her professionalism. He now had a significant grin.

Dearest B. Pierre,

Please reconsider. I'd be happy to telephone you so we could discuss this now.

That'd be quicker for you than a meeting on this matter---a matter very important to me for personal reasons.

C. Hexler

Less than a minute passed before the reply came:

Read what I just sent you. Then read it again to be sure you understand.

B. Pierre

Charlie raised his arms and cheered. He forced himself to focus, and typed:

Maybe I wrote at a bad time. You seem deeply hurt. I didn't mean to hurt your feelings. Do you need my help? Do you maybe even need somebody to talk to?

C. Hexler

Pierre hissed like a stepped-on python, thumped her desk hard, and wrote:

I don't NEED help from you, Hexler. And I don't get hurt by ridiculous views that might be childishly expressed. Show up in four days. Meanwhile, stop bothering me.

B. Pierre

Charlie again threw his arms in the air and yelled, "Yes!" He had almost brought out damning signs of immaturity. He reviewed a computer file and then typed with renewed gusto:

Dearest Blanche,

Of course you do not NEED help from me. I am merely trying to apply the wisdom of Agency Personnel Manipulation Soft Skills for Middle Managers Training Seminar OP-457-DC-VDK, Session 3, Module 2a. You no doubt will recall that effective middle managers should be alert for ways to encourage and tactfully support their senior managers when those senior managers are under exceptional stress.

Since I might not fully know the right words to use, please take this message and those preceding it as my heartfelt attempts to support you when stress might be getting a little too much for you. Like the instructor said, we all need to love ourselves.

So, cross your arms and give yourself a big hug!

Your good friend and faithful subordinate,
Charlie

Charlie had to try twice at clicking the "send" icon. He was laughing so hard his first attempt missed.

Her reply came right away. In his mind, he could see her throwing against her closed office door the less expensive items on her desk.

Don't call yourself my friend, Hexler. You're just an insufferable jerk who happens to report to me.

And you're not going to be reporting to me long, Hexler. I'm going to write up charges on you. Expect serious disciplinary action! SERIOUS DISCIPLINARY ACTION!

B. Pierre

He thought about having a drink in celebration, but couldn't afford the time to pour one. He wanted to keep the dialogue going while maximum adrenalin flooded Pierre's system, affecting her judgement. That wouldn't last much longer. It was time to take his best shot.

Dearest Blanche,

Charges? I'm confused! I'm hurt! What have I done wrong? Do you know something about me I don't know? Have you tried to show me my faults and help me grow as a career Federal employee proudly working for America? Have you considered my recent successes?

Let's both take a deep breath. I'll give myself a hug. You give yourself a hug. Then we'll start all over again with my request for vacation starting tomorrow. I'm sure that you and I together, acting in the spirit of workplace harmony which Agency Personnel Manipulation avows, can both come away from this moment feeling happy and professionally fulfilled.

Your faithful subordinate, who wishes

you success in your stressful job,
Charlie

Well, that was his best effort, Charlie thought, as he sent the email. She'd be off her adrenalin spike soon and thinking more clearly. If she were going to do something truly outrageous from a personnel standpoint, it would come now.

He hopefully watched his laptop screen and quickly was rewarded.

That's it, Hexler. You're FIRED for egregious insubordination. Contact your union rep if you want to appeal.
B. Pierre

Charlie not only got up and celebrated with a drink, but made it a double. He was going to quit, anyhow. Lars' offer was incredible. But now his leaving would be better still. Pierre's self-documented hubris might find its way to the personnel über-poohbahs monitoring all Federal employees. Why, even T*he Manhattan SomeTime*s might be interested!

Lars would be very, very pleased.

67

There were many Lars Brents in North America. Even more lived all across Europe and some others dwelt in Asia and South America. Brent thought that whatever kidnappers came for him wouldn't arrive until he wanted them to since Valhalla still had only a vague notion of where to find him. Further, Brent knew how to nullify facial recognition. He was very safe.

Accordingly, he and Charlie had time to deal with the women in their lives. The two men took separate flights to Vancouver, British Columbia. Charlie went straight from the airport to a good hotel near Little India. He was checked in and unpacked by two p.m. when Lars called.

"Charlie, I hear you're going to meet her at the restaurant?"

"Yeah. That's her idea. She has her office there since she entertains business clients so much. She's in government relations or something like that. Kinda makes sense to have an office beside a restaurant dining room."

"Sounds like you're all set, but I'll ask anyway: Do you need anything I can help with?"

"Nope. Just give my best to Mila."

Then Charlie was on his own. He felt prepared, having bought a new shirt at the airport. He thought about getting it laundered, but figured the rich scent of curry powder would mask new shirt formaldehyde. He just had to order the right dinner. Reassured, he ironed the shirt and let it air.

He'd bought a new tie to go with the new

shirt and would polish his old shoes. He'd wear his old blazer, which he loved, and a favorite pair of khaki-colored trousers that'd be okay. They were starting to fray a little at the cuff, but so what? He could afford new trousers, he told himself, but he was who he was. New trousers couldn't help much.

Indeed, new trousers might not matter at all. The woman was a stunner for sure, yet in his experience, stunners moved on. They'd stick around long enough for a Christmas present---one of them had, anyway---and then they'd find somebody who wasn't gone all the time. Somebody who could say what his job really was. Charlie long ago had concluded that extraordinary women liked men unhampered by long absences and national secrets. Agency demi-poohbahs stood no chance.

Charlie arrived at the restaurant early and waited for Louise Haranya by the front door. She entered, however, from the far side of the room, where the door to her office was. Charlie saw her right away. His intelligent eyes popped open a little. His strong jaw dropped a little. He could hardly believe how beautiful she was in person.

Other males his age in the crowded room must have felt the same way, for they turned to stare. The women with them thereupon frowned and one elbowed her husband. Louise made a better entrance than any actress Charlie had ever seen in the movies.

Louise Haranya in her four-inch heels was just the right height for Charlie. She wore a simple, modest black dress, but it fit her perfectly. Gold earrings and a thin gold chain were her only jewelry. Charlie thought it more jewelry than she needed given Louise Haranya displayed the best smile in the room. For that matter, Charlie thought hers the best smile in Canada. She moved with confidence and grace. Charlie considered her the most attractive woman he'd ever met. She was one of those women who were sexy without even trying.

He quickly regained his composure, and walked into the restaurant dining room to meet her, a smile on his weathered face. As he did so, Louise began forming her opinion of him. She thought he looked very athletic, even with a sport coat on. He had big shoulders, a trim waist, and strong hands. She liked his rugged look, straight posture, and confident manner. And his eyes! She already knew she could get lost in them if she weren't careful.

This, she thought, might be the man she'd spent more than a year hoping for.

As soon as they found each other, a waiter found them. He led them to their table and took drink orders. Louise chose the best white wine on the menu. Charlie ordered a whiskey she'd never heard of. He said it was from Texas. How, she asked, did he know about Texas? He'd lived there once, he said. He'd lived many places, but as far as he was concerned, a little Fort Worth, Texas distillery made the world's best whiskey. He was surprised to find it.

By then they were looking at menus, which were mostly in English, but sprinkled with Hindi words written in Devanagari script. She offered to translate the non-English parts. He said he spoke Hindi. He didn't have native fluency. Not yet. But he wasn't terrible, and actually enjoyed getting to practice the language. She brightened right up.

"Charlie, what you and I have now is the menu for tourists. If we ask for menus written entirely in Hindi, the waiter'll tell the kitchen. That makes a huge difference! The chefs' favorite challenge is delighting someone who's lived in India a long time."

She said it all in perfect Hindi.

"The kitchen will assume we've been living in India for years?"

He asked in Hindi that, while not perfect, was very close. She was pleased. Indeed, she was so pleased, she didn't switch back to English.

"Yes! If you waive to the waiter, he'll bring us Hindi menus!" Her eyes sparkled now.

They stayed in Hindi for the rest of the evening. He asked her to correct his grammar and pronunciation, but she found he needed only a little help. As she predicted, the chefs went all out. Charlie said it was the best Indian food he'd ever eaten. It was better, even, than what he had found in Mumbai's best restaurants. For him, that was totally unexpected.

Midway through the meal he leaned a little too far forward. The butt of his gun became just barely visible. She noticed.

"That's a Walther PPK, right?"

She showed no alarm and was clearly interested.

"Yeah. You're not supposed to see that. I'm told Canada officially frowns on guys like me going around armed. Might just be a rumor, though." He smiled.

"Is it a classic model or do you have the 1968 revision?"

He looked so surprised she had to laugh.

"It's not a trick question, Charlie. I've got a PPK at home, but mine has hot pink grips. And it's a classic. They're so hard to find now!"

"You know how to shoot a gun?"

He still looked surprised. This was, after all, Canada.

"I do. Mostly, Lars taught me. I'm good

using only the front sight when the target's up close. Say fifteen yards or less. Longer distances get harder for me."

"Have you had a gunsmith work on your gun's trigger?"

"No. How could that matter?"

With that they launched into an animated discussion of a German gun, while sitting in a Canadian restaurant, while eating Indian food, while speaking Hindi. She had good questions. He had superb answers---answers that drew on the same, colorful examples Lars had given her.

She soon realized Charlie must have been Lars' teacher! Lars had told her once when they went shooting that whoever had taught him how to shoot had also taught him how to hunt bad guys. Louise would forever remember that Lars alone had killed six deadly assassins intent on gravely harming her family.

She thus couldn't have been more impressed with the man in front of her! Charlie was intelligent, kind, and interesting. He looked John-Wayne-ish. The real-life Charlie Hexler most likely had better skills than the fictional James Bond. She'd take time to be certain, but she already felt Charlie Hexler was the strong, brave, and protective man she dreamed of finding. She felt herself falling in love. She already knew she'd fall hard.

Charlie felt the same way. Louise

seemed every bit as smart with business as Mila was with chemistry. Charlie liked smart women. And Louise Haranya was genuinely fun to be with. He didn't want the evening to end.

Finally, it was about to. The waiter said the restaurant would be closing in fifteen minutes. A Mr. Brent was paying for the meal and all gratuities, the waiter said. Would they like anything else before they left? It turned out they would not. The waiter retreated.

Charlie said, "This was my best dinner in many years. Thanks for joining me."

She graciously said it had been a wonderful evening for her. Then she waited to see how serious he was. She wouldn't be disappointed.

"I will, of course, make sure you get home safely. Maybe we could find someplace to meet tomorrow morning for breakfast?"

She liked that. He seemed serious. She said she'd be delighted to have breakfast with him. Soon they realized they both tended to go to bed around nine p.m. and get up around four-thirty a.m. It was another happy surprise for them.

He picked her up in a taxi at six a.m. Over breakfast, Charlie said he'd planned to spend the day seeing Little India and watching Bollywood films. Could she join him for at least some of that? Could she especially join him for dinner? And he could do other things in Vancouver if she wanted to. He was, he said, very flexible.

They spent the entire day together. They spent the next day together, too. Charlie was careful not to rush their relationship along. She was grateful for his restraint. That forbearance became something else---an important something else!---that she loved about him.

She found for Charlie a Little India tailor who Charlie later would declare a Canadian national treasure. Charlie ordered a new wardrobe, relying on Louise to develop for him the style she thought he should have. He was very pleased. Louise Haranya had flawlessly good taste.

He seriously kissed her goodnight on their second date. She kissed him back the same way. It took them fifteen minutes, and some of their best kisses ever, to say goodnight outside her front door.

The third day they watched a mix of John Wayne movies, James Bond movies, and Bollywood classics from the couch in her office. Her office had the best home theater system Charlie had ever encountered. Even so, they missed much of each movie. They were intently focused on each other.

Near the end of the third day, he told her he'd have to leave for about a week. No more than two weeks. He'd be helping Lars with some business he couldn't talk much about. It was a one-off project. After that he planned to retire.

To his surprise, she understood. She said she'd eagerly await his safe return and he should call her if it were convenient. He didn't have to worry about time zones, either. She wouldn't mind him waking her up at night.

It took every scrap of determination Charlie Hexler had to leave Little India the next day. Somehow he did, taking an early plane to Ottawa. He'd meet Lars there and help further construct a complicated trap.

68

Meanwhile, Lars Brent began his own three days in Little India. His time there would involve not only Mila, but also his personal chemistry laboratory.

His lab was the most expensive one-person facility of its kind in Canada, but nobody knew it. Brent had located it in a nondescript building ten miles from the heart of Vancouver, B.C., inside a mid-grade office park. The neighbors had no idea what went on in Brent's little business, which took up space comparable to a three-car garage.

One third---or roughly one garage worth---was given over to a storage room, in which Brent kept a gas chromatograph, a server, and the lab's fiberoptic Web interface. The interface was top-of-the-line, but neither unusual nor especially valuable. The chromatograph and the server, in contrast, were likely the most expensive in Western Canada.

Provincial tax collectors would have put Brent's business under a microscope had they suspected the value of these very high-end machines. Their tax collector manual, after all, claimed it took excellent income to support excellent equipment. Upon finding such equipment, the manual said, tax collectors should probe to fully expose the underlying taxable income.

Brent repeatedly had fooled the roving teams of Provincial tax assessors. He'd carefully removed labels from the server and scuffed up its front plate. The chromatograph received the same treatment plus two dents and an ugly scratch. Duct tape held shut an access panel missing its screws.

Conspicuously stored under and around the machines were various dog-eared operating manuals from a decade earlier. Brent had ordered them online from used bookstores. Refurbished circuit boards lay haphazardly in a shoe box Brent had labeled "replacement parts." Dust, partially removed decals, and a 1988 Calgary Olympics bumper sticker completed the illusion. His state-of-the-art machines easily appeared geezer-old and flea-market cheap.

Provincial regulators thought Brent tested and developed food additives for the Asian snack food market. Storage room shelves held not only boxes of Asian rice wafers, but also containers of flour, salt, spices, and so forth. Carefully labeled trays of rice wafers aged in a small, fourth-hand refrigerator salvaged from a student dormitory room long ago.

The wafers seemed part of ongoing analysis of a standardized rice wafer's vertical shear strength over time. A faded wall poster explained that, and further explained how retained shear strength indicated retained crispness. Brent could offer a supplementary explanation that quickly bored his listeners. He could be as dull as he was deadly.

His little business had been inspected months ago by Provincial revenue stalkers, who soon declared it unpromising from a taxation standpoint. Since the facility was dedicated to speculative research and not to proven production, the team's Senior Taxation Development Specialist saw little chance to seize significant tax revenue from it. She even looked disgusted by what she termed "the Third World equipment" used. Her team moved on in search of better turnips to bleed.

Next to the one-car-garage-sized storage

room was a conventional chemistry laboratory equally large. Part of the space held a small restroom with a special shower for washing hazardous chemicals from the body or the eyes, just in case an accident occurred. A cabinet near the shower held the second-hand respirator and third-hand moon suit Brent routinely kept ready. Various little bottles of chemicals fit snugly into a pair of ordinary bathroom medicine cabinets. Surprisingly, the chemicals were benign. Nothing toxic ever existed in the lab until Brent Lars combined harmless ingredients in unimaginable ways to make unthinkable poison.

Brent devoted much his lab space to a salvaged lab bench for wet chemistry. Specialized glassware was set up to drip one liquid into another. A Bunsen burner, an industrial sink, and a marble bench top completed the effect. His wet chemistry area looked like a high school chemistry lab too long afflicted with budgetary problems.

The remaining third of the building was rectangular empty space suitable for, say, a pair of king-sized beds had Brent been so inclined. The space's wall farthest from the wet chemistry area was an enormous white board. One could write on it with special ink markers or one could project images on it from a ceiling-mounted projector. The projector was what presenters anywhere in the world might use.

Brent's looked far older than it was.

He did his serious work out of sight in the cloud, where he rented world-class advanced processing power and abundant digital storage. He worked with his powerful applications and vast data by using a sophisticated dashboard that his ceiling projector displayed on the wall-sized whiteboard, which acted like a computer screen.

There was no mouse. Brent instead put a little white, reflective thimble on each index finger. Unobtrusive optical sensors in the ceiling and walls would precisely follow his hand movements. The ultra-sophisticated system also took his voice commands, but he found it easier to move the screen cursor around by waving his arms in the air.

Nothing in British Colombia rivalled his cloud-based computer system for capability and sophistication. Even the equipment at the Province's two big universities, its much bigger government, and its one large international company barely approached half of what Lars Brent's system could do.

He used his system to simulate chemical reactions. This meant the software imagined all the molecules in, say, a beaker of solution. Suppose an imaginary---or virtual---beaker held chemical A and chemical B, which would combine to form chemical C under the right conditions. Brent told the computer what the reaction would be by waving his arms like an orchestra's conductor. Drop-down menus then fell and rose from the top of his workspace and back---each menu movement precisely obeying the flick of a finger or the sweep of a hand.

He also could write and draw in the air with his fingers. Whatever he traced showed up on the whiteboard in the color of his choice. That was usually blue. Brent was partially colorblind between dark red and dark green. He avoided them.

As he worked, chemical symbols would appear on the screen, right where he'd placed them. Their characteristics, such as temperature or purity, were filled in by Brent using a pop-up box that opened when he clicked on the chemical ingredient. It was a standard object-oriented programming approach. Scientists and engineers around the world used it in one specialized application or another.

He drew in arrows to show, for instance, that chemical A combined with chemical B to make a compound C. More arrows showed what then befell compound C. Something like a tree diagram resulted, with various raw ingredients at the top of the big screen moving toward one finished ingredient at the bottom. The computer kept track of how many molecules, ions, or atoms had moved from each stage to the next, telling Brent precisely what happened along the way, nanosecond by nanosecond.

It was a truly marvelous system. Brent could simulate in cyberspace any chemical reaction problem anyone could address at a traditional chemistry lab bench. He could do it faster, cheaper, more accurately, and without any mess.

There were comparable simulation systems in use at all the world's Mega Pharma research centers. Needles knew how that would go. Scientists would have a sign-up list. They'd undergo formal training by a bloated IT staff desperate to justify its existence. That would mean too much training, retraining, and attendant delay. Meanwhile, corporate IT programmers would come up with pointless enhancements, routinely transforming productive bits of screen space into worthless eye candy. He had even heard stories of Human Resources crawling its threatening messages along the bottom of whiteboards at one company.

Mega Pharma research bureaucracies thus took the same software core that Lars used and, metaphorically, turned it into a barge. Lars, in marked contrast, kept his software in the nimble speedboat configuration the application's designers had intended. He in his lab could outperform Mega Pharma researchers every single time. It would not even be close.

So far as he knew, the entire world held only one other speedboat-like version of the simulation software. That was in the lab Mila Rossi had built with Mega Pharma grant money.

69 It was Saturday morning. Mila had finally loaded her two reluctant teenagers into the family's aging car. A picnic basket between her grumpy backseat passengers held snacks and sandwiches to get them through the day. They would sit in her office while she and Lars worked on making his exotic poison kill crucial seconds quicker than it did---though the teens did not, of course, know the lethal purpose of the Mom-and-this-Lars-Guy collaboration.

As soon as Mila backed out of her driveway, she encountered resistance. Her fourteen-year-old son went first.

"We can do our homework at home, Mom. Get it? *Homework*? As in work that's supposed to be done at home---*not mother's office work*."

"You know it's unsafe for you two to be home alone. Our house was broken into twice in the last five years. We live near Washington, D.C. It's not as safe as you think."

By now that response was automatic. She used the same words at least monthly.

The fifteen-year-old daughter took a different approach. "Mom, those jeans you're wearing are way too tight for somebody your age." She made a face toward the rearview mirror.

Mila sighed. "I might have left them in the dryer too long. They'll stretch back."

"And why are you wearing heels with blue jeans, Mom? You always wear flats or sandals to your lab."

"Says who?"

"Mom, I'm fifteen. I notice these things. You dressed up for this Lars guy, didn't you?"

"I dressed up to go to the lab. A research chemist can wear lots of things to her lab."

Mila now seemed faintly annoyed.

Her son said, "Mom, we all know you want to marry Lars-whoever-he-is."

"It's Lars Brent. To you, though, it's Doctor Lars Brent. He's a neurologist, a brilliant research scientist, and a former colleague. That's all you need to know."

The lab was still fifteen long minutes away. This was another one of the many, *many* times Mila really would like to have a genuinely good, loving husband who helped her raise kids. For now, though, all Mila could do was sigh. She did, and felt a little better right away. Sighing almost always helped her.

"When do we meet him, Mom? We get to help decide who our next dad will be."

"You'll see him today by videoconference. You can watch him through the big glass window separating my office from my lab."

"Swell. A videoconference interaction. Why can't he come here?"

Mila carefully negotiated a left turn arrow threatening to expire. Then she said, "He's Canadian. He lives in Canada."

"*Oh*. Well, that makes him *much, much* more interesting. Does he play hockey?"

"No. He does chemistry, biochemistry, neurology, and pharmacology."

"But he can't play hockey ... What kind of Canadian is he if he can't play hockey?"

"He's a very smart Canadian. You'll like him."

"Okay. If you say so. But remember, Mom, *real* Canadian men can play hockey."

And so it went. Three sighs later, Mila finally got her two, mildly aggravating teens into her office. Her son right away turned on her office computer and began to surf the Web. Her daughter almost said somebody needed to dust her mother's office, but realized in time who that somebody would be. Daughter remained silent, took a textbook from her backpack, and slumped into a chair as Mila walked from the office toward her lab.

Mila turned on more lights, turned on the technology, and pulled on the same little white index finger thimbles Lars would use. She donned a headset with a little boom mic at one side. Next she electronically connected her computer to his. He was already in his lab waiting for her. He waved.

He and Mila each appeared as a six-foot high color image on the far left side of the other's wall-sized whiteboard. Both also could appear in much smaller self images on their respective whiteboards so they could watch themselves. Both routinely suppressed their self-images, though, to maximize whiteboard space. Lars wore a headset like hers.

The rest of the whiteboard was bordered to create two wide columns. Mila's code, commands, pull-down menus, pop-ups and so on would appear in the left column. The right column would show the same items, but for Lars. Each could edit or mark up anything in the other's column.

They were almost ready to begin. Mila had to deal with their audience first. Her two teenagers had their noses six inches from her office window as they stared at Lars. Mila turned toward Lars, turned toward her office, waved to her kids, and spoke into her mic. Lars waved at the kids. Then he and Mila were back to their private conversation over their headsets.

Not hearing what they said bothered Mila's daughter. She thought conversation her mother had with this Lars man would disclose important clues about him. Her mother, however, used a headset! That hid all those valuable clues from mother's discerning teenaged daughter.

Did Mom really think she could deal with love on her own? thought the chagrined daughter. Mom didn't even watch reality TV. She didn't let them watch it either. The family knowledge base regarding romance seemed dangerously inadequate!

Her brother had retreated to her mother's office computer. He was playing some mindless video game that was little more than clickbait for unsophisticated boys, thought the daughter. It would be entirely up to her to guide their mother. Look at the jerk she'd married before! Their biological father had beaten Mom twice. Probably more. Mom wouldn't say. She'd been so ridiculously loyal to him and had tried so ridiculously hard. Even when their father was playing around with that dumb bimbo of his, her mother had still tried to save the marriage.

Teenage tempestuousness aside, daughter deeply loved her mother. If her mother were wrong about this man, her mother's inevitable pain would be great. Maybe even too great. Mom had to be right about this guy, daughter told herself. This was life and death stuff.

Daughter therefore would watch them closely. If this Lars guy were a loser, she'd figure it out from watching. Her mother might miss it---indeed, she probably would miss it. She was, after all, forty-two. But the teenage daughter promised herself that she, the dutiful daughter, would detect any looming problems. She had instincts for that, she thought. It was now up to her.

She moved to the office window, her nose almost touching the glass, and began her ever so serious vigil. Her brother stayed lost in his video game.

70

Kati Barska did well the first day: staying in her room, ordering room service, watching hallways and lobby with her computer. The meals sent up from the hotel kitchen were the only bright spots in her day. They had such a good chef! she thought. The food always arrived hot, too. She easily convinced herself Brent was wrong about using different restaurants.

The next day she was bored. She set half her computer screen for the hotel porn channel, even though it was in French. She set the other half to the hotel's hallways and lobby.

That morning she mostly watched the pornography, but she lost interest in it by noon. It was, she told herself, just the same old images of the same old body parts. One can only look at sex organs for so long. How, she wondered, did gynecologists and urologists ever endure their reference books, trade journals, and patient examinations year after year? Even dentists would have more fun gawking at those x-rays they took.

By early afternoon she'd switched from the porn channel to a game show channel. That held her attention only thirty minutes. She changed her screen over entirely to hallways and the lobby. If anything, she soon decided, the lobby feed had more plot to it than the porn channel. A homeless guy with a shopping cart came in, apparently to ask for a free room, and got thrown out. Two hours later an old lady's poodle got loose and the concierge chased it around the lobby for her. Great fun! Maybe the lobby was just having a good day.

Barska's eyes strayed upward and she began to think. Thinking felt like work to her then, but there was nothing else to do. Before long she remembered that Necromancer had promised her a big chunk of money if she sent him the hotel security camera video of Needles killing the two Volkovs. She'd not sent that particular video yet. She hadn't even contacted

Necromancer. After what Needles had told her, she'd been too afraid.

But a hundred thousand U.S. dollars was a lot of money, she thought. That plus what Needles had given her would pay for a new start. Maybe she'd even go to grad school someplace or maybe just pick up a couple of computer certifications that were in demand. These days the right IT certifications easily could be worth lots more than some college degrees. Especially if she were certified as some kind of exotic network security specialist.

The more she thought, the more it seemed a good idea to contact Necromancer. She'd never have to go near him or his guys, Barska assured herself. He'd do an electronic payment to her offshore bank account. She'd do an electronic file upload to their chatroom. That would be it. Because of her VPN, they'd have no idea where to find her.

She swilled a generous shot of whiskey and then downed another one. She told herself the first would clear her head. The second would bolster her resolve. Thus prepared, she went to the Dark Web.

Necromancer: Ready to trade video you need for cash I need. Meet me here in this chatroom at 1200 hours, Winnipeg, Canada time tomorrow.

71 Mila and Lars almost immediately forgot that teenagers might be watching them. The task before the two scientists presented sobering challenge. They would map out together Lars' entire process for making his needle poison. The twelve chemical ingredients and the forty-six formulation steps would eventually be arrayed in an arcane chain of simulation blocks on each whiteboard. He and Mila would work through one formulation step at a time. A few of the steps were simple, a few more were highly complex, and the rest were utterly daunting.

Lars was sure only Mila could quickly navigate the steps with him. This poison was far beyond anything ever created in a pharmacology lab. Even the world's several clandestine chemical warfare labs would have no idea how to proceed.

The world's most prominent pharmacologists could figure it out in time if he gave them instructions and coaching. There'd be much trial and error and much disbelief to overcome as they grappled with his work. They'd have to master an approach nobody on the planet but Lars would ever have attempted. But, in months, Lars told himself, they could get it.

Mila would grasp it all today. He was sure of that. He'd never met anyone like Mila.

They agreed that, for each step, Lars would explain the chemistry involved. Then he'd set up the necessary simulation code for that step on his whiteboard. Mila would independently develop her own version of the code. They'd compare and discuss results, modify their individual code blocks using the best of what emerged, and move on to the next step.

Lars said making the poison work ten seconds sooner might take them days of atomic-level design work. Or it might take hours. He told Mila he could never predict what would happen when they worked in the lab. She said she couldn't predict it either.

They began the coding. The block of simulation instructions for the first step looked like a chain of chemical symbols, joined by arrows, dotted lines, or symbols stranger still. Click on any symbol---or rather, point to it with the white thimbles they used---and a big popup box opened. Inside were dozens of parameters that had to be set. Just seeing an element in the chain didn't tell the element's full story at that moment. One had to open the element's popup box and read through the many parameters. Each popup box was, in effect, a tiny operating manual for its element at a particular nanosecond in the overall poison production.

They were building an elegant little

molecular world. Mila's daughter, like almost everyone else in the real world, would understand none of what appeared on the whiteboard. But she understood people well for her young age. She understood her mother exceptionally well. For hours she'd watch Lars and Mila work intently. She'd watch their faces and their body language.

She told herself facial expression and body movement would disclose all she needed to know. She was sure of that.

72

Kati Barska heard a knock at her door. She looked out the peephole and saw a harmless-looking old man: too little hair on his head, too many wrinkles on his face, too much weight at his middle. He wore a blue blazer with a paisley tie. The tie was unfashionably thin, as if to compensate for an overly thick middle.

She took out her cellphone and punched in the number for hotel security, but didn't hit "send." She opened the door as far as the heavy metal chain allowed.

"Yes?"

"Somebody named Necromancer hired me to bring you some money. He said you'd give me a drive thumb. Okay?"

The old man said it with a good smile.

"It's called a thumb drive."

"Whatever. I don't do computers. I'm old school."

He gave her a another good smile.

"Show me the money first."

He looked both ways and pulled a thick envelope from his blazer pocket. He opened the envelope just enough to quickly thumb through the bills for her. They all seemed to be hundreds.

"I'll also show you the thumb drive thing they gave me," he said

He held up an ordinary thumb drive still in its package.

"Give me the thumb drive," said Barska. "I'll load the video on it and hand it to you through the door after you hand me the money."

"Look, lady. I'm just a retired cop trying to make an extra buck. I don't know who you are. I don't know who Necromancer is. But he said I had to watch you download the file onto the thumb drive."

"Why?"

"Because I'm old school. I'm even proud to be old school. I don't know how to look at the thumb drive and see if files are on it. So, Necromancer said I had to watch you do whatever you do. I'm to ask you to show me what's on the thumb thing, too."

"Why's he using you if you don't know

computers?"

"Maybe 'cause I've been delivering special packages for years and being very honest about it. I've got a reputation now. That's my edge over young guys who know about drive thumbs." He smiled. This time it was a self-deprecating smile.

It worked. "Okay. Come on in." She slid the door chain back.

The gentle-looking old man walked inside with slow steps, and handed Barska both the envelope and the thumb drive. He shuffled to a chair and sat down while she counted her money. Then he started massaging one knee and complaining about arthritis. He warned her to start taking glucosamine pills early in life.

She smiled. He was just a harmless old guy in a land without guns. He probably didn't know the U.S. Army had taught her hand-to-hand combat. She could take him out if she had to. She was a U.S. Army Signal Corps female in her prime---a lean, mean, fighting machine if need be. He was just an old man with a bad knee. She was even an inch taller than he was!

73

Lars and Mila had been under her teenage daughter's microscope for almost two hours. Daughter had tentatively concluded her mother was radiantly happy, even though most of the time she saw mother's back rather than mother's face. Such happiness was highly unexpected given that Mom and Lars were doing chemistry, and chemistry wasn't even remotely fun. Daughter had hated the chemistry module in her science class. Half the chemicals smelled bad and the rest could hurt you. Chemistry was total yuck.

Lars looked as happy as her mother. Daughter found herself starting to like him. He smiled a lot. His eyebrows did a sort of twitchy thing every once in awhile as he listened intently to her mother. And he always listened intently! That was nice. Probably not lasting, but nice for now. He had this funny way of pursing his lips, moving them left and then right, or *vice versa*. And sometimes he puffed his cheeks out momentarily, either with or without pursing his lips.

He did those things when thinking about what Mom said. Sometimes he looked overhead, too. Sometimes he tipped his head. He seemed completely unaware of these mannerisms. Even so, daughter thought they often made her mother laugh. Not at him, but because she was so happy being with him. It would be her mother's happy little laugh, the laugh daughter never heard in the months before the ugly, painful divorce. Even though she couldn't hear her mother through the glass, it was good to see her laughing that way.

Her younger brother now stood beside her at the window. As usual, she thought, he was paying attention to all the wrong things. He only cared about the chemistry on the whiteboard. He watched it intently, which was bad enough. Worse still, he asked her questions about it.

Then he wanted to know why she couldn't answer his questions given she had taken the entire introductory chemistry module. He gave her that better-than-thou look he used when they played basketball against each other in the backyard. He always won. She always was annoyed when he did. She wondered why she kept playing.

Stubbornness. That was it. Her brother was immature, but she was stubborn. She'd work on that, she decided. She didn't like being stubborn. Being stubborn was for immature boys, rather many of whom were her age and in her classes at high school.

Lars held up his cellphone and pointed to it. He was asking her mother if she'd like some music. Daughter brightened up. Music class was her best class ever. She especially loved classical music, though she was careful not to tell any boys that.

Mother nodded approvingly. Suddenly her laboratory sound system, which reached into all parts of her lab and office, carried the majestic strains of Wagner's *Ride of the Valkyries*.

It was so out of place that daughter laughed. Her mother covered her own ears and shook her head in exaggerated disapproval. Lars thereupon did his bushy eyebrow trick, waved his arms, and began moving drop down menus up and down in time with the music. He did his puffy cheek thing, too, one cheek at a time. Ten seconds later he looked at daughter's mother for her approval of his music choice.

Mother was laughing, but still had her ears covered. Plainly, *Ride of the Valkyries* wouldn't work. He shrugged, stopped the music, and went back to his cellphone's playlist. Moments later the unlikely sound of the Bee Gees' *Staying Alive* filled the room. Lars closed his eyes and began doing ancient disco moves, but in his geeky sort of way. Everybody watching laughed, even daughter's dorky brother.

Her mother laughed hardest of all. Then she was dancing right along with Lars, who now had his eyes open. Mom was *amazingly* good! Daughter had no idea her mother could dance like that. The tight jeans probably helped. That made her hip movements work better. She was marvelous with her hips! Daughter took out her cellphone and began videotaping. She was determined to learn her mother's dance floor technique.

By then Lars and her mother were coordinating their dance moves. She would do what he did. Then he would do---or usually just try to do---what she did. For awhile they forgot all about their work. They were fully lost in the shared joy of being together.

Daughter realized her mother was dancing with her soulmate. It was such a beautifully romantic moment that tears ran down daughter's cheeks. She stepped back from the window so her brother wouldn't notice.

He didn't notice. He wouldn't have noticed even if she had stayed at the window. Her doubly dorky brother, as she sometimes called him, was back to looking at the chemistry on the whiteboard. For some reason known only to the doubly dorky, his sister thought, it fascinated him.

74

The stormtrooper-like man known as Security walked into Peeters' plush office and closed the open door.

"Barska's dead. Some Montreal Mob guy whacked her in her hotel room less than an hour ago. He got her computer and is sending it to me by one of their couriers. The thumb drive's coming, too. I'll get it all by late tomorrow afternoon."

Peeters leaned back in his big chair and

smiled. "Very good news! How'd they find her?"

"When she sent that last message to you, she used the same VPN server."

"That meant she could've been anywhere in the world, right?"

"Yes. But this mobster was a technological dinosaur. You see, the Mob had to call out some of their retirees to cover streets around the hotel. This old timer reasoned that if she was still using the same VPN-whatever-that-was tactics, she might still be in the same hotel."

"That's not an entirely logical argument."

"Indeed. But it made sense to somebody utterly clueless about computers. I mean, the Mob said the guy didn't even know how to turn off the machine. But earlier he had asked himself how Barska would set about staying in the same hotel for days undetected."

"She'd stay in her room for sure."

"She did. She also used a false name. But the Mob's techno-dinosaur paid one of the hotel food service guys for a look at room service orders. The dinosaur wanted to know if anybody had been ordering room service for every meal. That's sort of unusual."

"Hers was the only room doing that?"

"There were three others. One held a local hooker with an out-of-town client. The food service guy knew about the hooker right away. The other two rooms were for vacationing couples, each with one little kid along. Each kid came down with kid flu, so they all just stayed in their rooms. That left only a woman who stayed in her room."

"Then what?"

"The old guy followed the room service delivery person up later that day to that last room. He limped by Barska's door when she opened it."

"Limped?"

"Yes. Smart guy. He seemed harmless that way. He just wanted to see Barska's face out of the corner of his eye. It was her. The same brunette in the picture the Mob passed out."

"And the rest was easy?"

"Not real easy, but easy. He came back later claiming to be a retired cop and gave her the money. She downloaded the video and showed it to him on the screen. Then he overpowered her, did some painful things that won't leave marks, and learned her computer password. Once he was sure about the password, he washed five Sequilphaznost pills down her throat. She popped off right away. He rigged the scene to look like an accidental overdose, pocketed the money and the drive, and left with her computer. It all took him less than an hour."

"Very nice."

"One more thing. She had a big bottle of Sequilphaznost. That was unexpected, so he not-so-gently asked about them. She said Lars Brent had made them up for her. The Mob's sending Brent's pills to us with the computer and the thumb drive."

75

A half hour after their labs had become *de facto* dance floors, Lars and Mila decided to call it a day. They'd made remarkable progress. He thought they'd finish tomorrow morning. She thought they'd finish late tomorrow if he put disco music on again. They'd finish sooner, otherwise. Both were sure of success just ahead. They each loved big challenges like this.

Before they disconnected their video link, Mila brought her teenagers out to meet Lars. She turned on her room's microphone. No longer needing a headset to talk with Lars, she took it off. Then she introduced each teenager. He introduced himself to them, saying he'd looked forward to talking with them. They'd demonstrated so much patience in their glass cage!

The kids laughed and fell into easy

conversation with Lars. Mila sensed right away that he liked them. He asked Mila's daughter what, if anything, she'd enjoyed most about watching computer code. Daughter surprised herself, and pleased her mother, by saying she really liked watching her mother and Lars work together. They seemed such a good team! Lars and Mila both realized the daughter approved of him.

Soon they both realized the son liked the whiteboard chemistry. He probably liked Lars, too, but only wanted to talk about the software now. Mila let Lars answer her son's questions. Lars gave such clear, interesting answers that more questions bubbled forth. The young man seemed so intrigued that Lars asked if Mila had the tutorial for their software on her office computer. She did. Great! proclaimed Lars. There was an example about how to make gunpowder. Her son could work through it on her office computer tomorrow.

"Lars! *Gunpowder's dangerous.* Just have him simulate one of those solutions that grows crystals, or maybe changes color after five minutes."

He addressed her son. "Ah! You hear that? That's how my mom sounded the first time I made gunpowder. She even had that very same look on her face."

He turned to look wide-eyed at Mila. Her

kids shifted position so they could look at her, also.

"*What?*" asked Mila, who looked right back. She laughed in spite of herself.

"Mila, you can relax. I made gunpowder with my dad. He was a chemist, himself. He made sure we took as many safety precautions as your average moonshot would. I not only had a great time---we blew up a tree stump---but I acquired excellent lab safety habits that stayed with me from that day on ... Okay. Watch your mother. I sense a smile coming on."

The kids turned to look at Mila again. They were plainly enjoying the exchange. She made a face at Lars and wrinkled her nose at him. He liked her nose wrinkles.

She smiled, though. "Okay. But you only get to make virtual gunpowder. Simulate the explosions. They'll look like video game explosions. But no real gunpowder."

She wrinkled her nose at Lars again. She knew he liked it.

"Excellent," he said, focusing back on her son. "Once you learn all about gunpowder from the computer, I'll invite you two and your mother to Canada. In one, two, or three weeks, I think. I already know some stumps that are in the way. We can blow one up."

"Lars! No. *He's only fourteen!*"

"That's a perfect time for boys to learn

safe lab habits. I already know you're going to like what I'll say next, Mila."

She put her hands on her hips and frowned. "What?"

"I'll teach him all about safety when it comes to making black powder. Next he'll have to a pass a lab safety test you prepare. Use the same questions you'd give graduate students."

"Now, that part I like! Lars, my son will never pass a graduate lab safety test. He's only fourteen. And when he doesn't, you'll drop the subject?"

"Yes. If you want me to. But I already know he'll pass. He's smart for fourteen. He's got his mother's DNA for chemistry ... He might have your nose, too."

By now the daughter was laughing and the son was excited. "Please, Mom!" he begged.

Mila gave her son a warm smile. Then she gave Lars a very warm smile.

"Lars, I can agree to those terms."

"Yes!" shouted her son. His sister, meanwhile, displayed her grandest smile that month.

76

After a very good day in the lab with Mila and her kids, Lars Brent treated himself to dinner in one of the Little India restaurants he liked. He went back to his

Vancouver apartment and turned on his laptop. The early Grunt-Necromancer chatroom transcripts Barska had emailed him had been interesting.

It now was time to see what the datalogger on Barska's computer had collected long after the transcripted conversations ceased. He supposed Grunt would hide her computer soon, removing its battery when she did so. This might be his last chance to check her datalogger.

He found only one new message sent by Barska:

Necromancer: Ready to trade video you need for cash I need. Meet me here in this chatroom at 1200 hours, Winnipeg, Canada time tomorrow.

Brent cursed softly. It was a truly stupid move on Barska's part. He thought about contacting her, but it was already too late. Besides, she'd rejected his best advice once. She'd just reject it again, he decided. He could think of only two things that might be useful now.

First, he'd go through many hours of audio her laptop microphone had sent to his cloud account. Last year Dragon Lady had given him an app helpful for such a task. It would fast forward through the recording on its own, skipping over street noise, background TV shows, silence, and anything else clearly useless to him. The app would only give him human voices. Needles didn't expect anything profound. Encrypted chat was so much harder to intercept than cellphone calls, that he thought Barska's serious communications would all be sent that way.

He was right. He found nothing useful in the vast store of microphone audio, despite some brief mobster conversation at the end. Brent soon turned to the next thing that might help. He sent a message to the encrypted chatroom he and Charlie used now. It might be twenty-four hours before Charlie checked it, but that'd be soon enough.

Old Dog,

Saw your message. Congratulations on being fired. Those emails are perfect! You've definitely gotten better with age, I think.

Just in case the Agency guys in Ottawa will still talk to you, please ask them if they've heard anything about a female fitting Grunt's description. Checking the Ottawa morgues might be a good idea these days. Grunt may have been careless.

Needles

77

It was the second day of Mila's two-day consulting project. She and two eager teenagers arrived at her lab an hour early.

Daughter was pleased to see her mother again wore heels. She wore jeans that must have been in the dyer too long. Mother's knit top might have been in the dryer with them. There was, daughter thought, hope for her mother's budding romance.

Mila showed her son how to work the simulation software tutorial on her office's desktop computer. He'd have about nine hours to make and test virtual gunpowder, she said. He nodded, took his place in front of her desktop, and showed more enthusiasm than for his video games. Mila was surprised! Pleased, to be sure, but very surprised.

As Mila started her son, daughter finished her homework. She didn't have much, anyway. She said she might read a book. She might, but mainly she didn't want her mother to realize daughter planned to spend the entire day studying the evolving Mila-Lars relationship. She found their interaction compelling! It was, daughter thought, like a real-life romance novel.

Precisely at the scheduled start time, Lars video linked his lab to Mila's. She was waiting for him, headset and finger thimbles already on. They waved to each other, said something, and began. They soon were nearing the end of the multi-step chemical process they needed to model. The decisions grew harder.

Before long, they were disagreeing with

each other every few minutes. Sometimes they went from resolving one disagreement right to a new one. It hadn't been like that yesterday, daughter thought. She worried that mother was about to lose her boyfriend by being stubborn.

However, daughter soon grasped the dynamic at work. It was so unexpected! Even when the two disagreed, they clearly still liked each other. The frowns seemed contrived, as though just a shorthand for signaling disagreement of a position, not disapproval of a person. Smiles seemed entirely genuine and appeared at all the right moments. Lars gestured a lot with his hands, as Mila listened. Next he waited for her response, listening closely as she waved her finger thimbles. Then their disagreement cycle repeated itself.

Sometimes Lars agreed with her mother and they did it Mila's way. Daughter could tell that from body language, from facial expressions, and---more telling still---from which one corrected whiteboard code so it looked like code the other had written.

Sometimes her mother agreed with Lars and the opposite happened.

Sometimes they were at loggerheads and it all took longer. If that happened, mother always gave in to Lars. They did it his way. That must have been because he was the client and paying her, thought daughter. She'd ask her mother about that. Until then, it felt good that her mother wasn't being stubborn over something silly. Being stubborn over something big was a different matter, of course. That was okay. Daughter had boys in her high school classes who *should* hear nothing but *no* from her.

It took Lars and Mila two hours before their now identical code models were completed. It was time for a break. Mila left the lab to check on her children. She was pleased to find her son intent on his tutorial and making remarkable progress. At first, he didn't even notice she was in her office. This was the same boy who had hated, despised, and loathed---his words---his science course's minimal exposure to chemistry. Now he was hooked! His super-chemist mother felt very good about that.

Mila had turned to leave when daughter asked, "Mom, why do you always give in to Lars when you two disagree? You're just as smart as he is."

Mila laughed. "It's the easiest way to solve the problem. This isn't about who's smarter. This is about finding the best solution."

"I don't understand."

Mother smiled at daughter. "Well, Lars and I listen to each other well. He listens to me better than any man ever has."

"I can see that. *So?*"

"If his way and my way still differ, even after all that listening, then sometimes either way should work just as well, right?"

"I guess. *So?*"

"Then it doesn't matter which way we go. But if we have two approaches that look equally good to me, I just do it Lars' way. Why bother splitting hairs?"

"Then he always wins."

"Nobody always wins because there's no contest. Or perhaps you could say we both win since we both want the best solution."

"What if you think the choices aren't equal? What if you think your way's better?"

"Mostly, I'd just do what Lars' wants. It's the easiest way to show him he's mistaken."

"Does he ever admit you were right?"

"Always, once it's clear I'm right. But sometimes he turns out to be right. I end up agreeing with him as often as he agrees with me. We don't keep score. And you know what?"

"What?"

"Since we don't keep score, our game's much more fun."

Mila smiled again at her daughter, grabbed a bottle of water from the family picnic basket, and went back to her lab.

78 Half an hour later Lars and Mila finished building their now identical simulations. When they told the computer to run the simulations, it would follow cohorts of atoms, ions, and molecules through forty-six steps, combining them repeatedly into more complicated compounds. At the end, there'd be only two compounds: Lars's needle toxin and an almost undetectably tiny amount of unwanted byproduct.

"Let me get this straight," said Mila. "You and I are only trying to reduce the byproduct now. It's a contaminant we have to get rid of?"

"Yes. That contaminant slows down the neural cascade by ten seconds. If we make the poison totally pure, the neural cascade should occur almost instantly."

"So how much contaminant is tolerable?"

"I think two parts per billion."

"Lars, I again hope you realize almost nothing gets that pure in real-life. That's hard!"

"Yeah. That's *extremely* hard."

They went back over their code looking for ways to reduce the contaminant in the final compound. Mila kept shaking her head. Then she said, "Here---at step fourteen---is where the contaminant begins to increase. Do you filter the fluid you add at this step?"

"Twice. Afterwards I centrifuge the result and filter again. The fluid's as pure as a lab can make it when I put it in."

"But not good enough, right?"

"Yes."

She held her chin with one hand as her other hand scrolled code up and down. She let go of her chin to scratch her head. She shook her head, shook it again, and scrolled some more.

Finally, "Lars, I don't see a way. I'm sorry to let you down, but ... *wait!*"

She began talking to herself. Hope arose at Lars' end of the videoconference. He waited nearly a minute.

She by then had grown excited.

"Lars, go to step nine where I'm pointing."

She circled the step on the whiteboard, using her finger like a virtual ink marker.

"Why do you use that particular chemical to accelerate the reaction?"

"It's cheap. Nontoxic. Stable. Readily available. Why?"

"But that step's where the contaminant's precursor's created. It's a byproduct of making this essential intermediate compound, right?"

"Yes. Why?"

He still didn't get it.

"What if you used a permanganate here? And maybe just used chromium as a catalyst at the next step?"

Then he saw what she saw.

"Yes! That's all we need! *Mila, I love you!*"

"What did you say?" She went to half smile.

"I love you. I love you. *I love you* ... Is that enough?"

"Maybe. But I like hearing you say it." She went to full smile.

He said it five times more for her, throwing his arms out wide on the fifth time. They both stopped to laugh. Then she had second thoughts.

"*Oops!* Lars, what if my idea creates a new contaminant?"

"It might. It won't matter, though. There could only be one new contaminant and I already know what it is. It won't have much impact. Better still, it evaporates given enough heat."

"But, Lars, this whole forty-six-step process generates very little heat."

"Correct. I do some laser machining on the needles."

"*What?*"

"You don't know about that yet. I heat

the needle while removing its outer glass tubing. The new contaminant will evaporate right away. This'll work. Definitely."

They revised their models and ran the simulations, both getting the same compound at the end, along with the same data on compound properties. Lars looked carefully at the results. He, of course, knew his poison better than Mila, though she had almost caught up entirely. Mila was, indeed, very, very quick. It was one of many things Lars loved about her.

"I think we're done," he announced, a big grin again stretching his beard. "This is perfect. Instant neural cascade inducement. Undetectable poison. *I love you, Mila!*"

Mila brought the kids out to say goodbye. First, though, Lars and Mila's son had an animated discussion about black powder. The teen explained his simulation tutorial results. Lars said the young man seemed ready to learn graduate student lab safety procedures. Lars would be in touch about that in roughly a week.

He'd also send Mila an encrypted satellite phone. It'd loosely resemble what they'd once used years ago in Alabama, but would be far, far better. He might need to discuss their chemistry with her. Mila laughed and said she looked forward to receiving the phone.

Soon she and the kids left for the day. Once they were home, daughter took mother aside.

"Mom, did Lars say he loved you? Like over and over and over again?"

79

Once Lars had disconnected his video link with Mila, he went to work in his Vancouver lab. By now he had made so many needles that producing them was an efficient routine. That routine that evening went even quicker because of Mila's insight. It took him only two hours to make up seven needles using the revised toxin.

He holstered six in the little glass tubes he easily concealed in clothing and luggage. The seventh one he tested in the lab's gas chromatograph, which showed a contaminant well level below one part per billion. Even Brent was surprised. His new poison would be completely undetectable in a victim's system.

He went home to his apartment, just in time to hear his encrypted satellite phone buzz at him. Charlie's number appeared on what amounted to satellite phone caller ID. They went through their usual identification routine for a secure call.

Finally, Charlie said, "Ready for an update?"

"Go."

"Barska's dead. She was found in her hotel room by housekeeping. The police think she'd overdosed on those pills she took, whatever they were."

Needles was silent for a moment. "I guess I didn't give her good enough advice."

"Nope. That's wasn't the problem. My person in Ottawa somehow got a copy of the police investigation report. The investigation's still ongoing, but they think the killers found her through room service orders. One of the supervising chefs said she'd ordered something like a dozen meals in a row. One of the kitchen staff probably told somebody that. The staff are being questioned now."

"I feel a little better. I guess it's not my fault."

"It's definitely not your fault. Barska threw caution to the winds."

"She'd have had a big bottle of Sequilphaznost pills I made for her. She'd also have had her laptop. Were those two items on the inventory the cops made of her possessions."

"Wait a minute. I gotta dig that report out ... 'no' for both. Somebody took them?"

"I hope so."

He told Charlie that Barska's computer had a datalogger wired into its keyboard. There was also an open microphone on it, sending its audio recordings to the cloud.

"But don't you need a Wi-Fi connection to use the mic?" asked Blue Dog.

"The software for all this is in the datalogger, which installed it automatically. The mic software constantly looks for a Wi-Fi connection. It'll log in to any public Wi-Fi source. If a user connects to private Wi-Fi source, the mic will simply use it while it's available."

"But what if the bad guys turn off Barska's computer?"

"It won't matter. Not for a couple of weeks, anyway. The datalogger, not the computer's controls, now runs the computer. The datalogger will keep the mic on, using whatever power is left in the computer's battery. So little power's consumed the mic will stay hot for days."

"But don't you have to listen to what's being said, Lars?"

"Not until I want to. The data either goes to the cloud directly or it accumulates in the datalogger chip. What accumulates in the chip is sent to the cloud as opportunities arise. I can go through the cloud recordings at my convenience using a voice recognition utility."

Charlie was impressed. He sounded happy.

"I think you're telling me that whoever

took Barska's computer has bugged himself?"

"Yeah. Good way to put it. And I think we might add another piece to our plan."

"What?"

"Let's give Blanche Pierre an even bigger problem than firing you'll cause her."

80

The first step in giving Blanche Pierre a much bigger problem involved the Agency's intense internal counterintelligence. Charlie knew some of the Agency's email addresses. He picked one Kati Barska might reasonably have discovered. Lars then sent that address an untraceable message.

To: Section Chief, Headquarters Counterespionage

Subject: Likely Breach of Security at Agency Headquarters

I'm a former U.S. Army Signal Corps major, who was medically discharged in recent weeks. I accepted a temporary Agency job offered me by Blanche Pierre. Someplace you've got a file on me. The Army's got another file. You'll find I'm legitimate---or was so. I'm dead now.

I came to believe Pierre might be selling Agency secrets to the Chinese. To make a long story short, somebody---almost surely her---copied me on an innocent looking message she'd intended for someone apparently in Chinese intelligence. Dumb mistake. She'll figure out eventually that she erred. Then she might send killers after me and my computer.

Or maybe not. She might have some innocent explanation, like maybe the guy in China is one of your agents. Who knows? That's your problem.

My problem back then was I might get murdered soon. So, I set up a nice little robot. It will send you this message if, for some reason, I don't check in with the robot once every so many days. If you see this message, I'll be dead and you'll have a spy problem.

You might find my body around Quebec City. Good luck catching whomever killed me.

The Late Kati Barska
Major, U.S. Army Signal Corps

Charlie knew an email like this would trigger a very quiet, very intense investigation of Blanche Pierre. That might lead Agency investigators to Peeters, but probably not any time soon. Under obscure U.S. counterintelligence laws, Agency investigators now could have NSA add Pierre's voiceprints to the voice recognition screens constantly run on transocean telephone communications. If Peeters and Pierre frequently relied on burner phones, that might someday work. Meanwhile, other measures would be needed.

Charlie had one. He was highly confident at least fifty Agency employees knew, or could easily discover, Blanche Pierre's Agency email address. No Agency fingers would point to him convincingly. With Charlie's complicity thereby hidden, Needles waited a day for NSA to begin screening Pierre's messages to or from places outside the U.S. Then Needles sent an email to Pierre from one of Needles' anonymous, untraceable accounts:

To: Human Resources Director Blanche Pierre
From: Street Hustler
Subject: Invoice for My Silence

Hey.

You don't know me yet, but that's okay. You're the big shot Agency woman who got my best friend, Kati Barska, the spy job that killed her. Necromancer and you killed her. She told me you might. That's why she was hiding in Ottawa's Glass Wall place.

And the killer you sent to whack Kati took hundreds of Sequilphaznost pills she said some guy gave her.

I need the drug, too. Just like she did. Only nobody was giving me the pills for free like Necromancer and you were giving them to her. Also, no nice guy with a pill jar showed up out of nowhere to help me.

Therefore, Kati mailed me some of this nice guy's big bottle of pills. You know what? This Sequilphaznost stuff works for me. Kati said she'd share more of it. I'm schizophrenic in a bad way. I'm gonna need more of those pills. But you, asshole, had them stolen. You and your buddy Necromancer did that when you killed my friend, Kati.

Now I don't have access to pills. You got me into this mess. You're going to get me out.

I want fifty thousand Euros and five hundred Sequilphaznost pills. I'm okay for two weeks. You've got that long to gather up the pills and the money. I'll tell you how to deliver. I've first got to set up some way that's totally safe for me. I don't trust you and Necromancer. Not after the two of you killed Kati.

If you don't pay up, I'll tell the cops what you and Necromancer did. I'll tell the Agency and the FDA. I'll even tell the lousy Manhattan SomeTimes. *Then I'll start on social media.*

And guess what else: I know you're selling Agency secrets to China. Kati caught you, and that's why you and Necromancer killed her. You've got lots of money. So, big shot, pay up.

Have a nice day, asshole.

Blanche Pierre was worried as soon as she read the message on her office computer. She was twice as worried after rereading it. She'd no idea who Necromancer was. Even the name sounded ominous.

She called the Maryland phone number Peeters had provided. He said it would be like using a burner phone hooked to voicemail. Pierre left a voice message asking only if there were any discount liquor sales at the usual place at the usual time. It meant Peeters was to meet her in a Dark Web encrypted chatroom at a certain time when she'd be off Agency premises.

Needles and Old Dog were reasonably sure Pierre would contact Valhalla somehow. They also thought they had better than a fifty-fifty chance to intercept that contact once the Agency's internal counterespionage procedures were invoked. Unknown to ordinary citizens, the combined eavesdropping of the FBI and NSA was formidable.

Some would even say the combination was awe inspiring. The two agencies leased their own cellphone towers in major cities and had long ago placed data taps on undersea transmission lines. Some NSA satellites did little more than duplicate, process, and prioritize the endless messages routed overhead through space.

Yet even if the U.S. government intercepted damning electronic conversation between Pierre and Peeters, that information normally would be confined by law to a tiny portion of the U.S. intelligence community. Getting them to share any such information with Charlie and Lars was the next component of Brent's trap.

Such access could be acquired through a serious legal dispute. Each side of the dispute was entitled to see whatever relevant information the other side had. Americans knew this as the discovery process that preceded the initial jury session in a courtroom. Lars and Charlie each would file a lawsuit. Each suit during discovery would allow, the two hoped, at least one man's attorneys a good look at whatever Pierre-Peeters messages U.S. investigators had snatched from the ether and, if necessary, had decoded.

The next day, the Ontario attorney Brent had engaged filed what American lawyers would call a wrongful death lawsuit against Blanche Pierre, the Agency, and Valhalla Pharmaceuticals. The suit was brought on behalf of both Kati Barska's estate and Lars Brent. For Barska's estate, Brent wanted the three hundred thousand Canadian dollars she had in her possession when she died. For himself, he wanted the estate to repay him the same three hundred thousand Canadian dollars, which he said he'd loaned Barska.

The suit averred the money, along with Barska's computer, had been stolen at the time of Barska's death. The removal of these items suggested foul play. There was *prima facie* evidence that Pierre, Peeters, and Valhalla may have been complicit in the removal of these items. Each party would've wanted to cover up Barska's possession of Sequilphaznost pills.

Brent's suit said Barska had told him Pierre, herself, had arranged for Barska to improperly receive Sequilphaznost pills. Barska having such pills appeared flagrantly illegal under various laws governing clinical trials, the lawsuit noted.

Then there was the anonymous friend of Barska's---somebody called Street Hustler---who'd been in touch with Brent. Brent's suit alleged that Barska gave Street Hustler Brent's email address. Street Hustler had emailed him, claiming Pierre and somebody called Necromancer conspired to bring about Barska's death.

Street Hustler, Brent further said, might

have suffered from advanced schizophrenia. Her recent phone call to Brent suggested as much. She'd told Brent that, earlier in the same month, Street Hustler had sent Pierre an email describing the conspiracy Street Hustler alleged.

The suit asserted Street Hustler told Brent in subsequent telephone call that she was afraid to retrieve the money she'd demanded from Pierre. Street Hustler even told Brent three times that Pierre and her co-conspirator might kill her. She offered Brent half the money she'd demanded from Pierre if he'd pick up the money when it came. Brent said he'd referred her to the police, whereupon Street Hustler got angry and hung up.

Finally, the lawsuit added a particularly damning bit of fiction. Barska near the time of her death, the suit alleged, had told Brent about her correspondence with somebody called Necromancer. Barska had said, according to this bit of fiction, that she thought it highly likely Necromancer was Vlaski Peeters, who wanted her to spy on Lars Brent. Barska said she somehow had figured that out from comments Blanche Pierre made while issuing Barska's contract.

The lawyer added standard legal verbiage and then, on behalf of Lars Brent, asked that the Canadian Court, the U.S. Court, the Belgium Court, and the European Union

High Court order the preservation of email and any other messages either sent or received by Blanche Pierre and Vlaski Peeters for the past one hundred days. Brent's attorneys, of course, could receive copies of all such documents during the usual pre-trial discovery procedures.

It was a marginal case based largely on hearsay information, but courts made rare exceptions to hearsay rules. For example, if the best information available in a homicide or potential homicide were hearsay, it might be considered for whatever a jury thought it worth. Also, the allegations in Lars' case identified a computer, a sum of money, and an email message. Any of these might substantially bolster Brent's allegations. Merely knowing those items existed might be important to the court, Brent's lawyer said.

All this meant that, while Brent might or might not win this case, it couldn't be tossed out of court right away. That alone mattered to Brent. He didn't care about winning a case. He cared only about establishing that Pierre was communicating with Peeters.

81

Lars and Charlie resumed their preparations for the kidnappers they expected to attack Lars soon.

Lars bought a small log cabin in rural Ontario, nearly an hour outside Ottawa. The comfortable little structure squatted unobtrusively at the end of a two-mile dirt road, all by itself. It had a phone line, an electricity line, a flush toilet, and a well. Miles of otherwise virgin forest surrounded it. As that region's hunting cabins went, it easily was the most luxurious.

Lars put the utilities in his name. He further had the cabin's landline phone listed in the local, online phone book. The cabin's address would also appear on documents involved with Brent's lawsuit. These measures ensured the bad guys could discover where Lars Brent supposedly lived.

In mere hours, Brent, Charlie, and two of Dragon Lady's engineers installed a sophisticated alarm system at the rustic cabin, put hidden video cameras inside, set up hidden microphones, installed sensors, and hooked up a public address system. It was all powered by batteries and a well-insulated generator hidden deep in surrounding forest. A signal booster connected the gadgets by satellite to Brent's cellphone.

Both Lars and Charlie thought kidnappers would start their attack by cutting off the cabin's links to public utilities. The cabin was far beyond cell-phone service. Severing the victim's phone line would mean, to the attackers, that Brent couldn't call police. The bad guys, thereby would give the good guys a minute or so of warning that the assault had begun. Also, Charlie constructed a padlocked gate across the driveway, a mile from the cabin to give an additional half minute of warning.

Charlie, Lars, and Dragon Lady's engineers drove to the cabin in three vehicles, one of which was an old pickup truck recently licensed to Lars. When the engineers finished, Charlie and Lars departed the cabin along with everyone else, leaving behind the old pickup truck.

In between the three-vehicle trip out and the two-vehicle trip back, Brent hooked up a pair of chemical mines which Dragon Lady's husband, Kenneth, had helped him build. Brent provided the chemical agent and the propellant. Kenneth provided the radio-controlled valve to separately vent each chemical mine's contents into the cabin's interior, one at a time with twenty-four hours between the two discharges.

Needles and Old Dog would be waiting for the kidnappers, but waiting in Vancouver, where they'd be more comfortable than in the Ontario cabin. They'd deal with the goons by laptop remote control. It was like using a cruise missile, Charlie said, but without the missile.

82

Brent's lawsuit was still making its way to Pierre. She so far knew only about

Street Hustler's email, which she'd forwarded to Peeters. He read it with dismay, gazed out his office window long enough to smoke a cigarette, and called for the man known within Valhalla as Security. Security soon arrived, his stormtrooper expression in place.

"That's Barska's computer?" asked Peeters, pointing to the laptop Security carried.

"Yes. I went through it carefully, but didn't find any problems."

"Does anything identify me as Necromancer on this computer?"

"Nothing. But the laptop's booted up and ready to go, in case you prefer to take a look."

Peeters indicated he wished to make his own examination. Security walked to the big desk, set the open laptop before Peeters, and took a comfortable chair nearby. They spent several minutes in silence as Peeters scanned the machine.

"Nothing here looks like a threat. Did you check for hidden files?" asked Peeters.

"Yes. We've got a forensic app for that. There's aren't any hidden files that matter. Just ordinary operating system stuff like everybody else has."

Peeters sent a few more screens across the laptop.

"You plan on destroying Barska's

laptop?"

"Immediately after I leave your office."

"Not that soon. I need to have my core team think through this situation. Hold off until after that meeting."

"Something's come up?" asked Security.

"Yes. Lars Brent just sued us. This Street Hustler might become a witness. And it now looks like Pierre could be trouble. It's all getting complicated."

"Should I get a couple of killers lined up? Maybe make somebody disappear?"

"It might take more than a couple this time. But I need to get the team together before we do anything beyond just lining up shooters. I'll try for a meeting this afternoon. It might not be until tomorrow morning, though."

The microphone in Barska's computer, of course, captured all they said.

83

It became Charlie's turn to file a lawsuit. Charlie's suit was against Blanche Pierre for discharging him in violation of Civil Service Law, his union contract, and his civil rights under the U.S. Constitution. Charlie's lawyer also alleged mental anguish. Charlie found that part highly amusing, but the lawyer said it gave them more to bargain with.

The next morning Pierre was formally

served notice of the lawsuit as she stood outside her home. She acted unconcerned and drove to work. There she entered her Agency office sanctuary and closed the door. Pierre had her secretary clear Pierre's schedule for the next three hours. Make sure, Pierre said, nobody except her boss or her father-in-law disturbed her. All alone in her office, she tried to think through her present legal situation.

She started with Brent's lawsuit. It was bad enough all by itself, to be sure. However, she thought Valhalla would fix most of that. Peeters at the outset had strongly hinted that Barska and Brent would "soon be out of her life forever." Also, the rogue operation could be blamed on Hexler. He and Pierre had been alone whenever they'd discussed his mission. He'd no witnesses to what she'd said.

She'd also been careful from the start to have her minions furtively monitor Hexler's GPS locations during recent weeks. She'd somehow coax a damning pattern from his movements. She'd make Hexler the fall guy all over again.

Barska's contract had been put in writing. Yet it said almost nothing about the secret work involved. It was just a generic form Pierre had signed---one of many routine forms she signed every week. The details of Barska's contract all had been left to Hexler.

Other documents---some Valhalla guy called Security had provided these---would show Hexler, not Pierre, had handled all project funding. He supposedly got the funds from a phony offshore company. The Agency used dummy companies like that all the time to transfer money. That part would look normal to somebody in Pierre's position. Nobody would expect her to probe beneath the surface.

Pierre would say her personal involvement merely had been recruiting an outside operator Hexler'd needed for something he made sound harmless at the time. She'd be as surprised as anyone where he'd taken matters from there. Demi-poohbahs were uniformly expected to display good judgement and work with very little supervision. Who, she'd say, would ever imagine a long-term government employee like Hexler would launch the unauthorized operation he alone had contrived? He should've been worthy of her trust!

Yes, she thought, she could survive Brent's lawsuit with Valhalla's help. Hexler's lawsuit would be harder. Valhalla had no interest in helping her with that situation, which---from a professional personnel standpoint---was embarrassing. She'd been wrong in sundry ways, the entire little travesty was in writing, and she hadn't been able to correct her error.

She reminded herself she'd tried hard to correct it! She'd made at least five calls to each of three numbers Hexler might be expected to answer. He didn't answer. If he had, she'd have told him she was unilaterally converting his discharge to a three-day suspension. He should report back to work, she'd have said, on such-and-such a day.

She also sent the same message by overnight mail. Hexler, however, wasn't at his mailing address. Not only that, but he'd stopped his mail for a month. None of his neighbors knew where he was. None of his neighbors even knew who he was! Hexler had been careful not to interact with them over the years. It was as if he'd thought the less they knew about him, the better for him.

Giving him verifiable, personal notice he was no longer fired would've mostly offset her impetuous, unfounded behavior. The timely reversal would've turned a big, festering mess into a minor distraction easily overlooked by Agency senior executives owing her favors. She, after all, had covered up their minor distractions, or worse. If the Hexler situation stayed small, she told herself, the IOUs she held would be enough.

It probably wouldn't stay small, she conceded. Hexler's lawyers already had dragged it into the courts, where it might get much more attention than it deserved. How much more depended on what his lawyers spent on public relations and social media.

If various senior officials in the current administration, or even in other agencies took notice, she'd be in trouble overnight. While this indiscretion on her part wasn't by itself fatal to her career, it might become so given her nontrivial errors in years past. Then she'd again need help from her father-in-law, the U.S. senator about to retire at age ninety-four.

How much help would he be this time? she wondered. His health was failing in half a dozen ways she knew about. He drooled on himself, dozed off in front of cameras, and lost his way reading short, prepared statements. His comprehension had so diminished that he dared meet only with lapdog reporters from *The Manhattan SomeTimes*.

Besides all that, Hexler's lawyer had asked for Agency copies of any electronic communications she had with or about Charlie Hexler. The lawyer wanted chat. He wanted email. He wanted transcripts for all her relevant cellphone calls and satellite phone calls. He wanted somebody neutral to examine her computer. He even wanted email related to Lars Brent, whom Hexler had been overseeing. Hexler's lawyers wanted to depose her about all of that.

The Brent part of Hexler's suit was a surprise. Maybe a lawyer could have that suppressed. Maybe not. Anyway, she knew how the rest would go, and it would be bad enough. There'd be questions about her mental stability, how much she drank, what medicines she took, which other employees might have complaints similar to Hexler's, *etc*. All the while, she'd have to get her real work done.

She took time out to focus on hating Charlie Hexler, feeling strangely refreshed afterwards. She told herself she was in a mess, but so what? She knew how to get out of messes. Before long Hexler would be in the biggest mess of all, and he'd perish there. Blanche Pierre smiled at the thought and stopped worrying.

84 Vlaski Peeters quickly assembled his core executive team around his office's mahogany conference table. Security had Barska's laptop before him, opened up and booted. For Security, it was like displaying a bowling trophy, only better. He managed a crooked sort of half smile.

The Finance Director was a little toad of a man who, in keeping with Valhalla honorifics, was simply called Finance. His best facial feature was the pair of beady eyes behind his thick-framed glasses. Bushy gray eyebrows and an over-engineered nose filled out the center of his face. Puffy cheeks and a thin-lipped mouth completed his look. He'd have done something silly with his hair if he had any, but Finance was bald.

The rotund, fifty-something blonde known as Research wore a bright red pants suit under a big white lab coat. She went without makeup and slouched. She compensated by wearing heavy gold chains around her neck and thick gold rings on her sturdy fingers. From across the room, the rings looked like brass knuckles

The attractive woman next to her was a strong contrast. She was perfectly groomed, fashionably dressed, and ever articulate. They called her External Affairs. She oversaw both lobbying and public relations. A perennially charming public face of Valhalla, External Affairs enthralled Eurocrat regulators and a typically pliant press corps. She and Peeters were unquestionably the best liars in the room.

Finally, the Human Resources Director was present. HR, as they called her, was a thin woman with a plastic smile, gaunt face, and dim eyes. She dressed like an undertaker, spouted procedures like a bilge pump, and thought like a finger puppet. That last aspect had much advanced her career since the HR department served as Peeters' corporate Gestapo. Their job in large part was to spy on employees and fire the unenthusiastic.

Vlaski Peeters began the meeting.

"We may need to kill Lars Brent. I need a decision at the end of this meeting. Everybody got that?"

They all knew about Brent. They all nodded.

"Let's start with his poison, or maybe with his poisons. Explain that part, Research."

Research deftly knocked one hand's five gold rings on polished mahogany and began.

"You'll recall that Barska was supposed to learn all she could about Brent's magical poison. She didn't provide much. Nevertheless, we learned that he uses different dosages. A low dose delivered subcutaneously can anesthetize in minutes. This is what Brent used on Barska and the two Agency guys with her. A high dose of that poison---at least, we think it's still the same molecule---kills in seconds.

"We also know he has an antidote, at least for the low dose. He wiped poison on his hands and then put his hands on his victims. What knocked Barska and the two Agency guys out had no effect on him."

Research glanced at HR, who didn't seem lost yet.

Research said, "Having an antidote like

his is rare, but not unheard of. What's astonishing is the poison's speed at a higher dose. Nothing like it exists in the known world of pharmacology. I say that because of video the Mob killer took from Barska. It shows Brent killing two Volkovs, each of whom died in ten seconds. That's just about impossible without hooking the victim up to an IV first. Fentanyl is quick, but what Brent used kills far quicker. I'm convinced Brent's the first person ever to induce neural cascade."

"This part's critical," said Peeters. "Once again, what's neural cascade and why should we care?"

Research leaned forward a little. She knocked two hands worth of gold rings on the table this time. It was like giving herself a drum roll.

"Neural cascade's a pharmacological miracle. Until Brent came along, it was only an interesting theory bantered about by Valhalla's two lab geniuses. They never could produce neural cascade, though."

HR sensed a growing need to show interest.

"How does this neural cascade work?"

"Think of neural cascade as magic. First, an almost unmeasurably small amount of Brent's poison makes contact with one of the victim's nerves. The body, of course, has nerves just about everywhere. Any nerve will do. The poison somehow---nobody but Brent understands this part yet---makes each nerve cell touched do two things."

"This is really important," said Peeters.

He directed that to his entire staff since HR already seemed to be zoning out. HR never understood anything technical, thought Peeters. Her whole department was like that. Ruthless to be sure, but technologically as witless as jellyfish.

Research talked a little louder, thinking that might help HR.

"First, the poison tells the nerve cells touching it to commit nerve cell suicide, but not right away. No, no, no! The suicide must wait until the suicidal nerve cell tells its neighboring nerve cell to die. As soon as that message is delivered, the first nerve cell kills itself. Two steps: the messenger cell tells the neighboring cell to commit suicide and then, once the message's been delivered, the messenger kills itself. Clear so far?"

She looked around the table as though gauging group comprehension, but actually just checking on HR, who didn't yet seem bewildered.

"The neighboring cell follows suit. It gives the same suicide command to its own neighboring cell and then pops off. You get cell after cell playing follow-the-leader suicide. Brent's poison only affects the first cell in the long chain. After that, the cells kill each other."

"And that's why nobody found poison in the corpses? Only the first cell was affected, so only the tiniest bit of poison would be needed?" asked Finance.

"Maybe. There'd have been very little of it, to be sure. Just enough to trigger the first microscopic cell in the chain. However, it's equally likely Brent's using something nobody would ever think to test for."

External Affairs asked, "Do all the body's nerve cells commit suicide?"

"No. In time they would, but the poison sends its suicide commands to the brain by the most direct route. If the poison were injected between left toes, for example, it would go up the nerves in the left leg to the spine and into the brain before the cascade ever had time to reach the right side of the body. Brain death stops the progression."

Security asked, "And this neural cascade takes place how quickly?" Ways to kill always fascinated him.

"Consider it instantaneous. A neural cascade goes from, say, toe to brain as quickly as it would take the nervous system to report stubbing a toe. We're talking nanoseconds."

Peeters looked at HR and decided a last

summary might still be necessary.

"I hear you saying the poison starts a chain reaction, but only starts it. It's more what the nerves do to each other than what the poison does to the nerves?" he said.

Research looked pleased since HR finally seemed to get it. "Exactly!"

Finance took a turn. "Is there some physical way to know death was by neural cascade?"

"Yes. Over the years, we've examined eight such corpses. We now know---and nobody else in our industry even suspects---that cascaded nerve cell diameters are about five percent smaller than those for healthy nerve cell diameters.

"Counting the Volkov bodies, which I hope to acquire soon, we can expect to have eleven complete MRI scans that, under high magnification, all should display the reduced cell diameters. Six MRIs are from six Asian assassins who mysteriously died near Vancouver, Canada, five years ago. Those six are the earliest neural cascade kills we're sure of."

Peeters smiled. It was his greedy look.

"Tell us how much the authorities know about neural cascade."

Research smiled back with her own greedy look.

"Nothing whatsoever. The authorities learned nothing from the Volkov deaths. We haven't told anyone anything and only two of my researchers know about our neural cascade data. They're paid well to keep it secret."

"Any further questions for Research?" asked Peeters. There was none.

Peeters said, "So far we've learned that neural cascade exists, and only Brent knows how to cause it. Hold that in mind. We'll get back to that. But let's first talk about Valhalla's unhappy business prospects. Your turn, Finance."

The Finance director hit a laptop key and brought up his talking points. He also sat up straight, making himself an inch taller, but not tall enough to raise his shirt pocket fully above the table's edge. He really needed a modern steel-and-plastic office chair. Instead, he had an old-fashioned mahogany chair too low for his torso and too hard for his buttocks. He'd twice considered bringing a cushion to these meetings, but each time decided against it. Security would think him a wimp, and Research might imagine him having hemorrhoids.

"We're like most of Mega Pharma," intoned Finance. "We rely on patent-protected blockbuster drugs for the bulk of our revenue. Such drugs let us vastly overcharge Americans. We then sell the same drug everywhere else for pennies on the dollar. It's the very high prices for Americans that's essential. That's where the money is. Patents let us do that legally."

He was pleased HR seemed to understand halfway, which might be all he could hope for.

"This time two years ago we had ten patent-protected drugs. That meant ten ways to price gouge. Six months ago three went off patent, the generic drug companies immediately undercut our prices, and we now make much less off those three drugs.

"That leaves us seven patented drugs that dominate their markets. Three of them will go off patent late next year. Unless we find some wildly profitable new drugs quickly, we'll drop from number two in our industry---yes, we're no longer number one as of yesterday---to number eight or worse. We won't completely shut down, though. Before that, certain nasty competitors would buy up our stock and take us over. The Valhalla name would go away. Lots of Valhalla jobs would disappear, including ours. It would be brutal."

HR looked concerned. She hated job loss. Layoffs meant so much extra work for her.

Peeters took back the floor with a wave of his hand.

"We've now said that neural cascade is a pharmacological phenomenon only Brent Lars understands fully. We've also said we need new patented drugs. How might neural cascade help us get new drugs?"

It was back to Research. "We're not entirely sure. Some of this is untested theory. What I'm about to say comes from the two best scientists we---or others in our industry---have. These are the two guys who theorized years ago neural cascade was possible. They're now convinced that neural cascade's scalable."

"What's that mean?" asked HR before Security could. Security was a little better technically than she was, but not all that much so.

"It means that Brent might have one basic drug rather than several. A little bit of Brent's drug'll make you comfortable right away. In other words, all your worries disappear. Barska and those two Agency guys reported feeling happy as the poison began to affect them. Again, we don't know why, but all anxiety flittered away. They were laughing and smiling."

"Notice," interrupted Peeters, "that this drug of Brent's, suitably diluted, might dominate the market for anti-anxiety drugs overnight."

Research nodded enthusiastically and continued.

"And we think another dosage of Brent's

drug will put you to sleep. That's what he did to Barska and the two Agency guys. None had any side effects and Barska claims to have slept wonderfully well."

"Notice further," interrupted Peeters, "that this drug of Brent's might take over the market for sleeping aids."

This time everybody nodded.

Security asked, "How does he fine-tune dosages of this stuff? I thought only a few molecules of the poison killed? Even if you dilute it, you'd still get a few molecules of poison."

It was an insightful question. He surprised them all.

"An excellent point!" said Research. "Dilution might turn out to be the wrong word. It seems Brent has an inhibitor of some sort. Something that dials back his magical poison. Earlier, I mostly talked about cell suicide. However, attenuate Brent's poison molecule in some fashion only Brent understands, and you can send a different message. That message might be something like, 'Don't worry, be happy,' or 'Have a good night's sleep.' Instead, of one lethal message for nerve cells, you could pick from a range of messages and some would be nice ones."

She paused to gauge comprehension, looking only at HR. So did everyone else. HR didn't notice. Instead, she inspected the room's crown molding before finally nodding that she understood.

"And it gets better," exuded Research. "A little more of the drug will anesthetize you so effectively that you could undergo surgery, not feel a thing, and not move a bit as surgery proceeded."

"Notice we'd surely own the market for anesthesia overnight," said Peeters.

"Finally," said Research, "too big a dose---and we'd still be talking only a microgram or less given how powerful Brent's drug seems to be---would be a lethal toxin."

"Regrettably, the market for lethal toxins is somewhat thin," observed Peeters. "There are always a few lethal injections in state prison systems. There's good potential, too, for euthanasia in nursing homes. That might create some viable demand. Same for assisted suicide and organ harvesting. Brent's drug would be perfect for these markets."

"But all this is speculative, right?" asked Finance. "I mean, we don't know that Brent's drug could pass regulatory trials for any of these applications."

"Partially speculative. Only partially," said Research, remaining effervescent. "Brent essentially tested the lethal injection part on the Volkovs. He sort of tested the anti-anxiety and sleeping aid parts on Barska and the Agency guys. What's untested---according to our two blue ribbon theorists---is the anesthesia part. I won't bore you with molecular-level premises, but the tests we know about make it a very, very good bet that this drug's the best anesthesia ever."

By now, Finance's pallid face had its happy look. "We're talking three enormous ethical drug markets and one tiny one, right? And we'd own those markets?"

"Yes," said Peeters. "Something over half a trillion U.S. dollars a year of annual revenue if we get all those capabilities past regulatory trials. But we don't have to get them all past the regulators. At least, not right away. Each of the drug's big three markets is probably worth over two hundred billion U.S. dollars all by itself. One market alone will save the company."

External Affairs briefly displayed her full public relations glow. "We wouldn't have to worry about competitors buying us. We'd buy them!" She laughed happily at her insight.

HR asked, "Will Brent sell us rights to his neural cascade drug?"

All eyes turned to Peeters.

"It's doubtful. We'd offer him a good price. Yet Brent already could have made such a deal with just about any Mega Pharma company on his own. He might not want to sell."

"Why not sell?"

"He might not want the attention. A little background helps here. You see, we give a lot of money to a certain U.S. senator who has much to say about our industry. His daughter-in-law is Blanche Pierre, who's the HR director at the Agency. She has access to many interesting files. HR identified her for me."

HR smiled, showing her brownish-yellow teeth of a very heavy smoker. Peeters let her briefly continue the story for him.

"We did some research on Pierre years ago and found the link to the senator," HR said. "He made sure Pierre eagerly began working for us. And that gets us back to Brent's motivation to cooperate, I think."

With that, she looked toward Peeters, who resumed the lead.

"Pierre claims Brent's spent a dozen years killing high-end assassins. He's made five kills she knows about. Those were Agency-sanctioned and made over ten years ago. He's made other targeted hits for certain European intelligence agencies, but Pierre doesn't know details, except that she thinks the French and the Brits hired him."

External Affairs asked, "He's a serial killer who can't sell his secrets because he'd call attention to his career?"

"I think so," said Peeters.

"We could let him stay anonymous," suggested Finance. "We'd introduce the drug as our invention and pay him under the table from our profits. There's enough money for everybody."

"It would, to put it mildly, be embarrassing for us if his role were discovered. But there's a much bigger problem for us," said Peeters.

"What?"

"Whatever deal we offered Brent could be offered by our competitors. There'd be a colossal bidding war. Winning would be a pyrrhic victory for us, even if we could win. Buying this unbelievable technology from Brent won't work."

"So what can we do?" asked Research, as Security began to smile.

Peeters smiled, too. "We can take it from him. We'd kidnap Brent, interrogate him, and quietly kill him. The world would never even know he were gone. A few weeks later, we'd announce an amazing new drug family would be entering the regulatory process."

"But will he tell us his secrets?" asked HR. Her office relied on fear and knew its limits.

"Everybody talks in the end," said Security, with an evil smile. "Drugs and sleep deprivation. A little terror, hunger, and cold. All of it choreographed by experts borrowed from a bloodthirsty dictator. Everybody talks. Brent will break in a week or less."

"And that gets us to decision time," said Peeters. "Raise your hand if you think we should kidnap, interrogate, and kill Lars Brent to get his secret formulas."

They all voted to do so. HR chortled briefly when Peeters announced the group's unanimous decision. He then told Security to make the arrangements. Peeters said to use the Montreal Mob for the tough guys needed. Tell them, Peteers further said, to move quickly.

85 Peeters' entire executive meeting had been captured on the active microphone in Barska's computer. Charlie and Lars listened to the covert recording of that meeting while flying by chartered jet from near Lars' Ontario cabin back to Vancouver.

Lars turned in his airplane seat to look at Charlie, who sat across the aisle. "You know, Charlie, I never thought it would go this well."

"Same here ... Want more coffee?"

"No, thanks. I've had too much already."

Charlie rose, walked to the cabin's high-tech coffee machine, and returned with a fresh cup. It wasn't a double expresso, but nearly that strong. He sat down in his seat and took a long, appreciative sip. His neurons surged in response.

"Lars, I'm now thinking we don't need the lawsuits. We've linked Pierre and Peeters' just from the laptop mic, huh?"

Lars shook his head.

"They'd argue the recorded conversations were digital fiction. Valhalla'd just say the conversation never occurred."

"But we'd say otherwise, right?"

"Yes. Assuming we're alive. Assuming we could get the laptop. Assuming we could prove they took it. And on and on it goes. Charlie, you gotta realize that, if we're dead, their phony tapes defense wins by default."

"You and I aren't easy to kill, Lars."

"We're not. It might take a hundred killers to drop each of us, but they can afford two hundred killers."

Charlie reflected on that. "Maybe we should go to Europe and break some heads?"

"Not yet. Valhalla's goons attack the cabin soon. Let's deal with them first."

"Lars, that makes it time to think through our schedule."

"Meaning what?"

"Meaning how long can you and I stay in Vancouver and still wrap everything up within the timeframe we intend?"

"Charlie, I think you're in love."

"Nawh. I always look like this."

"Okay. I'll play along. Back to our timeline. We've shown the bad guys where to go. Peeters is telling them to hurry. I'd guess they'll show up in, what? Four days?"

Charlie said, "No sooner than three. Maybe four. We've at least three days to deal with the kidnappers coming for you."

"Okay. That means we don't have to leave for Europe until four days from tomorrow?"

"Yep. That works for me."

Both men had plans for the next three days. Each smiled.

86

Once they landed in Vancouver, Charlie and Brent went their separate ways. Charlie took a cab from the airport to his hotel, talking to Louise on his cellphone the entire time.

Lars got his own cab, made the short trip to his Vancouver apartment, where he called Mila on his satellite phone. It would be their fifteenth satellite phone call.

She answered on the second ring. Lars took that as a good sign.

"Hi, Mila."

"Hi, yourself! My daughter's just been

talking about you."

"Is that good?"

"I think so. Wait … I've got to go into my office and close the door."

She did so, to her daughter's disappointment.

"There. My daughter can't hear me."

"And what did she say about me?"

"She thinks I should marry you."

"I think that, too. Are you ready for a proposal?"

Mila sighed in pretend frustration. "You have to surprise me, Lars. We can't schedule a proposal. And it can't be over the phone. You're supposed to take me in your arms. I could recommend some good novels if you need inspiration."

"Nawh. I think I can get this right. What else did your daughter say?"

"She identified your many good qualities. Next she said I need tight skirts which are cut too short and tight tops which are cut too low. She also told me which websites to visit for lingerie."

"How old is she again?"

"Fifteen! I didn't realize she had these ideas inside her mostly innocent-looking little head! I told her she and I are going to have another serious talk. Soon!"

"I agree with her. Go easy on her."

"You would agree! But I might wear tight jeans for you someday. I mean, why not? My daughter says I already have."

"You look unbelievably good in tight jeans, Mila."

"Thank you. But I'm guessing my wardrobe isn't why you called."

"It isn't. I still need to tell you in detail what I've been doing for the past few years."

"Okay. We need a session like that."

"I also want you and the kids to visit Vancouver, Canada. I'll pay for everything."

"Oh … This is a nice surprise. When?"

"Tomorrow morning. I'll have a limo pick you up and take you to the airport. An executive jet will be waiting there. I'll meet you three in Vancouver."

"Tomorrow!"

"Yes. You'll be in Vancouver through the weekend. Even longer if you wish. Charlie'll be there, too. Along with the woman he's in love with. Her name's Louise."

"Charlie's in love?"

"Yes. Seeing him oblivious to everything but Louise is, all by itself, worth the trip."

She laughed. "Lars, I can get somebody to cover my classes, but I can't just up and leave. This is the D.C. area. Our neighborhood was safe once, but those days are gone. There are break-ins around here. I'd have to stop the mail, set timers for the lights, have a neighbor check for packages, and more. And then I still have to get the kids packed. That last part takes time."

"I'll have a security service send somebody to live in your house while you're gone."

"Lars! Then I'd have to clean up. I have two teenagers. Household disorder happens."

"I'll have a maid service clean up."

She looked at her satellite phone in wonder.

"You can do all that?"

"No. But I know somebody in Vancouver who makes such miracles happen. She's the concierge working for a powerful family out here."

"Lars, I simply don't know what to say!"

"Just say 'yes.'"

Again she laughed. "Okay. 'Yes' it is. Even though I can't believe I'm doing this."

"Can I get you to wear tight jeans again?"

"In the lab. Not in an airport full of strangers. But I have a skirt and top you might like."

"Would your daughter approve of it?"

His hopes soared.

"Maybe."

87 It took Security a day to make all the arrangements. He walked into Peeters' office.

"The kidnapping's all set up. Brent's living at an isolated hunting cabin deep in a forest north of Ottawa."

"It's hard to believe he lives in a cabin. They guy's got to be rich. Why a cabin?"

"That was my reaction. This place's much nicer than you'd think. The Mob had somebody sneak up and peek through a window. Comfy furniture. Rustic décor. Indoor plumbing and a desktop computer. Electricity and a landline phone. Also, one or two people in the nearest town said Brent's had several serious deliveries made in the past two weeks."

"He'll be there awhile?"

"Looks that way. It'd be a good hideout for him if he ever needed one. He probably has someplace nicer elsewhere, but for at least a week he'll be at the cabin setting it up. And so far this cabin's the only Lars Brent address we feel confident about."

"He'll be hard to locate if he leaves. We should move quickly."

"We already are. The Mob's sending six

guys and two vehicles. One's an SUV. The other's a panel van."

"A van can reach a place like this?"

"The driveway's only a dirt road, but in excellent repair. Brent had it brought up to Provincial standards."

"Mob guys will charge in during the night and tie him up?"

"They plan on sedating him. There'll be a small plane waiting thirty miles away. That'll take him to a private jet in New Brunswick. From there it'll be non-stop to a little Belgian airport. The interrogation team will be waiting in a farmhouse half an hour distant. Brent's body will be buried there once we're done with him."

"How long until we have his secrets out of him."

"Fifteen days from now at most. Maybe just ten days."

88

Mila could hardly believe how smoothly her morning trip to Vancouver went. The executive jet landed at a small Canadian airport mid-morning. Lars, Charlie, Louise Haranya, Jenny Haranya---who Charlie and Lars occasionally called Dragon Lady---and Jenny's two teenaged children met the plane. Jenny's teens were a boy and a girl the same ages as Mila's respective teens. Jenny had brought them along to help her show Mila's family Vancouver.

Lars made the introductions. Everyone seemed to like everyone else right away. As Lars had predicted, Mila thought it worth the trip just to see Charlie Hexler in love. Charlie seemed to smile all the time. He looked at Louise more than at everyone else put together. He even held her hand! Mila was delighted. So was her daughter, who liked romance in general.

Louise Haranya took charge. She and Jenny Haranya drove everyone but Lars and Mila to see Little India. The teenage boys would spend time there in what Charlie thought North America's best video game arcade. It was used by the Haranyas for market research. The boys would play the beta version of a new virtual reality combat game so advanced it didn't have a name yet. Charlie would advise on trigger control and sight alignment.

Jenny said she and the girls would do some shopping, with Louise leading the way. Louise, Jenny said, knew the best tailors in Western Canada. They and she'd been friends for years. Lars had arranged for Mila's daughter and Jenny's daughter to get matching, custom-tailored outfits if they could agree on what to buy. The girls enthusiastically said they could.

The happy little tour groups headed off,

leaving Lars and Mila alone by the plane. Moments later, a chauffeured limousine drove up. Lars opened the door for Mila.

"We're going to Little India. One of North America's most secure conference rooms is there. I've booked it for the rest of the day. I've also got dinner reservations for us at a ski resort restaurant overlooking Vancouver. We'll take a ski lift to it, even though there's no snow yet."

She told him it all sounded wonderful.

He might have said more. She might have said more. Neither did. The limo's privacy screen was up. They soon fell into one another's arms. She snuggled against him all the way to the Emporium.

Once inside the store, he led her through the Haranya family's high-tech consumer sales area, up the narrow stairway, and into the ultra-secure conference room he and Charlie had used. There, after several long kisses, he explained they were safe from surveillance. They sat at the table in two of the stiff wooden chairs designed for staying awake in meetings and not for romance.

"The furnishings aren't terrific. Secure rooms don't seem to include couches. Our private dining room at the ski lodge has a couch, though."

She laughed and squeezed his hand. She

left her chair, sat in his lap, and put her arms around him. It wasn't optimal positioning, but still an improvement over separate seating. Ten very happy minutes passed before chair sharing became uncomfortable.

"Mila, difficult as it may be---you're a profound distraction for me---we need to talk."

She whispered in his ear. "Okay. But I like distracting you."

She returned to her seat and crossed her perfect legs. She pulled her skirt hem well down to show she was serious about not distracting him. She smiled to show she was not all that serious about it.

"And I like your distracting me. But I have to tell you what I've been doing."

"Please do," she said. Mila already knew Lars and Charlie did the same work. She loved them both, nonetheless.

Alas, he started his story the wrong way.

"To begin with, I'm a criminal. In theory, I could be prosecuted for twenty-two murders."

She looked stunned. Mila was now fully serious, which visibly worried him.

Indeed, Lars instantly felt his choice of words the biggest blunder of his life. His entire world seemed to change. Instantly, and unexpectedly, he was at a tipping point.

"Mila, if you choose to walk away from

me, I'll understand. You have kids to raise and you're entitled to a good life. If you want me out of your life, I'll leave."

He waited, looking even more worried. To Lars, there was nobody on Earth like Mila. He sensed her slipping away. He could only watch his fate unfold.

She knew his heart, though. That mattered more than he then imagined.

"Lars, I know you've been hunting assassins again. You're a counter-assassin and maybe the best ever. Charlie couldn't tell me what you've done. But he could tell me you're the most ethical person in the world at what you do. He meant you've only killed evil assassins, right?"

Lars felt a surge of hope.

"Yes. Twenty-two of them, including the five I killed for the Agency under Charlie's operational control."

"Only bad guys? Nobody else?"

"That's correct. No collateral damage. I never took a job unless the client could convince me my target was a professional murderer, who had to die if innocent lives were to be spared."

"You were like Charlie? Like James Bond?"

She said it gently, sensing his discomfort.

There was love in her eyes.

"The work was the same. However, Charlie and James Bond worked for one government. They followed its orders. That meant they could live safely within that government's borders all their lives. Their government would protect them. I've worked for three governments and one family. I helped the family for free, but charged the governments at least three million U.S. dollars per kill. That's how I set up my lab."

She immediately saw his problem. "In the U.S., for instance, you wouldn't be prosecuted for kills on behalf of the U.S. government?"

"Yes."

"But you might still be extradited from Canada for kills you made working for another government? Then some country outside Canada. would prosecute you for murder?"

"It's possible. There are big, practical difficulties, though. Extradition's a slow process. And I'd get some behind-the-scenes help. The U.S. and the other governments I worked for don't want my career disclosed in somebody's courtroom."

"What governments did you work for?"

"Only three. Take the U.S. first. I did eleven kills for them, but the last six were not through the Agency. There are some very quiet little groups in the State Department and in the Department of Defense. The Agency's the public face for U.S. intelligence. It's where politicians and reporters go to ask questions. It also draws attention away from the two little groups that do the serious, silent killing. They're under black ops rules. That means no rules apply once the president approves the targets."

"I can't imagine anybody prosecuting you for those eleven kills, Lars."

"You're probably right. The Brits and the French used my services, too. Same situation. Altogether, I killed sixteen professional assassins while working for the U.S., the Brits, or the French."

"That leaves six kills. They were for a crime family?"

He smiled. "No. It was the Haranya family. You've met some of them. The family stays under the radar, but it's amassed an impressive little empire that operates worldwide from here in Little India. It's all legitimate and totally ethical. The Haranyas are quite astonishing that way."

"But they asked you to break the law?"

"They had no choice. The Montreal Mob's Canada's dominant crime family. People talk about Mexican cartels, but the Montreal Mob's at least as powerful and it's vastly more sophisticated. Canadian law enforcement's pretty darn good, but sometimes the Mob can outspend the police if they want somebody killed badly enough."

"The police didn't help the Haranyas?"

"Not enough. The Mob told them to pay protection money. Lots of it. Otherwise, one of Sanjay Haranya's sons would disappear. Sanjay went to the police right away. They did things to keep his family safe, but those things cost money. The Mob knew the police budgets wouldn't continue to protect the Haranyas. The Mob just sat back and waited."

"While the police protection was reduced, reduced again, and eliminated?"

"Just as the Mob wanted. Just as the Haranyas feared. The Mob sent Sanjay a message. They said six assassins were coming."

"He came to you?"

"Yes. We already got along well. The Haranyas did the alarm system for my lab. I'd also bought some spy gear from them. They figured out what I did for a living. Louise put two and two together that way. Her late husband once was an Indian government intelligence officer of some sort. She knew his friends. One of her many contacts pointed her toward me. She won't tell me who, but I'd bet it was a well-placed Brit."

"You stopped the assassins?"

"I did. Sanjay somehow located them. Maybe with electronic surveillance. Haranyas are superb at that. I drove a shuttle that picked the killers up at a private airport. I gassed them and left the bodies lying face up in a circle on a deserted beach, all holding hands. That way the tabloids were sure to run the story."

"And, of course, they all died of natural causes?" she asked. Then Mila smiled. His hopes rose further.

"That's what the police forensic guys said. It scared the hell out of the Montreal Mob. They thought Sanjay had some kind of Asian techno-voodoo. He sent them a message: Any more threats, he said, and their top guys would start dying from natural causes."

"And that was the last the Haranyas heard from the Montreal Mob?"

"Yes. The Mob still has no idea what happened to their six goons. With so much unknown, they dare not try again. Their risk would be huge. To the Mob, it's as though Sanjay can summon supernatural forces they don't understand."

"And those are the only kills?"

"So far. It'll take about a week to finish up what Charlie and I are working on. We might need to eliminate a dozen killers in the worst case. Charlie and I think it won't get that bad."

Curiosity, not concern, overcame her.

"Lars, what, exactly, are you and Charlie up to?"

"Well, it all started when Charlie checked whether I'd lied to him about a lab journal."

She looked at him with mounting curiosity.

"This takes some serious explaining, Mila. We should order lunch before I start. Lunch will be sent up from the restaurant across the street. The food's awesome."

89

He began his account after phoning in their luncheon orders. Mila soon was stunned.

"Okay so far?" asked Lars.

She briefly closed her eyes, seemed to talk to herself, and then said,

"Okay. I'm with you again ... *This is mind-boggling!* Do you contrive these scenarios just to challenge me, Lars?"

"Yeah. Just for you. The woman who as a nine-year-old child prodigy won chess tournaments against college chess champions."

"Only two tournaments. After that they raised the entry age." Her eyes twinkled.

"Okay. Here I go again, once more trying to impress the woman I love."

He soon did. She was back to alternating

between insight and wonder. Lunch arrived. Mila tasted it and said it was superb. It was easily that. The chefs all knew Dragon Lady. They also all knew the Haranya family's concierge, who'd pay the bill on Lars' behalf.

Even so, Mila barely noticed the extraordinary flavors and presentation as she ate. It was all she could do to comprehend the world Lars placed before her.

Above all that, she truly loved Lars. She'd kept him in the back of her thoughts for two years, never knowing where he was. Ever since her divorce, she'd occasionally dreamt about Lars being her husband and her children's adoptive father. Until very recently, it had seemed only the stuff of dreams---too much for her to hope for in this life.

But now Lars was offering her all that and unimaginably more. She sat there in silence, love in her heart, awe in her eyes. She just might be the most blessed woman in the World, she thought, as implications became clear. She at last fully understood.

He then realized she fully understood.

"So, Mila, what do you think about our prospects?"

"Lars, was that a *de facto* marriage proposal?"

"Not yet. I know you'll get mad if I don't do it right."

She gently laughed. "I will! You need a ring. Do you even know my ring size?"

"Yes. Your daughter texted it to me."

Another gentle laugh. "She would! She's determined you'll be her new dad."

"What about your son?"

"He's a boy. He still thinks more about video games than romance. But he likes you. After you and he blow up a tree stump, I think he'll want you around." She smiled at the thought.

Then Mila stood up and sat down in Lars' lap again. Ten minutes later they stopped so he could call for the limo. They went directly to the ski resort restaurant, where Lars tipped the restaurant staff well. The staff, in turn, made the private dining room available early.

Lars and Mila promptly sat on the couch. They spent the remaining afternoon in one another's embrace. Grand romantic interludes alternated with sensible problem-solving. An early question was where they'd live. He preferred Vancouver. Would she and the kids be happy there?

Mila was surprisingly open to moving. She said she worried about the safety of her children so near D.C. Also, the public schools weren't all that good, given that each of her teenagers had tested well above the genius level. Her kids seemed bored with schoolwork.

He explained that the Haranya family had started its own private academy. There were only about fifty children in it, but there was one teacher for every three students. Lars said the Haranyas were from India and valued education greatly. Sanjay's wife, a former schoolteacher, watched over the Academy like a hawk. Sanjay, himself, wrote whatever checks she asked for.

Every Academy kid---every last one of them!---was doing incredibly well. That greatly mattered to the Haranyas since their children would be running the family empire all too soon. And Mila's kids would be welcomed. He, Sanjay, and Sanjay's wife had already discussed that.

Was Vancouver safe? asked Mila. Lars said that, apart from some bad areas the druggies frequented, it was quite safe. The Haranya clan also deployed electronic security measures that would impress the U.S. Secret Service. Even in gun-hostile Canada, all the family's adults had concealed carry permits. Lars was sure Charlie would teach her kids martial arts if Mila wanted him to. Charlie was so good at hand-to-hand fighting that Charlie had never shown much interest in poisons, Lars said.

Would she and the kids need Canadian government permission to live in Canada? Yes, he answered. Louise was well-connected with various senior Canadian officials. She'd make sure everything went smoothly. She'd even get Charlie organized given a few weeks to train him. Mila said nobody could train Charlie.

It began to get dark outside. Lars led Mila to their dining room window, which looked out over the world below. She saw several ships anchored in the Pacific, waiting their turns at Vancouver's port. Massive, dark mountains lay to one side of their window, keeping silent vigil over the city below. To the other side sprawled Vancouver. It's lights were coming on now for the night, making the entire metroplex twinkle just for Mila. The peaceful, welcoming beauty of it all captivated her.

They took the last ski lift car down the mountain and climbed into their waiting limo. Its privacy partition was already up. Lars took Mila in his arms as soon as the door closed. She stayed in his arms for the short ride to her hotel.

Two minutes from the hotel they began disengaging. They let their passions subside. They adjusted their outfits. Such measures were important. Charlie had texted that he, Louise, and Mila's kids would meet them in the hotel lobby when they arrived.

Mila and Lars entered the lobby to find Charlie and Louise radiant. They could've been proud grandparents. Meanwhile, Mila's kids and Dragon Lady's kids chattered away like long lost friends. The four teens genuinely liked each other.

Mila's son asked Lars if his new friend could join them tomorrow to make gunpowder. Both boys looked eager as could be. Lars said they could if---and only if---his parents gave their permission, if the boys did the computer simulation first, and if Dragon Lady's son passed Mila's lab safety test.

Mila's daughter asked if she and her new friend could go shopping in Little China tomorrow. She said Uncle Charlie---Mila was surprised at this new appellation---would take them. Auntie Louise---another new appellation---would come along and knew a good tailor there. Mila's daughter promised to use her babysitting money for whatever she bought.

Before long, Mila's son and his new friend had Mila on the phone with Dragon Lady to explain gunpowder making and stump blasting. It was a delightful conversation for the mothers. Dragon Lady and Mila would become close friends in weeks ahead.

Louise turned to Lars as he watched it all. "Things are going well?" she asked.

Lars looked not only happy, but grateful. "Things are going very well. Thank you!"

Louise took Charlie's hand, looked his way, and smiled. "Our part's going well, too," she said. Then she turned to Lars. "Thank you!"

90 The Montreal Mob tried to move quickly to kidnap Brent. At first, things went well. One of the Mob bosses maintained a list of contract goons well-prepared for such work. He easily recruited six unprincipled ex-mercenaries and flew them to Montreal from various locations.

The client, whom the Mob knew only as Necromancer, provided the basic kidnap plan. It was a good one, two of the six mercenaries said. The two had participated in several successful kidnappings. Their advice was much respected by the others. For awhile, all looked well to the Mob boss in charge of the contract.

Then one of the two experienced kidnappers became severely ill. His malady seemed stomach flu or food poisoning. Either way, he'd need days to recover. Find somebody else, he told the Mob's recruiter. Otherwise, wait a week for him to get at least half his strength back.

The recruiter enlisted one of the Mob's regulars---someone who wasn't a temporary contractor like the others. Usually a regular like him didn't participate in contract jobs. His much greater, far more evil talent was reserved for the Mob leadership's in-house enforcement team. The five contractors quickly accepted his supervision.

He looked at their plan. A cabin like Brent's, he said, was easily turned into a trap. There was only one way in and out. Also, the surrounding forest could hide a battalion of men, assuming they knew what they were doing. The Canadian authorities had such men. So did Canadian subsidiaries of U.S. private security firms.

What should they do? the others asked. He said their plan seemed entirely adequate, assuming only Brent was at the cabin. He said they first should have a surveillance drone fly over. It'd be too high up for Brent to notice, but images sent from the drone would be excellent. The Montreal Mob, he assured them, could arrange such a flight. He requested it.

The drone flight caused a day's delay, but the video eventually emailed to the kidnap team was, indeed, excellent. They enlarged it on a laptop and gleaned all they could. Somebody surely lived at the cabin. A truck was in front. Lights appeared in windows. The tracks on the long driveway showed Brent had driven in and out.

They decided nothing whatsoever like the vehicles supporting an ambush team had used the road. Best of all, infrared imaging showed no warm bodies hiding in the forest around the isolated cabin. Their plan should work.

The six men zeroed their newly issued assault rifles. They packed the supplies and shackles they'd use. Also, an unscrupulous nurse instructed them on the sedative for Brent.

The kidnap team arrived in Ottawa that afternoon and rented two vehicles using false IDs. They'd strike Brent's cabin just before dawn the next morning.

91

While Auntie Louise and Uncle Charlie took the girls to Little China, Mila, Lars, and the two boys worked in Brent's lab. Dragon Lady and her affable husband, Kenneth, showed up mid-morning to watch. They, like Mila, much welcomed the boys' rapt interest. The two teens loved the software! It was, to future techies like them, far better than a video game. In remarkably little time, their several simulations arrived at the perfect proportions for the charcoal, potassium nitrate, and sulfur comprising black powder.

The boys eagerly took to the lab bench, where Brent had laid out the chemicals and tools in advance. He had them work with a wet mix so that, even if they somehow got a spark to it, the powder wouldn't go off. He made them follow a hundred safety procedures, something they took considerable care with. The boys worked uncommonly well together, as though born to comprise their *ad hoc* laboratory team.

Lars showed them how to safely dry the mix, which they gently crushed into the right grain size. Once the boys settled into a routine, their work went quickly. By lunchtime they had a pound of black powder, which went into a paper bag Lars carried in a knapsack. Everyone went to a fast-food place, but the boys were too excited to spend time going inside. Everyone used the drive through.

Half an hour later, they arrived at the unwanted tree stump. It was three feet across and two feet high. Lars used a portable electric drill to make a two-inch-diameter hole angled into the side of the stump and stopping inches past the stump's center. It took awhile.

He had the boys fill up five sandbags with dirt as he worked. He explained the bags would be piled at the mouth of the hole once it contained gunpowder. That would tamp the blast, keeping more of its force inside the stump for greater damage.

As the parents listened, Lars fully explained fuse to the boys. Dragon Lady was genuinely surprised there was so much to learn about fuse. She became as interested in the project as her son was. So did her husband, Kenneth. Super-chemist Mila answered their many questions while Lars worked with the boys.

The boys carefully poured their pound of black powder into the stump's two-inch-diameter hole. They inserted two fuses and plugged the hole with the paper bag. Sandbags were placed just the right way. The boys then had their parents move safely back. The boys took safety so seriously, the adults were impressed. Even Lars hadn't expected so much insight from two teenagers so soon.

The boys shouted "Fire in the hole!" three times. Lars said that was a customary warning that explosives were about to go off. Each boy lit a long fuse as Lars watched. Once both fuses were sizzling, the boys and Lars walked---no running!---well away and took shelter with the parents. Two minutes later, they heard a very loud blast.

Everyone gathered around the splintered wood that had once been a stump. The mothers took pictures first. Then everyone took pictures. Finally, Lars and the boys checked that no wood smoldered unseen. As the happy little group walked back to their two cars, Mila and Lars lagged behind. She took his hand.

"It's been years since my son's had this much fun. And he learned so much chemistry!"

Lars was pleased. "He's a good kid. You've done well with him, Mila."

"Thank you, Lars. He needs a dad, though. Someone exactly like you, I think."

92 Somewhere on the way back to Little India, the boys transitioned from being very happy to being both very happy and very hungry. Dragon Lady invited everyone to her family's home for pizza. Charlie, Auntie, and two hungry teenage girls soon joined them. The girls were as happy as their brothers and sometimes giggled at their newly shared secrets. Dragon Lady proposed an impromptu sleepover for the teens. That idea was a big hit with the kids.

Mila and Lars couldn't stay for pizza, but brought her teens' toothbrushes, pajamas, and such to Kenneth and Jenny's house. Lars and Mila already had reservations, Lars said, to dine at the upscale Perpetual Puddle Grille. Louise, he said, had assured him it was Vancouver finest restaurant. To no one's surprise, she knew the owner. Louise had helped Lars get the restaurant's private dining room on short notice.

Lars drove Mila to her hotel, picking her up an hour later. He found that, in only sixty minutes, Mila could transition from uncommonly beautiful to world-class gorgeous. She wore a little red dress that right away elevated his pulse. Mila definitely didn't need her daughter's advice on clothes, though he assumed Mila would probably receive it anyway.

Since he was driving them, and therefore

had his hands occupied, Mila was free to talk. She went on and on about how good the day had been, how much her kids loved Vancouver, and how kind Jenny and her husband were. Why, she asked, would anybody code name someone as nice as Jenny 'Dragon Lady?' She looked pointedly at Lars. He didn't know. Mila shrugged and chattered on.

She speculated that Vancouver might be one of the best places anywhere to spend a winter. The skiing in nearby mountains was spectacular! Did Lars know the fabled Flautist Resort was less than four hours away? He only sort of knew that. She nodded emphatically and asked him if he'd someday take ski lessons with her. The kids wanted to learn to ski, also, and Jenny said there were big discounts on lift tickets if you knew what to look for. Lars said he'd like that. They should get their calendars out and plan a trip for the winter.

She noticed they were no longer going toward the restaurant and asked why. He said he wanted her to see two Vancouver housing developments. It was only a short detour and it could be awhile before they'd have another chance.

Mila was pleased. She said she watched the *Real Estate Channel* often. Life outside the D.C. metroplex---or, at least, outside her part of it---was beguiling. And, by the way, did he like modern architecture? Not over-the-top modern, of course, but tastefully so? He did. She confirmed that as they drove past nearly two hundred beautiful homes.

Their restaurant's elegant private dining room didn't have a grand view, but it had two leather couches. At this point in their relationship, couches trumped views. Even so, they started off at the dining table. Dinner was extraordinary! It also came with a remarkable dessert having fewer than a hundred calories. Mila made a mental note to buy online the Perpetual Puddle Grille's cookbook.

After dinner, they sat on a couch with predictable results. Fifteen minutes later, he pulled back a little from her.

"Mila … did you know I can read your mind?"

"No, you can't." She said it with a happy smile.

"I can. You'll order the restaurant's cookbook when you get back to your hotel room, right?"

"Yes! How did you know?"

"Like I said, I can read your mind."

"Hmmm."

She wrinkled her nose at him and smiled.

"And since I can read your mind, I know this is the right time to propose."

He said it softly, love in his eyes and---from out of nowhere!---a jewelry box in his hand.

Mila teared up. She ignored the ring and looked only into Lars' eyes.

"Mila, I don't want to live my life without you beside me. I want you there as my wife, as my partner in everything that matters, and as the mother of my children. I want to adopt your kids. I want to wake up next to you each morning and fall asleep beside you each night. I want us to grow old together here in Vancouver. Mila, will you marry me?"

She was so happy she choked up and struggled to say yes three times. Mila wiped her eyes twice before realizing he'd opened the ring box. Lars took out a full-carat, perfectly cut, flawless stone that was more beautiful than she thought any diamond ever could be. She actually gasped. He pushed the ring gently onto her finger.

Mila had to wipe her eyes yet again before she could make out all the ring detail. It seemed to flash fire, even in the dining room's low, romantic lighting. She had never seen such magnificent jewelry. It fit perfectly. She remembered her daughter's role and smiled.

She said it was not only the most wonderful ring in her life, but the most wonderful day in her life. She thought her kids would be overjoyed when Lars and she told them. They'd bubble over with congratulations, Mila speculated, and then her daughter would want to study the ring.

They decided to tell her kids tomorrow. Long kisses and gentle caresses followed. They lost themselves in simply being together. Mere proximity felt so good to them. It already felt, Mila told herself, like being married.

They talked about schools for the kids, how Mila would move to Vancouver, and the research laboratory they'd start together. She made sure he knew she didn't care about the money that might, or might not, come their way. She'd want to be his wife even if they were poor as church mice.

Maybe, they decided, they'd buy the house they'd driven past that day---the one that was modern, but not too modern, and for sale. The one with the beautiful maples in front of it. Or maybe they'd just get an option to buy it and look some more. Lars said Louise and Jenny would provide excellent advice on Vancouver housing. Louise and Jenny together appeared to know almost everyone. Sanjay and his wife seemed to know the rest.

Lars said Sanjay and his wife were looking forward to meeting Mila---perhaps soon after he and Charlie finished up their current project. Mention of the project made Mila visibly anxious, even though she knew Lars and Charlie together would be formidable. Even Lars alone would be formidable, but she still worried.

Lars sensed as much, explained why this last job would be easy, and again promised he would retire. Well, sort of retire. He'd work in their Vancouver lab with her. She'd have to wear tight jeans, though.

That got her mind off dangers to come. She laughed, talked about his chemistry lab that would become their chemistry lab, and suggested they might set up a mini-chemistry-course for teenagers. He believed pre-teens also could benefit, but thought their parents should sit beside them during lab sessions. She agreed and offered further refinements. Memorable romantic interludes punctuated pedagogical musings. It was an enchanted evening.

The magic took Mila's mind off what Lars and Charlie had left to do. It would be far more dangerous than Mila could even suspect. Neither Charlie nor Lars wanted to worry Mila or Louise. The two men pretended the next few days would be easy.

93

That night early risers Charlie and Louise went to their separate bedrooms by ten p.m. It was a late night for them and they fell asleep quickly. Happy dreams ensued.

Mila and Lars didn't get to their separate bedrooms until the restaurant closed. They went back to Mila's hotel, where they took half an hour to say goodnight inside the door to her room. Lars took a taxi home. They were both asleep in their respective rooms by one a.m., each looking forward to announcing their engagement to Mila's children.

The teenagers lasted longer than anybody that night. Dragon Lady put girls at one end of the house and boys at the other. She told them they had to turn lights out and be asleep by two a.m. She later reported to Mila that they did, indeed, turn the lights off on time. However, she thought they probably whispered away in the dark until nearly three a.m.

At four-thirty a.m. Charlie, the first one up, was making hotel room coffee when his laptop dinged at him. Somebody's vehicle had driven over the seismic sensor at the entrance to Lars' cabin driveway. Seconds later another beep pattern sounded. That meant there were two vehicles on the driveway. A minute later, the cabin's power and phone lines were cut.

Charlie called Lars' cellphone. The attack on the cabin had begun.

94

The six kidnappers traveled in an SUV and a van. Since their reconnaissance had found the simple driveway gate, they were prepared. One man in the lead vehicle leapt out with a pair of bolt cutters, snapped the gate padlock's shackle, and pushed the gate open.

That brief delay gave Needles enough time to activate his laptop. As the second vehicle passed the gate, Needles was already connected to Old Dog by videoconference. Their laptop screens showed three little boxes, one for each of their faces and one to summarize sensor data. Most of each screen showed video feeds from the cabin's interior and exterior. So far, only the sensor data was of interest.

"They'll park a few hundred yards away and advance through the trees," said Old Dog. "Less danger of getting shot from the cabin that way."

"How many do you think there are?"

"Well, if they used a pair of vans---and that's what I'd use---they could get maybe eight men into a van. That'd make for uncomfortable travel, though. They'd also need room for their victim. That all means the most we'd see would be fifteen bad guys. The fewest would be about eight. Any fewer and they'd just take one van."

"I'm betting five or six goons divided up between two vans," said Lars. "That way if one van breaks down, they can get everybody into the other."

"Hadn't thought of that," said Charlie,

"but it sounds right. Let's estimate six for now."

The seismic sensors just before the cabin parking area still showed no activity. "That tells me," said Charlie, "they've dismounted. You've got time to make yourself coffee if you hurry."

"Good idea. I hereby hand the controls over to you."

"I hereby accept the controls."

Lars was soon back, sipping hot coffee as he sat down.

"I'm again taking the controls."

"The controls are yours," said Charlie. He gladly let Lars operate cabin devices since Charlie wasn't quite sure when to set off the first chemical cannister. The exact moment depended on where kidnapper stood in the room.

"You see that?" asked Lars. "The seismic sensor just inside the tree line at the parking area tripped. Somebody'll be stepping into camera view any moment now."

"Got it … and there he is. Far left of the outside camera field. Should see more soon."

Four men cautiously took up positions at the cabin front, two at each corner."

"I'd bet on one or two more around back," said Charlie. "Six goons overall still looks like a good number."

One of the four men in front began to

pick the front door lock.

"Dummies," said Charlie. "The door's unlocked. It sticks a little, but it's unlocked."

Thirty seconds later the door lock picker stood, took his assault rifle from the man holding it, and had the four men in front line up to burst through the door. Lock Picker held up four fingers, then three fingers, two fingers, and one. The four charged into the room as Lars and Charlie watched on the cabin interior's hidden video camera.

"Not a terrible entry," said Charlie. "But no bulletproof vests, no radio headsets, and no flash bangs. They must think a wimpy-looking guy like you is a pushover."

By then all the cabin rooms had been checked for anyone hiding there. When they found nobody, the leader called for the two men out back to join them. Soon they did, meaning all six men now stood within range of the gas cannisters.

"Here goes," said Lars, remotely activating the electronic valve on one cannister. The six men didn't notice the slight hiss.

Lars counted aloud: "Three …" He stopped his countdown at "two" when all six men immediately crumpled to the floor.

"Nice," said Charlie. "Is that what you used on my two Agency guys?"

"It's been enhanced. My favorite blonde

made it work faster."

"Will these six on the floor live?"

Charlie asked out of curiosity. He felt no sympathy for the goons.

"Yeah. I gave 'em a light dose. They'll be unable to move for days. They can't talk, either. They're wide awake, though. It's too soon to put them asleep."

"Why?"

"I have to wait for the cabin atmosphere to clear. A full day's wait should be long enough. Otherwise, too large a dosage builds up in the air. Setting off the other cannister now would kill them, even though the second dose is less potent."

"Got it. Can they see okay?" Again, he asked out of curiosity.

"Their vision's fine. They can blink their eyes. They can hear us."

"Time to give your Needles speech?"

"Yeah. Might as well."

He focused a hidden camera on the face of the goons' leader, who happened to be looking in the right direction. Lars zoomed the camera in enough to see the man's eyes blink.

Lars turned on the cabin's hidden speakers.

"My name's Needles. If you can hear me, blink your eyes twice."

The goon leader blinked. Lars assumed the other goons also heard him.

"It'll be at least four days before you can walk well enough to reach your trucks. Remember that there are bears in the area. If they find you helpless, they'll eat you. Stay in the cabin until you can walk and shoot a gun. Blink twice if you got that."

The leader, and presumably the rest, blinked twice.

"You've been given a dose of experimental anesthesia. In a week, you'll be good as new. No headaches. No nausea. No cognitive impairment. That last outcome means your brains will work just like they did before you were gassed. Blink twice if you understand.

The leader blinked.

"Since you won't be able to move for three or four days, the muscles you're lying on will start to ache. It'll hurt like hell, actually. I gave you too little gas to numb the pain. Consider that payback. Anyway, you'll feel lots of pain, but zero anxiety. In other words, you'll hate the present, but won't worry about the future. Blink twice if you understand."

The leader blinked.

"About a day from now, I'll give you a smaller dose of the aerosol. That will put you to sleep. You'll ache terribly when you wake up, but you'll sleep comfortably and pain-free until then. I have to wait a day. If I give you the second dose too soon, it'll kill you. Time to blink again."

The leader did so.

"You probably won't smell very good when you wake up. Your bodily functions will continue whether you want them to or not. That part's worth two blinks all by itself."

Two more blinks.

"Almost done. Tell your bosses I spared your lives, even though you'll wish you were dead before this is over. Even so, if you come after me again, I'll kill you. I kill guys like you as easily as you'd swat mosquitoes. You've no chance against me and my technology. Got that?"

"Two more blinks."

"That's it. Don't worry. Be unhappy. In fact, be miserable. Needles out."

Needles and Old Dog had the cameras and microphones transmit their feeds to Needles' very secure cloud. They might learn something useful. They knew the Mob would send other goons to rescue the six men. The Mob might not care about temporarily paralyzed goons, but would want to retrieve the assault rifles. Untraceable assault rifles were valuable in Canada.

95

Lars and Charlie were done with the cabin attackers well before breakfast. Charlie went to Louise's house. She was again cooking breakfast for them both. He looked forward to telling her about the cabin attack. Louise delighted in his adventures. Another good morning lay ahead of them.

Lars went in another direction and soon knocked on Mila's hotel room door. She was dressed and waiting for him. They had three wonderful hours together without her kids around. The teens were at Jenny Haranya's house, sleeping late after their overnight. Dragon Lady texted to pick them up at one p.m., after she'd fed them all breakfast.

Lars and Mila arrived at the Dragon Lady's lair on time. Mila had temporarily removed her engagement ring. She and Lars brought Jenny Haranya a big bouquet of flowers as a thank you for her hospitality. Jenny was pleased. Mila's teens meanwhile conversed nonstop with their new best friends.

Lars and Mila left, her kids in tow. The two adults intended to tell the two teens the adults were getting married. They'd be one family.

It took a half hour before the adults could say so. The teenagers first wanted to recount for Mila and Lars all their good times at Mrs. Haranya's house. Mila and Lars listened with much satisfaction. Mila's daughter hadn't even noticed her mother wore tight jeans and heels.

At the hotel, Lars had a conference room reserved for them. Once inside, the kids stopped talking long enough to order snacks from the restaurant's menu. The food soon appeared. Despite having eaten only an hour ago, Mila's kids dug right into the nachos set before them.

Mila slipped her engagement ring back onto her finger. She looked at Lars, who looked at his watch. They wondered how long it would take Mila's daughter to notice the ring.

It helped that the ring flashed beautifully given even a little ambient light. Mila's daughter noticed it in seconds, right after a three-watt sparkle. Her mouth dropped open. Her eyes welled up. She rushed to hug her mother and Lars at once. They sat close enough together that she could do that if she stood between them.

Her brother missed the ring entirely, having been focused on Canadian jalapenos. When his sister sprang toward her mother and Lars, he looked up. "What?"

Mila laughed softly, as she hugged her daughter back.

"Lars and I are getting married. We'll be one family." Mila looked radiant as she said it.

Her son got up, hugged his mother, walked around his sister---who as usual, he told himself, had taken the best spot without even asking!---and hugged Lars, as well. Mila smiled happily at Lars, who responded in kind.

Then Mila's daughter wanted to see the ring. She became so excited about it that even Mila's son got interested. Thus began a question-and-answer session that would last over an hour. When would the wedding be? Mila said that, given she and Lars already knew each other so well, the wedding would be in two months.

Could she, the daughter asked, be in it? That was a very eagerly posed question. Yes! Both kids would be in it, said Mila. Cool! replied the daughter, just before asking if she could help her mother shop for the dress. Mila said she could. The daughter then offered to help pick out bridesmaid dresses and flowers. Mila agreed to both.

The son asked if he and Lars could blow up another stump—not that afternoon, but someday. Lars explained they could, but the young man was now so good a chemist that black powder looked too easy. Lars thought they'd make a hundred grams of plastic explosive next time.

Mila pretended to be shocked. "Lars! He's only fourteen!"

It was token resistance. She already knew her son could do it under Lars' tutelage. It was probably illegal, but they'd be very discreet. Besides, given what Lars planned for Vancouver, the authorities wouldn't mind. Mila smiled at her very enthusiastic son. He just might become a chemist after all, she thought. Just like his new dad.

Lars explained where the kids would attend school, which was easy. Jenny's kids had already told them about the Haranya's private academy. The Haranya family matriarch, Mrs. Sanjay Haranya, herself, was in charge of it, said Mila's son. It was an exceptionally cool place.

Soon the daughter asked where they'd live. Mila and Lars explained that might be a hard choice. There were many neighborhoods with nice houses and lots of kids. Two such neighborhoods were within walking distance of Mrs. Jenny Haranya's house. The kids wanted to start looking there. The son already felt sure that area was the best in Vancouver for them. His sister emphatically agreed. Finding a house would be easy, she assured both adults.

Mila told them about the ski resort atop the nearby mountain. Would they like to take lessons there if she and Lars took lessons? "Yes!" both kids said together. Could they go there that afternoon? the teens asked. Just to see the place?

Mila looked at Lars. They'd discussed

the next part. It was to be their final inducement if the teens balked at moving. It had been his idea. It was to be his decision. She already knew how he'd decide, though.

"Not this afternoon," Lars said. "You see, I mostly get around using buses, taxicabs, and rental cars. That's easy to do in Vancouver. But our family's going to need a car. Actually, two cars. One for your mother and one for me. However, since your mother and I'd usually go places together, you two often would share one of the cars when you're old enough."

That was it. The kids were completely sold on living in Vancouver. The little family-to-be spent their afternoon car shopping. Lars said they should get something that would be safe, comfortable, and good in winter. And it couldn't be pink. Otherwise, Mila and the kids could choose however she saw fit.

Later he'd have whatever cars they chose discreetly armored and equipped with defensive electronics of all sorts. It was too soon to tell the kids that, but he'd told Mila.

96 Dinner that evening was pizza, eaten as a family in what Auntie Louise thought the best Italian restaurant near Little India. She was right. The kids, who all afternoon had debated almost nonstop which cars to pick, somehow stopped to eat pizza. They devoured it, said it was better than any back home in D.C., and asked Lars if they could return to the restaurant another night.

Mila smiled her approval at him. He agreed they'd come back in maybe a week. They'd invite Uncle Charlie and Auntie Louise to join them. He and Uncle Charlie would be back from their business trip then. That response fully satisfied the teens, who right away returned to debating which cars to buy.

Their refreshingly civil debate continued during the ride back to their hotel. Lars said goodnight to the teens and left them in their hotel room huddled around Mila's laptop, avidly visiting automotive websites. They barely noticed Lars take Mila's hand and lead her from the hotel room. He closed the room's heavy door. Three long, slow hallway kisses later, they said goodnight. Mila went back to facilitating teenage decision-making.

Lars returned to his Vancouver apartment. There he opened his own laptop and found Charlie's draft of their message to Vlaski Peeters:

Dear Mr. Peeters (a.k.a. Necromancer),

Please play the smaller of the two files I attach. It shows the six professional killers you sent.

Notice I only paralyzed them. They'll be

able to walk from the cabin when they wake up four days from now. They'll have brutally painful muscle aches and ugly bruising from immobility, but no medical examiner anywhere will find traces of unusual chemicals within them. I easily could have killed your goons.

The first video helps make my first point: I'm very good at eliminating assassins---far better than you and your team now can imagine. Remember that. You don't want me coming for you as an enemy.

I might, however, come as a friend. Notice the word "might." I'm trying to decide whether to kill you and your entire team, or to make you my allies. In the latter case, you can get far richer than you are now and live well into old age.

We need to talk about the two futures available to you and your team. Consider that my second point.

Before we have this conversation, though, play the longer file for your team. You'll soon discover that, as a practical matter you and your team are already dead if I say so. I don't have to kill you myself. I'd just send the audio file to the police.

There's more evidence to send with it. You see, I had a datalogger chip placed inside Barska's laptop. I also had full control of her laptop microphone, which is how I acquired the audio attached.

You and your team would go to prison. It wouldn't seriously matter how long your sentences were. You'd all die in the first month if I were to take out contracts on you. The killers would be your neighbors behind bars. They'd kill quietly and slip back into inmate anonymity.

The last time I checked, a convicted EU murderer serving life---and therefore with nothing to lose---would assassinate one of you for less than five thousand euros. I hope you again see that you don't want me as your enemy.

Have your entire team---their lives are at stake just like yours---in the principal airport for Marseilles, France. Go to conference room _____ on concourse ___ at _______ local time on Tuesday, _____ days from now. No cameras. No cellphones. No electronic surveillance. Expect me to check for surveillance when my accountant and I enter the room. You may have present no more than five bodyguards.

And that's it. Have a safe trip.

Needles

Needles soon had Charlie in a videoconference. Each man could see the draft.

"Nicely worded, Charlie. There must be some poet in you."

"Nope. It's the vitamin E."

"The conference rooms I picked are all inside the metal detector perimeter? That's why you didn't say no guns allowed?"

"Yeah. I expect ceramic knives and maybe the best tough guy talent EU mobs offer."

Lars asked, "When do you want to do this? Sooner's better than later for me."

"For me, too. Let's give Peeters forty-eight hours to get everybody there. How's that?"

"Perfect. I'll finish the email, encrypt it, and send the key separately."

As Charlie watched, Lars finished the message. He used some Dragon Lady spy technology on the result, entered the email address the datalogger had reported Grunt typing, and sent his message off. He expected to ruin Peeters' day.

97

Peeters played both email attachments in mounting horror before retrieving the emergency bottle of vodka hidden in his office. Twenty minutes later he had self-medicated enough to appear composed.

He gathered his staff in his conference room and passed out copies of only the basic email message. Those copies, he said, should be returned to him as soon as they were read. It was an unusual precaution, but everyone quickly understood why. He collected his handouts.

His staff stayed silent. They were already worried enough. Nobody wanted to assume the further risk of speaking before understanding the two attachments. They said nothing as Peeters played the attachments for them. Afterwards, Security and Peeters looked calm while the others looked terrified.

Peeters began with a reassuring smile. “This situation’s much easier than it seems.”

His team didn’t understand yet, which meant Peeters had a chance to seem brilliant before them. He liked that.

“Let’s begin with the obvious. This Needles person can only be Lars Brent.”

His staff nodded agreement.

“Next consider the people on the cabin floor. The video doesn’t link them to us, does it?”

His staff again nodded agreement.

“So, we don’t care about the video of men on the floor. Am I right?”

Some said “yes” and the rest nodded “yes.”

“Now consider the audio---the recording supposedly made of us plotting unmatched evil."

He had tried to elicit smiles at his artful wording, but only got a weak grin from Finance.

Peeters said, "That entire audio file could've been generated by one or two special effects wizards, giving digital life to a script some playwright conjured up. Am I right again?"

They all said "yes" this time.

"In order to prove the recording's genuine, prosecutors would need a witness. They'd need Needles. Is that correct?

That drew another "yes" chorus, this a little more emphatic than the last.

"And if Needles were killed, the prosecution's main witness goes away. Right again?"

Before everyone could nod along, External Affairs asked, "What if other, unknown persons heard the recording when Needles did?" She was the brightest of the lot.

"Well, their problem would be the same as the prosecutors' problem. Any presently unknown persons would only know what Needles told them. With Needles dead, their evidence gets much, much weaker. And don't forget, we upstanding citizens would all be testifying the audio file was false."

He smiled, as though it were conclusive. Conclusive or not, those present wanted him to be right. They easily nodded agreement.

“This means we can make all our Lars Brent problem---or at least most of it---go away by killing Lars Brent. Can we agree on that?”

They agreed, and looked to Peeters for guidance.

“I assumed we’d all reach the same conclusion,” he said. “I’ve asked Security to prepare for Brent’s assassination at the Marseilles airport conference room. Security, tell us your plan.”

The group shifted in their seats to give the burly man full attention. None seemed disturbed by killing Brent. Indeed, they were pleased the grim plan already existed. They knew from past experience that Security was good at such things.

Security cleared his throat. “It’s easy. I’ve lined up five superstar tough guys. Each with an elite ex-military background. They’ll be in the room with us when Brent and his accountant enter. Our five guys will jump the two of them and sedate them.”

“Might we want to hear Brent’s offer first?” asked External Affairs.

Peeters responded, “We’d want to hear it, but wouldn’t want the bodyguards to hear it. If they don’t know Brent’s information, they can’t use it against us."

External Affairs nodded, smiled, and said, "I like that thinking. Please continue."

Security sort of smiled back. "The sedatives will knock Brent and his accountant out in about a minute. Two bodyguards will carry each man from the room and through a nearby employee exit. The fifth bodyguard will walk ahead and tell anyone who asks that the two guys are being rushed to the hospital. He'll say it's poisoning and they need their stomachs pumped."

Finance asked, "Won't an alarm go off once they open an employee exit? Passengers can't use those exits in the airports I've seen."

"It depends on who gets bribed how much. This time it only takes ten thousand euros."

Finance looked satisfied. He crossed his thick arms over his thicker middle and awaited Security's next words of comfort.

Security said, "The bodyguards will have a rental van and a driver waiting nearby. The five bodyguards and the two unconscious guys will be driven outside the airport to someplace very secluded. I'll meet them and the unconscious guys will go into the trunk of my car. I'll take them somewhere else and you don't really want to know the rest. Just be assured Brent and the accountant will never inconvenience us again."

"I think that means," said Peeters, "that all our Lars Brent problems begin to go away the moment he and his bean counter enter the conference room."

He smiled his biggest smile and looked around the room for affirmation. His staff displayed comparably large grins.

Security's smile was a little off, just as it always was. He once had said executioners weren't suppose to smile, so why bother learning how?

98

Security was already well on his way to killing Lars Brent. He had long stayed in contact with certain ex-spies and ex-military personnel he'd met through Germany's black ops work early in his career. Some of the best retired killers in Europe were his friends. They, in turn, knew of other skillful killers just like them. He'd no shortage of excellent referrals whenever he needed to bypass Valhalla's in-house security officers and get truly lethal talent.

Soon after Peeters' staff meeting decision to kidnap and kill Brent, Security quietly slipped out of the room. Making sure nobody followed him, he went to a small, well-secured warehouse miles away. Valhalla had rented it through a pair of offshore shell companies. The building provided secure staging area for Valhalla Security's occasional clandestine projects.

Five very tough men in their forties and fifties awaited Security at the warehouse. All had long ago distinguished themselves with high-stakes contract kills, mostly in Europe's German-speaking areas. Security considered them his peers. They smiled when they saw him. He was an old friend, whose jobs paid very, very well.

Soon the five men took seats around the long table in what served as the warehouse conference room. Security put a thumb drive into the computer already hooked up to a projector.

"This is a short-fuse mission. We'll go through the plan first. Afterwards, I'll issue some special equipment."

As he said it, he'd pointed to five gym bags stacked in one corner.

"We'll be done here in two hours and you'll leave for Marseilles. The travel arrangements were in the envelope with your initial payment. Everybody clear on travel?"

Heads nodded. Travel was the easy part.

"Good. You'll be posing as freelance bodyguards. There's no uniform since you'll need to blend in with crowds during the exfiltration phase. But wear a sport coat with a turtleneck shirt. Everybody got the black turtleneck shirt I said to buy?"

More nods. These men did what they were told. Nobody here made rookie mistakes.

"The story is you're contractors helping me protect these five corporate big shots."

He projected his first slide onto a conference room wall behind him. Everyone saw pictures for Peeters and his key staff. No names appeared.

"I'll protect these five, myself. Forget their faces. They were never in the room, okay?"

More grunts and nods. It helped that only External Affairs had a face any of them might care to remember.

"Your real job's to subdue two people who'll walk into the airport meeting room after we and the folks on the screen are inside. Here's a sketch of the room."

He changed slides. Up came a big rectangle with a conference table at one end. There were two doors for the room, one of them by the room's conference table end and one at the room's other end. Apart from the conference table and its ten chairs, the room was empty space. Nobody could ever get vehicles through the doors, but---if one could do that---there'd be enough empty space to park two full-size luxury sedans side by side.

"I had some furniture moved out of the open area. That leaves more room for the short-lived attack you'll make."

Heads nodded. The extra space was a luxury they readily appreciated.

"You five guys and the people I protect will be in the room when your two targets enter through the door farthest from the conference table. They'll have to use that door since the other one'll be locked. The five VIPs I protect will be seated at the table. I'll stand between them and the fighting area."

He picked up the little electronic pen he used to write on the image and made a red X on the slide to show where he'd stand.

"Three guys will stand along the wall on this side of the door. Two guys will stand along the other side of the door. Spread out so you don't seem to be ganging up ready to fight. The three guys will go after Brent. The two guys will take out the accountant with him. Okay"

Heads nodded.

"We know nothing more about the accountant. It might be a man. It might be a woman. It might be a tough guy like us pretending to be an accountant. Until we know otherwise, assume it's a tough guy."

Heads nodded again. Somebody grunted, too.

"You can kill the accountant if you need

to. Try to do it without any blood. We can get cleaners if necessary, but it'd take an hour. I've never used these cleaners before, so I'm not sure how good they are. So, don't spill any blood, even if you break the accountant's head open."

One man laughed softly at that and two men smiled.

"The three guys go after our main target. We need him alive."

Security showed one of Barska's grainy security camera photos of Lars Brent.

"Sorry. That's the best picture available. But you'd expect that. This guy's a professional assassin and a damned good one. He doesn't let people take his picture. He had a neatly trimmed full beard when this image was made. He might've shaved off the beard. He wears glasses or contacts. The real tip-off is that he's not powerful like you guys. He has thin bones. He's skinny. And he's only six feet tall. Look at that picture, though. Try to remember it."

The five men focused on the picture, studying it, memorizing it. They had good recall for anything operational. Each man's eyes soon shifted from the screen to Security, who continued.

"This guy's named Lars Brent. He might call himself Needles. We wait until he identifies himself before we attack. Obviously, we don't want to jump the wrong guy. You must not attack until I give the signal."

"What's the signal, boss?" asked one of the men.

"I'll say 'Welcome to the Marseilles Airport.' Everybody say that so we're all clear."

They repeated the phrase. Security was satisfied with the single repetition.

"Once you have the signal, three guys swarm Brent. The remaining two guys swarm the accountant. Make sure the fight never gets within ten feet of the VIPs. They're the ones paying you lavishly for this job and, I hope, for future jobs. Keep them safe and happy. That's important."

Nods and grunts came in reply.

"Fritz, you've used hypodermic needles before on a mission. Anybody else?"

Two men raised their hands.

"That's perfect. Each of you three will have a hypodermic needle with knockout juice in it. Don't worry about finding arteries and veins. Just jab it into any big muscle. One needle full of juice per target. Then punch the guy a couple of times so he goes to sleep quicker."

Fritz laughed at the part about the punches. Knockout serum never did work fast enough.

"Now, we need to discuss equipment," said Security. "This Needles guy is dangerous with his hands. Don't let him touch your skin. He's got some kind of jelly he puts on his hands. If he touches you, you'll go to sleep in minutes. It's not fatal, but you'll black out."

"How good's that intelligence, boss?" asked one of the more experienced killers.

"It's excellent. We've a reliable account of two Agency tough guys being knocked out by Brent. He shook their hands. A few minutes afterwards they keeled over and woke up six hours later. But there's more intel on this guy. I've got a video clip of him taking out two Russian heavyweight killers in a hotel corridor … "

"Did this guy kill the Volkovs?" someone asked. News of the Volkovs' inexplicable demise had quietly spread among professional killers around the globe. The Volkovs had been at the top of the game. Some in the room had envied their skills.

"Yeah. Watch this."

He showed them Barska's video clip from Ottawa.

All five were hugely impressed. One asked, "The guy just touches them and they somehow die? It's that hand jelly of his?"

"Nope. No jelly this time. He's holding a needle in the palm of each hand. It might even be several needles in his palm. We don't know how long the needles are or what they look like. Consider each of Brent's hands like a king cobra's head. One strike and you die in ten seconds."

It was sobering news. He had more such news.

"One other video clip. There's some audio with this one. You'll see six guys sent to kidnap Brent lying on the floor of some hunting cabin. You'll hear him talk to them."

He played the video. By the end of it, all five men looked nervous.

"You know, boss," said the eldest man present, "this could be a good job for stun guns."

"You won't need stun guns. I've got some good news about knocking Brent out."

"Good news?"

"Yeah. Very good news, in fact."

Security looked at his watch.

"Tell you what: We're running a little ahead of schedule. Take a smoke break. Be back here in ten minutes for my good news."

99

While the men went outside the warehouse to smoke, Security checked again the five gym bags. The men came back on time, looking forward to good news.

"Ready for the sunshine and lollipops part?"

Some nodded. Some laughed softly.

"First, Brent won't enter the room intending to kill anyone right away. He first wants to see if they'll pay him gigabucks. It'd take him at least ten minutes to figure that out."

"You're saying Brent might come into the room without one of those snake fang things in each hand?"

Security nodded decisively. "Yep. He'll enter the room barehanded. He's not going to want a fight, anyhow. A fight means bodies to dispose of."

They understood how hard body disposal was. Anyone who could avoid it would.

Security said, "Here's more good news. You'll get to act first. You'll have surprise on your side. You can overpower him before he can pull one of his needles from his pocket or wherever."

"What about that hand jelly he has, boss?"

"He won't use it. It takes five minutes to work. You'd kill him twenty times during those five minutes. If he used anything, it'd be one of his handheld needles. That brings me to even more good news."

Security took one of the gym bags

stacked in the corner and lifted it onto their conference table. He unzipped it and removed what looked like a policeman's body armor vest, except that it was much more lightweight. He held it up.

"Here's the best news of all. This is new armor for prison correction officers. It won't stop a bullet. It's designed to stop homemade knives prison inmates might have."

"That's why we wear black? So you can't see this vest on underneath our shirt?"

"Yes. There's also a one-inch protective collar at the neck. A turtleneck hides it."

"We can get past the airport security screeners wearing that?"

"Every single time. This is the beta version for what comes out next year. Feel it."

Security tossed the vest onto the conference table. Five hands reached out to touch it.

"Whoa! ... This thing's really lightweight. I've got a rain parka twice as thick."

Security looked pleased. "The guy who sold us these has worn them through airport screening in five different European airports. No problems whatsoever."

"Boss, how's this thing stop a knife?" It was the eldest goon that asked.

"It won't stop a full frontal thrust from somebody your size who's got, say, a well-sharpened bowie knife. But it'll keep the knife from going deeper than a half inch. You might be sore a day or so, but there's no way the blade would reach any organs."

"What about a needle?"

Security smiled. "Brent absolutely cannot penetrate this vest with a needle … Ready for the rest of your armor?"

They were not only ready, but eager. Security pulled out an armlength sleeve made from some sort of shiny fabric.

"The sleeve's almost as good as the vest, but thinner. Slide one sleeve on each arm. Wear it under your turtleneck. The sleeve'll stop any needle Brent tries sticking in your arm. Block his hand techniques with your forearms, just like you already know how to do."

"What if he tries to stab our unprotected hands and fingers, boss?"

"He won't. Think about it. Sticking a needle into a moving hand's hard. Sticking it into a moving finger's harder---maybe even impossible. He'll first strike for your neck or upper torso. That's all he went for on the Volkovs. It worked then. He's not going to change his tricks for us."

Smiles broke out around the table. Just to be sure, Security asked them if they could take out an unsuspecting skinny guy before he could put his hands in his pockets. All said they could.

The eldest goon even prophesied their mission would be fun.

100 The Valhalla executives didn't take the company jet to Marseilles. They didn't travel under their real names, either. Security arranged for them both temporary identities and a private jet, which landed at a small commercial airstrip. Two limousines sped them to luxury hotel rooms ten miles away. They'd meet Lars Brent and his ill-fated accountant at the Marseilles city airport conference room tomorrow.

Concurrently, Lars and Charlie flew on their own private jet to the Marseilles city airport. They traveled under false IDs and stayed in a mid-priced motel five minutes from the airport. They ate dinner at separate tables in a restaurant near their motel, which meant one could better watch the other's back. That evening, when the hallway was clear, Charlie knocked on Brent's motel door. Soon both men were inside.

"Charlie, what's that in your hand?"

Charlie handed Brent a plastic clipboard three-sixteenths of an inch thick.

"It's approximately one and a half square feet of ballistic panel. Put that inside your briefcase. If they somehow get guns into the room, hold up your briefcase. It ought to stop the first shot. The idea's to close with the shooter before his second shot."

"I like this. Thanks. Can I reciprocate by giving you some of my needles?"

"No, thanks. I'm an old time Ninja sort of guy. I don't attack with dainty thorns."

"I knew you'd say that. And you've got the anti-surveillance scanner?"

"I do. It looks like an eBook reader. Louise's techie gave me an in-depth tutorial. It might be the only electronic device I'm really, really good with."

"I bet Louise loved aiding and abetting her big-hearted spook."

"She did. I now have a one-woman fan club."

"We've still got time to recon the airport conference room, if you want."

"Nope. Lars, if they're smart, they'll have some sort of surveillance outside it. Peeters has all the money in the world to spend on killing us. He'll even take unnecessary precautions."

"Then I guess we're almost done. Take off your shirt."

"Lars, I hate shots. Will this hurt?"

"No. I'm a physician, remember? Take

off your shirt."

Charlie halfway unbuttoned his shirt, before having second thoughts.

"This isn't gonna make my arm numb or sore or anything, is it?"

"Definitely not. You'll hit just as fast and just as hard. This shot's simply an antidote. It ensures the chemical agents I may be slinging around have no effect on you."

He gave Charlie the antidote injection. Charlie winced in anticipation, but barely felt it.

"Hmm. No pain. You might be good with needles, Lars."

"Very good. I could take out all five bodyguards and Security, myself, you know. Or you could take out half of them with my poison packets. You don't need to endure a slugfest."

"Nawh. Like we agreed, beating up their best tough guys makes the right sort of impression. Besides, if I don't do it James Bond style, what would I tell Louise?" He smiled.

"Yeah. What, indeed?"

Lars still handed Charlie two of his poison packets, just in case. Each looked like one of the little packets holding a moist wipe for cleaning eyeglasses.

"Remember, all you have to do is tear the packet open. Don't even bother removing the wet paper wipe inside. Then toss the torn packet so its contents get within twelve inches of the person's face. Do that before counting twelve from when you open the packet. The vapor will do the rest. The guy'll crumple and stay unconscious for about fifteen minutes."

"I'd rather punch him."

"I know. Your packets can be for emergency use only. Anyhow, Charlie, I guess we're done until tomorrow?"

"Yep. Sleep tight. We'll meet at breakfast. Twelve minutes before the restaurant here opens?"

"See you then." Lars went back to his room. It'd been a long flight, and he needed a good night's sleep. Tomorrow would be all about life, death, and trillions of dollars.

101

The next morning Lars and Charlie had breakfast at different tables before sharing a taxi to Marseilles' city airport. One of their charter's pilots met them and took their luggage to the executive jet Lars had chartered. Charlie and Lars walked through airport security carrying only their thin leather brief cases. With an hour's wait before entering the conference room, they found a coffee shop and sat at separate tables.

Security and his five-bodyguard team arrived at the conference room early. Security turned on an electronic scanner he'd brought with him. It was a less sophisticated version of what Charlie had. After they'd turned off their phones, one of the bodyguards counted aloud to fifty. Security's scanner confirmed no signals were being transmitted into or from the room.

Next Security ran a quick rehearsal. He stood near the conference room table, saying he'd personally protect the five executives. He had his goons take their positions around the room. Security quizzed them one last time on the plan.

What, he asked, had to happen before the men attacked? The stockiest of the bodyguards, who stood six and a half feet tall and weighed over three hundred pounds, answered. The man said Brent had to identify himself, either as Lars Brent or as Needles. Otherwise, they'd waste time snatching the wrong guy.

A scar-faced man got the next question. Security asked him who'd attack Needles. He said the three men standing along one wall would take out Needles. The other two men would take out the accountant.

And what triggered the attack? asked Security. The tallest man---actually, there were two men the same height; it came down to their hairstyles---said they'd only attack once Security said, "Welcome to the Marseilles Airport!" It had to be Security who said it. Nobody else.

What happened after the men were knocked unconscious? Security looked toward a heavyset man with a neck tattoo. He answered that the bodies would be carried first through the airport employee door nearby and then to the waiting van. If anybody questioned them, the team would say both men urgently needed their stomachs pumped.

For perhaps the fifth time, Security warned to attack quickly and violently. That way Brent couldn't deploy his little poison things. Strike for his eyes, his knee, or any of the usual non-lethal targets. Block any hand techniques Brent threw. It was only his hands that were dangerous.

Security then was satisfied his men were prepared. The solid door had only a little peephole, but it was enough to see Brent coming. Security told the man by the door to keep watch.

Fifteen minutes before the meeting, Peeters and his staff entered together. Security assigned them seats at the table. At ten minutes before the meeting, two caterers brought in a cart with pastries and coffee. Security wondered to himself what moron had asked for that silliness. The cart took up fighting space and provided hot liquid a target might throw.

It turned out the refreshments were entirely HR's idea. She said she had wanted to surprise them. She babbled through an explanation of how the "coffee" came from premium organic acorns naturally devoid of caffeine.

She was interrupted by the bodyguard at the door's peephole.

"Two guys are coming."

102

Charlie pushed open the door for Lars, who warily looked inside, realizing the peephole bodyguard would be behind him once he entered. With Charlie still holding the door, Brent gestured to the peephole man.

"You go stand by the far wall. I don't want you behind us."

Peephole man looked to Security for guidance.

"Do like he says," Security said with one of his deficient smiles. "We all like each other."

The bodyguard walked to the far corner, looking over his shoulder at Brent as he went. Brent and Charlie stepped in the room and Charlie let the spring-loaded door close behind them. Both he and Brent wore three-piece suits for the occasion. Charlie also had parted his hair in the middle and sported a garish bow tie. He had a little pink chrysanthemum in his collar's buttonhole.

Brent looked around, deciding which tough guys to leave for Charlie. Only a few seconds passed before Brent said, "My name's Lars Brent. I'm also called Needles. This is my accountant, Orpheus Ladysmith, IV."

Charlie liked his opponents overconfident. He'd picked for himself what he considered a truly wimpy alias. It worked. One of the hired goons sneered and another snickered.

"Welcome to the Marseilles Airport!" Security replied, not even attempting a smile.

Five bodyguards suddenly swarmed at Lars and Charlie. Security, meanwhile, stood between the Valhalla executives and a savage melee.

103

Security already had a serious problem. By telling the goon behind the door to move far from it, as Lars demanded, the door was left unblocked. Lars and Charlie only had to open it and flee into the airport concourse outside.

"Henchman!" Security called out to the goon now nearest the door. "Block the door!"

The man code named Henchman stood to Charlie's left and also was closest to Charlie. At Security's command, he put his head down and drove a big shoulder toward Charlie. The clear intent was to knock Charlie aside, letting the goon behind Henchman kill the hapless accountant while Henchman held shut the door. Nobody considered Charlie a threat yet.

It was a reasonable tactic, but failed an instant later. Henchman's massive shoulder made light contact with Charlie's left ribs, just as Charlie's left elbow slammed hard against Henchman's temple. The elbow strike could have been fatal, had Charlie been so inclined. Henchman went unconscious, crumpling to his knees and then to his face.

The score stood at Goons zero, Needles zero, and Orpheus Ladysmith, one—and a rather big one, at that.

The second goon on Charlie's side of the room rushed at him. He jabbed hard at Charlie's eyes as he came. It was a feint, meant to set up Charlie for a pile-driver-strong punch to the face. Charlie easily swept the feint aside with his right arm, which he raised with astonishing speed. Had anyone thought about it then---and nobody would in the heat of battle---Charlie was simply not normal. He was a statistical outlier, someone with lightning fast reactions only one person in ten thousand might match. The goon's forearm went partly numb from Charlie's block.

That left the goon in a very bad position. The arm he led with had been slapped aside hard, well away from the goon's face. It momentarily couldn't protect the goon's head. His other arm was drawn back ready for the lethal punch the goon had intended all along. In other words, the goon had both his arms at shoulder level and temporarily out of action.

If Charlie hadn't been so incredibly quick, it might not have mattered. Both the goon and Charlie had one hand drawn back, ready to strike. Tactically, it was like two Old West gunfighters drawing their weapons at high noon. He who hit well first would win.

Charlie was not only faster, but he struck with a textbook-perfect uppercut. The heel of Charlie's hand caught the goon under the chin, snapping his head back with what normally would have been deadly force. The goon's neck didn't break this time only because its heavy muscles were contracted, and took most of the blow.

It was, nevertheless, more than enough to stun the goon for a full second, meaning the man stopped fighting for one thousand vital milliseconds. Charlie needed less than three hundred milliseconds to hammer fist the goon's right collarbone. It snapped, taking the man's entire right torso out of the fight. The goon screamed, clutched has badly damaged shoulder area with his good hand, and twisted his injured right side away from Charlie's wrath.

Charlie judo chopped the man, dropping

him unconscious. The score became Goons zero, Needles zero, and Orpheus Ladysmith two---all in the first five seconds of play.

Even so, Charlie now was very worried. When he struck the goon's collarbone, he felt the slight padding underneath. Charlie then knew the men were wearing high-tech body armor Lars' needles couldn't pierce.

Charlie turned Brent's way and shouted, "They're wearing body armor!"

Charlie's warning was already too late.

104

Three men had come at Needles, two of them abreast of each other and one trailing behind. All three would've attacked side by side in a bigger space, but the room was too small for that, even with some furniture missing.

Two of the men---code named Ox and Bison---were bodybuilders with massive chests, each man several inches taller than comparatively frail Lars Brent. The third, called Troll by his drinking buddies, was just as heavy, but inches shorter than Brent. In terms of sheer mass alone, it was as though two soda machines and a gun safe rushed Brent in attack formation.

Lars instinctively stepped away from Charlie to give him room. Lars kept his back to the wall as he did so, ensuring nobody could attack him from behind. While Charlie had simply dropped his leather portfolio, which held a ballistic panel, when the fight began, Lars still had his in his left hand. He tossed it at the face of the goon nearest him, the man known as Ox.

Ox raised his beefy right forearm to slap the leather case away from his face. He did it as he charged, meaning he moved forward while slapping. For tactically vital milliseconds, Ox's right side was halfway unprotected by his right arm and his left side vision was halfway blocked by the portfolio. Lars stepped closer and used that fleeting instant well.

Lars' right hand came up, its palm slapping against Ox's naked fist. For a split second, the fist was immobile as the forearm muscles which had driven it one way yielded to forearm muscles that would retract it. Needles had enough time to drive a tiny needle deep between Ox's fingers.

It was truly a world-class-difficult move that nobody, except possibly Charlie, would think Needles could make. Neural cascade did the rest. Ox dropped unconscious in a second. Needles sprang away from Ox's collapsing body, which thumped to the floor nearby. As Needles moved, he deftly drew another needle from his belt.

He was ready to strike Bison, the other big attacker up front, and did so. He stepped toward Bison, knocked aside the fist protecting the man's bullish neck, and felt his needle break up against the soft body armor beneath the shirt collar.

Lars suddenly knew he was in big trouble. An instant later Charlie confirmed it with his body armor warning. Since toxic needles wouldn't work well, Lars' hand went to his belt to grab one of the little packets hooked there. All he had to do was tear it open and throw it near the man's face.

He didn't get that far. Bison punched hard toward Lars' face. The blow would have had a good chance of killing Lars or, at the very least, of shattering the thin bone around one eye. Lars survived such injury because musclebound Bison was lunging mostly forward while punching mostly sideways. His big chest muscles interfered slightly with his big biceps, and his big triceps slowed the arm down a little more. His muscles, in other words, impeded themselves. It was the reason Charlie preferred to fight bodybuilders.

Lars slammed into the wall, falling hard to the floor at Bison's feet, but kept his wits about him. Had Lars somehow been dazed, he never could've drawn another needle from his belt. But he did draw it, and, in almost the same instant, slapped that needle into Bison's leg just as the big man raised a foot to trample Brent.

This time the needle went through

ordinary fabric and deep into the Bison's calf. Bison looked down at Brent in surprise, and died just as quickly. In effect, Mila's work saved Brent's life a second time that morning.

However, his life was soon in dire danger. As Brent sat on the floor, just beginning to get up, Troll launched himself onto Brent, like a flying gun safe crash landing. Troll not only knocked the wind out of Brent, but got a choke hold on his unprotected throat. He lay full length on Brent, Troll's abundant weight easily pinning down the dazed, much smaller man.

Troll roared at Brent as he squeezed Lars' neck. The big goon had lost all control of himself. So angry was he after seeing his colleagues overcome that he meant to crush Brent's larynx, which would've been a fatal injury.

Troll actually got within a second of doing so. He failed because an instant sooner---just as Troll roared---Charlie Hexler kicked him hard in the head. Now Charlie and Mila both had saved Lars' life.

The score became Goons zero, Needles two, and Orpheus Ladysmith three. The entire Valhalla executive team looked close to panic when Security growled, "I'll handle this."

He drew a ceramic, long-bladed assassin's knife and turned toward Charlie

Hexler, who was breathing hard---too hard, thought Security, for an old man who'd simply been lucky so far.

105 Security might have attacked Charlie right away. Instead, Security waited. This was his moment, after all. The most important people in Valhalla were behind him, terrified, and dependent on him for their lives. He couldn't even imagine, Security told himself, the riches and privilege they'd bestow on him after he saved them from the old man and Brent.

Mostly from the old man, he told himself. Brent hadn't done so well that morning. He'd survived only because Security's guys had performed worse. They hadn't used the body armor to even half the advantage it should've provided.

So, Security told himself, he'd be a hero this morning. But first he'd build a little tension. Just like they did in those blockbuster superhero movies.

Charlie said, "You really think you need a knife against an unarmed old guy?"

Charlie calmly adjusted his bow tie as he spoke. He then looked at his watch, careful to keep its face turned away from Security.

"Damn! Some idiot got blood on my watch. Consider me very pissed."

Charlie smiled, though.

It was so unexpected Security smiled back in spite of himself. The old guy had style.

"You've done well for an old fart. You can die proud."

He waved the knife and moved two steps closer to Charlie. A good five paces separated them. They weren't quite close enough yet for Security to use his knife.

Charlie shook his head and waved one hand, as if pushing away a bad option.

"First hear the deal Brent has for you alone."

Charlie pulled back his suit jacket and reached into his shirt pocket with two fingers. He removed one of Lars' little packets. He tore the packet open and began cleaning his watch with the towelette inside. Lars said the chemical vapor on the exposed towelette lasted twelve seconds. Charlie counted to himself as he cleaned his watch's face. One ... Two …

"What do you mean?" asked Security.

From the floor to the other side of the room, Lars Brent said, "I'm thinking about your watching over Valhalla for me. Half this morning's intended as a job interview for you."

Charlie held his wrist up to the light, seemingly found a blood spot he'd missed, and kept on cleaning the watch with the towelette.

He still counted to himself: five … six …

Lars finished pushing Troll off of him.

"Damn, this guy's heavy. Where'd you find a minotaur like him?"

Lars propped himself on one elbow, making no further effort to rise. He knew where Charlie was heading, and didn't want to threaten Security by getting up. Lars merely looked at Security and tipped his head.

"Security, this is your lucky day."

By then Charlie's count had reached nine. He could wait no longer and rushed at Security, who predictably raised the knife and went to a fighting stance. He waited for Charlie to get within range, confident of an easy kill.

An ugly smile crept onto Security's face as Charlie tossed the towelette from just outside knife range. Charlie, meanwhile, said aloud for Lars' benefit, "ten … eleven … twelve!"

Lars leapt to his feet, tearing open a packet of his own. He sprang toward Security just as the man fell to the floor, somewhere between Charlie's count of eleven and Charlie's count of twelve. Charlie kicked the knife away from the unconscious man.

106 Security and five bodyguards lay on the floor. Lars turned to face Valhalla's five terrified executives, addressing them from the room's open area. He used a businesslike tone.

"Let's start with a housekeeping item. Orpheus will check how many are dead and how many are unconscious."

Charlie waved and began checking for pulses.

Brent said, "Orpheus will make sure any goons still alive sleep eight more hours."

As if on cue, Charlie took from his pocket a tiny plastic vial of what looked like over-the-counter eyedrops. Since the first goon he checked was alive, Charlie rubbed the man's neck with four drops of whatever the vial held. He then checked the other goons.

The five executives at the table looked at Lars in near shock as he walked to Vlaski Peeters' end of the conference room's long table.

"Stand up, Peeters."

"Why don't you sit down next to me, Mr. Brent?"

Peeters had recovered enough to mix a faint smile with a faint sneer.

Lars slapped Peeters across the face hard. It had to hurt. Then, before the astonished Peeters could respond, Brent slapped him three more times. Big, red welts were already forming on Peeters face. He raised his hands to protect himself from further battering.

"Let's try again, Peeters. Get it right, or expect a needle in your neck."

Peeters stood up. He stood erect, now just barely composing himself. It was hard to tell whether his eyes held more fear or hate.

Without warning, Brent viciously slapped the man's face again. Peeters stumbled back against the table, raising his hands again. He was too slow, though. Brent slapped him hard twice more, and then stepped back.

"Stand up straight, Peeters."

Vlaski Peeters did so. There was no mistaking his eyes this time. They held fear alone.

"Hands at your sides."

He did that, too. His staff at the table behind him watched in horror.

Brent pretended to draw a needle in his right hand, which he moved to shoulder-high, two feet from Peeters neck. Since none of the Valhalla executives knew what Brent's needles looked like, they imagined his empty hand held a kill needle.

"I think we finish this when you count to ten, Vlaski. Whole numbers only, starting at one. One number every five seconds. Got that?"

Peeters, who now expected to die, nodded. His death, he thought, at least would be quick.

"Start counting."

"One … two … three." He paused to swallow.

Brent stepped closer to Peeters. Brent's hand now was palm down, six inches from Peeters' ear. External Affairs gasped.

Peeters flinched, but kept on counting.

"Four … five …"

Peeters now seemed terrified.

"Six … seven … eight …"

Peeters patrician face, reddened and swelling from the slaps, quivered. Only Brent noticed.

"Nine …" Peeters swallowed and closed his eyes. "Ten."

Nothing happened for five seconds. Peeters opened his eyes and stared at Brent. Five more seconds passed as his fear gave way to confusion.

Ten seconds more passed.

Then Brent withdrew his hand. Still standing in front of Peeters, he said. "Consider those slaps payback for Barska. They were supposed to hurt. Did they?"

"Yes," came the reply.

The confusion in Peeters' eyes, if anything, was greater.

"The ten count was a little test to see if

you're good enough to work with me. I think you are. What do you think?"

Brent smiled. Relief flooded across Peeters' face. He felt as though he had just aged ten years. He cautiously smiled and said, "Yes. I think we can work together."

"Good. Let's make a fresh start of it."

Brent looked from left to right at the stunned executive team seated at the table.

"And that goes for all of you. We're starting over with each other. We now commence a very unusual relationship. Agreed?"

They nodded. External Affairs was so relieved, she smiled. Finance looked grateful, Research was surprised, and HR became nonplussed. One glance at HR's glassy-eyed stare, though, and Brent didn't care what she thought. He could tell a dummy when he saw one.

Brent said, "We should all sit down. Vlaski, you stay at the head of the table. My friend and I will sit at the opposite end. That way I can be sure Orpheus Ladysmith won't bite."

Brent smiled. The Valhalla types dutifully smiled back. Charlie, having sedated everyone who needed it, sat down next to Brent. He put his hands on the table, interlocked his fingers, and smiled. He still looked dangerous, bowtie notwithstanding.

Lars said, “Don’t worry about the guys on the floor. I’ve arranged for their disposal.”

The Valhalla executives all meekly nodded.

HR silently concluded Orpheus Ladysmith IV wasn’t an accountant. Maybe just a bookkeeper, she thought, who’d embellished his resume.

Brent said, “Once we’re done here, I’ll identify some special paramedics for you to call. Tell them to come get six men who suddenly became violent and seconds later collapsed. We’re not sure, we’ll say, but we suspect the six might have shared the same controlled substance earlier. That’s the story we all tell, agreed?”

They nodded.

“The police probably won’t believe it initially, but there’ll be no medical evidence to the contrary. These particular paramedics will support whatever story you tell. As long as we all tell the same story, that story will work. You’re all respectable citizens, right?”

The executives nodded.

“And the guys on the floor are much less respectable. Stick to the story and we’ll be okay.”

The executives nodded again. Even HR

seemed to get it.

"Next item. We share a very important common bond. I won't comment on Mr. Ladysmith, but the rest of us are killers. The rest of us conceivably---I think it's a long shot---face life in prison, if we aren't careful. I'm a professional assassin. You folks hired men like me to commit murders. We're all criminals. Got that?"

Everyone but Charlie nodded.

Brent said, "We'll get to details later, but here's another important point to keep in mind. I don't want drug industry regulators checking into my past. I need to stay out of the picture. That means I need you if I want to make billions of dollars for myself. You likewise need me to make your own billions of dollars."

Vlaski Peeters thought a moment and then dared speak.

"I seem to hear you saying that we've very strong financial incentives to work together?"

Finance and External Affairs already saw where Brent was headed. So did Research and Peeters, himself. HR wondered if Charlie were even a real bookkeeper.

"Yes," said Lars. "Very strong reasons. But that can wait until we cover some preliminaries. Perhaps we could begin with a question that gnaws away at me. Until now, nobody in the Mega Pharma world knew I existed. Nobody knew about my poison. How did you find out?"

Peeters answered. "I'm afraid it's a long story. Research, maybe you could start us off."

She cleared her throat and began without her customary ring knocks.

"Certainly. In our business, the world's government medical examiners ask us for technical help three or four times a year. That happens when they're baffled by a death under suspicious circumstances. No infections or diseases are involved since they can test for biological agents on their own.

"Most problems they bring us involve inorganic compounds found in the bloodstream. Usually, it's the same situation: The unexpected, poorly understood side effects of mixing compound A and compound B with compounds C, D, and whatever. Our scientists quickly sort those situations out with gas chromatography, simulations, and deep molecular knowhow.

"We began encountering occasional, mysterious deaths that almost surely were assassinations. However, each victim always appeared dead from natural causes. Something made him---so far, they've all been big male warrior types---die in seconds."

Lars asked, "How did you know the victim didn't really die of natural causes if there were no chemical evidence to the contrary?"

"At first, it was circumstantial. The victims were dangerous terrorist assassins. They were among the most accomplished killers the World's intelligence agencies knew about. They all seemed to die suddenly without wounds, electric shocks, bacterial or viral abnormalities, burns, trauma, or the like. The best guess was poisoning.

"We begin paying for a full-body MRI scan each time we encountered such a corpse. One of our two resident geniuses thought to look closely for nervous system abnormalities. He quickly found evidence bearing on what had only been an interesting theory the two developed years earlier. All the victims studied with MRI scans had died from what could, theoretically, have been neural cascade."

"And what, precisely, is that?" asked Charlie. He hadn't understood Lars' explanation, but they'd been finishing off a bottle of wine. He had an excuse.

"The poison makes contact with a nerve," Research said. "The body, of course, has nerves just about everywhere. Any nerve will do. The poison somehow---nobody understands this part except Dr. Brent---makes each nerve cell touched do two things. In nearly the same nanosecond it both kills itself and makes the nerve cells touching it do the same."

"And that's why," said Charlie, "nobody found Lars' poison in the corpses? There was so little of it?"

He looked genuinely interested. Lars looked surprised that Charlie had even asked.

Research looked at Lars. "Dr. Brent, I'm really stealing your thunder at this point. Stop me anytime you'd like to take over."

"Call me, Lars. And your explanation's fine. Orpheus likes it more than mine."

"Well, of course I do. Lars, you use big techie words. She speaks English."

It was just likable Charlie being likable Charlie, but that was enough. Ice broke. Tension subsided. Finance and External Affairs laughed softly in spite of themselves. Research thanked Charlie and went on.

"We at first thought no poison was found in the bodies simply because of the minute poison quantities. We did more sensitive tests. Yet our exceptionally sensitive testing still couldn't find anything toxic. That suggested we weren't looking for the right thing."

Lars asked, "Then how do you prove a neural cascade occurred?"

"Cascaded nerve cell diameters are about five percent less than healthy nerve cell diameters. But the difference is too tiny to see under an optical microscope. You need a full MRI and subsequent computer enhancement. It took us years to determine as much."

"I, myself, didn't know about the cell diameters. You and I need to have lunch someday," said Lars. He apparently meant it.

"Lars," Research said, "you might want to look at the MRI scans. I now have eleven MRI scans showing neural cascade. Six are from top-ranked Indian Subcontinent assassins who mysteriously died near Vancouver, Canada. That means the racial backgrounds are very similar."

Charlie said, "You know, I heard about those six. Which leads me to ask how much the various authorities know about neural cascade."

Research said, "As far as I'm aware, they know nothing whatsoever. We haven't told anyone. Outside this room only my two research superstars know about it. They're paid well to keep this secret."

Lars had hoped for that. "I applaud your insight into the business prospects for neural cascade. We've a good discussion ahead in that regard."

Research was wise enough to share the spotlight.

"What I've covered so far is how we knew what some genius was up to, all of which immensely impressed us. Vlaski should address the hard part: discovering that genius was Lars Brent."

Both Brent and Peeters were pleased with how she made the transition. Peeters began.

"We hired a big data analysis firm, but without telling them about neural cascade. At that point, we knew the dates for eight such poisonings. Since the poison was so secret, the big data guys assumed only one person used it. Further, the poisonings were far flung. Different cities. Different countries. Different continents, even. But always places where English or French or both were spoken.

"The data miners hypothesized a bilingual killer who traveled by air. The data miners looked at everybody flying to and from the kill sites during both the three days before the kill and the two days after. They especially looked at private jet manifests."

"Why five days?" asked Brent.

"They assumed one day to fly in, one day to scout, one day to kill, one day to lie low, and one day to fly out. The five days were either a good choice or a lucky guess. They still found only three persons who fit the profile, and none of them was named Lars Brent."

"I used a different false ID each time. That worked for awhile?"

"For awhile," said Peeters. "Then External Affairs had a good idea. Tell us about that."

The distinguished looking woman at the table said, "By then it was clear that our unknown assassin---you, Lars!---was truly world-class. But you still had to get clients somehow. We didn't think you'd work for organized crime. Why bother? Somebody like you could pick and choose. Organized criminals would be treacherous clients on their best days. Also, you could make much more money doing kills for intelligence agencies. The data mining guys guessed you'd work for the Brits, the French, and the Agency."

"Maybe you were the one who found Blanche Pierre?"

"Not directly. Her senator father-in-law's a political whore. We buy his votes and his services with campaign donations and bribes. He's long been our puppet. We told him we wanted somebody in the Agency to help us with a sensitive matter. He trotted out Blanche."

"She fingered me, as the movie cops might say?"

"Yes. She asked around. Once you get on the Agency's top floor, it seems they're not very good at keeping Agency secrets. Discretion's for the peons downstairs. Blanche knew you'd poisoned five people long ago. She said it looked like death by natural causes."

"Why not come to me directly?"

"First, we didn't trust Blanche. We still

don't. She only connected you to five deaths and they were all long ago. She could've been very wrong about you and somebody else could've made all the kills since then. We needed a way to test that you were the person with the miraculous poison. Given the business possibilities at stake, we spent lavishly on that test."

"You made up the story about somebody trying to turn Americans against Russians?"

"Yes. Vlaski and I wrote it. He's very clever about such things."

"Valhalla hired the Volkovs?"

Peeters said, "Security did that. We had to see if you were the one with the magic poison. We also hoped to learn something about how it worked. We needed somebody to spy on you for us while you went after the Volkovs. Pierre found Barska, who'd been very recently kicked out of the army. Barska also needed a drug we make. Finding Barska was the most sophisticated contribution Pierre made. For almost two entire days, we were highly impressed with Pierre."

"Where did the thirty-six million Canadian dollars for my services come from?"

Finance briefly raised his hand inches high. "From us. We have some secret slush funds."

"What did Blanche get paid?"

Finance shook his head. "The senator never told us. We sent five million dollars his way. Some piece of that went to Blanche."

External Affairs asked if she could raise a question. "Please do," said Brent.

"Thank you. I sometimes have to put up with Blanche Pierre and listen to her bitch. I'm guessing that this nice accountant with you is Charlie Hexler. Am I right?"

She smiled at Charlie.

Charlie looked at Lars. "Is it okay to identify myself?"

"Yes."

"You got it right. I'm Charlie Hexler. Pleased to meet you."

"Likewise," said External Affairs, with a gracious smile. "In the interest of our long, mutually beneficial relationship, I should warn you about something right away, Charlie."

"What?"

"Blanche Pierre despises you. That fact alone gave us very high confidence in your having exceptionally good judgement."

She sent forth a cheery lobbyist smile.

"Thank you. I'm honored to be despised by Blanche Pierre. And the contempt's mutual."

Lars said, "How did you choose the targets for the Volkovs?"

Peeters' staff turned to him. He smiled.

"It wasn't anything personal. Strictly business. You see, Lars, Mega Pharma's a dog-eat-dog world. The two CEOs ran impressive pharmaceutical companies that threatened to take over Valhalla in years ahead. I wanted to kill both of them before they went after my company."

"What about the Russian dissident?"

"She's in a clinical trial for the only promising drug in our pipeline. She's too unhealthy to live, though. Even our new drug won't be enough. If she died in some way unrelated to our drug, she'd drop out of the study results. Our trial numbers would look slightly better."

He looked at his staff for approval. It came quickly as a mix of smiles, nods, and HR's single thumbs up.

"Clever," said Lars. "I'm very impressed."

"Thank you," replied Peeters, as though accepting a career achievement accolade.

"Vlaski, tell me what you know about the commercial uses of my very special poison. That'll get us on the same page so we can talk business."

Peeters looked at Finance, who already had the appropriate spreadsheet on his laptop screen. Finance explained that, at low levels, Lars' compound would dominate the prescription antidepressant market. It would become overnight the world's leading happy pill since it had no side effects. Regulators would especially like that it was non-addictive. Totally safe, said Finance, who could already smell vast profits ahead. His bulbous nose twitched.

Then, he said without missing a beat, the formula at slightly higher levels should make possible an effective sleeping pill. But perhaps Lars could confirm that? Lars did, Finance hit some laptop keys, and his screen's excellent numbers became better still. He withheld the total, though, for suspense. Like Security, Finance had rudimentary instincts for theater.

Also, said Finance, one could increase the dose and use the drug as an extraordinary anesthesia. It promised to almost overnight completely dominate the singularly lucrative market for surgical anesthesia.

Lars thereupon said the drug had an antidote. Most errors made by an anesthesiologist could be corrected. With ordinary surgical precautions, the chance of anesthesiologist-caused brain damage would approach zero. And, of course, there were no other side effects. Everybody smiled.

Finance continued. He said the drug would supplant all compounds used in lethal injection. That wasn't a big market. However, given their patent would let them charge whatever they wanted to charge, Valhalla would make meaningful profits on executions. Also, the developing markets for assisted suicide, euthanasia, and organ harvesting had potential.

Lars asked how much money they---meaning Valhalla, Charlie, and Lars---could make each year altogether, once the drug's patent was in place.

Finance rapidly punched keys with his thick fingers, corrected his thick-finger typos, and checked his work. He looked up. Then he beamed.

"Total revenue would be at least six hundred billion dollars a year and gross profits should exceed five hundred billion a year. Those, by the way, are very conservative estimates!"

"Those match the numbers I had someone develop for me independently," said Lars. He referred to estimates Louise and Dragon Lady had compiled.

Valhalla executives all savored the moment. Visions of yachts, palaces, and private jets filled their evil heads. Even HR looked dreamily happy.

Valhalla's exultation ended abruptly when the conference room door burst open. In walked grim-looking plainclothes police officers, followed by at least ten uniformed police. Behind them, paramedics stood lined up with gurneys, ready to go.

A square-jawed man with one hand on his holstered gun, said, "Everybody's under arrest. Put your hands behind your heads."

107 It took almost an hour for preparations to transport Peeters, his staff, Charlie, Lars, and six immobilized thugs across Marseilles. The delay allowed French TV camera crews to get into position. Then came the dramatic spectacle of a twelve-SUV-three-ambulance convoy with flashing lights, wailing sirens, and motorcycle outriders. A French SWAT truck secured the rear.

Charlie thought the whole spectacle silly. So did the police officers transporting him. They told Charlie the best cafe for lunch near the jail. They said, all the same, that he should walk another two blocks to the second-best place by way of the police station's underground parking. The extra two blocks would put them well past reporters. French reporters, one officer explained, didn't walk far outdoors. He thought they worried about wind mussing their hair.

At the main police station, it took less than five minutes for the French to release Charlie. It took an hour for them to release Lars since the Valhalla executives, eager to save themselves, all said Lars was a professional assassin.

Even so, somebody in a very secret part of the French government's intelligence community told the police commandant to release Lars without any questioning. That was important, the high-ranking official said. No, neither he nor Brent would answer any of the police commandant's questions. Just make it happen immediately or resign immediately, the powerful official said, before abruptly hanging up.

Lars and Charlie walked from the police station, through its parking garage, and on to what really was a very good little restaurant. They finished their meal, checked in with their significant others by text message, and took a taxi to their private jet. Before long, they were aloft and *en route* to Washington, D.C.

The information they still needed should reach them during the flight. Charlie was sure of that. French interrogators were, Charlie said, unusually good by international standards. They were even outstanding! They'd lean hard on the Valhalla executives, regardless of any well-paid defense attorneys in the room.

Charlie was right. The information he and Lars awaited was radioed to them an hour outside of Washington, D.C. It was so good that Charlie smiled the rest of the flight. Their next big meeting would be in an Agency conference room. Pierre and assorted big shots would attend, Charlie said. Maybe some staffer from Blanche's father-in-law's office, too.

Lars mostly worked at his laptop while aloft. He had a complex document to prepare and only a little time for Sanjay and his attorneys to check over it before the jet reached Washington, D.C. One of the Canadian lawyers Sanjay had handpicked would meet them at the airport. There were, Sanjay had said, only three attorneys in Canada with the very high U.S. security clearance this man held.

Meanwhile, the Valhalla executives became increasingly eager to tell all they knew. They blamed each other so freely that transcripts from Kenneth's hole-in-the-wall gang, as the single technician now called himself, would prove unnecessary. He was disappointed, since his twenty-some-hole recordings had together captured every word in the room despite Security's furniture rearrangement.

Kenneth would pay the technician a *very big* bonus, though. He'd soon turn happy.

108 The show-down with Blanche Pierre took place at a long conference table in a plush Agency conference room. Brent, Hexler, and Sanjay's attorney sat at the foot of the long table. Blanche Pierre sat at the table's head, looking daggers at those opposite her. Pierre's personal attorney sat next to her, doodling on a legal pad. Charlie smiled at Pierre cheerfully, sure that would antagonize her.

In between the two table ends sat eight other attendees. The main one, who everyone had agreed would run the meeting, was the Agency's Inspector General. He had been in that job for fifteen years, knew all about everything relevant to it, and was much respected. His assistant sat beside him and would take notes on his behalf.

Next to the assistant was a staffer from Pierre's father-in-law's office. The staffer would make a short opening statement, would stay if he wished, but would probably leave. He said he had urgent constituent advocacy to perform and kept looking at his expensive watch.

A lawyer from the U.S. Food and Drug Administration was present. So was an attorney from the U.S. Patent Office. Both lawyers wore gray three-piece suits and had bushy brown hair. They looked like twins who shopped the same sales. Each firmly clutched a black plastic, government-issued ballpoint pen.

The State Department sent a mousy woman who twice volunteered that she spoke six languages. She was State's lead Canada desk analyst. It took six languages, she said, to keep up with increasingly polyglot Canada. Nobody else present cared.

A tall man from an unfamiliar think tank was there because, the Inspector General said, the think tank might establish their own inspector general position. This, for them, was research. They'd been invited merely as a courtesy. Nobody familiar with the world of U.S. black ops believed that, but the story worked with the FDA, State Department, and Patent Office attendees.

A digital recording machine sat on the table before the Inspector General. He punched a button on it and a light glowed to show it recording properly.

The Inspector General started them off.

"I'm Agency Inspector General Hennessy Willoughby. This is a meeting requested by Mr. Lars Brent regarding Agency Personnel Director Blanche Pierre. This meeting's being recorded, so we begin by going around the table, starting with Ms. Pierre. Tell us your name and the organization you represent so it's in the audio file."

They did. Back to the Inspector General. "I've been in this job a long time, but this might be my most unusual meeting ever. I look forward to it. We begin with a statement from the Deputy Chief of Staff for the Senior Senator from Montshire."

A tall, self-righteous young man cleared

his throat, sat up straight, and said, "I'm told that certain outrageous statements about Montshire's Senior Senator were recently made by persons now under arrest in France and facing grave felony charges.

"The statements are so unfounded, and the sources so untrustworthy, it might seem unnecessary for me to comment now. Nevertheless, not everyone knows Montshire's esteemed senior senator as well as I do. Therefore, I state for the record that the Senator is an honorable man, who has served both Montshire and America faithfully and well throughout his distinguished career.

"Further, I find deeply offensive the vulgar characterization of him as a 'political whore.' I further trust that everyone here shares my deep contempt for this baseless charge, and will do all he or she can to protect the Senator's well-deserved, highly commendable reputation. And that, Mister Inspector General, concludes my statement."

He swept a well-practiced, threatening glare across the room. The staffer was almost as arrogant as his imperialistic senator. The ploy was routine huff-and-puff in Washington, D.C., thought Charlie. The guy seemed only about average at intimidation, though he'd probably scared the mouse from State.

His threat delivered, the staffer excused

himself. The Inspector General thanked him for his remarks and then noted the man's departure for the record.

Hiram Willoughby said, "I next point out that this meeting is just that: a meeting. It's not a formal hearing. Nobody will be testifying under oath today. This is just to hear Mr. Brent's allegations. Neither he nor Ms. Pierre has to answer questions unless he or she wants to. We're just getting started, folks. All we want to understand this morning is what we're up against. Am I being clear so far?"

He was. Everyone nodded.

"Please begin, Mr. Brent."

Lars passed out identical packets.

"I will refer to certain documents. For your convenience, I provide copies now. The legal-sized documents are transcripts of recordings. Copies of the actual audio recordings are on a thumb drive. It's in a little envelope stapled to each packet."

The Inspector General spoke up.

"Mr. Brent's material is highly classified and subject to the usual restrictions. We've obviously not made a formal classification this soon, so treat these as Top Secret Plus Six for now. The materials cannot leave the room."

Lars waited for them to flip through their packets. When they'd all looked back up, he explained that twelve years ago he'd worked for the U.S. government in Alabama. His job was developing poisons for use by U.S. government assassins, if such persons were ever on the U.S. payroll. He was not at that moment, in any fashion, saying such assassins ever existed.

Heads nodded. They all knew what couldn't be said. Even the representative from State got it.

"I invented a remarkable poison. The details of that poison were kept in a laboratory journal. In other words, the recipe for the poison was kept there. After I finished testing the poison, I left the agency. The journal I kept was in my laboratory safe when I left."

"That's a lie," said Pierre. "Brent stole the classified journal and took it with him. He stole highly classified government property."

The Inspector General almost told Pierre not to interrupt, but Brent smiled gently and quickly went on.

"Please next look at Appendix Six."

Brent explained that Appendix Six was a certified photocopy of an inventory taken the day after Brent's resignation. He described the inventory procedure. Clearly, Pierre was mistaken, or worse, but Brent didn't say so.

He went to Appendix Seven. It was a certified photocopy, he explained, of the document's destruction certificate. It established that the journal---which had mysteriously been shown missing on the computer version of the paper ledger---had existed, had been destroyed, and came to the destruction facility from Blanche Pierre's office.

She turned red and started to speak, but her lawyer quickly whispered in her ear. She said nothing, but stayed red. Charlie hoped she'd suffer a minor stroke, but, alas for him, she did not.

"At this point, Mr. Inspector General," said Lars, "I recommend you confirm everyone in attendance is cleared for Top Secret Plus Twelve or higher. The man from the little think tank nodded to Wilcox. That made the request justified. Soon they had such confirmation.

Brent continued. "When I left U.S. government employment, I returned to Canada. The poison I'd developed for the government and field tested five times was good, but not good enough."

"What do you mean by field testing, Mr. Brent" asked Hiram Wilcox.

"I ask your permission, Mister Inspector General, to have Charlie Hexler explain that field testing. He was my control officer during those weeks."

"Hexler is incompetent and not to be trusted," said Pierre, venom in her voice. "He's also been fired." Her lawyer whispered again, apparently telling her to control herself.

Lars was unfazed. "In order to tell you the important things I need to say and you'd want to hear, I must use Charlie Hexler. But now his credibility has been challenged. I think I can, in less than five minutes, demonstrate that Ms. Pierre's outburst comes from unfounded personal animosity toward Mr. Hexler. May I digress?"

Wilcox, who never had thought much of Pierre, said, "Of course. A digression now might help us understand what you place before us."

"Thank you."

Lars turned to Charlie. "Mr. Hexler, please summarize for us your government employment as it relates to this morning's session."

Charlie did so concisely. He tried to be humble, but what he had done was enormously impressive.

"Have you ever had bad government performance appraisals?"

"Yes. Twice. Each time it was from Blanche Pierre."

"Did your compensation suffer from those appraisals?"

"Yes. I lost my annual raise each year."

"And why were the two appraisals bad ones?" asked Lars.

"Ms. Pierre said it was my fault that you stole your journal when you resigned"

"But we now see that the journal was there all along, correct?"

"Yes."

"And we now have reason to believe she knew the journal was there all along, correct?"

"Yes. It might have been in her office the whole time, based on the incineration records."

"Do you feel that Ms. Pierre has behaved professionally toward you, Mr. Hexler."

"Objection!" said Pierre's attorney, already trying to think of a reason for objecting.

"We're in an informal hearing," said the Inspector General. "There are no objections. You'll get your turn after you've heard Mr. Brent's case. Bring up your arguments then."

The attorney nodded and went back to legal pad scribbling.

"May I answer that question?" asked Charlie.

"Yes," said the Inspector General.

"I think Ms. Pierre behaved dishonestly, unethically, and deceitfully. Besides that, I have found her to be otherwise highly unprofessional."

"What leads you to think her highly unprofessional in other ways?" asked Lars.

"Why, that email exchange we had. I

tried to help her and she fired me."

That led to everyone reading the email exchange, which was another exhibit in the packet. The think tank guy laughed softly three times while he read. Hiram Willoughby smiled just as often.

Willoughby said, "Before anyone comments on this email exchange, let me ask Mr. Hexler if his discharge might possibly become a lawsuit someday."

"Yes," said Charlie. "It already has."

"Then," said Hiram Willoughby, with another smile, "this email exchange shouldn't be discussed further here. Mr. Hexler should have his union representative and his attorney present for such discussions."

"Thank you, Mr. Inspector General," said Charlie.

"You're welcome. To save us time, I'm willing to stipulate that Mr. Hexler is a fully credible witness as to whatever happened during Mr. Brent's field testing. Is anyone else willing to so stipulate?"

They all were. Pierre had no choice and her lawyer whispered that to her. She still turned bright red, again raising Charlie's hopes for a cardiac event.

Charlie went on to explain that Brent had been a hero, killing five professional assassins intent on murdering America's leaders. Good guys would have died, said Charlie, if not for the imaginative genius of Lars Brent. The man had extraordinary courage and reliability. He also was, in Hexler's opinion, the very best counter-assassin on Earth at the end of the field testing.

Charlie got a little carried away, but impressed those from State, the FDA, and the Patent Office. More importantly, the man from the think tank caught Hiram Willoughby's eye and nodded agreement with Hexler. Willoughby nodded back.

Lars said, "Mr. Inspector General, if there are no questions, I suggest we return to my basic story."

There were no questions. Lars went back to his tale.

"After I left government service, I set about inventing an entirely new poison. I created for what I believe the first time ever a phenomenon called neural cascade. This meant my poison killed without leaving any trace. It looked like natural death. I began working as a freelance assassin for the most secretive intelligence agencies of the U.S., the United Kingdom, and France. Under contracts with them, I killed eleven professional assassins by using my new poison.

"Appendix 2 explains how this activity came to Valhalla's attention. They realized they couldn't just buy my poison formula from me. In selling it, I'd attract attention to my past. My past very likely would've come up if I'd tried to establish I were the inventor.

"Valhalla concluded they'd have to kidnap me, forcibly interrogate me, and kill me if they wanted the recipe for my radically new drug. Such plans of theirs appear mainly in Appendix 4, which is the transcript of a recording I secretly made. Please look at that Appendix now. It's short."

He waited for them to read.

"Valhalla was prudent. They didn't want to kidnap me, murder me, and pursue clinical trials unless very sure my poison would work. They had Ms. Pierre pretend the Agency wanted me to stop three killers. The killers were sent by Valhalla, unknown to me."

"I didn't know they were from Valhalla," said Pierre. "Don't say I knew that!"

Brent ignored her, relying on her attorney's immediate effort to quell Pierre.

"Ms. Pierre arranged for an unsuspecting young woman named Kati Barska to work with me at stopping the three killers. Ms. Barska was there, however, mainly to spy on me and report to Valhalla as much as she could could about my poison and its effectiveness. Valhalla wanted to know that it worked and, if possible, how it worked."

"Mr. Brent, if I may interrupt?" asked Hiram Willoughby.

"Please do."

"I see a great many reports on activity underway throughout the Agency. I don't recall a report on you or this project you now describe."

"I suspect there was none. Ms. Pierre somehow got herself placed in charge of my counter-assassination effort. She had Mr. Hexler assigned to act as my handler in the field. The money came from Valhalla and not from the Agency budget. It was entirely a rogue operation, but only she and Valhalla knew that."

Willoughby looked toward Pierre. "Do you wish to comment, Ms. Pierre?"

Her attorney said Ms. Pierre was saving her remarks until having heard all of Mr. Brent's wildly inappropriate allegations.

Willoughby looked toward Brent, who said, "This might be a good time to look at page twelve of Appendix 7. Appendix 7 is the transcript of a meeting Mr. Hexler and I had with the Valhalla executive team. Mr. Hexler and I pretended to be criminals in that meeting, which was recorded by hidden microphones. If you look at page 12 of Appendix 7, I think you will find that Valhalla had Ms. Pierre run a rogue operation for them."

"Is there more information connecting

Ms. Pierre to Valhalla?" asked Hiram Willoughby.

"Possibly. In the wake of Ms. Barska's murder by Valhalla, Mr. Hexler and I sent Ms. Pierre an email from an imaginary person claiming to be Ms. Barska's friend. We also filed lawsuits. Ms. Pierre almost surely communicated these developments to Mr. Peeters. If the Agency can disclose what secret government surveillance acquired, Ms. Pierre's transmission might become available to your inquiry. Mr. Hexler and I don't know what's been intercepted. We therefore rely, at present, upon the Appendix 7 meeting Mr. Hexler and I had with Valhalla.

At that point, Brent said they'd heard the main points of his story. The detail, of course, was in the handouts and on the thumb drives. Did anyone present, asked Willoughby, have any comments or questions for him before Ms. Pierre presented her side of things?

The patent attorney said he'd need to set up a separate meeting with Mr. Brent. That meeting would consider the narrow question of whether Mr. Brent, given his government research work, owned rights to what he called the new poison. Those rights seemed extraordinarily valuable. The possibility of government ownership of those rights necessarily would need to be examined, but he didn't expect any major problem. Lars and the man exchanged phone numbers. Lars recommended tomorrow or the next day for their meeting.

The FDA attorney asked if Mr. Brent would begin the necessary clinical trials for his new drug. Lars said he would, but not for about three months. No more than four months. The attorney thereupon gave Lars his card and said the FDA might want to fast track the trials. Sometimes that was allowed if the social benefit appeared great enough. Since Brent's drug theoretically could wipe out misuse of opioids, the benefit seemed vast.

The mousy woman from State asked if Lars, who lived in Canada, would set up a pharmaceutical company there. He said he'd do so in Vancouver. She asked if he knew Sanjay Haranya. Lars said he did. Sanjay was one of Lars' investors. The woman was visibly impressed. In Canada, knowing Sanjay Haranya was far better than knowing six languages.

Each of the three persons tacitly affirmed Lars Brent and his story. Pierre's attorney grew more disheartened when each of the three spoke. He basically gave up altogether soon after the tall man from the obscure think tank asked, "Lars, there are six dead guys in British Columbia that somebody might need to explain. How does that get handled?"

He smiled, as though already expecting a perfectly good answer.

"I don't know. You see, Sam, there's nothing to connect me to the killings. No trace of poison was found in their systems. My old poison---the one Blanche Pierre had the recipe for---could have achieved that effect. Maybe she gave the recipe to somebody who tried it out."

Pierre's attorney started to protest, but the man called Sam stopped him with a wave of his hand. "Yeah, that mere possibility alone's enough ... You know there were murder warrants on all the six dead guys?"

"I didn't know that. Thanks for telling me."

"You're welcome. Each of the six was a stone-cold professional killer. Some unknown counter-assassin did the World a very big favor that night."

"That's good news, Sam. Thanks again."

"You're welcome again. One more thing, Lars. I sometimes see a couple of Canadians who matter a lot in my line of work. They tell me Canadian authorities will never, ever be looking into the deaths of those six bad guys. They said I could be absolutely certain of that."

"More good news! You know, Sam, you need to let me buy you dinner sometime."

"Yeah. That'd be good. Maybe we can

bring Charlie along. But now I've gotta go."

He stood, shook Hiram Willoughby's hand, said goodbye to Lars and Charlie, and left. It became manifestly clear that he'd no interest in hearing Blanche Pierre's side of things.

Her lawyer's heart sank. Concurrently, Pierre turned from beet red to pallid white as all hope left her. Charlie forever would treasure that moment.

109

Lars and the senior patent office attorney met the next day in a U.S. Patent Office conference room. Lars had brought Charlie along. The senior attorney had in tow a junior colleague, who specialized in pharmaceutical patents. Charlie thought she dressed like a prison matron and couldn't say "r" words like everybody else. Possibly a University of Montshire Law School grad, he supposed. His ex-wife went there and still struggled with "r" words.

"Mr. Brent, since we had a long-ish meeting yesterday, I think this might be a short session. I imagine you seek an Independent Origination letter from the U.S. government?"

He referred to a standard letter occasionally issued by the government to former employees who, entirely independent of government anything, invented something after leaving government employment. In effect, the letter meant the government would never assert full or partial ownership of the person's invention.

"Yes," said Brent.

"Then I turn to my colleague. Pharmaceuticals like yours are her specialty."

Prison Matron smiled better than Charlie thought she would.

"First, Mr. Brent---is it 'Mr. Brent' or 'Doctor Brent---that I should call you?"

"Just 'Lars' is fine."

"Thank you. And I'm 'Jane.'"

Charlie barely hid his surprise. His ex-wife's name had been Jane. It was a bad omen, he thought.

"Anyway, Lars, we together now confront circumstantial evidence that what you learned as a government employee made possible your discovery of neural cascade. And, by the way, congratulations on that discovery however you did it. Neural cascade already looks like guaranteed Nobel Prize stuff."

"Thank you. And what evidence does the government have that my time in Alabama contributed to neural cascade's discovery?"

"Can we stipulate, Lars, that while in Alabama you invented a poison that killed in what? Fifteen seconds?"

"It wasn't that fast. And may I ask now if you're cleared for Top Secret Plus Twelve discussions?"

She said she was and the senior attorney confirmed it.

"Good. I used the poison five times in the field to kill individuals formally designated as threats to America. These days those persons might be killed by drone strikes. Back then, the government sent me. In each instance, it took the victims approximately thirty-five seconds to die. The biggest one, an athletic male of around two-hundred and seventy-five pounds, took forty-five seconds to die."

"Your point, Lars, is that neural cascade, being much faster, didn't occur?"

"Exactly. The poison I used while a government employee was incapable of creating neural cascade. An entirely different molecule's required."

"Perhaps while a government employee you acquired knowledge critical to making that entirely different molecule? Perhaps you received essential knowledge from Dr. Mila Rossi in Alabama?"

"I didn't receive essential knowledge from Dr. Rossi. She'll confirm that if you contact her. She's now a professor working in the Washington, D.C. area. You also should know that she and I are getting married. She'll be resigning her teaching job soon and moving to Vancouver."

"Congratulations," said Prison Matron with a good smile. She began writing this new information on her legal pad. Her colleague added his own congratulations.

"Thank you," said Lars to both.

Prison Matron said, "So, I take it your position is that your new compound is entirely yours? You claim the government's not entitled to any ownership interest?"

"Correct. The government is not entitled to the relevant intellectual property rights. Of course, the government will see some social benefit. Opioids might not be prescribed again, for instance."

"Yes. No doubt your drug'll do a lot of good, Lars. And, I think that concludes my questions for you. What are your questions for me?"

Lars asked Prison Matron, "What written evidence does the government have that my work in Alabama directly or indirectly led to my discovering neural cascade?"

"Well, since a duplicitous moron apparently had your lab journal destroyed, it seems we have no written evidence. That journal was the only material record of what you formulated in Alabama. The answer to your question, so far as I'm presently aware, is zero.

Zero evidence. Next question?"

"Can you give me an Independent Origination letter today?"

"Do you plan on filing for a patent? As opposed to keeping your invention a trade secret?"

"I think the patent application will reach you in about a week. I'll be the sole inventor. However, since we're getting married, Dr. Mila Rossi will be co-owner for the patent. In other words, it'll be community property."

"Her co-ownership won't affect your originality claim. No problem there. And I have to look at your patent application before we can issue the letter. Your application will say in detail what you did and how you did it. We have to ensure that, based on such greater explanation, the government still has no intellectual property rights to your work. It's mainly just routine."

"Understood. Does there seem to be any problem so far?"

"Well, take this as no more than preliminary and unofficial, but I think you'll get your letter. I mean, how could you not get it? The critical record of your work in Alabama on any poison whatsoever was destroyed by the government, itself."

The meeting soon ended well. Charlie left the room with a very good impression of

Prison Matron, even though she still reminded him of his ex-wife.

110

The next thirty days were busy ones for Mila and Lars. Mila, now back home in the U.S., worked daily with realtors, movers, and lawyers. She resigned her faculty job after arranging an orderly transition. She sold her house in D.C., applied for a Canadian work permit, and did all her usual things at home. Her kids understood and didn't have a single quarrel. The house became so peaceful Mila thought her teenagers might be ill.

Meanwhile, Lars worked on his patent application. Sanjay, himself, found the best intellectual property lawyers in Canada to help Lars. The application was done in five days. Then the patent lawyers switched off with the corporate lawyers Sanjay had selected. They set up the Canadian company that would commercialize Lars' neural cascade discovery.

Canadian officials quickly issued the permits, trademarks, licenses, and such. Often they hand-carried the paperwork through the relevant Ottawa ministries. Why not? one lobbyist asked. At least a hundred superb, ultra-high-tech jobs would be created in British Columbia. Besides, the lobbyist said, Louise Haranya, herself, was pushing things along. Her personal involvement was a big deal! With such momentum, the legal work finished up early.

Well before then, Lars flew Mila and the kids to Vancouver to buy a house. Mila had done plenty of preliminary work with the realtor Dragon Lady recommended. Mila, Lars, and the teenagers found the perfect home in less than a day. Lars bought it outright. Mila and the kids picked furniture the day after. A week later, the house was ready for them all to move in. Only Mila and the kids moved in, though. Lars would do so after the wedding. He'd mostly just come for dinner until then.

All in all, Lars, Mila, and two enthusiastic teenagers had their hands full for three weeks. During those weeks, French investigators made commendable progress documenting Valhalla's wrongdoing, some of which went well beyond what Lars and Charlie had uncovered. Valhalla's executives still vociferously blamed each other in hopes of reduced sentences for themselves. All faced heavy sentences for murder, conspiracy to commit murder, attempted fraud, and more.

Blanche Pierre fared only a little better than Valhalla's executives. She lost her job, went to jail, and awaited trial for fraud and conspiracy to commit murder. The Agency would come up with its own list of charges. Her husband filed for divorce and her father-in-law ignored her repeated phone calls. Blanche

Pierre's fate looked so bleak that, for almost half a minute, Charlie felt sorry for her.

Amidst such far-reaching turmoil, Valhalla's directors appointed one of themselves to run the company temporarily. That lasted two weeks. Valhalla's stock already had plummeted on the news of unprecedented corruption at the top. The company's biggest competitor bought the shares for bargain prices and took over the corporation. At month's end, the name "Valhalla" had mostly disappeared from active commerce.

As all these events transpired, the European press paid rapt attention. Stories began to appear about neural cascade. Then European reporters linked Lars Brent to neural cascade, though details were few. He might, some speculated, be the inventor. Somehow, European journalists began calling Lars' cellphone number. He changed phone numbers, but they found the new one. He began using either burner phones or encrypted satellite phones.

The Lars Brent story grew by the day. Asian papers began carrying it. Days later, the august *Manhattan SomeTimes* started running stories about Lars Brent and neural cascade. Unable to find a picture of Brent, the *SomeTimes* commissioned an artist's sketch based on descriptions the *SomeTimes* had received from it usual anonymous sources and unidentified experts. The front-page picture that resulted looked like Charlie. Mila loved it.

Then Lars Brent's U.S. patent application was approved. He got his Independent Origination letter the same day. The patent office had rushed the application through in record time. The President wanted the drug in clinical trials yesterday, he said. He was determined to rid America of opioids. He already had ordered the FDA to get the clinical trials finished as soon as they could, consistent with acquiring accurate, valid results.

The senior patent attorney called Lars to congratulate him. That sort of expediting didn't happen in Washington, D.C. more than once or twice in a lifetime, the attorney said.

The next day Sanjay, his wife, Lars, Mila, Louise, Harry, and three corporate lawyers met for breakfast in Little India. They used a private dining room the dozens of reporters searching for Lars would never find. The nine talked over their situation and signed agreements.

In due course, Mila asked, "When do we finish this?"

"How about tomorrow afternoon?" responded Lars.

They discussed that prospect, finally deciding Mila, Charlie, Louise, and Lars would fly to Sweden the following day. The three lawyers would go, too. Sanjay said he'd have all the arrangements made within the hour.

111 Swedish pharmaceutical firm Olafsen Pharma was headquartered in Stockholm and operated world-wide. It offered a broad, surprisingly affordable range of medications, but nothing in regard to anesthesia, pain relief, sleeping aids, or anti-depressants. More than any company in the industry, Olafsen Pharma needed the drug Lars Brent had invented.

With it, Olafsen could fill big holes in its product lines. Not only that, but each such drug would completely take over its market since it was non-addictive, easy to use, quick acting, and without any known side effects. It also had an antidote in case of misuse.

As ethical drugs went, Lars Brent's patented neural cascade formula would reshape Mega Pharma all by itself. Number-twelve-ranked company Olafsen, if it licensed Brent's neural cascade patent, easily would catapult to number one in its industry within six months.

Lars Brent was coming to discuss exactly that licensing. CEO Sven Olafsen, the grandson of the company's founder, was thrilled. Sven Olafsen was a tall, middle-aged executive with Nordic good looks and boundless goodwill. He and his staff sat at the company's executive conference table when Lars, Mila, and the rest of their party entered the room.

"Welcome!" said Olafsen, as everyone stood. "Before we begin, may I ask which of you gentlemen is Lars Brent? We've not been able to find a credible picture of you."

Lars smiled and raised one hand briefly. "That'd be me."

Olafsen turned to his staff. "I want you all to know that this man saved my life. Dr. Brent, I'd have been in the first carload of passengers on that elevator rigged to blow up. You stopped the killers. You're a hero, Dr. Brent. I ask all of us on my team to welcome you with a special round of applause."

They did. It was hearty, sincere, and impressive. Lars was genuinely touched. Mila was so pleased she had to wipe one eye. Charlie and Louise beamed as the their three lawyers looked utterly baffled. No matter. Charlie would fill them in later. Since the Volkov project had never been a real Agency operation, he could speak freely about some of it.

Lars thanked Sven Olafsen and his team. Before he could say more, Sven was introducing his side of the long, polished teak conference table. Lars introduced those with him. Business cards were exchanged along the way. Everyone would be careful to get everyone else's name right, and the cards would help. Each card---even Lars' new one---had a photo on it.

Sven said refreshments could be brought in then or a little later, as Lars preferred. Later would be fine, said Lars. They'd started their morning with an excellent breakfast at their downtown Stockholm hotel.

They turned to business. Lars explained that his family and the Haranya family, along with a very dear mutual friend, would jointly own a new company called Scintilla Pharma. It would be headquartered in Vancouver, Canada and would pursue subsequent patents related to neural cascade. Louise Haranya would be Scintilla's CEO during the start-up years. Charlie Hexler would become Vice President for Corporate Security. Mila Rossi and Lars Brent would share the title of Principal Scientist.

Lars said, "Mr. Olafsen, since you, Sanjay, and Louise have already covered the basics by videoconference, perhaps we should now take your questions? I'd guess Louise will have to handle all the hard ones."

He smiled at Louise. She was good at this.

Olafsen was good at it, too. "First, please call me Sven. And all of us on my team hope you'll address us simply by our first names."

"And the same for those of us over here," said Louise.

She thus took charge of her side. Mila loved it. So did Lars. Neither liked talking about business. They were high-end theoretical researchers and fiercely proud of it. Hyper-exotic technology was their realm.

Charlie had a far better appreciation for administration than either Mila or Lars. Charlie, after all, had been a demi-poohbah.

Sven asked, "We understand---or we think we do---that Scintilla doesn't wish to manufacture or distribute the products neural cascade will make possible?"

"Correct," said Louise. "Our expertise is in research and development. We'll have a sophisticated R&D station in Vancouver working with a similar R&D station in Mumbai. We intend to invent new drugs, patent those new drugs, and license all this knowledge to someone else. Our highly preferred partner is your firm."

"Olafsen alone could make all the neural cascade family of drugs and sell them under its own name?" asked Sven.

"Absolutely. We want R&D in close proximity to production. Your Mumbai facility is ideal for that. We also would want---and we think you'd eagerly come to want---a new production facility in Vancouver, Canada. You'd find the Canadian government remarkably accommodating. Attracting a world-class employer like Olafsen is extraordinarily important to them. I'm reliably told you'll be offered an astonishingly good deal."

She smiled exactly the right way. Louise had started out in sales.

"Of course," said Sven, "we can't arrive at specific license fees without much more clarification. But the rough ranges Sanjay and I discussed look entirely feasible. Frankly, there's so much money to be made here that we all should be very happy if we're sensible."

"So, Sven," said Louise, "it sounds like we can make this work?"

"Without question. We have a considerable amount of data ready for your people now. We believe we can get whatever else you need quickly."

"I take it you've seen the patent application?" Louise asked.

"Yes! Lars, I wish you could have watched my best scientists go through it. They were---what's the right Canadian word?---dazzled, I think. Yes! They were utterly dazzled by the brilliance of your work. They hope to meet you and Dr. Rossi before your return to Canada."

Lars looked to Mila, who spoke for them both. "Thank you. I was dazzled, myself, by his work. Lars and I'd love to meet your scientists. I'd bet we and they think very much alike."

They broke for refreshments, for many conversations, and for checking email. Mila found her kids, who were staying at Jenny's house, had asked if they could order pizza for everyone. They could, Mila wrote back. Use the credit card she'd left for them. Best of all, the message had been addressed to Lars and Mila both. Next time she'd make sure he answered.

Before long, Louise and Sven were blocking out next steps, assigning dates, and otherwise producing a viable work plan. The staff---including Olafsen's entire legal department---began crunching through vital details. Sven had lunch sent in so the progress continued unhindered.

The group---now already becoming a formidable team under Sven and Louise's artful direction---had a singularly productive afternoon. They had valuable conversations that evening, as well. Louise took everyone to dinner at the restaurant Sven picked.

At the end of the day, both sides knew a remarkably good arrangement would emerge. At the end of the month, it did. Lars and his principal investors received their first licensing fee. It was for ten billion U.S. dollars. A larger sum was likely next month, with far more thereafter.

Mila and Lars got 60 percent of the licensing fees. Sanjay and his wife received 20 percent, which mostly would go to the Haranya Family Foundation. Charlie and Louise got 10 percent each. When the deal was announced, Olafsen common stock's price skyrocketed. At the end of the next trading day, Olafsen stock was worth seven times what it had been worth that morning, which meant Sven, his family, his employees, and his investors also did well.

Mila, who had struggled financially for two years, suddenly had more money than she ever could have imagined. Able to buy any luxury in the entire world, she didn't. When they got back to Vancouver days later, she and Lars finally celebrated. They ordered pizza, made popcorn, and watched a movie at home with their kids.

Epilogue

It took less than two months for Peeters and his evil team to be sentenced. Each one was to spend several consecutive lifetimes in prison without parole. The weeks they'd spent giving sworn testimony against each other made prosecution easy. Lars' and Charlie's evidence made prosecution foolproof. The Valhalla executive cases would become mandatory reading for law school students and criminal justice students throughout the European Union.

Lars and Mila became man and wife two months after their engagement. It was a beautiful wedding attended mostly by the happy Haranya clan. Charlie was best man. Dragon Lady was matron of honor.

Although Mila had reserved the final decision for herself, she had let her daughter pick the wedding party's dresses. Mila's son and Dragon Lady's son did the taste testing for the possible wedding cake recipes. It was a tough decision, the boys said. They spent almost an hour eating cake samples before they could decide. They took all the leftover cake home with them.

Mila was an absolutely stunning bride! Her teens were impressed and Lars was spellbound. Mila's daughter looked exceptionally beautiful, too. Even her brother said so. That especially pleased his sister since the Haranya Academy they now attended had some very interesting boys her age.

Those boys all came to the wedding with their parents. The boys were smart, athletic, good-looking, kind, and well-behaved. Days ago she'd even overheard one of them whistling Tchaikovsky's *1812 Overture!* These Canadian boys were *definitely* not like the boys in her Washington, D.C. metroplex high school. Well, she admitted to herself, not like *some* of them.

Two days after the wedding, while Mila

and Lars were still on their honeymoon, Charlie asked Louise to marry him. Lars and Mila both had known it was coming, but didn't think Charlie would propose until they returned. Charlie couldn't wait. Louise was just as eager. Lars and Mila both would be in the wedding. So would their kids. Afterwards, Charlie and Louise would depart for an extended honeymoon in Mumbai. They would also look at the Olafsen manufacturing site there and meet with key managers.

While the Hexlers were away, career civil servant Ruby Dobbins and her husband finally retired to Mudpuppy Beach, Florida. The Dobbinses easily made friends there. They started the little garden they never had time for in Alabama. They adopted an old, loving dog blind in one eye. They learned to play bocce ball and joined a seniors' league.

Ruby's husband tried oil painting, but had so little talent he gave it up a month later. He sold his art supplies to Ruby in return for two meaningful hugs and one plate of homemade cookies from the next Mudpuppy Frontier Girls' annual bake sale. Preferably chocolate chip cookies, he said. Or oatmeal cookies or brownies or sugar cookies or any sort of sandwich cookie. Ruby also could substitute a troop's candy bars or whatever for cookies.

Ruby happily complied. She had a new

part-time job that she loved and that paid exceptionally well. For one, two, or three days a month, or more---as Ruby saw fit---she ran Mudpuppy Acquisitions, LLC. Her job was to buy half of whatever each Frontier Girls troop in the Southeastern U.S. sold at their fundraisers.

She told wide-eyed little Frontier Girls, their grateful leaders, and the girls' pleased parents that Mudpuppy Acquisitions would take care of professionally packaging and shipping the purchases. Some would go to the Little India district of Vancouver, Canada. Most would go to local nonprofit groups serving the elderly, to ex-inmate rehabilitation services, or to families in need. Wherever the sundry goods went, a rich Canadian would pay all the costs.

Lars had given Ruby an excellent salary, a generous car allowance, and a lavish travel *per diem*. She could take her dog and her husband with her. As she deemed feasible, Ruby was to spend at least two thousand dollars on each Frontier Girl fundraiser within driving distance. Within broad limits, spending more, or increasing her service territory, would work fine, too.

She was to send Charlie's share of the cookies to Louise, who would ration them. Charlie had no willpower when it came to cookies.

About the Author

Randall Jarmon started out as an English major at heart, but ended up with an engineering degree. It left him with a lifelong interest in technology.

He once received more than his share of elite military training. Those years were a good way to learn about tactics, weaponry, martial arts, and so forth.

He has worked in a world-class manufacturing setting and a world-class R&D center. Part of the fun for those with technical backgrounds is determining when the technology in his stories goes from fact to fiction, if it ever does so. The shifts will be subtle. Expect to miss some.

He earned a pretty good MBA. Later he earned a doctorate (in Management) well worth having. Among other things, he now easily explains the complex organization of human effort. Look for good plots clearly set forth.

Randall Jarmon and his wife divide their time between Arizona and Texas. They have two children, six grandchildren, and a golden retriever.

He has written other novels. If you liked *The Thin Man's Poison*, you might also enjoy *The Rainstorm Revolt*, *Among the Ruthless*, *From* Us, or *Flat Light*. Each is available as both an eBook and a paperback. These are standalone novels you can read in any order.

MIKVELK Publishing, LLC
mikvelk.com
December 2023

Afterword

Thank you for reading *The Thin Man's Poison.* Mikvelk's a tiny firm, so you can be sure every reader matters to us. We're trying hard to earn not only your repeat business, but also your positive reviews.

This book brought back pleasant memories of my working in Vancouver, Canada over a decade ago. There is so much to like about Vancouver. I suggest adding a trip there to your bucket list if you've not yet visited Vancouver.

As always with my novels, I'm especially grateful to my wife, Carolyn, who has made helpful suggestions on earlier versions of this manuscript. She loves a good suspense novel and will stay up late into the night reading. A writer can get some good advice, I think, from persons so inclined.

Of course, any flaws in the manuscript are my fault alone.

Randall Jarmon

MIKVELK Publishing, LLC

mikvelk.com

S.D.G.

###

www.ingramcontent.com/pod-product-compliance
Lightning Source LLC
La Vergne TN
LVHW021219080526
838199LV00084B/4262
9798987954249